Journeys of Choice:

Joanna's Crossroads

Journeys of Choice:

Joanna's Crossroads

Melissa Warner Scoggins

fW Publishing / Marietta GA

Journeys of Choice: Joanna's Crossroads
All Rights Reserved Copyright ©2009
Melissa Warner Scoggins

This novel is a work of fiction. Names, characters, places, and incidents are either the product of the author's imagination or are used fictitiously. Any resemblance to actual events or locales or persons, living or dead, is entirely coincidental.

For Information, please address:
FW Publishing Company
P.O. Box 93 / Marietta, GA 30061-0093
Email: fwpublishing@mindspring.com
website: www.firstworkspublishing.us

Cover Design by Audra Pettyjohn, Graphic Artist
Evolution Designs, Dawsonville, GA

Library of Congress Control Number: 2008943464

ISBN: 978-0-9716158-7-8

Printed in the United States of America

For my parents,
Ann Bradin Warner and Arthur E. Warner,
who gave me life—and who to this day
show me how to live it well.

However the path may turn,
wherever the road may lead,
Make my way straight, O Lord,
make it straight indeed.

Rev. Dr. Henry D. Scoggins
May 18, 2004

Acknowledgements

When, on my 49th birthday, I vowed I would write a novel before I turned 50, I thought my greatest challenge would be coming up with the story I wanted to tell. As it happened, the "bones" of the story came to me quickly (I would say how, but that's another story). Finding the time to write, well, that was a challenge. Finding the courage to let other people read my work was an even bigger one. But by far the greatest hurdle for this new author was finding someone to publish it. I accordingly am deeply grateful to FirstWorks Publishing Company, Inc., for believing I had something to say and being willing to take a chance on me.

When it came time to work with an editor, an unholy fear took hold of me and sent my mind reeling. What if I don't like her? What if she tries to change my story? What if...well, you get the picture. Working with Diane Martin turned out to be a gift from a very gracious God. She "got" my story right away and every work session was productive. I never once felt criticized, even when she said "you're holding back" or "let's punch this up a little." This book would not be what it is today without her help.

Joanna's story would never have come to life were it not for the patience and encouragement of my loving family. My husband, Rev. Dr. Henry D. Scoggins (a/k/a "Hank"), kept my theology on solid ground and came up with Joe's nickname. My son, Matthew McClenahan, said "go for it, Momma," and started planning how to spend my royalties. My daughter, Elizabeth Scoggins, gave me a living example of the strength and humor I wanted Joanna to have. Matt and Elizabeth also learned to cook.

I had the blessing and unquestioning support of my parents, Dr. Arthur E. Warner and Ann Bradin Warner, who to date are and will remain the only other people to have read the first draft of this manuscript. My cheering section also included: my brother, Arthur E. "Bud" Warner II; my sister, Dr. Patricia J. Warner; my friends Lynda Northern and Margot Henderson; and my uncle, John "Bud" Bradin, who also has writing in his soul.

Other folks guided, encouraged, prayed and helped me in countless ways. I cannot name them all, but they know who they are and they have my deep gratitude.

And last, but really first, I thank the God who made me and saved me, who guides and sustains me, who wonder of wonders, loves even me. And you.

Prologue

One by one they arrived, bearing pies and cakes, hams and fried chicken, jars of pickles, freshly baked bread, jugs of lemonade. The trestle tables set up under an ancient magnolia creaked under the bounty.

"This isn't a picnic," Matthew Garrett declared, "It's a feast!"

"Go on with you, Reverend," a woman laughed. "It's just good plain cooking."

"Papa..." The dark haired girl tugged on her father's coat sleeve.

"Yes, Joanna"

"May I have a piece of chicken?"

"You know the answer to that, Josie. Of course not. We'll all eat together."

"But, Papa, I'm..."

"Hush, Josie. You'll wait like everyone else."

The child sighed.

"And no sulking, Joanna. You know how I feel about that."

"Sulking won't make things better," she quoted, "but it will make you look like a mule."

Matthew Garrett suppressed a grin. "Exactly. So why don't you go help Miss Wheeler carry her basket? The sooner all the food is here, the sooner we will eat."

Joanna wrinkled her nose. "I don't like Miss Wheeler, Papa."

"Shush!: Matthew Garrett quickly glanced around to see if anyone had overheard. "Don't say such a thing, especially not here."

"But it's true, Papa. And you tell me always to tell the truth."

Again, Matthew Garrett forced a smile away from his lips. "So I do, Josie. But you don't have to say what you're thinking the moment you think it. Now, go help Miss Wheeler. And stop pestering me!"

He bent for a kiss Joanna proffered, then watched her scamper off. *Oh, child of mine*, he thought, *that quick mind of yours is apt to land you in a peck of trouble one day...*

Chapter One

January 1885

Virginia, with its rolling hills and thickets of pine trees, looked much like North Carolina. Joanna could easily imagine herself back in Raleigh. *But what will Indiana be like? Surely such a foreign place won't resemble home,* she thought, then whispered, "Home."

That word again, piercing Joanna's heart anew. *I can't keep thinking about the past and all that happened,* she thought, turning her cheek firmly against the leather seat, pulling her coat over her like a blanket, and willing herself to sleep. Sleep took over...

* * *

Her father's eyes... how Joanna loved them. Almost coal black, with lashes thick as curtain fringe. Wise eyes, as quick to discern a wounded spirit as to notice an injured bird. Tiny creases walked their way to his temples, creases that deepened to furrows when a smile lighted his face.

He was smiling now. "Come here, my little Josie," he said, patting his knee, "and tell me all about your day." Joanna climbed up, remembering to position her skirt over her knees, as her mother had taught her, and with excitement filling her voice, she began the telling of her day. She felt so safe, snuggled in her father's arms.

* * *

Metal screeched against metal in the sudden slowing of the train.   Her eyes blinked open in that twilight place between waking and sleeping, where neither seems real. *Papa? Where are you?* A sudden stop pitched Joanna forward into the leather back of the seat in front of her. *Papa? Where are you?*

She felt her heart pounding, and then, she realized how cold it was and briskly rubbed both arms. *I'm not eight years old, sitting on Papa's lap back home,* she thought *I'm all grown up and alone heading to a place I've never been before.*

Joanna shivered, not from the cold, but from a chill that had taken root in the pit of her stomach months earlier. *I have no home...* She put a few coins into her coat pocket, and went to the conductor standing between the connecting cars.

"Richmond, Virginia!" the conductor bellowed out and turned, nearly knocking Joanna off her feet. He reached out, grabbed her arms, and steadied her, then hollered again: "Fifteen minutes for refreshments!"

Joanna carefully descended the snow-covered metal steps and took her place in the line that formed for the refreshments. She took a deep breath—glad for the quietness the train had denied in the endless hours since she left Raleigh; glad for the light of day after hours in that dusty, dreary parlor car, and gladder still to be breathing the fresh air, even if it was a biting, frosty air.

"No *real* woman wants the vote." The voice was male, loud, and confident.

"Sure 'nuff, taint no *real* woman." Another voice, also male, mocking.

Joanna craned her neck in the direction of the men's derision. There was no other lady in line ahead of her and the worn looking woman selling buns and coffee wasn't showing her colors with a ribbon or sash.   It wasn't until she reached the service window that she saw the newspaper stand and read the headline: *The Strong Minded Women Are in the City.* Beneath the headline was a grainy picture of a woman she knew to be Susan B. Anthony.

"Board!" The conductor's voice boomed above the howling wind. "Five minutes to departure!"

Joanna's hope for a reviving cup of coffee vanished. She

hurriedly pushed a coin through the window, murmured *thank you* to the clerk, and shoved the dry bun into her pocket. Her foot barely reached the first metal step as the conductor blared out, "All aboard! Final call!" Joanna grabbed hold of the arm rest on the seat as the train lunged forward.

Many hours and several states later, the conductor's voice roared once again. "Appleton, Indiana! All out for Appleton!"

Joanna stole a hurried look through the soot-covered windows, donned her coat and bonnet, gathered up her belongings, and headed for the door. A blast of frigid air laced with snow and ice pellets pushed her down the walkway beside the train. Another gust sent her carpetbag airborne ahead of her. *Welcome to Indiana, Joanna, and why is your red muffler in your trunk and not around your neck?* She grimaced, clutched the collar of her coat tight around her throat, and leaned over to retrieve her bag. Her fingers had barely grasped its handle when a much larger, gloved hand covered hers.

"I'll get that for you, ma'am." The voice was low and indistinct and when Joanna looked up, the reason was obvious. A woolen scarf swallowed his face and neck, leaving only his eyes visible—eyes so blue, they were almost purple—and glinting a smile even though his mouth was hidden.

Joanna said nothing; neither did he. And then, they both—almost in unison—began to speak. They stopped mid-sentence, then began again, and wound up laughing. The sound of their laughter was like the ringing of a church bell and it warmed Joanna like a fire crackling on the hearth.

He pulled the scarf from his face. "I'm Edgar McGill, Laura's brother. She sent me to fetch you," he said, still smiling. "I knew who you were the minute you got off the train." Edgar thought it best not to share what came to mind the moment he saw Joanna Garrett standing in the alcove between the two cars: *She looks like a china doll... and look at those huge dark eyes. She's way too pretty to be a schoolmarm, and mighty spunky to be traveling all alone... all five-foot of her.* "We've been waiting for you, Miss Garrett."

Joanna looked puzzled and Edgar McGill jerked his chin toward the boy perched on the edge of the platform. "That's my son, Joe."

"He and I have something in common..."

This time, Edgar's face showed a puzzled look.

"My friends sometimes call me Jo, though my mother always calls me Joanna; and, of course, my students call me Miss Garrett."

"Well, Miss Garrett, let's get you to the house before this

snow blows up into a real storm. Laura will have my hide if you catch cold and can't be at the schoolhouse come Monday morning." He beckoned to his son, who leaped from the platform and raced to his father's side. "Run up to the station, Joe, and get the foot warmer for the wagon." Without a word the boy obeyed.

Edgar pointed to Joanna's carpetbag. "Is this all you have—mighty light for someone planning to stay a while."

Planning to stay a while? Of course I'm staying... I can't go back. The voice inside her head was stern. *Don't think about that. Let it be.* "No, Mr. McGill, the rest of my things are in a trunk in the luggage compartment. This is just what I had to have with me."

"I'll put this satchel in the wagon and come back for your trunk. Why don't you step inside the station, where it's a little warmer, until we're ready to leave?"

Joanna did as Edgar McGill suggested and unconsciously wrinkled her nose as she entered the one-room station. The station agent, puffing a half smoked stogie, was hunkered over a table close to the coal stove. He looked up and nodded before returning to his paper shuffling. Joanna skirted the few well-worn benches—she had sat enough to last her a month of Sundays—and walked to a soot-encrusted window where she watched as two men handed her trunk down to Edgar. He had no trouble hoisting it up onto his shoulder as if it weighed nothing.

Her eyes followed Edgar, taking in his steady, sure-footed gait as he headed for his wagon. His long legs exaggerated his lanky frame and he had towered over her, but, then, most people towered over Joanna Garrett. She caught herself staring and abruptly turned from the window, only to face another pair of startlingly blue eyes.

"Miss Garrett, I'm Joe McGill. Pa's got your trunk in the wagon and I've got the warmer for your feet right here," Joe said, holding a blanket tucked firmly under one arm. "Ready?"

Joanna smiled. "Lead the way, Joe."

Edgar helped Joanna into the front seat of the buckboard wagon. His son tucked the brick warmer at her feet, then laid a quilt over her lap before clambering up onto the back seat.

Joanna had never felt such bone chilling cold, nor seen icicles as thick and long as the ones clinging to the station's roof. The wind, snow and ice clearly declared, *You're not in North Carolina anymore, Joanna Garrett!*

Edgar clucked to the bay mare, snapped the reins, and they were off; the horse trotting briskly, holding her head high as blows of steaming exhale rushed from her nostrils.

Should I be making conversation? How could they hear me with this wind sucking my breath away? Joanna was so weary after the countless hours on the train, that all she wanted was to get to her new lodgings, jump into a warm bed, and go to sleep. Joanna suddenly realized she didn't know just where she would be sleeping. Laura McGill's letter had said only that Joanna would be staying with Laura's family, unless a room freed up in the town's only boarding house.

Joanna turned to Edgar and pulled her collar from her mouth and chin. "Mr. McGill, I forgot to ask where you're taking me."

"Home, of course," he said without turning his head.

Home—that word again. Deep roots and journey's end, a welcome fire, and loving arms—exactly where Joanna wanted to be, but where she couldn't return. "Do you mean at your home?"

He nodded. "You'll be staying with me and Laura and Joe at our place."

How she longed for a place of her own, no matter how small, rather than being a month-to-month border with families whose children attended school. She would hate packing up and moving every few months, but she knew she had no choice in the matter, at least not right away. "So, I'll be boarding with your family for a month or so, then moving on."

"Not exactly."

"Not *exactly*—" she hesitated.

"You'll be staying with us until the school board decides whether to fix up the old Gordon place for you."

She looked up at the darkening sky. *I might actually have a house of my own! Thank You, Lord.*

The town had disappeared as soon as they left the depot, and the three rode for half an hour through the rolling countryside thick with pines and hardwood trees, with only an occasional house along the rut-filled road. Just when Joanna thought she couldn't take one more jostle or bump, Edgar manipulated the reins and the horse turned off, down a winding lane. It was too dark to see much, but after a few moments, Joanna glimpsed a hint of a light through the blowing snow. They rode on toward the light and Joanna saw the two-story frame house that seemed to beckon, *Come along now.*

Edgar drew his horse to a stop, just in front of the stairs that ascended to a wide and deep-set porch. "Joe! Hop down and help Miss Garrett out of the wagon!"

Joe did as he was told and took Joanna's hand. "Mind your step, the ground's a little icy." Joanna smiled at his grown-up tone.

"Go on in, Miss Garrett. Joe and I'll put up the horse and bring your things in. Laura's inside."

She climbed the few steps to the porch and paused at the door. *I can't just go in, even if Mr. McGill told me to.* She hadn't been raised just to walk into someone's home without knocking. She poised her hand, ready to knock on the door.

It opened, and a tall, slender woman with light brown hair and dark brown eyes stood in the doorway. She was wearing a red checked apron, smudged with flour, and a broad smile with a dimple in her left cheek.

"I've been waiting for you, Miss Garrett! Let's get you out of the cold." She took Joanna by the arm and drew her into the front hall where she swiftly brushed the snowflakes from Joanna's black wool coat. "I'm Laura McGill... I can't tell you how happy I am that you're here," she said, continuing to brush the snow. "Come into the kitchen where it's good and warm."

Joanna took off her gloves and pushed them into one of her coat pockets and followed Laura through the front room, down a short hallway and into the kitchen. Her jaw dropped as she took in the high-beamed ceilings from which dangled pots of all sizes; a long oak table, and a tremendous stone fireplace next to which stood a six-burner stove. "Oh, what a splendid room!" she said, her eyes savoring the cozy look and feel of the place.

"I love it, too," Laura said. "This was once the entire house. My grandparents built it and lived right here in this room with my mother and her baby brother. Sometimes, I imagine my mother being rocked to sleep beside that hearth or my grandmother knitting by its light at night. It's my favorite place in the whole house."

Joanna understood why. The room drew her in, warming and welcoming her to stay a while, and chat. She could easily envision a woman rocking her baby beside the stone hearth and she wondered what Laura's mother looked like. Was she the one who gave Edgar and Joe their almost violet eyes, or were hers dark like Laura's? Did the McGills get their height from her? Joanna's open mouth was nearly a question mark, and then, the back door blew open.

"It's really coming down now, Aunt Laura! Pa and I put the rope out to the barn just in case the storm gets worse overnight. What's for supper? When do we eat?"

Edgar glanced at Joanna, shaking his head. "Miss Garrett, I'm afraid you'll have your hands full with my son."

"Don't worry, Mr. McGill. I can handle as many boys as can fill my classroom. And I like questions. They're the best way to learn."

Joe looked at Joanna as if he had found a new friend. His father looked at her as if she were crazy.

Laura brushed past both of them and set a steaming mug in front of Joanna. "I hope you like coffee as much as you like questions. We have it morning, noon, and night, especially in the winter. Cream and sugar are on the table. And, Joe, we're having stew and cornbread for supper. They're almost ready, so go wash your hands. And, you, too," Laura said, gently shoving her brother.

Edgar said grace in a way that reminded Joanna of her father. When her heart began to race, she took a deep breath and forced herself to focus on the plate of food. The crusty top of the cornbread gave way to its soft underneath and the hot stew and coffee warmed her from the inside out. Dessert was a slice of hot, dried apple pie served with a hunk of cheddar cheese on the side.

"These go well together," Joanna said.

"My father would be pleased to hear you say that, Miss McGill. He always said he needed a piece of cheese to cut the sweet of the pie," Edgar smiled. "My mother laughed at him, but she served cheese with every apple pie she made. Laura does, too."

When Laura rose to clear the table, Joanna stood up, too. Laura shook her head and took the plate and stew bowl out of Joanna's hands. "No, ma'am. You have to be exhausted after your long trip. Edgar will show you to your room while Joe helps me with these dishes. We'll be done in no time."

Joanna *was* exhausted. She had found it almost impossible to rest on the train, with the constant clatter and coal soot blowing everywhere, and the presence of two men in what she had hoped would be a ladies parlor car. Not that Joanna minded men, it was the way they had looked at her, giving long and appreciative stares when she took her seat. Their eyes followed her every move. Joanna, with her high bosom and rounded hips, was accustomed to having men notice her, but something about those two had left her trembling, perhaps, because she was traveling alone, and farther than she'd ever been before.

After Edgar showed Joanna into a small bedroom on the upper floor and went back downstairs for her trunk, she sank down on the bed with a sigh, hardly able to wait to get undressed and crawl under the layers of quilts. She sat, tracing the stitching on the top one, until Edgar returned with her trunk.

"If I didn't know any better, I'd say you had bricks in here," he said, smiling up at her. Her dark eyes glanced to his. There was no mistaking the weariness in them, but there was something else he couldn't name. Sadness, perhaps, or fear. He felt the urge to reach out to her, to reassure her she was safe, but propriety stopped him. "Do you need anything else, Miss Garrett?"

"No, I'm fine," she said, through a weak smile.

"Then I'll be saying goodnight. You must be more than ready to unpack your bag."

As soon as she heard Edgar's boots clumping down the stairs, she pulled a nightgown and robe from her carpetbag, along with her hairbrush and a well-worn Bible. She took off her clothes, seeing for the first time just how grimy they were, and hung them over a straight-back chair in front of a small roll-top desk. She splashed some water into the washbowl and shivered as she quickly scrubbed her face, neck, hands and feet. *Just a spit bath tonight.* Tears filled her eyes with the memory that phrase evoked. She drew on her gown and turned down the bed covers, sighing with pleasure as she anticipated crawling under them.

A knock at the door startled her and she pulled on her robe and opened the door.

Joe was clutching a bulky, blanketed object. "Aunt Laura wanted you to have this bed warmer, Miss Garrett."

"Thank you, Joe. This will be a great comfort." He nodded and stared at her for a moment, then ran for the stairs.

Joanna giggled. *Good thing I didn't have any curling papers in my hair — the sight of his schoolteacher in night clothes was too much for him.*

She wedged the warmer near the foot of the bed before removing her wrapper and climbing in. She lifted her Bible, opened it to *Proverbs* and softly spoke aloud the passage she had recited before going to sleep every night for the past month: *"Trust in the Lord with all thine heart; and lean not unto thine own understanding. In all thy ways acknowledge Him, and He shall direct thy paths."*

She sank back into the pillow and looked up to heaven: "Dear God, I don't know why I had to come here, and I don't know if I've strayed from Your path, but I do trust You with all my heart and I'm trying to believe that I am where You want me to be. Thank you for the kindness of these good people who have welcomed me into their home. Thank you for bringing me smiles and laughter tonight when tears were all I expected. I pray that I will fulfill Your purpose for me and be a blessing to others in this new place." Her lips formed the word, *Amen,* but Joanna was already asleep.

Chapter Two

Joanna's eyes shot open. *Where am I?* She snatched her woolen wrapper from the bedside chair and raced to the window. She parted the curtains, leaned close, and blew a peephole through the ice-covered pane. Bare, icy limbs of an oak tree scratched at the shutter, and far in the distance a horse grazed on a hillside rimed with glistening frost. *Yes, I'm in Indiana. This is the McGill farm*, she told herself, *and I'm three days away from starting my new job at the Henry Township School.*

She shook herself. *Enough lollygagging, Joanna Garrett. You may be a guest here, but you needn't be a burden to these nice people.* She drew several skirts from her trunk, finally choosing the checked wool in shades of red and brown, along with a red blouse, and a dark leather belt. Not her newest outfit, but one she loved, something familiar and comforting in the midst of all this newness.

In the light of day, Joanna took in the room more fully. Whoever it had belonged to liked things cozy and bright. A braided rag rug covered the wood floor and the small roll-top desk held an inkstand and pens, and a sheaf of paper, even a blotter. The white muslin curtains were embroidered with red and pink roses, which also adorned the globed china lamp on the bedside table. After a final check in the mirror, Joanna made her bed, locked her trunk, made one final check in the mirror, and walked out into the hallway. "Oh, I'm so sorry, Mr. McGill," she said, embarrassed that she hadn't looked down the hall, and avoided bumping into him. "Good morning."

"Mornin' to you, Miss Garrett. Laura's downstairs, and Joe and I'll be joining you as soon as I get that lazy boy up," he said with a grin, heading for the loft where Joe slept.

Edgar had awakened before dawn to a mind racing with expectation. *Just one more day until the dance in town. One more day until I hold Lucy Sheppard in my arms.* The next thought came swiftly and unbidden. *And maybe, just maybe, one more day until I finally get the chance to kiss her.* Edgar wouldn't admit, even to himself, how often he dreamt about Lucy, her blonde hair cascading down onto her bare shoulders, her wide blue eyes slightly closed, her lips against his. No other woman had caught Edgar's eye, much less quickened his pulse, since Bessie died. He feared he would never again feel the love he had felt for his Bessie. Even more, he feared that he would.

Edgar had no idea where he stood with Lucy. More than one woman had made it clear that she'd be willing to take Bessie's place—in Edgar's life and in his bed—but Lucy Sheppard wasn't one of them. She would promenade with him at square dances and accept a cup of punch at a church social, but she did the same with Jim Owens and Cal Turner. *So why is Lucy the one I dream about? Is it because she isn't chasing me? Or because she's so different from the women who are?*

Lucy's widower father owned the town's weekly newspaper and Lucy worked there, writing chatty pieces about Appleton's social life, such as it was. Last year, she had talked her father into hiring an itinerant photographer to take pictures of the fire at Dave Calhoun's place. Everyone had gladly paid extra for the special edition with those photographs. Lucy was something, all right, and Edgar wanted to find out what that *something* was.

"Joe! Wake up, son!" Edgar tousled Joe's light brown hair. "It's past six o'clock. I've already started the chores!" Joe pulled the quilt up over his head, but Edgar yanked it off.

"All right, Pa, all right! I'm getting up," he moaned, rubbing his eyes as he rolled off the bed, wrapping the top blanket around him. "I'll be downstairs in a minute."

"You better be, son," Edgar said, reaching to ruffle his son's hair again. "I know how hard it is to get out of bed some mornings, but the cows can't wait. When school starts next week, you'll have to hustle to get your chores done and get to class on time."

"I won't have to worry about being late, Pa—not when I'm riding with my teacher!"

Edgar was still grinning when he passed through the kitchen and saw Joanna setting the table for breakfast. *Boy, she's a little thing. I bet I could put both my hands around her waist and pick her up, easy as pie.* He felt the rush of a flush at the thought and hurried past her without saying a word.

"Breakfast will be ready when you are, Ed," Laura called after him. "Where's that lazy nephew of mine?"

"He's up—but he better be down here before I get to the barn. I don't know what got into him, sleeping late. He's going to be in for a shock next week when he has to do chores *and* get ready for school by seven-thirty."

A minute later, Joe bounded into the kitchen, pulling his suspenders up over his shoulders, and reaching to pluck one of the rolls from the tin Laura had just taken out of the oven.

"Wait till breakfast," she scolded, lightly smacking his arm. Joanna noticed, though, that Joe had successfully seized a roll as he raced for the lean-to. She tried, unsuccessfully, to suppress a smile.

"My younger brother—the one next to me in age—was always ravenous in the morning," she said. "I used to sneak him a slice of bread when my mother wasn't looking."

"How many brothers do you have? And do you have sisters?" Laura knew very little about the woman chosen as the first teacher at the new township school.

"I have two brothers, one older, one younger. They're back home in North Carolina."

"You're the only girl?"

"Indeed I am. And my brothers would tell you I'm spoiled rotten because of it!"

"Must have been hard for you to leave them. I can't even imagine life without Ed and Joe."

I couldn't imagine it either, until I had to, she thought. "Tell me where the silverware is and I'll finish setting the table."

"Have some coffee first, Miss Garrett," Laura said, handing Joanna a mug and pointing to the pot of bubbling water on the stove. "I can't remember whether you take cream and sugar."

"I use both, and please, call me Joanna. The coffee smelled so good when I woke up, and I thank you for such a pleasant start to my day. I was always the first one up at home, so I made the coffee and everyone else got to savor the delicious smell." She reached for the sugar bowl and put a spoonful into her cup. She saw that Laura noticed. "I always do it this way. My grandmother said coffee tastes better if you put the sugar in first."

"My mother said the same thing!" Laura flashed her ready smile once more. "I drink my coffee black, but you just watch that brother of mine. He'll put the sugar in his cup as soon as he sits down. And, Joanna, please call me Laura."

Edgar and Joe came in from the barn and the four sat down to Laura's breakfast of eggs, home cured bacon, and those wonderful rolls that Joe couldn't resist. Edgar reached for the sugar bowl first thing. Joanna caught herself before she burst out laughing, and shot a glance at Laura, who nodded with a grin.

I like it here. I like these people and I hope I'm going to like the town and the school as much,.

As soon as breakfast was over, Joanna joined Laura at the sink. One washed, the other dried and the dishes were soon back in the cupboard.

"Now, what else needs doing?" Joanna asked.

"I'm not going to want you to move into the Gordon place, Joanna! It's been a long time since I had any help in this house!"

"Now wait a minute, Aunt Laura!" Joe's eyebrows furrowed. "I thought you said I was as good as you are at sweeping the floors!"

"So I did, Joe, but, as good as you are, I have a feeling Miss Garrett might be even better."

"If nothing else," Joanna interjected, "I've had more experience. Could you tell me more about the Gordon house, Laura? Mr. McGill said the school board hasn't yet decided what to do about it."

"Oh, they're still fussing about spending time and money on that place, especially after the other teachers boarded with different families for a month at a time. But several women, myself included, felt we needed to give our teacher a little privacy. We thought a man with a family couldn't very well stay at other folks' houses." Laura bit her lip. "Oh, Joanna, I didn't mean that the way it sounded! We didn't think boarding would be fine for a woman either."

"I didn't take it that way, Laura." she smiled, quick to reassure this young woman, whom she already liked. "Tell me about the house."

"Well, it's about a mile from town and has a little bit of land with it—not enough to farm, but enough for a real nice garden and some flowers, too, if you've a mind to." She knew from the sparkle in Joanna's eyes that the new schoolteacher would have roses, along with corn and tomatoes. "You'll have just a half mile walk to the school, which is the last building on that side of town.

The house isn't big, but it has a good-sized front room and a kitchen and two little bedrooms. The front porch needs fixing and the whole house needs a coat of paint come spring."

"It sounds wonderful. I would love to have a place of my own." Joanna's eyes widened in the realization of what she had said. "Oh, Laura, how rude of me! I didn't mean to make it sound like I'm unhappy to be here."

"No offense taken, Joanna—it seems we both suffer from foot-in-mouth disease! You just spoke from your heart. Any woman would prefer a place of her own to living with a different family every month. I couldn't do it."

"Couldn't do what, Laura?" Edgar asked, joining the women in the front room where they sat talking. "I didn't think there was *anything* you thought you couldn't do!"

Laura grabbed a cushion from the horsehair settee and whacked her brother with it. "We were talking about living with different people every month, the way poor Miss Lambert had to do—that's what. Living with you two is bad enough. At least I know all your bad habits, like the way you always run your fingers through your hair when—"

Edgar's hand covered her mouth. "Now, Laura, don't be telling Miss Garrett our family secrets. We don't want her packing up and moving out on her first day with us."

"I don't think there's any chance of that, Mr. McGill. I don't have any place to go, and besides, I'm enjoying myself here. My room is the prettiest I've had in some time, and I'll venture a guess that I have your sister to thank for that."

"You sure do, Miss Garrett. That was Laura's room when we were children and she had it all fixed up as a study before we knew you'd be coming to stay with us," he said. "That was going to be her writing room."

"Now who's telling our family secrets?" She laughed and turned to Joanna. "I'm very happy you like it and find it comfortable."

She must really love to write, Joanna thought. *I wonder if she'll tell me about it when we get to know each other better.*

"When do you want to take Joanna into town, Ed? Shall we go this morning, or wait until we go to the dance tomorrow?"

A dance? That's the last place I want to meet the students' parents.

"Well, I've finished the chores," he said. "So I can take you before dinner if you'd like."

Laura came forward on her chair. "It's a square dance at the Grange. The Ladies Aid Society is trying to raise money for a pipe organ for the church. Everybody pays a twenty-five-cent admission. The ladies will be selling coffee and punch and cookies, and raffling off some pies and cakes. I baked some gingerbread that's cooling in the pie safe."

"I'd love to go to town and see everything in daylight," Joanna said, "if you're sure that won't inconvenience you, Mr. McGill. I am eager to see the schoolhouse, too."

"Just give me a few minutes to make sure Joe knows what I want him to do and then we'll be on our way," he said, then turned to Laura. "We'd better put some bricks to warm so you and Miss Garrett won't be too cold. There's not much snow, but it's frigid out there and the way the clouds look, it's not going to get any warmer."

Fifteen minutes later the three were in the wagon that had brought Joanna to the farm the night before, the bay briskly trotting north toward town. The women, buttoned into coats with hoods, their hands covered in woolen mittens, were snug with hot bricks at their feet and blankets over their laps. Edgar had fewer comforts. His flannel shirt and overalls were topped with a leather coat lined with lamb's wool, and he wore a checked cap pulled low over his ears. A few strands of his dark brown hair escaped the cap and curled on his neck.

Joe must have gotten his light, straight hair from his mother, Joanna thought. *I wonder what happened to her?*

"We're almost to the Gordon place," Edgar called out. "Do you want to stop, Miss Garrett?"

"Yes, I'd love to peek in the windows if you think it would be all right."

"You can probably do more than that." The pink and gray scarf around Laura's face muffled her voice." The house was wide open the last time I was here. There's nothing anybody would want to steal."

Edgar pulled up in front of the one-story clapboard house, gave his sister a hand down, then took hold of Joanna's red-mittened hand and helped her down from the wagon. *My, she's tiny,* he thought again, *and so pretty.* He suddenly blushed, thankful the wind and cold could be blamed for his flushed cheeks. "Mind the steps," he warned as they walked up onto the sagging porch. "They're a mite uneven."

Laura turned the doorknob and stepped aside for Joanna. She walked inside what might be her home and her heart sank. The interior almost made the outside look good. Two small windows shed miniscule light into a dark, damp smelling front room, and the kitchen was no better. No stove, no sink, just a Hoosier cabinet missing its doors. *No wonder the school board doesn't want to fix up this place,* Joanna thought. *It's a mess!*

"It doesn't look like much, does it?" Laura touched Joanna's shoulder. "Let's see the rest of the place."

From the lean-to attached to the kitchen, the women saw a dilapidated barn and what once might have been a chicken coop. Then they inspected the two bedrooms. One was a little larger than the other and, for the first time, Joanna thought the house might not be completely hopeless after all. Though the bedroom was dark, like the rest of the house, it had a large window, facing east, and walls of knotty pine. She could position her bed—when she had one of her own—facing the window, so she could watch the sunrise as she awoke; she loved to greet God with the dawn. She turned back to Laura and saw that Edgar had joined his sister at the door. *How like they are, and how unlike. Both tall, one olive skinned and the other fair; one with almost violet blue eyes, while the other's were a warm, dark brown.*

"It needs a little work, but I believe it will be a good place to live."

"A *little* work?" Edgar's eyebrows shot up. "It's dark and damp and that porch is downright dangerous." Laura glared at him and he scratched the top of his head. "But it's got a good roof and it is close to the school house, and it would be all yours."

Joanna sighed and gave them a wide smile. "All mine."

The schoolhouse gave Joanna immediate cause for joy. It was, obviously, brand new; its boards were almost white, and the school yard was all dirt and no grass. That it was a two-story building surprised Joanna, who had been told she would be the only teacher for 30 pupils. The shiny new bell hanging at the entrance tempted her to pull its rope cord. *No, I'll wait till Monday, when I'll give it a good tug!*

Edgar tried the door; it was locked. Joanna peered through a window and saw rows of double student desks and the teacher's desk at the front. *My desk. Come Monday, I'll be the teacher in this bright new building. I hope I can give the children what they need.*

They took a quick turn through town, heading down what seemed to be the main street that, even in the bitter cold, was filled with people—women shopping with children in tow and men unloading goods from wagons, or standing in shop doorways. Joanna took note of two dry goods stores, the apothecary, the boarding house that Laura mentioned, a hardware shop and bakery, two saloons, and a fancy hotel with a sign that read: *The Morgan House - Nice Rooms and Good Food.*

Several people waved at Edgar and Laura, and more than a few folks stared at the petite stranger in the bright red hooded coat and red mittens.

I wish I had worn my black tam coat and gray scarf, Joanna thought, nervously squirming on the wood seat

"Everyone knows who you are," Laura said, as if reading her mind.

You could be draped in widow's weeds and they'd still stare at you, Edgar thought.

Joanna however leaned back on the seat with a sigh when they headed south from town.

Edgar dropped the women at the front door and drove to the barn, where he put up the horse and gave her a bucket full of oats. He ran the wide field that lay between the barn and the house, feeling the wind cutting through his coat. The sky, which had been a light gray that morning, was now filled with ominous, low-hanging black clouds.

"Looks like more snow," he said, rubbing his hands together as he hurried into the warm kitchen. "Toad, we'd better cut some more firewood and fill the coal scuttles, and make sure there's plenty of hay in the barn. Let's get on it right after dinner."

After a meal of potato soup and rye bread, and more of Laura's good apple pie, Edgar and Joe left to tend to their chores. As soon as the women were alone, Joanna asked Laura the question she'd been itching to ask during dinner.

"Why on earth does Mr. McGill call his son *Toad?*"

"That's a good story," she laughed, "but I should let Joe tell it to you. He's heard it so often that he thinks he remembers when it happened, but he was just a newborn babe at the time."

"All right. I'll ask Joe to tell me the story when we're alone."

That opportunity came sooner than she thought.

Chapter Three

Joanna bolted upright around midnight when the shutter outside slammed her window, ripped off, and landed on the roof with a thud. She heard footsteps in the hall and recognized them as Edgar's. She listened for another door to open. If Laura got up, she would, too. But all was suddenly quiet and Joanna nestled back under her quilts, shivering and wishing the brick at the foot of her bed had remained warm.

It was still dark when she rose, so dark that she thought it might still be nighttime. She parted her curtains and peered out. It was indeed morning, but the clouds hovering overhead were such a mass of gray and black that virtually no sunlight pierced them. Edgar had accurately predicted the snow. Down it had fallen, all night and now, the next morning, with large flakes and smaller ones laced with particles of ice.

She dressed as fast as she could, blowing on her fingers to warm them so she could fasten the buttons on her bodice.

All three McGills were already in the kitchen when she joined them downstairs, each with a cup of coffee; an empty cup waited for her.

"Good morning," Laura said. "Have some coffee to warm yourself. I haven't been up long enough to have this room heated."

"Did the storm do much damage?"

"We were lucky, Miss Garrett," Edgar said, focusing on his cup of coffee. "Some of the fence behind the barn blew down, but the stock are safe and the barn wasn't damaged. You must have heard that shutter fly off your window and land on the roof. The noise could have awakened the dead."

"It surely woke me! That howling wind sounded almost human. I've never experienced a snowstorm like this."

"I bet you haven't, living in North Carolina," Laura said. "You probably don't get much snow down there."

"Not anything like this. We had a big storm when I was a little girl, and, oh, my brothers and I had such fun in it! You should have seen the snowball fight we had. Papa got so angry when he saw my brothers pelting me with snowballs—" She paused. "Of course," she said, sheepishly, "I was throwing snowballs at them, too!"

"You were in a snowball fight?" Surprise filled Joe's voice.

"There wasn't much my brothers did that I wouldn't try."

"But—you're a school teacher!"

Joanna laughed. "I am now, Joe, but I wasn't then. I was just a 10-year-old girl having fun. Unfortunately, that snow was gone almost as fast as it came. But, I have a feeling *this* snow might be here until Easter."

"Welcome to Indiana, Miss Garrett," Edgar said with a grin. "Too bad you didn't come in summer time so you could see how pretty this place is. Winter isn't our best season."

"Winter would be all right, Pa, if it wasn't so doggone cold!" Everyone laughed.

What a happy household, Joanna thought. *I'm glad to be here, even for a little while.* She stood at the kitchen window and watched Edgar leading the way to the barn, turning around every few seconds to make sure Joe was still holding onto the guide rope. The snow swirled so fast and thick that the barn was invisible.

"Now I see why Mr. McGill put that rope up. Will they be able to do any work in such a storm?"

"They'll do their chores in the barn—feed the stock and milk the cow—but Edgar won't be able to do a thing about the fence and the shutters until the storm lets up."

"What about the dance tonight?"

"I expect they'll still have it, unless this turns into a real blizzard," Laura said. "Why, if we let cold and snow stop us, we wouldn't do much all winter!" She paused. "I'm not going, though, and I don't think Ed will either, even though he's been counting the days."

Joanna started to ask the obvious question, but thought better of it. *A lady friend, no doubt.*

* * *

Wilmington, N.C. - June 1883

Joanna stood by the window, its shutters open to the breeze, drinking in the scent of gardenias and jasmine.

"A penny for your thoughts."

"Are you sure they're worth that much?"

"They are to me," he said.

At that, she turned trying to suppress the smile that so wanted to appear. "Why, Mister Brodie, what a thing to say! I thought a big Raleigh attorney would have a better grasp on the value of money."

Nicholas Brodie leaned closer, far enough to maintain propriety, yet near enough so only Joanna could hear him. "If we were out in the garden, behind that hedge of gardenias, Miss Garrett, I would show you *exactly* how much I value your—thoughts."

Joanna seldom blushed but did so now. "Then, I can only be thankful we are in the parlor, Mister. Brodie."

Nicholas took Joanna by the hand and led her into the drawing room, where the furniture had been moved to the room's perimeter to accommodate the guests. The musicians on piano, violin, and bass were playing a Viennese waltz. He glided Joanna across the polished floor, so gracefully and with such ease that more than a few heads turned. Some eyes admired, while others envied Joanna's charm and beauty, and Nicholas' confidence and form.

And then, there were the snippets of conversation Joanna caught between two ladies as she and Nicholas swept by. "Don't they look fine together? ... They're a handsome couple."

Nicholas and I—a couple?

It was long after midnight but Joanna was still keyed up and wide-awake. She heard her parents talking in their room next door. They must have forgotten to shut their door or, perhaps, they assumed she was fast asleep. Joanna knew she shouldn't be eavesdropping, but...

"Didn't Joanna and Nicholas Brodie look wonderful dancing together?" Mrs. Garrett queried her husband.

"Josie always looks wonderful—whether she's dancing, or just sitting still."

"I think they make a perfect couple."

"I know *you* do, my dear."

Joanna caught her father's inflection.

"Well, of course, I do!" her mother reaffirmed. "Nicholas Brodie is a fine young man, from a good family. He would be a good provider and just think of the home our girl would have! Don't you agree?"

"Mr. Brodie certainly has a promising law career and I gather he moves in very high society," her father said.

"I think Mr. Brodie will soon ask for our daughter's hand."

I do, too, Mama.

"I'm afraid you're right, Helen."

"*Afraid* I'm right? Matthew, don't you want Joanna to marry Mr. Brodie?"

Joanna held her breath, waiting for his reply that was long in coming.

"I want what is best for Josie. I like Nicholas Brodie well enough. I just... I just don't know if he would be the best husband for our girl."

"Matthew! Whatever do you mean?"

"Nicholas Brodie is a smart man and, I think, a good one. But our Josie needs something *more* in a husband."

"And what, pray tell, does that mean?"

"Oh, I don't know exactly, Helen! Perhaps, more... more... *grace*."

"I'm sure I don't know what you mean."

"I'm not sure I do either, my dear." Joanna heard his deep sigh. "Let's go to sleep."

* * *

Appleton, Indiana - January 1885

A blast of frigid air with whirling snow blew Joe and Edgar into the lean-to. Edgar's neatly trimmed mustache was white with ice and only Joe's blue eyes were visible above the muffler that covered his face and wrapped around his neck. He looked like one of the mummies in the history book in Joanna's trunk. Laura grabbed a broom and swept the snow off the two of them. As soon as Joe was out of his coat, he made straight for the cook stove and pulled a chair up beside it.

"Not so close," Edgar cautioned. "You need to thaw slowly or you might burn yourself."

"Maybe you should have a cup of coffee to warm you up, Joe," Laura said. "Or would you rather have tea?"

"Coffee sounds great, Aunt Laura! Can I fix it myself?"

"You mean *may* I fix it—and no, son, you may not," Edgar said. "The last time you fixed your own cup you had a little coffee with your sugar. Let your Aunt Laura fix it, or we'll be out of sugar before this storm blows over."

Joe rolled his eyes but eagerly accepted the steaming cup Laura set on the table for him—just as he liked it, half coffee, half hot milk, and plenty sweet. She handed a mug to her brother, too.

"It must be worse than I thought, Ed. It's a good thing you and Joe laid in plenty of wood yesterday."

A snort from Joe turned all eyes to him as he choked on his coffee, then burst out laughing.

"What is wrong with you?"

"I can't help it, Pa." Joe said, slapping his knees. "You should see yourself! You've got icicles on that old caterpillar under your nose and they're melting, and the thing looks like it's trying to run off your face!"

Edgar turned red and hopped up, peering at his reflection in the polished surface of the coffeepot. Joanna tried not to laugh, but Laura cackled along with her nephew. Joe's description was all too apt. It did look just like a fuzzy brown caterpillar crawling across Edgar's lip—an elderly caterpillar at that.

"That's enough out of both of you! It's a sad day when a man can't get any respect in his own home!" Edgar shook his head and stalked out of the kitchen, his boots pounding the floor as he headed upstairs to his room.

The remaining two McGills were still laughing and Laura was wiping tears with her apron.

"He really is angry, isn't he?" Joanna asked.

"No, he's not," they both said.

"He's just pretending to be," Joe said. "I call that old mustache of his a caterpillar all the time."

"Maybe he is a little angry, Joe, " Laura said. "After all, it's one thing to tease him when it's just us, and quite another with Miss Garrett here. She must think we're all a little crazy, and rude, too."

"I think nothing of the sort," Joanna said. "You're very at ease with each other and you like to have fun. I'm delighted to be in such a happy home."

When the dishes were washed and the kitchen tidied, the two women went upstairs.

"Let's just give everything a lick and a promise this morning," Laura said at the top of the stairs. "It's really cold up here."

Joanna had just finished in her room when Laura called out: "Joanna, will you come here a minute? I'd like to show you something."

Laura's room was yet another surprise in this house filled with the unexpected. The walls were a cheery robin's egg blue and the furniture—bedstead, table, chair and high dresser—were bright white. Blue and white gingham curtains fluttered at the window and a matching coverlet lay on the bed.

"Your room feels like springtime, even now in the midst of winter!"

"I need bright and pretty things around me," Laura said, "especially when everything outside is dull and gray." She motioned Joanna to her side and extended a photograph in an oval gilt frame. In it were six people— an older couple standing together behind a chair, a younger man and woman standing beside them, and a young woman seated in the chair, holding a baby. Joanna didn't recognize the older people or the seated woman, but she knew the others in a heartbeat.

"Why, that's you and Edgar! And that pretty baby must be Joe! Are those two handsome people your parents?"

"Yes, and thank you for calling them handsome. I always thought my mother was the prettiest woman I've ever seen, and my father the best looking man. This was taken at the newspaper office when a traveling photographer came through the year Joe was born. My father wasn't one for extravagances, but he made an exception that day. I treasure it so." Laura touched the frame lovingly, almost caressing it. "You'll think me strange, but, sometimes, I sit here and talk to Mama and Father... I feel as if they're right here with me."

"When did they die?" Joanna saw tears well up in Laura's eyes. "I'm so sorry. I didn't mean to—"

"It's all right, Joanna," Laura said, wiping her tears. "I haven't cried for them in a long time, I probably need to. They died eight years ago in an influenza epidemic. My father died first and my mother, who had nursed him day and night, died two days later."

"Oh, Laura...".

"It was awful, losing them both at the same time. But it was even worse when Joe lost his mother."

"I assumed that had to be her," Joanna said, gazing down at the photograph, "she's looking at him so tenderly. And all three of them dying in the epidemic... how dreadful!"

"It was horrible," Laura said, lowering herself onto the chair beside her bed. "I hope I never go through anything like it again. But Bessie didn't die of influenza. She died a few days after giving birth to a baby girl. There was a problem with the delivery. Doc Peters was tending to the sick way on the other side of town. He couldn't get here in time... we just couldn't stop the bleeding. It was a month after my parents died, and was a terrible blow. We were all so eager to have new life in the house, and then we lost Bessie and the baby. Edgar was devastated."

Joanna knelt, took Laura's hands in hers and held them tightly. Laura's eyes were now dry but Joanna was weeping. Silence reigned for several minutes, then Laura spoke in a near whisper.

"I don't know what made me tell you this today. Maybe it was what you said about us being a happy family. There was a time when I thought we would never be happy again. Hearing you describe us that way gladdened my heart."

"Grief never completely goes away," Joanna said, "but life goes on, and with God's love and the passing of time, there is healing. Thank you for sharing this with me. I feel as if I've known you and Joe and Mr. McGill longer than just these two days."

They walked downstairs, finding both Joe and Edgar in the kitchen; Joe holding a book and Edgar stretching what appeared to be a strip of leather.

"Pa's going to fix Dolly's harness, Aunt Laura. He wants me to read to him while he does it."

"We'll join you, Joe. Just give me a minute to get my knitting."

"And I'll run upstairs and get my handwork, too," Joanna echoed.

The clock in the front room chimed nine times when Joanna pulled a chair into the family circle, where Laura was already knitting something soft and blue. "What are you reading, Joe?"

"*Treasure Island*. I just hope there aren't too many big words in it. I'm not so good at reading."

"You'll do fine—and we can help you with the words you don't understand. I know you're going to like this book. It's a wonderful adventure and Mr. Stevenson paints pictures with his words. You'll be able to see Jim and Billy Bones and—" Joanna abruptly stopped. "I don't want to give away the story."

While the storm raged outdoors, the group inside heard only Joe's voice, the crackling fire, and the click-clack of knitting needles. Every so often Joe stumbled over a word like *schooner* or *Hispaniola* or *frigate*, and one of the adults corrected him. At the end of the first chapter, Joe put the book down, walked to the fireplace and rubbed his hands together. Suddenly, he began marching around the room, saying, *"Fifteen men on the dead man's chest – Yo-ho-ho, and a bottle of rum!"*

"Simon Joseph McGill, you stop that!" Edgar's tone was stern. "That kind of language may be fine coming from a pirate, but I don't want to hear it from you!"

Joe froze in mid step, crestfallen.

Laura put down her knitting and stood up. "Come help me peel some potatoes and carrots for soup, Joe. We'd best get started if we want to eat dinner by noon." Joe was still nodding his assent when they heard the lean-to door bang shut.

"Why, whoever can that be, in this weather!" Laura said. Edgar was already out of his chair and on the way to the kitchen, harness in hand.

Joanna wondered if he meant it for a weapon or if he simply didn't think to drop it before running to the door. *Don't be silly! No one would break into a house in the middle of the morning and during a blizzard. The storm and Mr. Stevenson's rousing tale have kindled your imagination!*

Edgar returned, accompanied by another man wrapped in a fur coat and covered with snow. Both faces were grim.

Laura looked up, then jumped from her chair. "Jim! If you're out in this storm, there must be trouble. It's Mary, isn't it?"

The man nodded. "I hate to ask you on a day like this, but can you come, Laura? Mary's been having pains all night. I'd go for Doc Peters, but I don't think I'd make it in this weather. Emma Johnson is sick herself or I'd have gotten her." Edgar and Laura knew what Joanna didn't, that Emma Johnson was the local midwife.

"Of course I'll come. Just give me a few minutes to get my things together," she said and flew up the stairs. Joanna hurried to the kitchen to gather food.

"Jim, go on into the kitchen and warm up. I'll go hitch up Dolly," Edgar said and turned to Joanna. "Miss Garrett, would you fill a foot warmer for us? And maybe get Jim here a cup of coffee?" Edgar was out the door with Joe at his heels.

She poured the cup of coffee and placed it in front of the visitor. She didn't know his last name but couldn't very well use his given name because they hadn't been introduced. "That will warm you up," she said and tried a smile. "I'm Joanna Garrett, the new schoolteacher. I'm staying with the McGills for a while."

"If I were thinking straight this morning, I'd of known that. I'm Jim Langston." He sipped the hot coffee, clutching the cup to warm his reddened hands.

Joanna went to the pantry and began filling what looked like a peach basket. Tea, a loaf of bread, Laura's gingerbread, a jar of jelly and a larger jar of chicken and noodles went into the basket, She covered it with a red-checkered towel tucked firmly down so the food wouldn't be dampened with snow when it arrived at the Langston place, wherever that was.

Laura rushed in, carrying a satchel, and stood beside Jim Langston. He gulped down his coffee.

Edgar hurried in a moment later. "I gave your horse some water, Jim, and Dolly is hitched to the wagon. Grab that foot warmer, Joe, and put it in the box for your aunt. I'll carry your satchel out, Laura, while you get your coat on."

It suddenly dawned on Joanna that Edgar was going to drive Laura to the Langstons. "We'll look after things... don't worry," she said firmly.

"We'll be fine, Pa, " Joe said, stepping next to Joanna. "I'll do the afternoon milking if you're not back in time."

Edgar cuffed the boy lightly on the shoulder. "I'll be counting on you, son. Wrap up well and keep a good hold on that rope, whatever you do."

"I will, Pa."

"I'll watch out for him, Mr. McGill." Joanna turned to Laura and hugged her. "I'll be praying until you're back home again."

She and Joe stood at the lean-to door watching Jim Langston help Laura into the wagon and Edgar snap up the reins. They waved until the horse and wagon disappeared from sight, though no one was looking back.

Be safe, Joanna prayed. *And, Lord, please let that baby and mama be safe, too.*

Chapter Four

The kitchen loomed large and empty after everyone had left. *What should we do? Anything to keep us from thinking about the storm or how Mary Langston is. But what?*

"Miss Garrett?" Joe tapped her shoulder. "Aunt Laura was startin' to fix dinner when Mr. Langston burst in. Shouldn't we be cooking? I'm getting hungry."

"That's just what we should do, Joe. I'll try my hand at making some potato soup and maybe some cornbread, too."

"I'll peel the potatoes. I'm good at it."

The iron kettle soon simmered on the back burner, filling the kitchen with its fragrance and warmth. "That needs to cook for a while, then I'll put the cornbread in the oven and we'll eat. Shall we read some more while we wait?"

"No Ma'am. I'd hate to be ahead of Pa and Aunt Laura. I'd probably tell them what was going to happen next and ruin the surprise of it. Plus, I might get rowdy again and I'd hate for that to happen."

Rowdy—what a word, she thought, quickly covering her mouth with her hand so Joe wouldn't think she was laughing at him. "You're right, Joe, we should all enjoy sharing the book on these cold winter nights. Would you like me to read from another book, or would you like to play dominoes or maybe checkers?"

"I love checkers!"

"Then checkers it is." She went upstairs and fetched the fine wooden board from her trunk. Two heads were soon bent over it, pondering the next move and waiting to see what the other would do. When the clock chimed eleven-thirty, Joanna headed to the stove. "I'd better get the cornbread in the oven, Joe, or we'll be having dinner at supper time."

Joe watched Joanna grease an iron skillet. "Are you going to bake it in *that*?"

"I sure am. My grandmother made the best cornbread in the world and *always* baked it in a cast iron skillet."

"I've never seen Aunt Laura do it that way."

"That's because it's the way we make cornbread in the south, Joe," She washed her hands and took her seat at the table again. "Now, whose turn is it?"

"Miss Garrett! You know you have to remember who played last or you might lose your turn!"

Play continued in silence, two sets of eyes focused in serious concentration. Joanna didn't try to let Joe win, but win he did, triumphantly taking his teacher's last checker and jumping to his feet.

Joanna stood up and made a mock curtsey to him. "Well played, Joseph McGill. And well timed, too. That cornbread should be ready, so if you'll get us some bowls and cutlery, I'll dish it up and we'll eat dinner."

Ten minutes later they were back at the table with steaming bowls of potato soup in front of them. Joanna served Joe a piping hot hunk of cornbread and placed a piece on her own plate, then said grace. She was pleased to see Joe bow his head and close his eyes.

Joe savored every morsel, alternating bites of soup with nibbles of cornbread. He suddenly stopped and looked into Joanna's eyes. "What do you think Aunt Laura and Pa are doing now?"

"I don't know, Joe." She put down her spoon. "I'm guessing your aunt is busy with Mrs. Langston and your father is helping Mr. Langston do chores."

"I wonder if it's still snowing?" He walked to the window in the front room. "Hey, it stopped snowing! The wind stopped and the sky isn't gray anymore. I think it's over."

"I'm so glad," Joanna said, joining Joe at the window. Before them lay a vast field of white, broken only by the gray walls of the barn and the very top tips of evergreens that hadn't been weighted down with snow. It was a scene straight from a *Currier and Ives* Christmas card. "How beautiful. So pure and clean looking."

"I guess it is, if you haven't seen it before. It's not a good snow for sledding, though. Too fluffy."

They returned to finish their meal. Joanna had asked Joe about the school where she would begin teaching in just two days. He told her about his classmates—the ones he liked and the ones he didn't—and about the work the previous teacher had assigned, how he liked geography and hated spelling, and what games the children liked to play.

"Miss Granger only gave us one recess every day and she took it away if anybody acted up. I didn't think it was right to punish all of us when just a few were misbehavin'. You won't do that, will you?"

"I try to be fair, Joe. I think it's important for my students to get exercise and fresh air during the school day. If weather permits, I like to take a break in the morning and a longer recess after lunch. How does that sound?"

"That sounds great!" Joe's blue eyes danced with delight as his lips broke a wide smile that was so like his father's. "I think you're going to be the best teacher we've ever had!"

I hope he still feels that way when I give him grammar to parse, and arithmetic to do, and those dreaded spelling words!

Joe went to the barn to do chores just before dusk, while Joanna fixed supper. When they sat down to another meal alone together, Joe said grace.

"God, thank you for this food and for Miss Garrett who cooked it so good. Please help Mrs. Langston have her baby safely and let Pa and Aunt Laura get home soon. Amen."

With supper done and the dishes washed and put away, Joanna pondered how to pass the time until they went to bed. "I was wondering if you would like to look at a book I brought with me," she said. "It's a history book with wonderful pictures of different peoples and places. Have you ever seen a mummy?"

"No, ma'am. I don't even know what a *mummy* is."

"Well, let me get the book and you can find out."

Joe spent nearly an hour devouring the section about ancient Egypt, pronouncing that the mummies looked *disgusting;* oohing over the Sphinx, and occasionally reading a choice tidbit aloud.

When the clock sounded its ninth chime, Joanna put her sewing away and joined Joe at the window. "I don't think they're going to come home tonight, Joe. It's awfully cold and I don't think they'd start a long drive this late at night."

"Pa wouldn't stay the night unless he had to," he said with certainty. "He'd want to get home to the stock—and to us."

"Well, we won't bring them home any faster by looking out this window, so let's go up and get ready for bed."

She followed Joe upstairs, waiting while he changed into his bed clothes, then climbed the few stairs to his bedroom in the loft. There wasn't a door, so she called out to him from the top step. "May I come in, Joe?"

"Sure."

The room clearly belonged to a young boy. The loft, triangular in shape, held Joe's bed against one wall, a desk and chair against another, and shelves along the third. A few shelves held clothes, but most were stuffed with an assortment of toys, books, birds' nests, sticks, and rope. Joe was already in bed.

"I wanted to say good night, and to thank you for being so much help and such good company today, even if you did beat me at checkers."

"Beat you twice," he said, grinning, "and I'd of beaten you again if we'd played after supper!"

"I don't know about that," she said, "but I'll give you another chance soon." She wanted to tuck the boy in, but felt it wasn't her place. "I hope you sleep well. I'll see you in the morning," she said, ready to descend the steps when Joe called out to her.

"Yes, Joe?"

"Do you think Mrs. Langston is going to be all right?"

Joanna turned and saw real fear on the boy's face. *And no wonder, when his own Mama died having a baby!* She pulled the only chair in the room close to the bed and sat down. "I hope so, Joe. Is this her first baby?"

"No... they have Jimmy, who's ten, like me; and Abigail, she's about five, and Billy is just a little thing."

"Then, I think Mrs. Langston will be just fine."

"Good. I'd hate for Jimmy to lose his Ma." The unspoken *like I lost mine* hung in the air.

Joanna was at a loss as to how, or if to address the subject. She wanted so much to wrap Joe in her arms and hug him close. Instead, she brushed the hair from his eyes and patted his hand where it lay on top of his quilt. "I would, too, Joe. And I'm so sorry you lost your Mama."

A flood of tears welled up in the little boy's blue eyes, but he brushed them away with the back of his hand. "It's not as bad as it was. I just got to thinking about her today because of Mrs. Langston. I been thinking about Pa, too. I bet it's hard for him to be there."

Joanna had thought that also. Had Edgar spent the day reliving the birth and death of his own daughter, and the death of his much loved wife? "I'm sure there are a lot of things running through your father's mind today, but I'm also sure he's glad to be there to help their family. Now, why don't you close your eyes and get some sleep and I'll do the same. And come morning, we'll probably have good news about a new brother or sister for your friend, Jimmy."

Joanna lifted the chair and set it back at the desk, then headed for the stairs.

She had just made it to the landing when Joe called out again.

She turned.

"I just want to say thanks. Thanks for playing checkers and for getting your book out for me and..." He paused. "Just thanks for everything."

"You're very welcome, Joe McGill. Now, go to sleep."

Chapter Five

Once again, Joanna woke during the night, sitting bolt upright in bed with the hair on the back of her neck prickling. Someone was moving downstairs. She carefully drew on her wrapper, pulled the pistol from her carpetbag and went swiftly, but silently, to the door.

She paused, barefooted, at the top of the staircase. The sound below had stopped. She hugged the wall, tiptoeing down each step and paused, again, as she reached the floor below. Still no noise—until she heard whistling.

Surely no burglar would be stupid enough to whistle while he robbed us. It must be Edgar. She pushed open the kitchen door.

Edgar nearly dropped the whistling tea kettle. "Miss Garrett! You scared the daylights out of me. I thought you and Joe would be fast asleep at this hour."

"*You* were scared to death? It's the middle of the night and I wake up hearing someone moving around down here. I didn't know *what* to think!" Her dark eyes flashed.

"You mean to tell me you thought it might be a thief and you trotted down here—" his eyes focusing on her tiny bare feet, "—in your night clothes to see who it was? You might have been killed!"

"Not very likely, Mr. McGill," she said, lifting her hand. "I'm a pretty good shot, even in the dark."

Edgar dropped the kettle; it clattered onto the stovetop and tipped over. He quickly righted it, then turned back to Joanna. "I thought the excitement of the day was over when I got home tonight, Miss Garrett, but I was wrong. This beats all! A gun-toting school teacher in my own kitchen. Now I've seen everything. Where did you get that thing?"

"My grandfather taught me to shoot when I was a young girl, Mr. McGill, and a friend bought me this pistol when I took a country school miles from the nearest town." Joanna remembered it well...

* * *

Elizabethville, N.C. - February 1884

"Nicholas, I don't need a gun."

"You do."

"No. I don't. It's not as if I'm in Indian Territory."

"Yes, but you're miles from the nearest town. And I don't like it."

Joanna's back stiffened. "You don't like *what*?"

"Any of it. I don't like you out here all alone, and I don't like you taking this school without talking to me first and—"

"Why can't you just say it? You don't like me teaching."

"No. I don't."

"And what would you have me do after working so hard and getting my teaching certificate?"

"Marry me." Nicholas Brodie took hold of Joanna's shoulders and pulled her to him.

"Your father has already given his permission. Joanna. Marry me and come to Raleigh, and then you won't have to teach school."

She pulled free of his hold. "We've been over this before. I *want* to teach, Nicholas. Married women can't teach, you know that."

"Indeed I do, and I thought marriage was a blessing, not a curse."

"You would."

"And what do you mean by *that*?"

"Nothing. You wouldn't understand."

"There's a great deal I don't understand, Joanna."

"I know." *I hardly understand myself.* "But I thank you for being concerned for my safety."

"I love you, Joanna."

"I know."

* * *

"Is that a *Derringer?*"

"Yes, Mr. McGill, it is. I've never aimed it at anyone, but I certainly wasn't coming down those stairs tonight without it!" Joanna sat down at the kitchen table.

"Miss Garrett, you astonish me." He joined her at the table, lifting the teapot in the air. "Have some tea?"

The sight of Edgar with the teapot poised in his hand contrasted so vividly with their conversation that Joanna couldn't help but burst out laughing. Edgar joined her.

"With pleasure, Mr. McGill. But where's Laura, and how is Mrs. Langston?"

"Mary Langston had a little girl late this evening, and they're both fine."

Joanna sighed. "Thank You, Lord."

"Laura wanted to stay the night so she could keep an eye on Mary and cook some food to tide them over for a few days. Jim said he'd drive her home this afternoon, but I told him I'd come back for her. Jim's exhausted, too."

Joanna saw the weariness in Edgar's blue eyes. "Joe and I were thinking about all of you and praying Mrs. Langston would have a safe birthing. I'll do some baking in the morning and send some bread with you, if that's all right."

Edgar nodded.

"And since it is *almost* morning, I think I'll say goodnight now, Mr. McGill." She put her cup in the sink, then headed to the door.

"Miss Garrett?"

Joanna turned around to him. "Yes, Mr. McGill?"

He looked long and hard at her then cleared his throat. "I just wanted to say thank you for watching over Joe and taking care of the house, and coming down here when you knew you might be in danger."

"You're welcome, Mr. McGill."

Joanna was nestled under her quilts when she heard Edgar

pass her room. *He's going to check on Joe.* Sure enough, a few moments later she heard Edgar's footsteps pass her door again and descend the steps. *He's a good father. He reminds me of Papa...*

* * *

Elizabethville, N.C. - March 1884

She was washing the chalkboard when she heard the schoolhouse door open.

"Hello, Josie."

"Papa!" Joanna ran to the door and threw her arms around her father. "What are you doing here? Is everything all right at home?"

"It is, and your mother sends her love."

"Then why are you here?"

Matthew Garrett took his daughter's hand, led her to a bench and sat down beside her. "I wanted to be sure everything is all right with you."

"You came all the way from Wilmington—"

"I came all the way from Raleigh, where I had a synod meeting."

Joanna grinned. "Well, that makes me feel better!"

"And is everything all right with you, Josie?"

She patted her father's knee. "I'm fine, Papa."

"School is going well?"

"It couldn't be better. The students seem to like me. I've learned so much about them, and you simply wouldn't believe how much progress they've made this term. There's one little girl, Papa—she's so eager to learn and so quick. I have to work to stay ahead of her, and none of the others can keep up with her."

"Sounds like a little girl I used to know. Is this child also prone to interrupting and asking lots of questions and does she have trouble sitting still?"

"I never interrupted you, Papa!"

"Me, no. Your teachers, yes. Remember Miss Wheeler in Sunday School?" Her father continued, his voice pitched several octaves higher. "'Reverend Garrett, I am distressed to have to tell you that Joanna was sent to the corner *again* this morning. She cannot seem to learn that she mustn't talk while I am speaking.'"

Joanna giggled. "At least I was awake in her classroom, which is more than I can say for most of her pupils."

Reverend Garrett shook his head. "So, school is going well. What about your living arrangements? Are you lonely?"

How do I tell my father I love having a little house all to myself? "No, Papa, I'm not lonely. I go into town every week to shop and I've made friends with the woman who runs the lending library... I treat myself to tea in the hotel every so often, where I see interesting people. And some of my friends come to see me every now and then."

"Is one of those friends Nicholas Brodie?

Joanna colored. "I haven't seen Nicholas since February, Papa."

"And how do you feel about that?"

I've tried not to think about Nicholas, much less feel anything. "I'm...confused."

"Confused about what?"

"I miss him, but—" The two sat in silence while Joanna considered what she would say next.

"But what, my dear?"

"Nicholas asked me again to marry him, Papa. He doesn't like me teaching here—I don't think he likes me teaching at all! He seems to think I should be leaping at the chance to marry him and be a lawyer's wife and have a fine house to manage."

"Marriage isn't exactly a curse, Josie."

"That's what Nicholas said."

"And you disagree?"

"No, not really, Papa. I want to be married. I see how happy you and Mama are—and I want a home and children. I—I just don't want to be married *now*. I like teaching and I'm only twenty-two and..." *And I like not having anyone telling me what to do!*

"Did you say this to Nicholas?"

"Not in so many words. I think he was angry that I wanted to stay here on my own, though. I don't think he cares *why* I want to do it.

"Give him time, Joanna—and if you don't want this relationship to end, write and tell him so."

"And if I do—want it to end?"

"Don't write him."

Joanna threw her arms around her father's neck, sniffing the familiar scents of pipe tobacco and bay rum. He held her tightly. "I can always talk to you, Papa. And you always understand."

"I try, sweetheart. Now, can you leave this place long

enough to have supper with me? And is there room here for an elderly minister to rest his weary bones for a night?"

* * *

Appleton - January 1885

Joanna was in the kitchen brewing coffee and baking biscuits when Joe burst through the door.

"Is my Pa home? And Aunt Laura?"

"Your father came home late last night, Joe. He's outside doing chores. Your Aunt Laura stayed at the Langstons, but she'll be home later today." She saw the questioning look in Joe's eyes. "*Everyone* is all right, Joe. Your friend, Jimmy, has a new baby sister, and Mrs. Langston is just fine."

When the door to the lean-to opened, Joe ran and flung himself into his father's arms before Edgar had a chance to take off his coat and gloves.

"What's all this?" Edgar said, easing Joe back into the warm kitchen as he shook the snow from his cap and coat. "I wasn't gone that long, son," he said, smiling and rubbing Joe's tousled locks. "That coffee sure smells good, Miss Garrett. Let me get a cup and sit down, Toad, and you can tell me what you did while your aunt and I were gone."

We spent an entire day alone together, Joanna thought, *and I never asked Joe about that nickname!*

"You should see that book, Miss Garrett has, Pa, 'cause you won't believe the pictures in it... dead people wrapped in sheets, big statues shaped like dogs with heads like people—I never seen anything like it!"

Edgar shook his head at his son's grammar but relished the curiosity and delight that showed in his son's eyes. He sipped his coffee and glanced up at Joanna, who turned as if to correct Joe's English, but didn't. *She must be a really good teacher if she's already got Joe this excited about a book.* "I'd like to see it, Joe. I've never seen pictures like that myself. Maybe we can read it when Aunt Laura gets home."

"Can I go with you to get her, Pa? It's not snowing anymore and I could help Jimmy chop firewood if they haven't got enough laid in!"

"You mean *may* you come? I don't know, Toad. Seems like it might be better for you to stay here and do the chores if I don't get back in time."

"I really think it'd be better for me to come along, Pa. It might do Jimmy good to have me there for a little while."

Edgar knew full well that Joe just wanted to be with him and, truth be told, he'd be glad for his company. "All right, son. If Miss Garrett doesn't mind being alone here, you may come along."

"I don't mind at all," she said. "It will give me a chance to get organized for school. Gracious me, I've been so caught up in the storm and the Langstons' troubles that I almost forgot classes begin tomorrow!"

"That's settled, then," Edgar said. "Joe, you help Miss Garrett get these dishes cleared up, and we'll head out as soon as I check the fire in the coal stove and finish up in the barn." He raised his gaze to Joanna. "We should be back before dark for sure."

Joe started clearing dishes from the table while Joanna opened the oven to check on three dried apple pies. She lifted the pies out of the oven and placed them on the cooling rack. The intense aroma of cinnamon and sugar filled the room.

"So that's what smells so good," Joe said. "Are we taking those to the Langstons?" He eyed the pies hungrily, even though he had just eaten oatmeal and biscuits.

"Just two of them, Joe. I thought I'd keep one for us." She began pumping water into the kettle to heat it for the washing. Joe carried the last of the dishes to her, then took the table cloth into the lean-to to shake off the crumbs.

"Joe, there's something I've been meaning to ask you. Your father keeps calling you *Toad*, and I wonder if you'd be willing to tell me why."

Joe groaned and sank into his chair. "I just knew you'd ask me that some day! I wish my Pa wouldn't call me that in front of you. I hate that stupid old name!" He covered his face with his hands and leaned his elbows on the kitchen table.

"If you don't want to tell me, that's all right. It really isn't any of my business. It's just the most unusual nickname I've ever heard."

Joe sighed. "I might as well tell you, Miss Garrett. Just about everybody knows anyway. Here's what happened: When my mama's daddy, my Paw Paw Button, saw me right after I was born, I was all shriveled and puny looking. My pa says it's because I was born a little too soon. Anyway, my Paw Paw said, 'Why, the boy looks just like a little hoppy toad!' And I've been Toad ever since."

"That's a wonderful story, Joe! Only somebody who really loved you could give you a nickname like that. I promise, though, that I'll always call you Joe—or Joseph— unless you tell me otherwise."

Father and son were warmly wrapped and in the wagon with the two freshly baked apple pies that Edgar said would *tempt his senses all the way to the Langston homestead.* Joanna waved them off, without worry this time, then climbed the stairs to her room, where she began poking through the schoolbooks, lesson plans, and ciphers in her trunk. She glimpsed her Bible on the bedside table.

"Today's Sunday!" she said, realizing she had lost track of time in all the excitement. "I wonder if the McGills usually go to church." Laura had said grace at dinner, as had Joe when the two of them were alone, and Laura seemed to appreciate Joanna's prayers for Mary Langston. Joanna well knew, however, that grace at mealtime and praying in times of need didn't mean folks went to worship on Sunday, much less that they really knew the Lord. Her own grandfather had prayed loud and long when he was ill, or crops were bad, or a hurricane was coming—but he never set foot in a church, except for Christmas Eve services and the baptisms of his grandchildren. Her grandmother, though, was another story. Joanna smiled just thinking of her.

She took her Bible downstairs and pulled a rocker close to the coal stove Edgar had stoked before leaving. She had set herself a goal of reading the entire Bible in one year—that was last September—and to accomplish this she read from the Old and New Testaments, Psalms and Proverbs every day. Today, the verse that spoke to her heart was Psalms 32:8: *"I will instruct thee and teach thee in the way which thou shalt go: I will guide thee with mine eye."*

"Thank you, God," she prayed, "for the encouragement of Your word. Help me to teach my pupils what You would have them know, and please, Lord, guide me in all that I do."

The sound of bells drew Joanna's attention from the pot of soup she was stirring. She hurried to wash her hands before running to the back door. She met Joe and Laura head-on as they came into the kitchen; she resisted the urge to hug Laura, and instead helped unwind Laura's muffler from from around her neck, then brushed the snow from Joe's overcoat. The kitchen was aglow in the last sunshine of dusk and the light from a kerosene lamp sitting on a lace doily in the center of the table. The room seemed to reach out and embrace its returning family.

"Welcome home, Laura, and welcome back, Joe. How was your journey?"

"It was great, Miss Garrett! Pa let me drive most of the way there and Jimmy and I had a real battle in the snow and I got to eat some of the pie you sent!"

"It was a much better trip today, Joanna," Laura said. "No wind making it harder for good old Dolly to pull the wagon, no snow in our ears and noses, and best of all, no anxiety. Yesterday, I just wanted to get there as fast as we could."

Joanna handed Laura a cup of coffee and pulled out her seat at the trestle table. "You sit down, Laura, while I finish supper. I bet you didn't get much sleep last night," she said, noticing the dark circles under Laura's eyes. "I'm just so thankful that you got there in time," she went on, "and that Mrs. Langston and her new baby girl are both safe and well. I know the Langstons are grateful for your help."

"I did what any good neighbor would do, but I am glad Jim came here instead of going into town. A few more hours and Mary Langston would have been too worn down to care anymore."

"Don't let her fool you, Miss Garrett," Ed said, his voice coming from the lean-to, "it made a *big* difference having Laura there instead of some other woman. She makes folks feel better just by being with them." He came into the room and inhaled deeply. "Does it ever smell good in here!" He lifted the lid on the iron pot. "Is that vegetable soup?" When Joanna nodded, he rubbed his hands together and reached for a spoon.

"Edgar McGill! Don't you dare sample that soup before it's served! You're as bad as your son when it comes to snitching before meal time!"

"Pardon me," he said snootily. "I was simply overcome by the fragrance and the call of my empty stomach!"

Joanna laughed, mightily pleased by his compliment. "Why don't you sit down with Laura and have a cup of coffee and I'll have supper on the table before you finish it."

Joanna ladled the soup into a tureen, took off her apron and joined the McGills. Edgar bowed his head and asked the blessing. "Lord, we haven't forgotten that today is Your day and we weren't where we should have been to worship You. But I think maybe we were where You wanted us to be, some of us helping a neighbor, and the other helping us. Thank you for Miss Garrett's hands that cooked this fine supper and for Laura's heart that reached out to Mary Langston and her baby. Bless this food to our use and be with us in the morrow."

Joanna's eyes had flickered open and briefly focused on Edgar as he prayed. *Who is this man? He looks like a farmer but he talks like a poet.* Her eyes were closed again when the next through came, but she still flushed. *And he's a very fine looking man.*

Joanna filled the soup bowls, hoping no one had noticed her reddened cheeks. "I have a question about school tomorrow. How am I going to get there? And what time does school start?"

"That's two questions, teacher."

"Joseph." His father's look quelled further sassiness. "I'll drive you and Joe to school; we should be there by eight o'clock., if you want the room warm before your students start arriving. The school bell rings, or, I should say, you ring the bell at eight-forty-five. So, we better leave by seven-thirty."

"I hate to take you away from your work," she said.

"I'd be taking Joe anyway this winter," he said. "Come spring, he'll be walking to school."

"And by then, Joanna, you should be in your own house and be close enough to walk to school yourself!"

After apple pie and more coffee, Joanna excused herself and went upstairs to finish packing her school bag. When she returned to the kitchen, Laura had set the table for breakfast and was busy measuring coffee into the pot on the stove.

"The morning goes a lot better if I get a few things done the night before."

"I do the same thing at school. Before I leave at the end of the day, I straighten up and put the books I need on my desk and write my daily schedule on the chalkboard. Mercy! Is there a chalkboard?"

"There are two! Sam Bailey was in a huff about it, but Minnie—that's Sam's wife—told him to stop behaving like a cheapskate, that by having two chalkboards, the students can do twice as much work. Sam pinches pennies and—" Laura paused through a grin, "he doesn't like change!"

"I'm thrilled to have such a modern classroom. I can't wait to see it tomorrow," she said, unconsciously wringing her hands.

"You can't wait," Laura said softly, "but you're nervous, too. I know I would be if I were in your shoes."

Try scared witless! I'm brand new here, I don't know my students, nor my classroom—I have to make this work. I have nowhere else to go... I can't go back to Wilmington.

* * *

Wilmington, N.C. - November 1884.

"You can't leave—it's the day after Thanksgiving, it's almost Christmas, Joanna. Your school is closed for the holidays and—"

"I can't stay here, Jonathan," she said, anger and hurt controlling the way she forced her clothes into her satchel.

"But this is your home. And I'll miss my only sister, even if she is a nag sometimes."

A smile flickered across Joanna's lips. "I can always nag you by mail."

"Please come home for Christmas. You'll help me cut down a tree, you'll bake your famous cookies, and we'll all go to church. You love the Christmas Eve service."

"I wouldn't be welcome at church, Jon. Not after today." *I may never again be welcome here at home*, she thought.

"Don't say that. You're always welcome at church. Papa would never turn you away."

"No, Papa wouldn't turn me away," she said, "but he wouldn't be happy to see me."

The conversation she had with her parents earlier in the day had shaken her deeply:

"I'm shocked, Joanna," her father had said. "Truly shocked."

"I'm sorry, Papa. But I don't see what I did that was so wrong."

"You don't see *anything* wrong with traveling to Washington, DC—without telling anyone? You don't see *anything* wrong with going to that meeting with radical women who want to vote?"

"No, Papa, I don't."

"But Joanna," her mother interrupted, "a woman's place is in her home, caring for her husband and her children. I can't imagine wanting anything more."

You can't, Mama—but I can.

"God created women for a special purpose, Joanna," her father said, "as a helpmate for man. I've always preached that woman is man's helper—not his servant. Think about what it would be like if all women stopped running their households and caring for their families."

"I'm not saying they should stop doing that, Papa, and neither are the women who want the vote."

"Oh, my dear, dear Josie," her father said, "You're very

wrong about that, and thank the Lord these women are few in numbers. But back to my point. What would a home and a family be like without a loving mother in it?"

"Papa, I know how much Mama does for our family, how hard she works, and how much she loves all of us."

"The family as we now know it can't survive, Josie, if no one is willing to tend it. Our own family wouldn't survive without your mother's hard work and her devotion to us, and to God."

"Women fulfill God's divine purpose, Joanna," her mother said.

"*God's* purpose—not man's," her father said in his pulpit voice.

"I believe that, too. I just don't understand why you think allowing a woman to cast a vote somehow hurts a woman or her family—or obstructs God's purpose."

"It's not just the vote, Joanna," her mother said, "it's what may follow in its wake."

"What do you mean, Mama? I want to know what you think about all this."

"Oh, Joanna," her mother said, hesitating and looking to her husband. "I don't—"

"What do *you* think, Mama?" Joanna persevered.

Her soft-spoken mother sat down in the high back Victorian chair beside the fireplace. "I grew up in a different time, Joanna," she said, shaking her head in contemplation, "with certain customs and proprieties for men and women. To think of women having the right to vote—well, it's a responsibility."

I don't really know how Matthew will feel about this, she thought, *but I have to be honest with my daughter, give her the response she will understand and reflect upon.* Helen Garrett understood the look on her daughter's face and resigned herself, then slowly slid back on the horsehair tufted seat.

"Joanna, I believe that even the suffragettes have no way of knowing where their movement will lead them—or, for that matter, how it will redound to women in the future." She paused and smoothed her skirting.

Joanna remained silent, as did her father.

"If women are granted the right to vote, which I think may happen, in light of the right being given to former slaves... where will it lead? Once women have that right, what else may happen? Will they want to compete with men for employment—or have to do so? And if they do become employed and work alongside of men, will the men want to marry them? Will women forego motherhood to maintain a parity with men?" She furrowed her brow. "What then becomes of women whom God ordained to participate with Him in procreation? Our Heavenly Father did not give man that gift, my dear daughter—and it is a wondrous, amazing gift. That should never be overlooked, diminished, or forgotten."

Mrs. Garrett stood up and went to Joanna. "These are the things I *think* about, Joanna, and I hope you will as well. I want you to be happy and to marry, my child. I want you to be a mother—not just because you love children, but because you will be a *wonderful* mother, as I believe God intended you to be."

"But Mama, think about what Nanny West and Nana Garrett did during the war. They kept everything going while the men were off fighting. They did all kinds of things the men had done. They were still womanly, and still mothers and wives."

"That was a very different time. My mother and your father's mother did what they had to do—not what they wanted to do. War changes everything."

"If mothers are going to have sons, and women have brothers and fathers and husbands who might be killed in a war, why shouldn't they have the right to decide who leads the government that declares that war?"

"Joanna!" Her father was dumbfounded.

Joanna pressed on. "Why educate women if we aren't capable of thinking and making logical decisions about who would be a good President, or what would be a good law? Did you ever consider, when you sent me to Peace Institute, that I might learn to think for myself?"

"We sent you to college because you are incredibly bright—perhaps, *too* bright," her father said.

"I am your daughter—created by God, as you always told me. If I am bright, as you say, Papa, God made me so."

"Of course, God gave you the mental acuity, Joanna, and your mother and I wanted to nurture your God-given abilities. We knew you had the potential to be a wonderful teacher, as you have become. But you know good and well that working as a teacher must stop if you marry."

"*If* I marry? Do you think no man will marry me?"

"That's not what I meant Joanna, and you know it."

Her mother cautioned her husband with a touch on his arm. "Joanna, think about what I posed a few minutes ago. If you get more involved in this suffrage business, will you be able to marry?"

"I'm *not involved,* Mama. I just went to that convention to hear the speakers and I came back. That's all." Joanna turned and faced the open hearth; it was easier not to see the look in her mother's eyes.

"Yes, you came back," her mother said, "and to what? A broken engagement, that's what."

Joanna spun around and drew a deep breath. "Yes, Mother, Nicholas broke our engagement when he found out where I had been. And if he hadn't broken it, I would have. Nicholas never wanted me to teach and never understood why I was drawn to teaching."

"I don't understand it either, Joanna, not when you had a good man with a bright future who wanted to marry you. You wouldn't have had to teach."

"Helen—" her husband spoke in a gentle tone, but his inflection made his meaning clear: *say no more.*

"Well, now I do *have* to teach," Joanna said. "But I won't teach around here!" She had stalked out of the drawing room, defiant to the end.

Her brother came up and hugged her. "But where will you go, Joanna?"

"I don't know, Jon. Maybe to Raleigh. They have plenty of schools in Raleigh."

"Don't go, Joanna. Stay here and work this out."

"I'm not sure it can be worked out, Jon."

* * *

Appleton - January 1885

"I guess I am a little anxious, Laura. I don't know how many pupils I'll have, much less where they are in their studies and, of course, no one knows me."

Laura went to her at the stone hearth and looked deep into Joanna's rich brown eyes. "I know you're just what our school needs, Joanna. You'll be fine," she said. "And if you have any trouble with the big boys, you just tell Edgar and he'll set them straight."

Laura's caring look, gentle touch, and kind words went straight to the lonely hollow in Joanna's heart, nestling and filling the emptiness that had been there since she left North Carolina, her friends, and her family.

"Thank you so very much, Laura."

There's more to you, Joanna Garrett... I know it.

Chapter Six

Sunrise fought the dark of dawn and the winter wind danced through barren branches tapping the minutes Joanna lay shivering beneath the window pane. She felt her heart begin to pound. *It's the first day of school... What if they don't like me... won't obey me? What if I lose this job? What if...*

"Stop it," she whispered. "Worry never helped anything. Remember what Nanny West always said: If it isn't big enough to pray about, it isn't big enough to worry about. Nanny had a saying for everything," she told herself, turning down the quilt, "and most of her wisdom directed her listener straight to scripture."

Joanna smiled, closed her eyes, and turned her palms heavenward. "Lord, you know I'm afraid and you know I don't want to be. Please take this fear from me. Send Your Spirit into me so that I may draw on Your strength and wisdom and patience. I trust that I am where You want me to be. I thank You for this new school and pray You make me a blessing to my students today. I love You, Lord. Thank You for loving me. Amen."

She tilted the white porcelain pitcher, emptying the last of the water into the basin, and washed. She dressed with considerable care, then assessed herself in the beveled mirror. She pulled the brush through her gleaming black hair one last time, adjusted her bodice decked with pearl buttons marching down the front like soldiers on parade, and moistened her glistening lips. "Well, I'm as ready as I can get."

Joanna has just finished tying her muffler when Edgar drove up with Dolly hitched to the wagon. Laura hurried into the front room carrying heated bricks and a tin dinner pail. She handed both to Joe, then turned to Joanna. "Now, don't be nervous. Remember, you're bigger—well, older anyway—and you know what you're doing. Try to have a little fun, too."

"Fun— at school? You gotta be kidding, Aunt Laura!"

Laura glared at him and inclined her head toward Joanna.

"Sorry, Miss Garrett! No offense meant. "

"None taken, Joe. Fun probably isn't the first word that comes to mind when you think of school. But we'll try to have some anyway."

The morning was clear and sunny and the snow glinted so brightly, it almost hurt Joanna's eyes to look at it. Joe sat beside her, talking a mile a minute about the friends he was eager to see, and sooner than Joanna expected, they were at the schoolhouse. "Mr. McGill," she said as Joe helped her down from the wagon. "Are we going to be able to get in? The door was locked on Friday."

"Now, Miss Garrett," Edgar said, plowing through the snow, leading Joanna up onto the porch, "do you think I'd come all this way if we couldn't get in? Jim Langston's been working here and gave me a key on Saturday." He drew a shiny brass key from his pocket and inserted it into the lock. "I should've told you." He pushed the door open and stood aside, letting Joanna enter first. "Meet your classroom, Miss Garrett!"

Her lips parted in surprise as her eyes took in the entirety of the room. The spaciousness of it was punctuated with shiny desks—double ones bolted to the highly-polished planked flooring—and tables and smaller chairs forming rows that led to the front of the room where her desk sat. Each desk had a slate resting on its top and, sure enough, there were two chalkboards.

Joe had scurried in after Joanna and was checking out the seats at the back of the room. "Miss Garrett! Here's where Jimmy and me can sit, and John and Charles can sit right across from us!"

"It's Jimmy and I— and your teacher will decide where everyone is going to sit," Edgar said, tempering his son's precociousness. "Now, come get Miss Garrett's school bag while I bring in her trunk."

Joanna walked to the chalkboard behind her desk, lifted the piece of chalk, and printed: *Welcome to winter term! I am Miss Garrett and I am very happy to be here!* She drew a few snowflakes and a shining sun to offset the words.

Edgar dropped the trunk beside her desk. "Is this where you want it? Or should I move it closer to those shelves over there?" He jutted his head in the direction of the side wall, the one without windows.

Joanna hadn't noticed that the wall to the right of her desk was lined with floor-to-ceiling shelves. They had been hidden by the door Edgar had pushed aside as she stood in the entranceway.

"Here is fine. I'll have to sort out what I'll keep at my desk and what will go on those shelves. I've taught in schools that had no desks and were half the size of this room. This is luxury!"

"The school board went all out on it," Edgar said proudly. "We're expecting Appleton to grow a lot in the next few years—now that we're a main stop on the B & O Railroad," he said. "There's an upstairs yet to see," he said, pointing to the staircase at the end of the shelved wall.

Joanna looked skyward. "Maybe I can take a quick look before the children start arriving."

"They're here already, Miss Garrett," Joe shouted from his vantage point at the front window. "Mr. Greer and his kids just drove up! And there's the Samuels coming up behind them."

"I'd best be getting out of your way," Edgar said. "Is there anything else you need before I go, Miss Garrett?"

"How about our dinner pail, Pa? We'll be mighty hungry if we don't have something to eat before we get back home. Aunt Laura wouldn't like that after she fixed it so nice."

"Come on out and get it, Toad," he said, and turned to Joanna. "Have a good day, Miss Garrett, and don't take any guff from the big boys. I'll be back at four o'clock to get you."

She followed Edgar to the door and saw two little girls pass him on the steps. "Come in out of the cold," she said, stooping down to them. "I'm Miss Garrett, your new teacher, and tell me who you are."

Joanna spent the next fifteen minutes repeating those words, then went outside and gave the bell a hearty tug. She loved the sound, an almost pristine peal that echoed through the crisp cold morning air. When she came back inside, the room was eerily quiet and thirty-five pairs of eyes followed her to her desk. Joanna drew a slight breath... *Remember what Miss Simpson always told us at Peace— they're more nervous than you are.*

"Good morning, everyone," she said, mustering a firm and

resonant voice. "You already know I'm your new teacher. I'm also new to Indiana and very glad to be here. And, I am really looking forward to getting to know each and every one of you."

A hand shot up from the back of the room. "Miss Garrett! Are you going to let us sit wherever we want to? That's what our old teacher did!"

"No, she didn't!" ... "Josh Baker, that's a lie!" came the chorus of voices.

Joanna hushed them with her hand and a smile. "Josh," she said, looking right at the boy, "never doubt that I am going to do things my way, not as any of your previous teachers did." *I always do things my way... it's why I'm in this classroom.* She ignored the accusations of lying; she would speak to Josh about that privately. "As for our seating arrangements, I'm going to get all of your names and ages, and then I'm going to seat you in groups according to your grade level. You may choose your seat mate, and you may keep that seat as long as both of you behave. Does that sound fair?"

"Yes, Ma'am!"

"All right. Now, let's get started." She asked each of the youngest students their names and whether they'd been to school before and if so, where they were in their primers and arithmetic books. One little girl couldn't—or wouldn't—speak, she was so frightened. *I'll take her aside later,* Joanna thought. *I know what it's like to be scared and confused...*

* * *

Wilmington, N.C. - October 1868

Joanna sat on the brick steps of her front porch, her face buried in her hands. She was crying.

Matthew Garrett came walking up the long brick path. "What's the matter, Josie?"

"Nothing, Papa," she said, refusing to look up at him.

"Then why are you crying?"

"I don't know, Papa."

Yes, you do... you just don't want to tell me, my sweet girl, he thought. "All right," he said. "Then may I sit with you?"

Joanna nodded and wiped at her tears as her father sat down beside her, his long legs extending nearly to the path below. Several silent minutes passed between them, and then Joanna spoke.

"Papa, may I ask you a question?"

That's my sweet girl... He lifted her tear spattered hand. "Of course you may."

"Why do I have to go to school?"

"Well, you don't really have to, but Mama and I want you to."

"Why?"

"Because God put a good brain inside your little seven-year-old head and God wants you to use it. School is where you can learn all kinds of wonderful things."

"If I don't have to go, would it be all right if I stayed home with Mama and Jonathan?"

"Did something happen at school today, Josie?"

Her little arms shot into the air and wrapped around her father's neck, and she burst into tears again. Matthew cradled her in his arms until her tears subsided and she could speak without those hurt-filled gasps. "You know that boy, James Pritchard, who lives near Nanny?"

"I do."

"He pulled my hair when Mr. Davis wasn't looking, and when I screamed and smacked James on the nose, Mr. Davis made me go stand in the corner."

I'd have loved to have seen that, Matthew thought, pressing his lips tightly together, repressing the urge to burst into laughter. *James Pritchard needed somebody to take him down a notch and my little girl was the one who did it!* "Did James have to stand in a corner, too?"

"No! That's what made me so mad, Papa. Mr. Davis sent James home!"

"Let me be sure I understand you, Josie. You're mad because James got to go home while you had to stay there and stand in the corner?" He loved the conviction that fired his daughter's eyes.

"Yes! It was awful, Papa. When Mr. Davis let me go back to my seat, everyone stared at me and some of the boys snickered when I walked by. I was hume..leeted!"

"You mean hyoo-mil-ee-a-ted?"

"Yes, Papa, that's what I mean! I just know everyone will tease me if I go back. I might cry— and then, I'll just want to die."

Oh, my dramatic child. Always taking things to the extreme. "And, Josie, what do you think happened to James when he arrived home early from school today?"

"I don't know, Papa," she said, her huge brown eyes gazing

into his. "He probably had a glass of milk and some cookies and then played outside!"

He looked skyward and bit his lower lip to hide yet another laugh. "Do you think his mother and father were happy that Mr. Davis sent James home?"

"No! And, if I were them, I'd be very happy if he stayed at school forever!"

"Joanna..." He said her name slowly and deliberately.

"Oh, Papa, all right... I suppose his parents were mad at him."

"Do you suppose they might have punished him?"

"I guess so." She sniffled again and thought for a moment. "Would you be angry if Mr. Davis had sent me home, Papa?"

"Not angry, Josie, but your mother and I would be very, very disappointed in you."

"And would you punish me?"

"Well, I would have to—wouldn't I, Josie?"

She leaned back against the step. Matthew Garrett could see his little girl contemplating the meaning of his words.

"Maybe I can go back to school tomorrow," she said, coming forward on the step and looking up into his eyes. "And will you walk with me to school tomorrow, Papa?"

"Of course I will, my little Josie."

She hugged her father again. "I knew you would understand," she said, and ran off to find her brothers.

* * *

Appleton - January 1885

Joanna progressed quickly through the older students, finding that some weren't yet in upper level *McGuffey Readers* and most had never studied history or geography. *What on earth did that other teacher do all day?*

"Thank you for being so quiet and well behaved while I was getting us organized. Now, let's get you settled into your seats," Joanna said, heading to the back of the room where the older boys and girls had already chosen seat mates. In twenty minutes she had the upper grades settled. Joe sat alone at a double desk, saving the seat beside him for Jimmy Langston.

"Would any of you older girls like to help me organize the primary class?" Several hands shot up in the air. "Wonderful! Now, let me see, you're Sarah," Joanna said, pointing to the slender girl with her tawny hair in braids, "and you're Emily," she said, looking directly at the dark-haired, heavyset girl sitting a row in front of Sarah.

Each nodded confirmation and came forward.

"Sarah, why don't you help the children select their seats. And, Emily, will you get—let me see, eleven of those red Readers you'll see on the shelf over there?"

As the noon hour approached, the primary students were seated with brand new *McGuffey Readers* in front of them. "You've done an excellent job following my directions," Joanna said. "It's almost twelve o'clock and I don't know about you, but I'm getting hungry. Let's stop for dinner now." Heads nodded and dinner pails clattered from the floor to the desktops. "You may sit wherever you like while you eat, and when you're done, if you'd like to go outdoors for a few minutes, you may do so."

She looked around the room of famished students. "Would anyone like to say grace?" Again, hands went skyward into the air.

The classroom buzzed with munching, drinking, talking, and a good deal of laughing. Joe brought Joanna her share of the dinner Laura had packed for them, then returned to his friends. She opened the waxed paper parcel and found slices of ham nestled in two of Laura's oversized biscuits, some bread and butter pickles, and a thick slice of apple pie with a piece of cheese tucked beside it. She walked to the water bucket and filled a tin cup, thinking: *I would love a cup of tea or coffee right now. I must remember to buy a kettle for the stove when I get to town.*

As she walked back to her desk, she noticed that the little girl who had been crying earlier was sitting alone and not eating. Joanna glanced to the floor below her seat. There was no dinner pail. She walked over to the child. "Emma?" She put her arm around the girl's thin shoulders. "Do you not have any dinner?"

Tears welled in big brown eyes then flowed down her chapped little cheeks. "No, Ma'am. My pa didn't pack me any."

"Well, then you must let me sit with you because I have more food than I can possibly eat, and if we share it, it won't go to waste." Joanna pulled a chair close to Emma's desk and placed one of the ham biscuits and some pickles on a napkin before the little girl. She went back to the water bucket to fill another cup and when she got back, just one piece of pickle and one bite of the biscuit were left.

"I see that you like Miss McGill's cooking as much as I do." Joanna broke the remaining biscuit into two decidedly different sized pieces. "Let's share this other biscuit and then we'll have some pie." While they ate, Joanna asked Emma about her family and learned that Emma's mother was ill and had gone back to her family in Boston some months earlier, leaving her husband to care for their three little girls. Her father worked at the lumberyard and had a small claim a few miles north of the McGill place.

At the conclusion of their forty-five-minute break, Joanna put on her coat and went out to the covered porch and rang the bell. Students slowly made their way back inside. She rang the bell again, ten minutes later. The four oldest boys lingered on the porch, then came in, talking loudly, and in no hurry to take their seats. *This is a direct challenge,* she thought. More than one teenage boy in past classes believed he could disrespect her authority.

"Boys," she said, her low voice firm and direct, "I ring the bell to begin class—which means you *immediately* return and take your seats. You show no respect for me or your fellow classmates by delaying the learning process." Jake Trimble tossed his head cockily, took his seat, and winked at the boy beside him.

Joanna spent the rest of the afternoon listening to each student read, enabling her to determine at which level each child would begin in their *Readers;* she then put arithmetic problems on the board to check their skills at addition and subtraction. She dismissed the class at three-thirty and fifteen minutes later, the room was empty, except for Emma and one boy whose name Joanna could not recall.

Joe came and stood beside Joanna at her desk. "That's Caleb Matthews," he whispered to her. "His pa works at the lumberyard with Emma's pa. I 'spect Mr. Matthews will be here soon to pick up Caleb."

Sure enough, a few minutes later the door burst open. The biggest man Joanna had ever seen strode into the classroom and headed straight for her desk.

"I'm Stinson Matthews and you must be our new school teacher, ma'am. Pleased to meet you." His enormous, work-roughened hands engulfed hers. "I'll be taking Caleb and Emma now and I'll try to get here earlier tomorrow. We got real backed up at the yard today and I didn't notice the time," he said and turned to the two children. "You younguns get your gear on and I'll be waiting for you outside." Stinson Matthews was gone as quickly as he had arrived, Caleb and Emma in tow.

Joanna sighed. *I'm done! It went well... Thank you, God.*

"Miss Garrett, I think you should sit down for a minute... you look tuckered out!"

"I am tired, Joe. Will you sweep up for me while I get ready for tomorrow?"

"Sure thing!"

Before the clock chimed four o'clock, the sound of Dolly's bells broke the stillness of the late winter afternoon.

Joe ran to the window. "It's Pa and Aunt Laura is with him!" Joanna went out onto the porch, clutching herself against the bite of the frigid wind.

"Laura!" Joanna motioned her into the school room. "Come warm yourself."

"Edgar and I ran over to check on Mary Langston," Laura said, heading straight for the stove, yanking off her mittens, and warming her hands. "It got late, so I told Edgar just to drive straight here. Hey there, Toad! How was your first day with Miss Garrett?"

"It was great, Aunt Laura. You should have heard Miss Garrett tell Jake Trimble to mind his *p's and q's*! She sounded like Reverend Goodman when he gets going on Sunday morning!"

"I don't think I was quite *that* fervent, Joe, but thank you for the compliment." She leaned close to Laura's ear, "I just had to let some boys know who's in charge. They're bigger than I am and getting to the age where they don't like anybody—most especially a woman—telling them what to do," she said, running her arms into the sleeves of her black coat, then tying her scarf. "I'm ready to go if you've warmed up enough."

Dolly pranced in the school yard, heavy puffs of steam streaming from her nostrils.

Edgar hurried to take Joanna's bag as she came down the steps. "How was your first day with the cream of Appleton's crop, as well as its dregs?"

The two women spoke simultaneously: "That's no way to talk!" Laura said, climbing onto the wagon.

"The day went well," Joanna said, pausing when she reached Edgar, "very well, in fact."

"Good! I'm glad," he said. "I wouldn't be in your shoes for love—nor money!"

It's certainly not for the money, she thought. *It must be love...*

Edgar took hold of her arm. "Miss Garrett? Is anything wrong?"

"No, Mr. McGill. I was just thinking..."

He nodded with a quick smile. "Those must be mighty serious thoughts."

You don't miss much, do you, Mr. McGill?

Chapter Seven

Friday came before Joanna could turn around.

"Next week we will begin studying history and geography," she said, "along with arithmetic and our reading and writing." The groans she expected came prolonged and heavy.

"I know you haven't studied these subjects before," she said, smiling as she walked up and down the aisles among the students, "so I don't expect you to be thrilled. I do want you to think about what geography and history really are." She pointed to a boy about eight years old. "Jacob, do you know where your grandparents came from?"

"Their farm," the boy responded. The rest of the class tittered.

"No, Jacob, not where they live now, but where they were born."

"No ma'am," Jacob answered.

"How about the rest of you? Do any of you know where your grandparents or great-grandparents were born?" Several hands flew up.

"My grandmother came from Ireland on a ship, Miss Garrett"

"My great-grandfather was born in Germany, but my Nana was born in Indiana, I think."

"My mother's family came here from France."

"And do you know where those countries are? Do you know any of their customs, or how to speak their languages, or what crops they grow?"

Puzzled faces punctuated their collective *No.*

"Well, that's why we're going to study history and geography. We'll find out where your families came from... we'll see where those countries are, and we'll learn about their way of life. That's geography. Then we'll learn about what happened there a long time ago. That's history. We're going to learn," she said, lowering her voice to a near whisper, " all about *you.*"

That afternoon—after everyone had left, including Joe, who had gone home with Jimmy Langston—Joanna sat at her desk surveying the empty classroom. It had been a good first week, She had anticipated having such a large number of students of varying ages, which ranged from timid little Emma Patterson, who had just turned five, to Jake Trimble, who was sixteen and two heads taller than she. What Joanna had not expected was that some of her students, even older ones, had not been to school before and many who had, were not where she thought they should be in their studies.

I don't know if my predecessor simply wasn't a good teacher, or if something interfered with her teaching, but things will be different now.

Edgar came for Joanna promptly at four o'clock and bundled her into the seat beside him. It was the first time they had been alone together and the fact that she noticed this made Joanna uncomfortable. It was a relatively warm and windless afternoon, so the two could talk and hear each other easily, yet it was several minutes before Edgar uttered a word.

"I went into town today," he said, "to fetch some lumber to repair the shutters, and I heard the Ladies Aid Society is holding their dance tomorrow. A few folks came last Saturday in the storm, but the band couldn't make it, so they just ate the cakes and drank the punch and put the dance off for a week." Joanna heard excitement in Edgar's voice. "I imagine Laura will want to go, and I know Joe will be ready for some fun. What about you?"

She hesitated. *Do I want to meet people at a dance? Do I dare dance? I love to, but I can't sashay around the room with the town's bachelors without raising some eyebrows. I've had my fill of raised eyebrows and disapproval...*

* * *

Wilmington, N.C. - November 1884

Nicholas Brodie paced around the drawing room of Joanna's family home. "I don't believe this, Joanna."

"What can't you believe, Nicholas?"

"What do you mean, *what can't I believe?*" He suddenly stopped pacing and bent over her as she sat stiffly in her father's armchair. "I can't believe you would do such a thing! I thought you were smart, Joanna. I thought you had better sense. And, worst of all, I can't believe I had to find out from one of my partners, over supper!"

"And what embarrasses you most, Nicholas? That your colleague knew about it before you, or that I went to the convention?" Joanna spoke calmly but there was ice in her voice.

"I am not embarrassed that you went to the convention," he said, leaning closer to her face. "I am appalled. And I am angry."

"What have I done to deserve your anger? I took a trip last March. I heard some speakers and I came home. I've done nothing else."

"You *took a trip* and *heard some speakers?*" Nicholas stifled a laugh and began pacing again. "You make it sound as if you went to the Lyceum to hear Mark Twain. You went to Washington, D.C. on the train, Joanna—you and Margaret Richardson. You went to a woman's suffrage convention. And who knows whom you heard speak—that scrawny Anthony woman, or her prodigious friend?"

Joanna remained seated, while fighting her contempt for the man who professed his love for her. "Why must you malign them, Nicholas? What is so awful about them? And, further, do you even know what either of them has said or written, or why they have done so?"

"I don't need to hear or read their diatribes to know what they say. They both spew the same thing, over and over again: *Give woman the vote.*"

"They say much more than that," she countered. "If you read them, Nicholas, you'd be impressed with their logic. They write very much like you do. They support their position with well thought out arguments and reasoning."

"How can you compare *my* legal discourses with the rantings of two women who want to vote with men, who probably wish *they* were men?"

"If either Miss Anthony or Mrs. Stanton wishes she were a man—it is only because men are the only ones in this country with the right to vote."

"Is that what you want, Joanna? You want to walk into the polling place and cast your vote along side me?"

"I don't know. I don't know enough about it yet."

"So you plan to do more of this? Read more pamphlets, go to more lectures? I am flabbergasted, Joanna. Flabbergasted and appalled." He shook his head.

"What right have you to be appalled by anything I do?" Sparks almost flew from her huge brown eyes. "I am *not* your wife."

"No, you are not—and not because I haven't asked you more than once."

"And... do you want to ask me to be your wife now?"

Nicholas stared at her. Their eyes locked, both ablaze, and then he lowered his gaze and turned away.

"Go back to Raleigh, Nicholas."

* * *

Appleton - January 1885

"Not too big on dancing?" Edgar asked after a long silence. "You won't be the only one there who doesn't dance, if that's what's worrying you. Lots of people come just to get out of the house and talk with folks they haven't seen for a while."

"I do like to dance, Mr. McGill, but, to tell you the truth, I'm concerned about how people will react if I do. That probably seems silly to you."

"No, it doesn't. My friend Luke Goodman said something like that to me when he first moved here."

"Luke Goodman?" Joanna glanced sideways at Edgar. "I have two students named Goodman. Is he their father?"

"He sure is, Miss Garrett, and a mighty fine preacher, too. Laura and I are good friends with Luke and his wife, Carrie. If you come to the dance, you'll meet them."

"How did Reverend Goodman resolve the dancing dilemma?"

Edgar laughed. "Luke told me he'd been a man longer than he'd been a preacher, and the man in him liked to dance and fish and do some other things people might not think a minister ought to do. He said he was going to be himself, and his wife was going to be herself, and people would have to take them as they are." He turned to her. "You might want to try that approach yourself."

Be myself? I'm not sure that's such a good idea—not if people in

Appleton are like the ones back home. "I'll take your advice, Mr. McGill. I'll go to the dance."

"Something smells might good," Edgar said, peering over Laura's shoulder at the pies she was taking from the oven. "And I bet I'm going to have to pay to taste of any of it."

"You're right, brother dear, it will cost you a nickel a slice at the social tonight to find out if I did a good job or not. I better not catch you breaking off a piece of the crust either. That goes for Joanna's cake, too."

"I shouldn't tell you this," Joanna said, watching Edgar eyeing the sugar-crusted top of the pound cake that was cooling on a rack beside the stove, "but I baked two cakes, that large one for the social and the other for us. It's too hot to eat now, but I thought we might have some this afternoon."

"See there, Laura, someone in this house knows how to show a man a little kindness." He spun around and bowed to Joanna, then took her hand and kissed it. She was so startled she almost dropped the plates she was carrying to the table.

"You're in mighty high spirits, Edgar." Laura eyed him suspiciously. "It wouldn't have anything to do with a certain lady being at the social tonight, would it?"

Edgar turned bright red. "No more than your wearing a new dress has anything to do with catching some fellow's eye."

Laura blushed this time and dished up the soup. They had almost finished eating when Joe burst in through the lean-to, with Jimmy Langston and his father close behind.

"Hey, Pa! Hey, Aunt Laura! Hey, Miss Garrett!" The boy's blue eyes flashed excitement. "Jimmy came along because he wants to go to the dance tonight but his ma and pa can't go, so we thought maybe he could come with us and spend the night and then..."

"Whoa, there, son!" Edgar ruffled the boy's tawny hair. "Slow down a minute and let Mr. Langston get a word in!"

Jim Langston didn't take off his coat but accepted the coffee Laura offered. "The boy's talking a mite fast, but he's got all the right points in," he said. "I heard about the social when I went to town yesterday for some groceries, but Mary's not up to going yet, of course, and Jimmy here would like to go, if it wouldn't be a bother to you. I don't really think he wants to dance. He just wants to eat more pie and cake than is good for him."

"We'd be more than glad to take Jimmy," Laura said, "We'll take him to church with us tomorrow, too, if that suits you."

"I'm hoping to get to church myself," Jim Langston said.

"I'm feeling mighty thankful for Mary's safe delivery and I'd like to be in the Lord's house to tell Him so. I'm mighty grateful to you, too, Laura."

Tears sprang to Laura's eyes, and to Joanna's, and Edgar cleared the sudden lump in his throat. "I hope you'll all be in church tomorrow," he said. "But if you can't make it, I'll bring Jimmy home right after dinner."

Jim Langston left, carrying a jar full of the the soup Laura made for supper, along with a loaf of bread. Laura turned to the boys, who were dangerously close to the pie safe where the evening's desserts were resting.

"All right, you two," Laura said, "keep away from there! Have some dinner and as soon as chores are done, it'll be time to start filling the washtubs for baths," Laura said. Moans and groans were their replies. "Don't act so surprised, Joe McGill! You know it's always bath night on Saturday and we have to take them early so we can leave for the social right after an early supper. I want everybody washed and dressed by four-thirty—not a moment later!"

Edgar and the boys met the deadline and were in the front room when Laura descended the stairs. Edgar gave a low whistle, taking note that the rosy color of her new dress suited her fair coloring and admiring the way her hair was piled high on her head, a pearl comb tucked into one side.

"You look lovely, Laura," he said, taking her by the hand and twirling her, "and if you weren't my sister, I'd be the first one to put my name on your dance card!"

"If we had dance cards, and if you weren't my brother, I'd let you," she said. They were still spinning when Joanna came down the staircase. Her gown, molded close through the bodice, flared to a full skirt. The light danced across the shimmering royal blue satin and the blue and white stone jewelry at her neck and ears. Edgar stopped dead in his tracks, mesmerized.

"Jumpin' Jehosophat, Miss Garrett," Joe almost shouted, "you look just like one of those pictures in Godey's Lady's Book!"

Joanna beamed. "Why, thank you, Master McGill! And, if I may say so, you and Jimmy are looking very handsome yourselves." The boys, dressed in starched white shirts and dark pants, tugged at their neckties and shuffled their feet.

"You look absolutely beautiful, Joanna. That dress must be the latest fashion, and how you sparkle in that color," Laura said.

Edgar remained dumbstruck, as his thoughts raced round in

his head: *No man could possibly ignore you... that figure... those eyes,* he thought, his eyes drinking in the loveliness of her. *There are no words to describe you but breathtakingly beautiful. Maybe I gave you bad advice about coming to the social and dancing to your heart's content.*

When Edgar found his voice, he managed to restrain the thoughts that played havoc with his senses. "You look very nice, Miss Garrett. I'm honored to be accompanying two such lovely ladies to the social."

"If we're going to get there on time," Joe said heatedly, "we better eat supper and get going!" He and Jimmy raced to the kitchen and the adults followed. Twenty minutes later, Edgar and the boys were hitching Dolly to the wagon, while Laura and Joanna put the few dishes they had used in the sink.

"They can wait till morning to get washed," Laura declared. "I'm not going to risk getting this dress wet, even with an apron over it!" She and Joanna took one last look in the hall mirror before donning their outerwear for the chilly drive into town.

Joanna lost count of the number of wagons, buggies and horses tied to hitching posts up and down Main Street. "I had no idea there were so many people in Appleton," she said to Laura.

"Oh, people will come from all over tonight, not just those who live in town. I hope there's room in the livery stable for Dolly."

"Don't worry about that," Edgar said, turning down a side street. "I paid Jeff Peters ahead of time so we'd be sure to have a place. I'm not worried about Dolly being out in the cold, but I didn't want you and Miss Garrett to have far to walk in all your finery." He pulled into a large barn, where a short round little man ran up to take Dolly's reins.

"Evenin', Edgar, Miss Laura, Ma'am. I saved a place for you right over yonder." Jeff Peters' breath came in visible puffs as he spoke. "Why don't you ladies hop down and then I'll put Dolly in her stall." He reached for Joanna's hand. "You must be our new schoolteacher. My boy, Tom, is in your class and he's been talkin' 'bout you all week. Now I see he's right about at least one thing. You are a sight prettier than Miss Lambert was!"

Joanna felt the warmth of a blush and wondered if she would be doing so all night. *Perhaps,* she thought, *I shouldn't have come at all.*

It was a short walk to the Grange. Edgar led Joanna and Laura through the crowd of men gathered out front. The hall was aglow with paper lanterns, colorful streamers and bouquets of paper flowers. Two ladies sat behind a table near the door, collecting the twenty-five-cent admission fee. Edgar reached into his pocket and pulled out two dollars.

"Keep the change, ladies," he told them. "This is for a very good cause."

Once inside the hall, Joe and Jimmy made a beeline to a group of children congregating by the food. A tall, sandy haired man waved at Edgar from a table.

"There's Luke and Carrie," Edgar said, "Let's join them."

Luke Goodman stood up as the threesome approached. "Edgar, Laura, it's good to see you! Seems like a month of Sundays since we last met." He extended his hand to Joanna. "You must be Joanna Garrett. I am delighted to know you." He pointed to a smiling woman seated beside him, whose fair skin and auburn hair loudly proclaimed her Celtic roots. "This is my wife, Carrie. We've been hearing lots of good things about you from our children. Don't let those two rascals give you any trouble."

"I'm so pleased to meet you both," Joanna said, returning Carrie Goodman's warm smile, "but I wouldn't describe your children as rascals, Reverend Goodman. Perhaps not angels, but definitely not rascals."

Laura sat down beside Carrie and the two soon were deep in conversation. Edgar chatted with Luke for a few minutes, then excused himself, saying he wanted to visit the dessert table before all the best items were taken. Joanna noticed, however, that he didn't head in that direction. Instead, he weaved in and out among the dancers, his eyes scanning the crowd. Joanna caught herself staring at Edgar and when she turned back to her table mates, she found Luke Goodman gazing thoughtfully at her. He was a handsome man, with a thick crop of wavy, light brown hair, high cheekbones and gray eyes. Joanna imagined him standing in the pulpit, a fine figure in his black robe and clerical collar.

"So, tell me how you find life here in Indiana, Miss Garrett. Is it much different from North Carolina?"

Joanna's brows shot up at the mention of her home state. "How do you know I come from North Carolina, Reverend Goodman? Does my accent give me away?"

Luke laughed. "Well, it's a pretty good clue, but I confess that I know where you're from because I asked the chairman of the school board. That makes me one of six people in Henry Township—all of whom are here tonight, by the way—who know a lot about you, Joanna Garrett."

She gasped inwardly. *What does he mean by that? Can he*

possibly know? She quickly recovered herself. "I like Indiana very much, Reverend. The McGills have made me feel like part of their family, and the first week of school went very well. The biggest adjustment so far has been the weather. I've never seen so much snow."

Before Luke could respond, a bevy of people surged toward their table. He leaned toward Joanna. "Looks like word has spread that you're here. Get ready!"

Joanna was soon surrounded with people introducing themselves and shaking her hand. There was Ted Garner, the town's banker, and his wife, Julia, along with Richard Werner, owner of one of the general stores, whose wife, Celia, a loud and overbearing woman, wore an enormous green feather in her hair.

One fellow, a gangly man of about thirty who seemed uncomfortable in his coat and tie, introduced himself as Harold Akers. "You've got three of my kids at the school, ma'am. I hope they've all been behavin'," he said. "My oldest, Adam, did pretty well with our last teacher, but my twins, Samuel and Samantha, can't even read yet and they're almost eight years old. I'm counting on you to change that."

"I'll do my best, Mr. Akers," she said firmly, "and if your children do the same, I'm sure your twins will be catching up with their older brother in no time."

"You won't have that problem with my children," a voice proclaimed from the depths of the throng surrounding her. "My Agnes and Phillip will be at the top of their classes, I assure you." The voice belonged to Celia Werner and Joanna noticed some eye rolling from women near her. "How do you intend to challenge students like my children?"

Joanna started to answer, but Luke Goodman broke in.

"Now, folks, I know you're all eager to get to know our new schoolteacher, but let's give Miss Garrett a chance to breathe. I'm sure she'll be glad to talk with you later about the specific needs of your children. Right now, why don't we let her sample Mrs. Stark's excellent punch and taste a few of the pies and cakes you ladies brought." Luke took Joanna by the arm and led her toward the food tables.

"Thank you, Reverend," she said. "I was overwhelmed back there, but I didn't want people to think I didn't want to know them, or don't care about their children."

"It hasn't been all that long ago that Carrie and I were newcomers here, Miss Garrett, so I understand what you're going through. Your coming to Appleton is the most exciting thing that's happened here in quite a while." He looked at Joanna appraisingly. "And, I might add, you're a very pretty young woman—that alone makes you an object of interest."

Several men had eyed her already; the last thing she wanted was to have other women jealous of her.

"I thank you for the compliment, Reverend, I didn't realize I would stand out so much. I guess I just wasn't thinking."

"Don't fret. Just try to relax, be yourself and let folks get to know you. You'll be just fine."

They reached the dessert table and Joanna saw Edgar at the far end of the line, facing a woman whose back was to Joanna. She wore a dress of silvery white silk that clung to her slender but rounded figure, and her blond hair was caught into ringlets on the back of her neck.

Luke followed Joanna's gaze. "That's Lucy Sheppard. Her father owns the newspaper and a lot of land. Lucy works with her father at the paper, even writes a column giving the *feminine* viewpoint every now and then. You two have something in common. Lucy is also a well educated woman."

She glanced toward Lucy again, and saw Edgar take her by the hand and lead her onto the dance floor. "They make a handsome couple," she said

"Oh, they're not a couple," Luke said, heaping a plate with pie and cake and cookies. "Edgar is a friend of mine and I think I'd know if he was seeing Miss Sheppard."

But didn't you see Mr. McGill's face when they started dancing? Joanna wanted to ask Luke. *Lucy Sheppard is definitely the reason he was so eager to be here.*

Between them, Luke and Joanna toted laden plates and four punch cups back to their table, carefully winding their way through the crowd. An older couple sat in the chairs Luke and Joanna had vacated. The man, white haired but spry despite his age, stood up.

"Keep your seat, John," Luke said quickly. He drew up two empty chairs from a nearby table. "Have you met John and Frances Lane, Miss Garrett?" Joanna shook her head that she hadn't.

"John is a retired minister," Luke said, "he preaches for me if I have to be away on a Sunday. Frances teaches our children's Sunday School class, and a fine job she does, too." He leaned across the table to kiss Frances Lane on the cheek. She looked to be about seventy, with a round face and pink cheeks.

"I'm so glad to meet you, Miss Garrett," Frances said. "When the weather warms up, I want you to come to tea so we can get to know each other. Our daughter, Rachel, was a teacher before she married. She so enjoyed it. I hope you do, as well."

"That I do, Mrs. Lane," Joanna assured her. "I love children and I love learning and I love having work that combines the two."

Conversation flowed easily among the four friends at the table. Joanna listened and commented every now and then, but her eyes were on the dancers. Laura left on the arm of a man Luke Goodman identified as Cal Turner, and Luke and Carrie soon joined them on the dance floor. The band was playing a polka and underneath the table, Joanna was tapping her foot in time with the beat.

"If I were a younger man," John Lane said with a grin, "I'd be asking you to dance, Miss Garrett."

"If you were a younger man, John Lane, we'd be on that dance floor together," his wife said, her eyes twinkling. "Remember how we used to beg the band to play just one more tune at the square dances? My, that was fun!"

Luke and Carrie returned and reached for their punch cups. "Dancing is thirsty work, John, no question about it," Luke said. "But I surely do enjoy it." He turned to Joanna. "Miss Garrett, may I have the pleasure of the next dance?"

"I would love to, Reverend," she said, "if it's all right with Mrs. Goodman."

"Please do, Miss Garrett," Carrie said, motioning them onto the dance floor. "My husband is much more of a dancer than I am, and I'll be glad to sit the next three or four dances out."

Luke swung Joanna into the moving circle, gracefully spinning her around the floor as the band switched to a waltz. He was an excellent dancer and all eyes were fixed on them as pastor and schoolteacher gracefully swirled and dipped to the music.

"Miss Garrett, everyone seems to be looking at us. What do you think makes us so riveting—the grace of our dancing, or the fact that you're a teacher and I'm a preacher?"

"The latter, most definitely. I wasn't sure I should be dancing tonight, but Mr. McGill told me I should. I do love it so."

"I can tell, because you're quite good at it. And, think of this: if you can't dance with a clergyman, with whom can you dance?"

"How about a gentleman farmer?" said a deep voice from behind them. Edgar quickly cut in and whisked Joanna away before Luke uttered a word.

"So, Miss Garrett, are you enjoying yourself?" He deftly directed her steps with the slightest pressure at her waist. "Or do you feel rather like a goldfish in a bowl?"

"Both, Mr. McGill. I've never had so many people watching every move I make. I feel a bit uncomfortable," she said, catching sight of Lucy Sheppard standing at the edge of the dance floor, her stare—more akin to a glare—fixed on the both of them. "But the Goodmans and the Lanes are delightful, and the music is wonderful. I'm glad I came."

"I am, too," He twirled her under his raised arm as the song came to an end. Before the band struck up the next tune, another man cut in on Edgar and whirled Joanna across the dance floor. His turn didn't last long, though, because Cal Turner cut in to lead Joanna in a polka, followed by Jim Owens, who deftly managed an old fashioned square dance. When yet another man came up as the square dance finished, Joanna held up her hand.

"I do appreciate your offer, Mister—is it Mr. Calhoun? But I simply must... catch my breath... before I can move another step."

"I'll get you a glass of punch, Miss Garrett," Cal Turner said with a slight bow.

"I'll get you some cake to go with it," Jim Owens added, dashing toward the dessert table.

A breathless and rather embarrassed Joanna returned to the table where Luke and Carrie Goodman sat with Laura and the Lanes.

Luke stood up as she approached the table. "Well, it seems you're the belle of the ball, Miss Garrett. I didn't realize what I was setting you up for when I took you onto the dance floor."

"You did so, Luke Goodman," his wife said, jabbing his arm with her index finger. "A man of the cloth shouldn't tell a bald-faced lie like that. You wanted Miss Garrett to dance and have a good time, and you knew no other man would be the first to ask her!"

Luke turned beet red and bowed his head in a penitent way. "True, my dear," he said, lifting his head with happy, laughing eyes. "I only hope Miss Garrett can forgive me."

"There's nothing to forgive, Reverend. You were right that I wanted to dance, but I had no idea there would be so many dance partners."

"A woman as pretty as you, new in town, and unmarried—and you didn't think the bachelors would be lining up to spin you around the dance floor?" John Lane's comment caught Joanna by complete surprise. "You underestimate yourself, and them, Miss Garrett."

The rest of the evening flew by with more talk, more dancing, more meeting of new people, and more punch. Joanna couldn't believe it was almost ten o'clock when she glanced at her watch.

Carrie and Luke Goodman had long since departed, as had the Lanes. The band was still playing, but only a few couples were on the dance floor, and the Ladies Aid had stopped refilling the punch bowl. Joanna pointed to her watch when Laura looked her way.

"Gracious me," Laura said, standing up and looking for Edgar. "I had no idea it was this late! If we don't leave now, we won't be home until after midnight! Where are those boys?"

Laura spotted Edgar across the room, dancing with Lucy Sheppard, and waved at him. In short order their group gathered in the vestibule, donned their coats and walked to the livery stable. Edgar soon had Dolly hitched to their wagon with foot warmers in place. They arrived home just after eleven o'clock. Half an hour later, all were sound asleep.

Chapter Eight

Tired though they were the next morning, the McGills, Joanna, and Jimmy were sitting in the fourth pew, gospel side, when Luke Goodman walked down the aisle behind the choir of the Appleton Presbyterian Church. The entry of the choir, singing, was something new and not uniformly well received.

"Reverend Jackson never did such a thing," several had remarked on the first Sunday the choir processed; "I don't see the point of it."

Luke had laughed when Carrie told him what she'd heard. *The point,* he had thought, *is that I need them to realize I'm not Reverend Jackson, and to accept me for who I am, the pastor God called to serve in this place and time.*

"I'm really looking forward to hearing Reverend Goodman preach," Joanna whispered to Laura.

"You won't be disappointed."

Laura was right. Luke Goodman had a marvelous speaking voice, rich and deep, and he knew how to use it. At one point, when Luke had been speaking softly and then raised his voice, the old man in front of Joanna jumped. Luke's sudden change of timbre had wakened him from his customary nap.

Joanna liked Luke's message, too.

"We've all heard the Ten Commandments," he said, "and I'll put before you that most of you can recite them from memory." Heads nodded. "For those of you who cannot—yet—you'll find them in Deuteronomy."

"We live in community," Luke continued, "and we need standards to follow. We need to know how to care for each other and how to behave one toward another. Luckily, we don't have to look far for the answer. God gave it to His people in the Ten Commandments, and He enlightened us more with the gospel. Read the Commandments, my brothers; live the Commandments, my sisters; and when we do, the kingdom of heaven will come a little bit closer here on earth."

Luke stood at the front door after the service, greeting each parishioner, hugging some, and patting others on the back. He grinned when Joanna walked up.

"Well, well, if it isn't my dance partner! I'm glad to see you this morning, Miss Garrett! And you, too, Laura, and Joe." He tousled Joe's hair as he spoke.

"I liked your message very much, Reverend Goodman," Joanna said. "It made me think I should put the Ten Commandments up in my classroom. My students could use a daily reminder that all of us live under God's sovereignty."

"Amen to that," Jim Langston said, joining Joanna and Laura on the steps. "When you have a new baby safely delivered in your house, you really feel God's presence in your life." He shook Luke Goodman's hand. "Now, I'd best be finding that boy of mine and getting on home." Jim crossed the lawn and whistled to Jimmy, who was standing with a group of boys under a barren oak tree. "Let's go, son!"

Laura and Joanna were waiting with Joe while Edgar brought Dolly from the livery stable when Joanna felt a tap on her shoulder. She turned.

Lucy Sheppard took a step closer, extending her kid gloved hand. "I saw you at the social last evening, Miss Garrett, but we were never introduced. I'm Lucy Sheppard." Her green-eyed gaze was direct and penetrating. "I would love to come one day soon and interview you for our newspaper. I know everyone is most anxious to learn all about our new school mistress."

"I'm pleased to meet you, Miss Sheppard. There's not much to know about a country school teacher, but I would be glad to speak with you. Perhaps you could come by the school one afternoon when classes are over."

"I could do that, Miss Garrett, but I had thought I might impose on the McGills to permit our interview at their home. You are staying there *temporarily*, I gather?" Lucy's slight emphasis on the word was not lost on Joanna, or on Laura.

"You're welcome to come to the house, Lucy," Laura

interjected, "though you might want to meet Joanna at the school so you can see what she's done there. You might even want to bring that photographer with you. Joanna's photograph would make for high sales of the *Clipper*." Laura took Joanna's arm and squeezed it. "As Jeff Peters said last night, Joanna's *'a sight prettier'* than Ruth Lambert was."

Joe tittered. Joanna hoped the January chill had already reddened her cheeks. Lucy, however, was looking elsewhere. Edgar had just pulled up in the wagon and was staring at Lucy Sheppard, as if he'd never seen her before. He hopped down and tipped his cap.

"Morning, Lucy," he said.

Laura coughed and covered her mouth. If Edgar had not been riveted on Lucy, he would have seen the daggers in his sister's eyes, as Joanna had.

Edgar really likes this woman, Joanna thought, *but Laura can't stand her. I wonder why.*

"May we give you a ride home, Lucy?"

"Why, thank you, Edgar," Lucy said in a much softer tone than she had used with Joanna, "but I have to stop by the newspaper office and then Cal Turner is picking me up. He's taking me to the hotel for Sunday dinner. In fact, I should be getting on or I'll keep Cal waiting." She brushed past Edgar, close enough that he caught a whiff of the heavy rose scent she favored. "I'll be calling on you soon, Miss Garrett. A pleasure to meet you."

Edgar watched Lucy walk away, and Laura watched him watching her. Laura shook her head in disgust.

"If it's no trouble, brother dear, Joanna and I are ready to get out of this cold and back to our own dinner. Could you please take us home?"

"Of course, I'll take you home, Laura," he said. "I'm hungry."

"Yes, I can tell..."

After dinner Joanna did the unheard of and went to her room for a nap. Edgar also headed to his bedroom.

The first thing Edgar did upon entering his bedroom was trade his dress boots for leather slippers, what his grandmother had called *bedroom shoes*. He went to his large oaken desk and extracted a sheaf of papers bearing the name Pennsylvania Academy of Fine Arts and began reading. He pulled a sheet of paper from the center desk drawer—reading, then writing—and, suddenly, slammed the papers onto his desk and stood up, running his fingers back and forth through his dark hair. "What am I thinking of?" he said aloud. "I can't do this. I have Joe and Laura to care for... I can't give up the farm to take—"

He walked to the window and pushed aside the curtains and stared out at the snow covered fields. "I'm a farmer, just a plain old farmer. I'll never be anything else." He shoved the papers back into their pigeonhole and flung himself onto the bed. In moments he, too, was asleep.

While Joanna and Edgar napped, Laura and Joe sat at the kitchen table, deep in a game of chess and treating themselves to thick slices of Joanna's pound cake.

"This is really good, Aunt Laura," he said, crumbs falling from his mouth as he took a swig of milk. "It's the best pound cake I've ever had."

"I agree, Joe, and I know Miss Garrett's secret. When she takes the cake from the oven, she turns it out onto a tea towel covered with white sugar. That's what gives it this crunchy sweet crust."

"Well, I hope she makes it again soon. I would of bought a piece at the social if I knew it was this good!"

"What did you have last night, Toad? I'm sure you and Jimmy ate and drank as much as you could!"

"Gosh, we had fun, Aunt Laura!" Joe's blue eyes danced in the joy of remembering. "First we tried some of the pies. Mrs. Lane made a great pecan pie and Mrs. Garner had a cherry one with two crusts. Then we had some punch, then me and Jimmy..."

"*Jimmy and I*," she corrected.

"Jimmy *and I* and Ben and Jacob went outside and had a spitting contest. It was so cold, our spit froze before it hit the ground. You shoulda been there!"

"I'm sorry I missed it," she said through a wry smile. "What did you do then?"

"Well, old Mr. Dawson got after us for being outside, so we came back in and sat for a while and watched the dancing. Gosh, some of those people looked funny!" He slapped his knees and cackled. "Did you see Mrs. Werner? Every time she whirled around, that feather in her hair bobbed and bounced—she looked just like a peahen!"

Laura repressed a giggle. Joe's description was all too accurate, but she didn't want to encourage speaking disrespectfully of his elders.

"And did you see Pa and Miss Sheppard? They were sashaying around, and Pa kept staring at her, and he looked real mad when Cal Turner cut in on them." Joe imitated his father's frown. "But, then, Pa went and cut in on Reverend Goodman and started dancing with Miss Garret. Didn't she look pretty last night? I never thought schoolteachers could be that pretty."

Laura remembered Ruth Lambert and thought, *I'm not surprised. Ruth was a kind person but no one, not even her own mother, would have called her pretty. Joanna is something else entirely. She's beautiful inside and out, and will definitely catch some man's eye — if she hasn't already. Maybe it would be better if the school board doesn't fix up the Gordon place. Joanna might be better off under our roof for a while!*

Joe was hunched over the chess board, waiting for Laura to move, when Joanna joined them in the kitchen. She poured herself a cup of coffee from the always full pot, then sat in the rocker by the hearth and watched them play. Laura made her move and Joe reached for his queen, moved it and hollered, "Checkmate!"

Laura threw her hands up in disgust. "I cannot believe I let you win," she said, going into the pantry. "I should have known better than to make that move!"

"Oh, come on, Aunt Laura!" Joe followed her into the pantry and tugged on her sleeve. "Admit it. I played better than you did and I won!"

"And you're humble about it, too," Joanna added. "It's always good to see a humble winner."

"All right, all right," Laura said, "you won fair and square. Now, get out to the barn, milk the cows and feed the horse. I don't know where your pa is, but chores need to be done when they need to be done!" Joe scooted out to the lean-to and was soon on his way to the barn. Laura watched him from the window, then turned to Joanna.

"He's a good boy. I love him as if he were my own. I hate to think there may come a day when Edgar remarries and I have to give up Joe."

"Is Mr. McGill planning to remarry?"

"I don't know that he's *planning* on it," she said, "but he's been paying a lot of attention to one woman for a while, and from the way he gets moony every time he's near her, I think it may be serious."

"Lucy Sheppard?"

Laura rolled her eyes in obvious disgust. "I'm afraid so. You couldn't help but notice how Edgar went looking for her last night and how he stared at her this morning. I think he's falling for her—though I wish it was *any* other woman, but her."

"May I ask why?" Joanna hadn't particularly liked Lucy Sheppard's arrogant demeanor, but Laura's feelings went beyond dislike.

"Lucy Sheppard is a wolf in lamb's clothing. She's got half the men in town thinking she's sweet and helpless— the *only* thing she has going for her is that she's pretty—not beautiful, mind you—though I think *tempting* is the more appropriate description." Laura was letting go with feelings she had bottled up for some time. "Underneath that blonde head is a mind that has to be in charge of everything and everyone, and underneath that milky white skin lies a heart of ice. Lucy Sheppard cares about her newspaper and about Lucy Sheppard, and that's all she'll ever care about." Laura chopped at the bread with such a vengeance that Joanna worried it would end up in crumbs.

"You both are so close and he loves and respects you. Won't he listen to you?

Laura put the knife down, put her hands on her hips, lifted her brow, and stared Joanna in the eye. "How many men in love have you known, Joanna? Have you ever known one who would accept being told about the faults in the woman he *thinks* is the only one for him?" Laura didn't wait for Joanna's answer and spun around to the cutting board.

Yes... Nicholas Brodie.

"I just keep hoping—and praying—that Edgar will see it for himself before he does something foolish. I cannot imagine that woman as a good mother for—"

Edgar yawned as he approached the kitchen. Both women began bustling about.

He looked from one to the other. "Laura, you look like the cat that swallowed the canary, and Miss Garrett, you look as if butter wouldn't melt in your mouth. What are you two ladies up to? And why didn't anyone come and get me at chore time?"

"We've just been having some nice girl talk with both you and Joe out of the way for once, Edgar. I didn't come get you because your son is perfectly capable of handling the evening chores alone." She began slicing the cold ham. "Why don't you go out and see how Joe's doing, and leave me and Joanna to get supper on the table? I think we're all going to want to get to bed early tonight after being out so late last night. At least I will," she said as Edgar headed toward the lean-to, "because I haven't had a long nap!"

Chapter Nine

Two weeks later, Joanna was alone in the classroom on a Thursday afternoon, setting up a table with books, maps, pencils and paper so the children could begin a geography study the next day. She was rummaging through the storage shelves for colored paper when she heard the door open.

"Joe... I thought you'd be outside for another fifteen minutes enjoying the sunshine."

"I could go back outside and wait fifteen minutes before entering, if you prefer."

Joanna spun around. "Miss Sheppard... Please come in."

Lucy stepped over the threshold and Joanna went to her, shook her hand, then shut the door. "I wasn't expecting you today."

"I know you weren't, Miss Garrett." She removed her hat, a dark green felt, and placed it on one of the children's desks along with her coat and gloves. "I was on my way back from Hanover and as I approached the schoolhouse, I decided this would be a perfect opportunity to have our little chat."

"I'm glad you came by," she said, regretting she had to break the Ninth Commandment to preserve social graces. "But I'm afraid I don't have much time to talk. I leave at four o'clock, she said, glancing up to the wall clock, "as you can see, it's almost that now."

Lucy's gaze traveled from Joanna to the clock on the wall. "Perhaps you could change your schedule—" Lucy said coolly. "Unless you're not eager to have our little community know more about its new schoolteacher."

She knows what happened back home. Joanna was grateful that Lucy's back was to her as she tried to compose herself.   "I'm flattered that you think people might find me interesting, Miss Sheppard. I'm willing to speak with you. We simply need to plan for a day when I can drive myself to school, so I don't inconvenience Joe and Mr. McGill."

Lucy spun around. "Edgar?" Her voice was cool. "And why would what you do affect Edgar McGill?"

"Hey, Miss Garrett, look what I found!" Joe said, holding a quivering black and white puppy. "I found it out by the well. Where do you think it came from?" He didn't see Lucy Sheppard when he bolted into the classroom.

"Hello, Joseph."

The boy jumped at the sound of her voice.

"Why on earth did you bring that dirty little beast in here? The school board didn't pay dearly for this beautiful new building so it could be sullied by a mangy dog."

"Miss Sheppard... What are you doing here?"

Joanna maneuvered herself between Lucy and Joe, and knelt down to the dog he held. "Miss Sheppard came to interview me for the newspaper, Joe. I didn't know she was coming either, so we were both surprised." She stroked the puppy's head. "Why, this little fellow can't be more than a few weeks old! It shouldn't be away from its mother."

"I know, Miss Garrett, and I looked everywhere for its mother, but couldn't find her. I couldn't just leave this puppy out in the cold, could I?" His blue eyes carried a heartfelt appeal.

"Of course not, Joe. But why don't we set him—or her—in the wood box? That way we won't risk a mess in the classroom?"

Lucy stepped to one side as Joe and Joanna passed her. "Well, it seems that matters more important than my interview need to be addressed." She went to the student desk where she laid her wrap. "I'll try to come again at a more *convenient* time." The tone of her voice made clear it was *her* convenience that mattered, not Joanna's.

"Do come back," Joanna said quickly. "In fact, let's choose a day right now." She went to her desk and her weekly calendar.

"Let's see—would next Wednesday suit you? It's a testing day, so the students will be leaving early, which should give us plenty of time together. And I'll drive myself to school."

Lucy pulled on her green leather gloves. "I'll have to check my own calendar and see if Wednesday is suitable. I'll let you know Sunday." She fixed a penetrating look on Joanna. "You do attend services regularly, don't you, Miss Garrett?"

"Yes, of course I do. I was fed by Reverend Goodman's sermon. My week goes much better if I begin it by worshipping God." She extended her hand to Lucy. "Letting me know on Sunday will be fine. Thank you for stopping by."

Lucy turned and strutted out the door.

Joe looked at Joanna, wide-eyed and a bit shocked. "Gosh, Miss Garrett, did I do something to make her mad? I didn't even know she was here until she spoke and about scared the life out of me!"

"You didn't do anything wrong, Joe. Now, let's have a look at that puppy." The two were sitting on the floor, stroking the still trembling dog, when the schoolroom door opened again. *Don't tell me she's come back!* Joanna thought. It was Edgar.

"What are you two doing on the floor? And was that Lucy Sheppard I saw driving off?"

"Pa!" Joe picked up the pup and ran to his father. "Look what I found, Pa! Can we take it home? Please, Pa? I've been wanting a dog for the longest time and you said it'd be good to have one on the farm, for a watchdog."

"Slow down, son." He took the puppy from Joe. "This pup can't even be a month old. Where did you find it?"

Joe told his story again, adding that he had been high in an oak tree when he heard a mewling sound near the tree trunk and climbed down to investigate. "It was just lying there in a hole in the trunk, Pa. It was shaking all over. I had to bring it inside—" He looked up at Joanna. "—didn't I, Miss Garrett?"

"You surely did, Joe," Joanna said softly. 'You couldn't leave it outside in the cold." She walked to Edgar's side. "Mr. McGill, that was Lucy Sheppard you saw. She came to interview me for the paper. She wasn't pleased that I didn't have time to speak with her today."

Edgar grinned. "Lucy can be a bit temperamental," he said. "She'll be back. I'm sorry I missed her."

Joe shook his head at his father. "Miss Sheppard hates this dog, Pa. She called it *a dirty little beast* and said I shoulda left it outside." He touched Joanna's sleeve. "Miss Garrett didn't think I shoulda left the puppy out in the cold."

Joanna tousled Joe's hair. "No. I didn't. We couldn't let the poor little thing freeze outside once we knew it was there." She looked inquiringly at Edgar. "It can't stay here. It will have to be fed often, and I'm only here during the school day."

Edgar looked from Joe, hugging the pup to his chest, to Joanna, who was looking at Joe and the pup with affection. He sighed. "I expect we better take the animal back to the farm with us—"

Joe whooped with delight and quickly reined in his glee when the pup let out a frightened squeal.

"I'm not going to take care of it, Toad. You found it, and it will be *your* responsibility. Understand?"

"Oh, yes, Pa! I'll take good care of it, and I just know it's gonna be a good dog." He nuzzled the pup's muzzle. "Aren't you, Patches?"

"*Patches?*"

"It just came to me, Pa," he said, pointing to the multicolored splotches on the dog's fur. "See how there's black and white and they're all mixed up? It looks just like a patchwork quilt."

"I like it," Joanna said, stroking the pup, "and it will work whether this is a boy or a girl!"

Joanna finished setting up the geography table and put a few papers in her satchel while Edgar carried the foot warmers out to the wagon. She turned the key in the lock and felt a tug on her coat sleeve. Joe looked up at her with a smile that said *thanks*. He carried Patches down to the wagon in the wood box and Edgar reached in with a piece of sacking and positioned it beneath the pup. Joanna smiled. *You like that puppy as much as Joe does, even if you don't want to admit it!*

"What a precious little mite," Laura said, wiping her hands on her apron and taking the pup from Joe. "Wherever did it come from?"

Joe told the story again, ending with, "Miss Sheppard was there, Aunt Laura. She told me to leave Patches outside in the cold!"

Laura glanced to Joanna and lifted her eyebrows. "Why does that not surprise me?" She patted the pup's back and it rewarded her with a lick of its tiny pink tongue. "But I am a dog lover and I am so happy you found this little fellow before he froze to death."

"We don't know if Patches is a boy or a girl, Aunt Laura."

She lifted the pup and gave its belly the once over. "Patches is a boy, all right. Run out to the barn, Joe, and get one of the calf feeders. We'll warm some milk and give this little fella a meal."

Laura laid the pup in the wood box. "I'll have to find another place for him to sleep. You'll need this at school tomorrow or you'll run out of firewood before the day's half over."

Joanna put a pan of milk on the stove to warm for the pup, then poured two steaming mugs of coffee. "A nice piece of pound cake would go well with this," she said, setting a cup before Edgar.

"We still have cake?"

She nodded, went to the pantry and returned with a thick slab of the cake. "I was saving it for dessert tonight, but you look as if you could do with a little sustenance right now." She cut a slice and handed it to him. Edgar broke off a piece and raised it over his coffee.

Joanna laughed. "My grandfather always used to do that and, oh, how it made Nanny mad. 'William,' she'd say, 'that cake's not dry and it's got plenty of flavor. Why do you want to mess it up by dunkin' it in coffee?'" She smiled again. "But he'd just tell her, 'Jo, my love, it's not what the coffee does to your cake that I like, it's what your cake does for the coffee.' Nanny would laugh and swat him with her dish cloth, smiling as she did."

"I think I would have liked knowing your grandfather, Miss Garrett. Sounds like a smart man." He held his plate out for another piece of cake. "You referred to your grandmother as *Jo*. Are you named for her?"

"I am, and proud to be. My grandmother is— was—the finest woman I've ever known." Sadness crept over her. "I still miss her, and she's been gone almost five years now."

Edgar stared into his cup in the silence that prevailed until he looked back at Joanna, his violet-blue eyes filled with melancholy. "I know how you feel. My wife died when Joe was two years old. You'd think by now I'd have gotten over it." He absentmindedly broke off a piece of cake, but didn't eat it. "In most ways I have, but some days, I get to thinking about Bessie and my heart feels like it's going to explode." Awareness of what he was saying suddenly struck him and he abruptly stood up. "I better go see what's keeping Joe." He grabbed his jacket and was out the door.

"Just the thing for Patches," Laura said, returning with a wicker basket. "It started out as a laundry basket and turned into a baby basket. Bessie used it to bring Joe outside when we were working in the garden. You would have liked our Bessie, Joanna. She was a wonderful wife and mother."

"Just before you came in, Edgar—" her face turned an unexpected crimson. "I mean Mr. McGill was talking about his wife."

"Edgar talked about Bessie?" Surprise hit her and Laura plunked herself into a chair. "He *never* speaks of her—not even to Joe. I can't remember the last time he mention Bessie." She leaned forward. "What did he say?"

Joanna recounted the conversation and her eyes filled with tears. "It made my own heart ache to hear him say it, but then, he suddenly ran out to the barn."

"Edgar's good at running away from his grief. He mourned Bessie for years, but refused to talk about it. Then, after Luke Goodman came to town and he and Edgar got to be friends, it seemed like Edgar let go of some of the pain and started healing. He's been more like his old self, but he still doesn't talk about Bessie." She reached for Joanna's hand. "I'm glad he talked to you, Joanna. I'm glad he has a good woman to talk to, someone who isn't his sister." She leaned back and gave a scoffing laugh. "I don't see Edgar opening up to Lucy Sheppard that way, even if he can't take his eyes off her. And I can't see her caring."

"I never told you *why* Miss Sheppard stopped by today..." Joanna was deep in the story when Joe and Edgar came in with the bottle feeder. Laura went to the stove and checked the temperature of the milk. "It's *just right*." She filled the bottle while Joe went to the basket where the puppy lay softly snoring.

"Sorry to wake you, boy," he said, kissing the puppy's head, "It's supper time." At the first taste of milk the dog's eyes widened, lapping it up in great gulps. "Look, Aunt Laura, look, Miss Garrett! He likes it!" The boy watched contentedly as the pup drank every drop. Joe held up the feeder. "He needs more!"

"That's all he should have right now, Joe," Laura said. "He'll be sick if he drinks too much at once. But don't worry, you'll get plenty of chances to feed him. He'll have another bottle after supper and probably another before we go to bed. And—" She patted both boy and dog on their heads, "you'll have to get up and feed him during the night, too!"

Joanna stroked the dog's soft, mottled fur. "You're a lucky little fellow, Patches. You've got a good owner in Joe, and a good home here."

Joanna lay in bed thinking about how happy the McGill house was, despite the lack of a wife for Edgar, a husband for Laura, or a mother for Joe. *What will happen if Edgar marries Lucy Sheppard ... and what will happen to me when I move out?* She relived those brief, tender moments with Edgar, who had bared the heartbreak of his soul. *He's a good man, a good father and a good brother. He'll make a good husband if he ever decides to marry again, and Lucy Sheppard will be one very lucky woman.*

Chapter Ten

Laura stopped short of entering the kitchen when she saw Joe standing by the stove, cuddling the pup, and waiting for the milk to warm for Patches. *A farm full of animals and the boy still needs a pet.*

"Aren't you the early bird," she said. "Has that little one been outside yet?"

"I took him out when I went to get the milk, Aunt Laura. He was whining something fierce, so I thought maybe he really needed to go out." He carried dog and bottle to the rocker while she poured the milk into the feeder. "How long do you think I'll need to bottle feed him?"

"Well, Patches looks to be no more than three or four weeks old," she said, handing the feeder to her nephew. "Puppies usually nurse for at least six weeks, so I'm guessing you've got two weeks of feeding, unless you can teach him to drink from a bowl sooner."

Edgar walked in grinning. "Looks like that dog has done what I haven't been able to, son—he got you out of bed *before* sunrise without being called." He said, thumping Joe's head. "C'mon out as soon as you're finished and give me a hand with the milking."

"Bye, buddy," he said, planting a kiss on the pup's head.

"You be good today, you hear?" He turned to his aunt. "I never asked if you'd mind taking care of Patches while I'm at school, Aunt Laura." His eyes carried a pleading look. "You don't, do you? And if you get behind with any of your chores, I'll do them when I get home." He picked up a shirt from the pile of mending near the hearth. "I'll even help you with the sewing!"

Joanna stood pouring a cup of coffee; Laura looked up at her and both women laughed. Laura took the shirt from Joe . "Thanks very much, Joe, but I don't think I'll be calling on you to darn socks or sew on buttons. I'll feed Patches for you and take him out, and we'll figure out some fair trade." She leaned over, hugged the boy, and kissed his cheek. "Have a good day at school, both of you."

As soon as Joanna arrived at school, she covered the lesson table with a red checked cloth that bulged over a big hump in the center. It lay in a peculiar way, rising over other smaller bumps as well. She planned to introduce geography after morning recess; her strategy was to arouse her students' curiosity, as well as pique their enthusiasm. She knew she had succeeded when the students kept glancing to the table as they went to the blackboard to diagram sentences. Caleb Matthews tried lifting a corner of the tablecloth, but Joanna frowned and shook her head discouraging his unsanctioned attempt. Even the older pupils tried sneaking peeks, all the while feigning disinterest.

Joanna was pleased, but maintained her control and waited until after recess, when she gathered the students around the mystery table. "Littlest ones in front, please, so everyone can see." She sat on the edge of her desk. "Now, class, who knows what the world looks like?" She called on Jake Trimble, who rarely raised his hand.

"Any fool knows that, Miss Garrett. Just look out the window—it's covered with trees and grass and fields." He snickered and leaned toward his pal, Harry Watson, who had just started to school the week before. "A teacher oughta know that!" A few pupils giggled.

"All right, Jake," she said. "You know what southern Indiana looks like. But what about South America? Or Europe? Does anyone know about those countries?"

Agnes Werner waved her hand. "I do, Miss Garrett." She flounced her red braids and threw Jake a withering look. "I've seen pictures in a book Mama has, and there's an ocean between us and Europe, and the one between us and South America, too."

"That's right, Agnes," Joanna said with a smile. "How would you like to see those oceans?"

The room echoed their uninvited replies: "Are we going on a trip?" ... "You can't show us that, Miss Garrett" ... "No one knows what the whole world looks like," and "Yes, show us!"

Joanna waited until they quieted down. "If you want to see the *whole* world, I can show it to you, but I'll need some help." She peered over the cluster of students. "Emma and Samantha, will you come and help me? And Josh and Albert, too." She positioned one student at each corner of the table. "Now, when I say *go*, I want you to lift up your corner of the tablecloth. Then I'll want you, Emma and Samantha to bring your corners together, and Josh, you and Albert do the same, and we'll see what's under there."

The students leaned forward, all eyes intently focused on the table.

"All right," she said. "One, two, three, GO!" Eight hands whisked the tablecloth as high in the air as their arms would reach, akin to a magician unveiling a rabbit in his hat. A chorus of *oohs* and *ahs* filled the moments as eyes went wide as saucers staring at the center of the table, where a huge round, colorful object sat perched on a shiny brass stand, nearly two feet tall.

"This," Joanna said, "is a globe. It shows what the earth looks like and we can see every country in the world on it." She spun the globe and pointed. "This is our country, the United States of America." She called Agnes to the table. "Can you find Indiana on the globe, Agnes?" The little girl leaned over the globe and studied it. "There it is, Miss Garrett!" she said, sticking her finger on an orange colored rectangle. "And look! There's Ohio right beside it! My aunt lives in Ohio!"

A tidal wave of students surged toward the globe, but Joanna motioned them back to their places. "Everyone will get a turn to look at the globe up close," she said, "but first I want to tell you a little bit about our world." She showed them all the continents and pointed out Germany, France, and England because she had learned that many of the students' families had come from those countries. She pointed out how large the United States was and how it had grown from the time of the Revolutionary War. Twenty minutes later, the youngest pupils were getting restless.

"Now, let's have the primary class come up and look at the globe." A few older students moaned. "While they do that, I'm going to pass around some books for the rest of you to look at. See if you can find a map of the world in them." She handed Joe and Jimmy Langston a stack of thin, brightly covered books to distribute.

The next hour was spent with students taking turns spinning

the globe, then bringing it to a stop with a poke of a finger and seeing what country it landed on. Joanna answered questions and indicated the different countries and explained what languages were spoken in them. It was past noon when Joanna announced dinnertime.

A chorus of voices protested. "But we're not done yet!"

"You'll be back at the globe soon," she promised. "In the meantime, I have another surprise for you. After dinner, I want you each to choose some colored paper and we'll trace the map of the United States and other countries from the textbooks. When they're finished, we'll put them on the walls and invite your parents to come and see them."

Their beaming faces told Joanna that her students not only liked her spur-of-the-moment idea but were eager to show their parents how well they were doing.

When she rang the bell to dismiss school several students lingered near the globe. *Good*, she thought. *I was right to start geography on a Friday. They'll be even more anxious to get back to it on Monday!*

Saturday dawned bright and unusually warm for February and Joanna and Laura took full advantage of it to work in the flower garden. It was too early to plant, so they cleared away piles of dead wet leaves and removed the annuals from last year's planting. Joanna was raking near a wooden swing when Laura let out a delighted squeal.

"Joanna! Come and see," she said, pointing to several tiny green stems poking through the ground, then knelt down. "My crocuses are coming up! And so are some of the new daffodils I bought from Mr. Greenwood! Oh, I just can't wait to tell Edgar that I've got flowers coming up already!" She looked up at Joanna. "He told me I was wasting my money on those bulbs!"

Joanna smiled. "What was it that Robert Browning wrote?" she said, closing her eyes. *"If you get simple beauty and nought else, You get the best thing God invents."*

"If that's not the joy of a garden, I don't know what is."

The two women finished their yard work and returned to the house to feed Patches and fix a light dinner. Edgar and Joe had left early to attend an auction near Columbus and wouldn't be back until nightfall. Over tea and biscuits and wedges of hoop cheese, Laura and Joanna planned the rest of their day.

"I really should do some mending," Joanna said. "I've fallen sadly behind on it."

"And I should sort through Joe's clothes and see how many new shirts he'll need come spring. The boy grows so fast that his cuffs are way above his wrists before I can turn around." Laura twirled her spoon in her coffee cup and nibbled on a biscuit.

Joanna sighed. "I should mend," she said again "but I really don't want to. I want to do something *different*, or go somewhere. I think I'm getting spring fever."

"I think I've got cabin fever *and* spring fever."

Joanna raised her eyebrows inquiringly. "What is *cabin fever*?"

"Sometimes I forget you're from the south, Joanna, where you have much milder winters. *Cabin* fever is when you start to think you'll go crazy if there's one more snowstorm... one more dull gray sky, or one more week when you can't leave the house."

"Why don't we go to town today, or drive over and visit Mary Langston? I bet she'd welcome talk with other women, and we could help with the baby."

"There's the slight problem of transportation. Edgar and Joe drove Dolly to Columbus."

Joanna slapped her palm against her forehead. "I completely forgot!" She mused for a moment, then banged the table so hard their mugs jumped. "I have to buy a horse. I'll need one when I'm on my own and, in the meantime, I could drive to school, and you and I can use it when your brother needs Dolly." She stood up and plunked her dishes in the sink with vigor. "I'll tell Mr. McGill tonight. I'll need his help to choose a dependable animal." She turned around to Laura. "What do you think?"

"I think you're terrific! You're independent and willing to take risks, and when you run into a problem, you look for a solution."

Laura's words pierced Joanna. She turned back to the sink of dishes. *If that were true, I'd still be in North Carolina. I solve problems by running away from them.* The memory was as vivid as though it had happened yesterday...

* * *

Raleigh, N.C. - December 1884

"Joanna! Are you in there?" Abigail Wheaton called out from the hallway.

Oh, no. I can't see anyone now—especially not Abby.

"Joanna!" Her friend's voice accompanied the knock at the door. "Come caroling with us!"

Joanna quickly shoved the envelope under the bed pillow, took a deep breath and wiped the tears off her cheeks. "Y'all go on without me, Abby."

The door opened and Abby poked her freckled face, red-haired head inside and saw Joanna sitting on the edge of the bed, a handkerchief at her nose. "Go without you? But you're the only one who can sing tenor if none of the men from Wake Forest come," she said laughing it.

"I don't feel like singing tonight."

"Are you sick?"

I am if a broken heart counts. "I'm... I'm not sure, Abby."

"I can't hear you, Jo."

"I said I'm not sure, Abby. I just don't feel right. Maybe I'm catching something." *God forgive me for lying. It's the least of my sins.*

"I'm sorry, Jo. Do you need me to get you anything before I go?"

"No, thank you. Maybe I'll be able to have some tea later."

"All right, then. But everyone will miss you."

"I'll miss being there, too. Have fun." Joanna listened until she heard Abby's footsteps running down the stairs. She pulled the envelope from its hiding place and unfolded the two sheets her father had penned. She'd almost memorized its contents...

2nd inst., December 1884

Dear Joanna,

This is a very difficult letter for me to write. I will ask you to forgive me for not coming up to Raleigh to speak with you in person, but Advent is simply too busy a season for me to undertake the journey from Wilmington.

To the point, your mother and I were shocked beyond belief when we read the enclosed article published in the Petersburg Progress in Virginia. Nicholas Brodie brought it to us. You cannot imagine what a sad and awkward meeting that was for us. His shock and disbelief were so great that he wept before us.

He was mortified, Joanna, and deeply concerned about what people who know you both would think of him, an aspiring young lawyer. Your going to that convention in Washington last March was bad enough — as I am sure you remember from our conversation then. But, Joanna! To be arrested as a suffragette! You cannot conceive of the shame your mother and I feel.

Under these circumstances, we believe it would be best if you not come back to Wilmington. Our parishioners will undoubtedly question how your mother and I ever let this happen. Our friends, though they be true, may doubt the propriety of your upbringing when they learn how far you have strayed from all we taught you, and how far from grace you have fallen. The course you have chosen is a damning one.

We will pray for you, as always. We hope with everything that is in us and will fervently pray that the Joanna we knew and loved will return to us. Write us if, or when, she does — when she returns to a Godly path and accepts the hand of our Lord and Savior, who will set her right again.

Yours in Christ Jesus,

Papa

The newspaper clipping, dated November 25, 1884, was short and devastating. Every word chilled Joanna as she held the ink-ladened article in her trembling hands...

SUFFRAGETTE'S SPEECH LEADS TO RIOT

Suffragette leader Elizabeth Cady Stanton gave another one of her sensational speeches at Lyceum Hall in Petersburg, Virginia, Thursday last. A group of Mrs. Stanton's fervent followers was taken into custody following a riotous outbreak and clash between pro- and anti-suffrage attendees and the local police. A group of women was held overnight in the Petersburg jail. Among the nearly fifty arrested were several "ladies" from outside the Old Dominion -- Martha Frye of West Virginia, Evelyn Zimmer of Indiana, and Joanna Garrett of North Carolina, to name a few. It is a sad day, indeed, when women—the mainstay of our families and communities—involve themselves in such frivolous and contentious matters. Will this issue force husbands, fathers, sons, and brothers to find ways to deal with their women, whose aspirations are so dangerously far-fetched and impractical? We hope and pray not, as our still-healing country cannot endure another national tragedy.

"Oh, Papa... it's not what you and Mama think," she wept. "This newspaper article is all *wrong,* but I'll never be able to convince you of that... *You've buried Josie...* She fell back onto the bed, hid her face in the pillow and cried a torrent of tears in the pain that choked her heart.

Joanna didn't know how long she had lain there; the tear-soaked pillow only confirmed that her tears had flowed incessantly.

She sat up, wiped her wet face, and knew what she had to do. "Maybe Susannah will know about a teaching post—one far away, where no one has seen that newspaper, or read its distortions and half-truths."

* * *

Appleton - February 1885

"Joanna?" Laura went to her at the sink and touched her shoulder. Joanna jumped in the sudden shock of reality. "Are you all right?"

She dried her hands in the dish towel, "I'm sorry, Laura, I must have been lost in thought."

"I was saying that your solution to the horse problem won't help us today, because we're stuck with sorting clothes and mending."

Joanna untied her apron and plunked it on the counter. "No, we're not! My grandmother said work will always be waiting for you, but pleasure can be fleeting. Let's do something else." She suddenly remembered the ream of paper and the inkwell in the roll-top desk in her bedroom. "Do you like to write?"

"Whatever gave you that idea?"

"Well, there's that pretty little roll-top desk in my room filled with writing materials and... somehow I had the idea that it was your desk." She snapped her fingers. "Now I remember! It *is* your desk! Mr. McGill said my room had been your childhood bedroom and that you had fixed it up as your study." She smiled triumphantly at Laura. "He told me that you had planned to use it as your writing room, and you said you still planned to. So, Miss McGill—what do you write?" She tapped her foot and gave Laura her best "I'm the teacher and you'd better answer me" look.

Laura untied her own apron and waved it like a flag. "All right, all right, I surrender! I do love to write. I wrote several pieces for the town paper—before Lucy Sheppard took over the women's page. I've been working on a story I hope to send off to a publisher in New York."

Joanna felt the excitement in Laura's voice.

"You're the first to know this, Joanna Garrett, and I don't want you to say a word to *anyone*. I may never get that story finished and, of course, I may not be able to sell it anyway. I don't want to disappoint anyone but myself if I fail." Now Laura looked serious. "Promise me, Joanna. Promise this will be our secret."

Oh, Laura, if you only knew what I'm hiding, she thought, *you'd know just how good I am at keeping secrets.* "Of course I'll promise. But *you* have to promise me that you'll spend this afternoon writing and that you'll feel free to use your study while I'm staying here. I don't want to be the reason your story doesn't get written!"

"I promise, teacher. I'll go upstairs as soon as I put these dishes away, and I won't come down until it's time to start supper."

Joanna took the apron out of Laura's hand and shooed her off. "You go now, and don't come down until I call to tell you supper's ready." When Laura didn't move, Joanna gave her a gentle shove. "Off with you." Laura reluctantly obeyed, left the room, but poked her head around the corner.

"You must be something in the classroom, Joanna. You may be a little thing, but one can sure tell when you mean business!" She pulled her head back just in time to dodge the dishcloth Joanna threw at her.

True to her word, Laura spent the entire afternoon closeted

in Joanna's room. *It's a glorious day to be doing anything,* she thought, *and an even better one to be doing what I love.* Laura had always loved words and had always been good at putting them together. Her mother's cedar chest was full of cards Laura had made and poems she had penned. She had excelled at reading and writing in school, and one of her teachers, an elderly, bearded scholar who lived in Appleton for a few years, had encouraged her to write for publication. "You have real talent, my girl," he had told her, "and talent should never be wasted. It comes from God, and using it is our way of thanking God." Laura had taken his advice, which was when she had written her first articles for *The Gazette.*

After her parents and Bessie died, Laura had assumed the job of mother and housekeeper and her writing, naturally, had fallen by the wayside. She had resumed the practice only a few months before Joanna's arrival. Edgar knew Laura enjoyed writing, arranging her old bedroom as a study, but how stunned he would be to hear she had begun a novel. She could hardly believe it herself.

Laura heard Edgar and Joe return shortly after the clock chimed four o'clock. *I'm not going downstairs and risk incurring Joanna's wrath, however mild it might be. I wonder what she's telling them.* She picked up her pen and went back to work.

Laura was so engrossed in her writing that she jumped nearly a foot off the chair when she felt something touch her shoulder.

"I'm sorry I startled you. I tapped on the door, but you didn't answer," Joanna said. "I even called your name when I came in." She saw the pile of paper filled with Laura's neat writing and smiled. "It looks as though you've had a productive afternoon."

"Oh, Joanna, it's been simply grand! I don't know when I last spent a solid afternoon just writing. I have a long way to go still, but my story seemed to come to life today." She removed the reading glasses perched on her nose, stood up and stretched with delight. "I know it's not everyone's idea of a good time, but I *really* had fun today," she said, gathering up her handwritten pages.

"Leave them there, if you want to. I promise I won't read them. I've been doing my schoolwork at the bedside table, where I have more room to spread out."

Laura put the papers into one of the slots in the desk and rolled down its oaken top.

"And, remember, Laura... I want you to come in here and

write whenever you want to. This is *your* special place—I'm just its temporary occupant."

"I'm going to hate to see you go," Laura said as they walked downstairs. "I've gotten so accustomed to having you here that I forget you're just visiting. It's like you're a member of our family."

Joanna remembered Laura's words as she prepared for bed. *I feel the same way and, oh! how good it feels to be part of a family again. How I'd love to be part of this family. And just how would that happen?* She looked at her image in the mirror.

Only if you married Edgar—

Her hand flew to her mouth, as if she had said the words aloud, and closed her eyes.

I can't entertain such a thought... No man will marry me if he learns the truth about me. Oh, Mama, I hope you're wrong...

Chapter Eleven

"I think you should get a horse, Miss Garrett," Edgar announced on their way to church. "I've been keeping an eye out for a good one for some time."

Joanna's heart fluttered. *I've been on his mind,* she thought, *as he has been on mine.*

"Come spring, I'll be out in the fields and I won't be able to make the drive to school twice a day."

"Have you ever owned a horse, Joanna?" Laura asked.

Joe interrupted: "What kind do you like? An Appaloosa, maybe? Or a quarter horse?

"I've never owned a horse, Laura, but I know how to ride. And, Joe, my favorite horse is a Paint."

"Jeff Peters up at the livery stable has some horses for sale, and a couple of them are Paints," Edgar said.

Joe slapped his thigh. "Hey, Miss Garrett! If you get a Paint, your horse will match my dog! They could be *Matches* and *Patches!*"

The four were still laughing when they arrived at church. Joanna and Laura passed Celia Werner, deep in conversation with Minnie Bailey. Celia, ever flamboyant, was wearing a sea green scarf around her neck and the ubiquitous feather in her woolen hat.

"Oh, Miss Garrett," Celia called, "I've been wanting to speak with you." She waved Minnie away, rather as a queen dismisses a servant, and followed Joanna up the steps. "It's about that geography lesson you taught last week."

Joanna's heart sank. The last thing she needed was a parent already upset with her teaching methods.

"I thought it was simply marvelous! My Agnes has talked of nothing else but your fancy globe since arriving home after school on Friday. I am so glad we *finally* have a schoolmistress who will challenge our brighter students." She patted Joanna's arm. "I hope you will continue in this vein."

"Gracious me," Laura whispered when they were seated in the McGills' usual pew. "You've certainly impressed Celia Werner, and that's no small *fait accompli.*

Joanna turned on the seat to face Laura. "I love your French accent!"

Laura rolled her eyes. "I want to see that globe myself!" Edgar tapped her on the shoulder, urging her to move further down on the seat. She looked up to see why he needed more room—there was Lucy Sheppard, standing in a green wool dress sprinkled with pink and white flowers and a hat of pale pink, lined with the dress fabric.

Laura nudged Joanna, who slid over to make room. Lucy nodded to Joanna as Edgar guided Lucy into the pew which, much to Laura's chagrin, placed Lucy right beside her. The rose scent Lucy favored nauseated her; she hoped she wouldn't have a raging headache by the time services were over.

At the conclusion of Luke Goodman's message on the transfiguration of the Lord, he announced that an evening service would be held on Ash Wednesday. "This is the official start of Lent," he said, "a time for introspection, a time for growth and the beginning of our journey to Easter. Come, and let us start that journey together."

"We've never done that before," the woman to Joanna's left muttered. Joanna heard similar remarks as she left the sanctuary, including Lucy's comment that "an Ash Wednesday service is inappropriately papist."

Lucy walked into the narthex and spotted Joanna, who was putting on her coat and chatting with Laura and Carrie Goodman. "Pardon me," Lucy said, "but I need to speak with Miss Garrett." She strutted away, in her customary fashion, leaving the distinct impression she was inconvenienced having to wait for Joanna.

Joanna barely reached her, when Lucy began: "I have

checked my engagement book and I find that Wednesday afternoon is an acceptable time for our meeting. Shall I be there at, say, two o'clock?"

Joanna nodded. "Miss Sheppard—" but, again, Lucy swaggered off, then abruptly stopped at the side door and turned back to her. "Do forgive me, Miss Garrett, but Edgar has kindly offered to take me home and I don't want to keep him waiting. I don't mind walking," she added with a contrived laugh, "but Edgar seems to think it's too cold and I might take a chill." With that Lucy breezed out the door and down the steps.

Laura let out an audible *humph* with the roll of her eyes. *"Take a chill?* That woman *gives* me a chill! I suppose we're supposed to just wait in the cold until my brother comes back to get us? Knowing Lucy, she'll have him carry something into her house, and then she'll insist he have a cup of coffee—it'll be an hour before he finds his way back here, *if* he remembers us at all!"

Carrie came up and put her arm around Laura. "You don't have to wait in the cold, Laura. You can stay right here in the church. Luke has a meeting with the deacons and that will take a while. I am sure," she added with a grin, "that Edgar will remember to come back for you—eventually." Carrie's mischievous response tickled Laura and Joanna; they were still laughing when Luke joined them.

"Care to let me in on the joke? I could use a little humor after being lambasted about the Ash Wednesday service."

Carrie told him what had happened, painting a colorful picture of Lucy inveigling Edgar into her house.

Luke laughed. "I have noticed that Lucy is showing quite a lot of interest in our Edgar all of a sudden. What I wonder is—" he said, looking straight at Joanna, "Why?"

Joanna felt her face flush. What she also couldn't see was the way the pale pink shade had so quickly turned the deepest red.

"Luke, you're embarrassing Miss Garrett," his wife chastised. "Now, tell us *why* people are so upset about the Ash Wednesday service."

"I, for one, am thrilled to have a midweek service," Laura said.

"Down home we always had Ash Wednesday services," Joanna said. "and I was glad. Lent always makes me look closely at myself and think about how God might want me to change."

"Thank you, ladies," he said. "I am glad to know that at least a few members of the congregation understand Lent isn't just a time for Roman Catholics to give something up and sing songs from the 14th Century." He was expounding on why some

Protestants found Lenten services too reminiscent of Rome and the Pope when Joe burst into the narthex with the Goodman children, Grace and David, close behind.

"Whoa, there," Luke called out to them. "Let's not be running in God's house! What's got you all so excited?"

"It's snowing, Papa!" Grace said. "Come see! Great big flakes and falling so fast!"

"It looks like a real storm," Joe said. "There's a big dark cloud in the west and it's moving this way."

Luke and the three women went to peer out the doorway. Sure enough, a heavy snow was falling and black clouds hanging low in the sky were moving in fast.

"Only a child could get excited about snow at the end of February," Luke said. "I'd be happy if we didn't see another snowflake until November."

"I hope Edgar can take his eyes off Miss Sheppard long enough to pay attention to the weather," Laura said. "A fine time for him to be off gallivanting, with a storm rolling in."

Joanna was oblivious to everything, except the children running through the churchyard trying to catch snowflakes on their tongues. She pulled on her mittens, tossed the end of her red scarf around her neck, and practically ran down the side steps. Joe ran to meet her.

"Look, Miss Garrett!" He flung his head back and opened his mouth. "They fly right in and melt on your tongue. Try it!"

She arched her back, trying to catch a huge snowflake when she heard a gasp behind her. She turned. Two men stood staring at her. *The deacons!*

"Miss Garrett?" It was Harvey Greer, a school board member, as well as a deacon. "What are you doing?" For the life of her, Joanna couldn't think of a single thing to say. Fortunately, John Lane came forward.

"It appears to me that you can take the schoolteacher out of the classroom, but you can't take the classroom out of the school teacher. It seems Miss Garrett is teaching a science lesson in the church yard." He winked at Joanna as he stood behind Harvey Greer. "Snowflakes are quite interesting scientifically, aren't they? All those different shapes, but all with six sides." He came down the steps and stuck his own tongue out. "A bit cold, don't you think?"

Joanna could have kissed him. Harvey Greer shrugged his shoulders, tipped his hat to Joanna, and continued into the church. She moved to John Lane's side and gave his arm a warm squeeze. "Bless you," she said. "I don't know what came over me, especially on the Lord 's Day. I feel like a child caught with her hand in the cookie jar!"

"Childlike is just what you were, Miss Garrett," John Lane said, "and childlike is a good way to be sometimes. Our Father in Heaven likes to see His children enjoying His creation." He patted Joanna's arm and went in to his meeting.

Joanna reached the front of the church just in time to see Edgar drive up, his face beaming. *He's smitten with Lucy Sheppard. It's written all over him.* She joined Edgar at the wagon and Joe ran up behind her.

"Let me wipe off the seat before you get in, Miss Garrett," Edgar said. "Joe, go get your aunt. We need to hightail it home before this storm gets any worse." Edgar pulled a small broom from the wagon box and brushed off the seat, then covered it with a blanket. "Now you can get in," he said, reaching for Joanna's hand. Their eyes met for a brief moment, and Joanna felt her pulse racing. *Oh, for pity's sake,* she chastised herself. *Stop making something out of nothing!*

The closer they got to the farm, the heavier the snow fell, blanketing the fields and trees, their boughs dipping lower than they had ever hung before.

"I don't think I can take another big storm," Laura groaned. "I know it's just the end of February and we often have snow in April, but I am so tired of it." Her eyes widened. "My crocuses! Do you think the snow will kill them?"

"Mr. Greenwood wouldn't have sold them to you if they couldn't make it through an Indiana winter," Joanna assured her. "They'll be fine."

The snow fell heavily throughout the afternoon, but when Edgar came in from doing the evening chores, he announced that it was tapering off.

"Good,"Laura said. "I was afraid we were going to be housebound for a week."

"I'm glad, too," Joanna said. "The snow is beautiful, but I have so much planned this week and I'd hate to think school might be closed for a few days."

Much later, Joanna would recall these words and note the irony in them. Though the week had begun without incident, it might have been better if the storm had closed school—permanently.

Chapter Twelve

Joanna was bewildered to see people waiting on the schoolhouse porch when she arrived at eight o'clock. Sarah Bailey was there, with the two Greer boys and their father.

Edgar turned to Joanna with a questioning look. "Were you expecting anyone to arrive early today, like a member of the school board?"

"No." She clambered down from the wagon without waiting for a helping hand. *I hope nothing's wrong,* she thought, almost running to the porch, where she fumbled to unlock the door. "Please come in, Mr. Greer... children. We'll get the fire started and have the room warm soon." She closed the door. "Is there anything wrong?"

Harvey Greer had never brought his children to school before, which particularly unnerved her after their encounter in the churchyard. "Albert? Charles? Is there something you wanted to talk about?"

The boys, uncharacteristically quiet, each took their father by a hand and led him to the geography table. Both pointed to the globe. "See, Pa?" Albert's face was alive with excitement. "I told you it was as big as the flour barrel and covered with pictures and bumps! It's the whole world in one place, just like I said!"

"As you can see, Miss Garrett, there's nothing wrong, except that my sons insisted I had to see this globe of yours. They talked about nothing else *all* weekend long. The only way I knew to get us onto a different topic of conversation tonight at supper was to come and see for myself what all the fuss is about." He bent over the table for a closer look. "It really is a wonderful specimen. Quite the largest I've seen—and the most detailed. It must have set you back a pretty piece."

"It was rather expensive, but when I saw it in a shop in Raleigh, I knew I had to have it. I saved up for months, but it was well worth it."

When other children started arriving, Harvey Greer coaxed Joanna to the door. "Forgive me if I frightened you, Miss Garrett." His deep voice and clearly articulated words befitted one of the town's two lawyers. "I am far from displeased with your work here in Appleton. On the contrary, I think you must have a real gift for, and a love of, teaching. Someone simply doing a job would not spend her own money on a learning tool for her students." An unexpected smile warmed his usually somber expression. "Continue in this vein and you'll have a long career here, if you want one." He tipped his hat and left.

Joanna rang the bell, feeling both irritated and relieved. The cause of the sense of relief was obvious. The irritation came from her reaction when she saw Harvey Greer on the porch. *You were afraid,* she told herself, *and you doubted yourself. That's not like you.* She sighed. *I'm so wary and feel so vulnerable. It's not a good feeling.* She gave the bell another hard tug. *I can't change the past,* she thought, *but must I be chained to it forever?*

Edgar left the schoolhouse and headed to town, to Annie Campbell's house off Main Street. Annie, a middle-aged spinster, had run the post office out of her home for over twenty years. She hadn't been the youngest postmistress in Indiana, though. That honor went to Ella Rickenbaugh in Celina, who was eighteen years old when she was appointed in 1880. The postal authorities had made an exception for Ella, saying that, although she wasn't of legal age, she wanted the job and was known to be 'dependable and trustworthy.' No one in Appleton questioned Annie Campbell's trustworthiness either.

Edgar rang the little bell on the wooden counter. Annie, a tall, spare woman with her hair in a bun, hurried from behind a drape that separated her living quarters at the back of the house.

"Morning, Mr. McGill," she said. Edgar smiled, and Annie Campbell flushed. There was that enigmatic *something* about Edgar McGill that made women of all ages keenly aware not only of his good looks but also the strength of his masculinity. There was also the typical female curiosity: *Why hasn't that handsome man ever remarried? What—or who— is he waiting for? If Lucy*

Sheppard, with all her money, hasn't landed Edgar McGill all these years since his wife died—well, then, there must be something wrong with her!

"What may I do for you, Mr. McGill? Mail's not in yet, of course."

"I know, Miss Campbell. I'm here to send a package." He handed Annie a small flat parcel covered in brown paper and wrapped with twine.

She looked at the address on the package. *"The Pennsylvania Academy of Fine Arts, Philadelphia.* This will cost you a bit, I'm afraid. It's right heavy, for a letter."

"That's all right, Miss Campbell. I'll pay whatever it costs."

Annie put on a pair of spectacles, placed the envelope on the scale and pursed her lips as she read the weight. "Just over ten ounces, Mr. McGill. So that'll be sixteen-cents"

Edgar reached into his pocket and withdrew the coins. "I'd like a receipt, please, Miss Campbell." While Annie busied herself stamping the package and writing Edgar's receipt, he stroked her white cat, Elliott, who reclined in his usual spot on the counter.

"This should arrive by the middle of next week, Mr. McGill. Are you expecting a reply? Do you want I should send Henry out when it comes?" Henry, Annie's nephew, served as her special delivery man.

"That won't be necessary, Miss Campbell," he said, petting Elliott once more and putting his cap on. "I'll just check back when I'm in town. You have a nice day, now."

Annie walked to the window and ever-so-slightly pulled back the white lace curtain. She stood there until the wagon pulled away. Then she went to the bin where she had placed Edgar's package and withdrew it. "Now, I wonder what this is all about?" she confided to Elliott. Annie Campbell might be able to keep other people's business private, but that didn't mean she wasn't curious.

Edgar walked into the kitchen and helped himself to a cup of coffee. Laura was busy with the Monday wash.

"Been to town..." Laura was stating a fact, not asking a question.

"I wanted to get some seed before prices start going up. I should've told you I was going, in case you needed something. I just didn't decide to go until I dropped Joe and Joanna—I mean Miss Garrett—at school."

I'll applaud the day when either one of those two is willing to use the other's first name!

"I've got a problem," Edgar went on. "The heifer has been trying to calve all day and I don't want to leave her. Could you go get Joe and Miss Garrett? Or would you rather take over with the cow?"

Laura flicked a wet shirt at him. "You know I'd rather fetch Joe and Joanna. Just let me get these clothes on the line and slip a pan of beans into the oven to start baking for supper."

Fifteen minutes later, Dolly was trotting down the lane toward the schoolhouse. Joe ran to the wagon as Laura drove up. "Let me show you where I found Patches, Aunt Laura!" She thought Joe couldn't have been more excited if he were showing her where he had discovered a vein of gold. Then the two walked up to the schoolhouse and found Joanna on the porch, her hand shading her eyes, and searching the school yard.

"There you are, Joe—and, Laura! What a nice surprise! There's nothing wrong with Mr. McGill, I hope?" Joanna's fear betrayed her.

She's wearing her heart on her sleeve and she doesn't know it. "Edgar's fine. He has a heifer ready to calve and couldn't leave her."

"Come inside and get warm."

"This room looks a sight different than it did the last time I was here," Laura said. "Just look at those wonderful pictures!" The primary class had been busy with artwork for the Open House, the walls papered with their drawings of birds, bears and a few animals whose breed she could not identify. "Oh, and there's that globe!"

"Look, Aunt Laura, how it spins and, see—all the countries are in different colors."

"I never went to school in a room this inviting," Laura said. "You're lucky to have such a bright, pretty place to learn. And you're even luckier to have Joanna for your teacher."

"I'm the one who's lucky, Laura." *Luckier than I ever believed possible...*

* * *

Raleigh - 3rd of December 1884

The light snowfall had turned to rain, a torrent of rain with bulbous drops that pounded the windowpane as Joanna paced Susannah York's small study.

"I have to find work."

"You have work, Joanna. The board has already offered you a contract for the spring term."

"Do you honestly think *that* offer will stand?" Panic filled Joanna's voice.

"They haven't revoked it, have they? You know very well, Joanna, that not everyone reads the *Raleigh News & Observer*."

"I'm sure Governor Jarvis does!" Her panic was growing in intensity. "Do you think he'll want a convict teaching in a North Carolina school, when he was a teacher himself? After he's worked so hard to push the legislature to establish normal schools, and set statewide standards for teachers and curriculum?" She shook her head, and wispy tendril curls bounced.

"I know what Governor Jarvis has done to promote public education," Susannah said. "Remember, we both attend the Edenton Street Methodist. I know the Governor and his wife well. But don't make what happened in Petersburg worse then it was, Joanna. You're not a convict—and neither am I. We spent one night in jail on a false charge."

"Fine. Do you think the school board will keep a teacher who was *arrested* at a woman's suffrage convention?"

"I don't think they will find out about it, Joanna. The article in the *News & Observer* didn't identify you as a schoolteacher." *By some miracle, it didn't even include my name*, Susannah thought.

"But what if they do? What if we get midway through the term and some parent hears, *your Miss Garrett is one of those radical women*. Do you seriously believe they will let me keep teaching?"

"Oh, for heaven's sake, Joanna! You're not a radical— you're not even close to being one. I don't see you sporting a yellow sash or passing out Mrs. Stanton's tracts on Fayetteville Street."

"Tell that to my father—and to my mother." She sucked in her breath and ceased pacing. "Tell that to Nicholas."

Susannah went to Joanna. "I haven't said this to you before, but I am going to say it now." She took hold of Joanna's shoulders and looked her straight in the eyes. "Nicholas Brodie was not—and never will be—the man for you, Joanna. You were right to refuse him three times."

"That's not what my mother thinks. She said I was foolish to let Nicholas get away."

"With all due respect to your mother, you would *never* have been happy with him."

"My mother seems to think that's not the point. She says no one will want to marry me now."

"And do you think she's right?"

"Maybe." Tears welled in Joanna's eyes. "Nicholas had known me his whole life, but he ended our relationship when he read about the arrest. He said, 'I thought I knew you, but I obviously don't. Men don't like strong-minded women.'"

"May I remind you, Joanna, that I was once married? I think most people who know me would consider me *very* strong-willed *and* strong-minded." She smiled, trying to inject a little levity into the conversation.

"That's not the same thing, Susannah. You weren't a professor when you and James were married. And you certainly weren't a suffragette!"

"And, as I said earlier, neither are you."

"It doesn't matter whether I am or not," she insisted. "What matters is what people *think* I am. If they *think* I'm a suffragette—in their eyes I am one."

"And would that be so awful?"

Joanna stared at her friend. "Have you joined the National Woman Suffrage Association?" The two stood silent for a long moment.

"No. But, as I told you on the train on our way back from Petersburg, I do agree with their principles."

"Then why haven't you joined them?"

"Because you're right about what people think. I very well might lose my position if I made my views public. College professorships for women are hard enough to come by."

"Then I'm right to look for a job somewhere else," Joanna said softly, resigning herself to the reality she faced. "It must be somewhere far away, where no one knows—or can possibly find out that I went to that convention, or anything about the arrest."

Susannah heaved an exasperated sigh. "If you feel that strongly about it, Joanna, I do have some contacts in other states. Let me write a few people and see what we can find."

* * *

Appleton - February 1885

Joe showed Laura his latest work in penmanship. "Just look at the loops on those letters! Miss Garrett says they're better than her own." He lowered his voice. "But, that's not saying a whole lot. Miss Garrett's handwriting isn't much better than mine."

"Shush, Joe," She glanced to Joanna. "She might hear!" A hearty laugh told her it was too late.

"Joe's right. My handwriting *is* terrible. I do have some talents, thank the Lord, but good penmanship isn't one of them.

Luckily, I don't have to know how to build a train engine to describe how they work, and I don't have to make pretty letters myself to teach my students how to make them." She lifted Joe's hair from his brow. "And, I might add, I always print when I write on the blackboard, and my printing is pretty good!"

"Have you had any word about the progress on the repairs to the house?" Joanna asked, setting the last dinner plate in the cupboard.

"Not a word," Laura said, "but I feel sure the men are working as fast as they can, given the weather. Believe me, anybody working for Sam Bailey, Harvey Greer, and Ted Garner knows he better not be caught lollygagging."

"Why's that?"

"Sam Bailey once caught a fellow drinking beer during his dinner break and Sam ran the man off the job. And I do mean *ran him off.* The poor fellow couldn't hightail it out of there fast enough with Sam flailing a two-by-four at his back."

"So, the house might be ready by Easter?"

"Yes, but you can always change your mind about living there."

"Gosh yes, Miss Garrett!" Joe said. "It'll seem real strange not having you here at home with us." A sudden sadness covered the boy's face.

"It will be strange for me, too." *Funny, I desperately wanted a place of my own... But not now... as fond as I am of you all... Laura's companionship and Joe's humor and—* she took a deep breath. *and dear, sweet Edgar...* She looked up and saw that Laura was on the verge of tears.

"I'm glad you've enjoyed my company, Joe," she said. "Actually, I was a little worried that you wouldn't like having your teacher living in your home."

"Well, if you'd a been like Miss Lambert or old Mr. Connors, it would have been a different story. I can't imagine living with her or that old goat!" He wrinkled his nose.

Laura knelt down to him. "Don't be disrespectful! Ruth Lambert was a very kind woman and Gerald Connors certainly meant well. He couldn't help how he looked."

"He looked like an old billy goat," Edgar said, catching only the tail end of their conversation as he came in from checking on the heifer.

Joe and Joanna burst out laughing. Edgar looked from one to the other. "What? What's so funny?"

"That's what I said, Pa, and Aunt Laura got after me for calling him an old goat!" He looked at his aunt. "See? Pa agrees with me!"

Edgar playfully cuffed his son's head. "It's one thing for one grown up to talk about another that way, but it's something else entirely when a child does it. You listen to your aunt." He looked down at Joe's paper. "What's that you're doing? Long division?"

Joe nodded.

Edgar whistled and sat down at the kitchen table. "I didn't start doing that until I was a lot older than you. Is everyone in your class doing long division?"

"No," Joanna said proudly, "just the brighter ones." The boy beamed at the unexpected praise. "Joe's very good at arithmetic, and if he keeps working the way he has been, I'll have to find someone to tutor him when he gets in the upper class. He'll be ready to take on work that's way over my head."

"I'll teach you what I learn, Miss Garrett," Joe promised. "Then you'll be able to teach it to everyone who comes behind me."

"I'll accept that offer, Joe. Maybe you'll join me at the schoolhouse and we'll teach together."

"No, ma'am," Joe quickly and fervently responded. "No offense, Miss Garrett, but I don't think I'd take to being cooped up in school all day. No, ma'am, I'm going to be a farmer—like my pa and his pa before him."

"You don't have to be a farmer, Toad, just because I am. You can be whatever you want to be—an engineer or a lawyer, or a lumberjack if you want to work outdoors. You don't have to be stuck on this farm for the rest of your life."

Joanna was perplexed by the undercurrent of anger in Edgar's voice. It was more than apparent he had hurt Joe's feelings.

"But, Pa, I love the farm. I've always loved it. I don't want to be anything but a farmer."

"If you feel that way, son, I'll be more than glad to let you take over the morning milking for me. It'd be a real treat to sleep in one morning. In fact, I'll trade places with you tomorrow. You stay here and work on getting the tools ready for spring planting and check on the heifer and her calf and I'll go to school." He looked over to Joanna, who was staring at him. "Or am I too old for school?"

"You're never too old to learn, Mr. McGill," she said softly, "but I don't think the Henry Township School has much to offer you." She untied her apron and folded it. "I can still teach Joe a few things, though, and he'll be an even better farmer, or whatever he decides to be, after he finishes school."

"Would anyone like more coffee before we turn in for the night?" Laura stood at Edgar's side, pot in hand, obvious in her desire to change the subject. "Or maybe a glass of milk?"

Edgar stood up and kissed his sister on the cheek. "No coffee for me. I'm going to call it a night." He gently squeezed Joe's neck as he walked behind his chair. "There's nothing wrong with being a farmer, son. Farmers feed the world. But, there's nothing wrong with being something else either."

"I'm going to say goodnight, too," Joanna said, declining one of the two glasses of milk.

Joe accepted one and drank it down without seeming to notice what he was doing.

Laura shrugged her shoulders and sat down with the remaining glass. "Your pa's not mad at you for wanting to be a farmer."

"He sure sounded mad, Aunt Laura."

"I know, honey, but it's himself he's mad at, or maybe his own father. Your pa loved school and wanted to continue his education." She looked into his questioning eyes as she sipped the milk. "Grandpa Henry needed help on the farm, and then, when Grandpa died, your pa had to take over. So, you see, what your pa said tonight wasn't really about what you're going to be—it was about what *he* wanted to be. Does that make any sense?"

"Sort of..." he said, a ring of milk covering his upper lip. "But if Pa doesn't want to be a farmer, why doesn't he do something else? And why isn't he happy that I want to take over the farm one day?"

Laura wiped his lip. "Two good questions, Joe. Right now your father has you and me to take care of, and the farm is the way to do that." She reached for Joe's hand and brought it to her cheek. "As for you taking over one day, I think he'll be both proud and happy when that day comes."

The two put their glasses in the sink and went upstairs to get ready for bed. Joe was in bed in his nightshirt when Edgar called from the top of the loft steps.

"Joe? Are you awake?" Edgar's voice was low. "May I come up?"

Joe jumped into bed. "Sure, Pa."

Edgar came and sat beside Joe. "I'm sorry about tonight, Toad," he said, stroking the boy's hair from his eyes. "I'm not mad at you for wanting to farm. I just want you to know, you don't have to be a farmer if you really want to do something else."

He stared into his son's blue eyes and fell silent.

"I know, Pa" Joe reached up and threw his arms around Edgar's neck. "Aunt Laura explained everything. It's all right."

"I love you, Joe," he said, hugging his son with all the love he had for the boy. "I always will."

"I know, Pa. I love you, too."

Edgar walked downstairs and gently closed the door to his bedroom. He stood staring at his desk, and then went to it, pulled open the desk drawer and reached in for the catalogue from the Pennsylvania Academy of Fine Arts. The postage receipt Annie Campbell had given him fell onto his desk. The catalogue opened to the page with the corner turned down. His eyes followed the print: *Our students spend two years studying the fundamentals of drawing, painting, sculpture, and printmaking...*

"Two years, he whispered, "How can I do that? Who would work the farm? How would I support all of us?" He tucked the pamphlet at the back of the drawer. "A pipe dream—nothing but a pipe dream."

Chapter Thirteen

It was after seven o'clock when Joanna came down to breakfast on Wednesday.

"Good morning, sleepyhead," Laura said, her back to the door.

"Good morning, Laura. May I help with anything?"

Laura turned. "Sure—" Her mouth dropped open. "Gracious me! Just look at you!"

Joanna stood in a black dress with a contrasting collar of red velvet and matching piping that ran down the front to its hem. A wide red leather belt cinched her tiny waist and her black hair, usually worn in a bun, was twisted into a loose mass and looped into a red chignon. With her matching black boots and the tiny hoops at her ears, Joanna was a sight to behold.

"That dress is absolutely stunning!" Whoever made your clothes back in North Carolina was a real artist."

"Why, thank you kindly, ma'am," Joanna said, dropping into a deep curtsey. "I made it myself."

"You didn't!" Laura tossed the dish towel on the counter and moved to inspect the dress more closely. "If you ever give up teaching school, you can make a handsome living as a dressmaker.

Your work is impeccable. And, pray tell, why are you so dressed up this morning?"

"Lucy Sheppard..." she said, lifting her eyebrows. "The interview?"

"I completely forgot! Lucy comes to interview you today!" Laura patted Joanna's hand. "You did just the right thing. There's *nothing* Lucy Sheppard values more than her own stylish self." Laura laughed with a wink. "I'd love to be there when Lucy walks in. It may be the first time she finds herself speechless."

Joe burst into the kitchen, his spelling book tight at his chest. "Morning, Aunt Laura!" He sat down beside Joanna, without looking at her, and pointed to the book. "Miss Garrett, could we go over my spelling words while we eat breakfast? I want to get a perfect score on my test today."

"I'd be glad to, Joe."

The boy looked up to smile his *thanks*. His eyes nearly bulged in their sockets. "Gosh! You look pretty! Like a redwing blackbird."

"Joe McGill," his aunt said, "that's a very nice compliment, and you're right, Joanna does look especially pretty today—but, young man, you didn't even say *good morning* to her before asking her help." She placed his glass of milk and two raisin muffins slathered with butter on the table. "Now, kindly start over."

Joe's eyes never left Joanna as he stood up and made a mock bow. "A very good morning to you, Miss Garrett," he said solemnly. "And, may I say you look quite pretty today?"

Joanna giggled.

"And, if it would not be too much trouble, would you be so kind as to assist me with some spelling after we partake of my aunt's delicious muffins?" He bowed and sat down.

Laura doubled over with laughter. "Where did you ever learn to talk like that?" she asked when she had recovered enough to speak. "You sound like someone from the theater!"

"Why, thank you, ma'am. You are most gracious." Laura giggled again and Joe reverted to his 10-year-old self. "It's how they talk in a book Miss Garrett's reading to us."

"You've obviously been paying attention," Joanna said, "and I can't tell you how much that pleases me. But why don't we go over the words on the way to school? I can call out the words while you drive."

"Can I really? He suddenly frowned. "But why isn't Pa driving us to school like he always does?"

"This is the day Joanna stays late to talk with Miss Sheppard, and you're going home with David and Grace Goodman, remember? We'll bring you home after church service tonight."

"I clean forgot! But, how will you and Pa get to town? Miss Garrett will have Dolly and the wagon."

"Jim Langston is coming by for us. He's bringing Mary and the children to church tonight. In fact, they're coming to supper with us." Her hand flew to her mouth. "Joanna! Your supper!"

"Not to worry, Laura. "I thought I'd dine at the Morgan House. I've heard they have excellent food."

"They do! Pa took me and Aunt Laura there a few times. You'll like it."

The clock in the front room chimed the half hour and Joanna jumped up. "Gracious! The time! We'd better get going, Joe. I don't want to be late—especially on an exam day."

True to her word, Joanna let Joe take the driver's seat. She quizzed him on spelling as they rode and was relieved to see they had arrived before the children.

By nine o'clock the students were hard at work on the first examination, arithmetic. She wrote the older children's questions on the board, but quizzed the younger ones orally. She caught Freddie Schmidt chewing on the end of his pencil and little Emma Patterson just staring into space. *I'm worried about that child.*

By the morning recess, both the arithmetic and reading tests were behind them. Joanna allowed an extra five minutes in the crisp air and sunlight, then called them in for the spelling test. She had decided to use a method that worked well in her last school: give the oldest students their test first, then have two of the best spellers in that group call words to other classes. They finished well before dinnertime and, as soon as the first students finished eating, Joanna rang the little bell she had used to signal the end of the testing period.

"Children, I want you to know I am very proud of all of you. I wanted to do something special to thank you for paying attention and working hard, so—" She reached under her desk and pulled a basket she had successfully kept hidden from Joe. "I brought some homemade pound cake for a treat! You may each come up and take a piece, but don't eat it until *after* you finish your dinners!"

The room erupted with the sound of boots slapping the hardwood floor and children shouting when nudged out of place in the line forming in front of Joanna's desk. "One at a time," Joanna said, "And mind the younger children!"

Emma Patterson took the piece Joanna offered, her brown eyes went wide in anticipation, and returned to her seat. Joanna watched as little Emma broke off a small piece of cake and put it into her mouth. As the sugary crust melted on her tongue, Emma's closed her eyes with a smile. She ate another small piece, then wrapped what was left in the kerchief that held her dinner.

The child is taking that one slice of cake home to share, Joanna thought. *I've got to find a way to send what is left of the cake home with Emma.*

A few wagons were already waiting at the hitching post when Joanna rang the bell dismissing school a little before one o'clock. Carrie Goodman was in one of them and waved at Joanna, who quickly walked over to greet her.

"Luke had to ride up to Madison for a presbytery meeting this morning, so I got to come."

"Do you have time to come inside for a minute, Carrie? I know Grace would love to show you the drawing she did last week."

"I really shouldn't... I left bread rising, so I better gather the children and skedaddle back home." She bit her lower lip and thought for a moment. "Oh, a few more minutes won't make much difference, I guess." She followed Joanna into the schoolhouse.

Grace ran to greet her mother, throwing her chubby arms around Carrie's legs. "Mama!" she cried. "What are you doing here? Come see my desk!"

David's greeting was reserved, but his shining eyes made clear he, too, was glad to see her. He led Carrie to the geography table and spun the globe.

"I've never seen one," Carrie said, turning around to Joanna, "but Luke said he used one in college." She leaned over the globe and touched the blue space that denoted the Atlantic Ocean. "It's hard to believe we're surrounded by all this water. The ocean must be something to see."

"It is something to see, Carrie, and something to hear," Joanna said, almost wistfully. "The water seems to magically fade away into the distant horizon... while waves rhythmically, and without end, lap the sandy shore. It's almost hypnotizing. Sometimes the water is a transparent blue, other times a deep green, and—in a storm—it's almost black." Her eyes had a faraway look. "I love the ocean."

"I can almost see it myself by the way you describe it," Carrie said. "I'm so glad I came in to see where my children spend their day. It's such a cheerful room," she said, looking around, "and a happy place to learn." She gave Joanna a quick hug. "And you must be a good person to learn from."

Joanna followed the Goodmans and Joe outside and searched the school yard, seeing only a few boys still playing tag. When Joanna went back inside, several girls were huddled around a desk and Emma Patterson was in tears. Her carefully wrapped cake lay in crumbles on the floor around Emma, who was on her knees, trying to pick up the pieces.

The girls had their hands over their mouths looking from one to the other. Joanna didn't know if they were trying to suppress laughter or trying to hide the fact that they had snitched some of Emma's cake.

Joanna hurried over and drew little weeping Emma into her arms. "There, there, Emma. We'll soon have this picked up. Don't worry..." She looked to the group of girls peering down at Emma. "Emily, will you please get the dustpan and broom? And why don't the rest of you girls get your coats on and go outside. I'm sure your parents will be along for you any minute."

Emma sat silently, tears still streaming down her face, while Joanna swept up the crumbs and emptied the dustpan into the waste bin beside her desk. She returned to Emma and lifted the weeping child onto her lap.

"Emma, please stop crying. I have something to show you, but you won't be able to see it if your eyes are full of tears." The little girl used a corner of her pinafore to dab at her eyes. "That's better. Now come to my desk and I'll show you what I've got." Joanna lifted the basket from under her desk and showed Emma the generous portion of remaining cake.

"I have all this cake left, and I don't know what to do with it." She rubbed her chin with a questioning frown. "I can't eat it all by myself, and I don't want it to go bad." After a moment the small hand tugged her sleeve.

"Miss Garrett, maybe me and my brother and sister could eat that cake for you, if I was to take it home with me."

"What a good idea! I would be *so very* happy if you would do that for me, Emma. Now, let's see what you can carry it in." A small pasteboard box of colored paper sat on her desk. "Here's just the thing, but we still need something to cover it with." Emma ran to her desk and brought back the kerchief. "That's perfect, Emma."

A short while later, Stinson Matthews arrived. Joanna waited on the porch until Emma and her box were tucked safely into the wagon beside Caleb and his father. She waved them off, made sure the school yard was empty, drew in a few deep breaths of the fresh, cold air and returned to her desk.

She anxiously glanced at the wall clock—it was nearly two o'clock. *Lucy Sheppard will be here any moment—and I'm not ready.*

She gave the classroom a once over and, satisfied it was tidy, filled the teakettle and put it in on the stove. She pulled a small hand mirror from her purse and wiped away a tiny inkblot on her cheek, then ran her tongue over her lips to moisten them. Her hair was neat, but she patted it nonetheless, then smoothed her dress, and announced to the empty room: "I'm ready. Bring on the lioness."

Chapter Fourteen

Within moments, a knock sounded at the door and Lucy Sheppard walked in carrying a leather satchel. She closed the door behind her and stood motionless, obviously waiting for Joanna to acknowledge her presence.

My, my, Joanna thought, *she certainly does like to make an entrance!* "Miss Sheppard, how nice to see you!" She stood up and went to Lucy and extended her hand.

Lucy removed her white kidskin gloves and accepted Joanna's hand.

"I knew you would be prompt, and so you are. Please, take off your coat and hat and come by the fire to warm yourself before we begin our talk."

"*Interview,*" Lucy said, slipping out of her coat and strutting to the chair by the stove. "What I'm here to do is *interview* you, Miss Garrett—we're not having a cozy *chat*. I am here on business, not pleasure."

Joanna resisted the urge to laugh in Lucy's pretty, but haughty face. "Would you care for some tea—or would that be inappropriate for a business meeting?"

Lucy hiked her brow, but returned Joanna's smile with only the slightest upward tilt of her mouth. "Tea would be fine, Miss

Garrett, and is rarely inappropriate." She surveyed the classroom while Joanna poured two cups and set them on the table.

"Now, shall we begin?" Joanna asked, after Lucy declined both milk and sugar. "I know you're a busy woman and probably need to get back to town as soon as possible. It's kind of you, and the newspaper, to take such an interest in the new schoolmarm."

Lucy reached for her satchel, withdrew a leather-bound notebook, and several pencils. She opened the notebook and placed it in her lap. "You're right, I am busy, but I am not about to hurry away. No, indeed," she said, giving Joanna a long challenging look, "I have set aside the entire afternoon to find out *all there is to know* about you, Joanna Garrett."

Oh, please, God, help me.

"I thought, perhaps, you could start by telling me all about yourself. Where do you come from?"

"I was born in Wilmington, North Carolina."

"And how old are you?"

Joanna employed her true southern charm. "A lady never tells her age, Miss Sheppard."

"True, Miss Garrett." *I can find that out from Harvey Greer,* she thought. *She must have told the school board how old she is.* "Does your family still live in Wilmington?"

"My parents do, and one of my brothers is still at home."

"How many brothers and sisters do you have?"

"Two brothers, no sisters."

"What does your father do?" Lucy looked up from her note taking. "Is he also a teacher?"

"No, my father is a Presbyterian minister, though he retired a few years ago and now spends most of his time writing."

"You're a *minister's* daughter? Did your father approve of your becoming a schoolteacher?"

"Yes, he did. My father encouraged all his children to do whatever they felt called to do."

Lucy furrowed her brow. "What do you mean by *called*?"

"I mean God's leading in our lives, Miss Sheppard. God has a path planned for each of us and it is our job to discern it, and then follow it."

"You can't be serious." Lucy shook her head. "Only ministers receive a call from God, and frankly, I wonder about some of them."

"I disagree. I believe God calls each of us to the work He wants us to do, not just those who serve Him as preachers and teachers of the gospel."

"Surely you don't think God has a plan for the town butcher," Lucy argued, "or that a farmer or a tailor, or even a businessman such as my father is *called* to that work."

"Do you find it so hard to believe God loves and cares as much about your father and his newspaper as he does about my father and his church?"

I find it hard to believe God even thinks about my father, Lucy thought, *much less loves him.* She changed the subject. "Did you study to be a teacher or are you self-taught?"

"I studied for several years."

"Are there normal schools in your home state? Or did you have to travel north?" Lucy's tone inferred she thought the latter was Joanna's only choice.

"There are indeed normal schools in North Carolina, Miss Sheppard." She was annoyed, but tried not to let it creep into her voice. "And there are also excellent universities. I attended Peace Institute, a college in Raleigh."

Lucy dropped both her notebook and pencil and hurriedly leaned over to retrieve them, then stared at Joanna. "You are a *college* graduate? You went to college with men, and have a college diploma?" She surveyed the walls, as if the lack of a framed sheepskin would prove Joanna was lying.

"I didn't go to college with men, Miss Sheppard. Peace Institute is for women only. It was founded in 1857, by a group of Presbyterians who wanted to form a school *of high grade* for women. My grandfather was one of those founders, and my father was very proud that I was able to attend Peace." She forced a hint of a smile. "And, yes, I have a diploma, but you won't find it here. It's in my room at the McGills."

"Miss Garrett, I came here thinking I would write about you in my weekly column, telling where you're from and how you like it here and such. But there's more to you than I had anticipated. I think you may be a front page story." *Just wait until Father hears about this!* she thought. *When I present this story, he won't be able to call it a nice little ladies' piece this time!*

Joanna sensed something in Lucy and it made her blood run cold. *The last thing I need is to make headlines in a newspaper!* "Miss Sheppard," she said, striving to stay calm. "I can't be the only female college graduate in Jefferson County. I'm an ordinary person, just a teacher trying to do her best by her students."

"Miss Garrett, you are anything but *ordinary*." She picked up her notebook and poised her pen over it. "First, I want to hear about your college life, and then we'll move on to where you've taught."

Joanna sensed defeat and yielded the next hour to Lucy's interrogation. She replenished the teapot and was showing Lucy the globe when a racket sounded at the door, and then it flew open and banged the wall.

A slight, dark haired man with an enormous handlebar mustache struggled under the weight of what appeared to be a box-shaped camera attached to a long wooden-legged tripod.

"Mr. Giannini!" Lucy placed her tea cup on the saucer and headed for the door. "I was beginning to think you got lost."

Mr. Giannini leaned the tripod against the wall, bowed to Lucy, lifted her hand and bestowed a kiss upon it. "Missah Sheppard—" His English was heavily spiced with his Italian roots. "Issah pleasure, as-ah allaways, to see you." His eyes drifted to Joanna. In only a moment, he drank in her glistening lips, the shine of her black hair, and the red dress that so vividly contrasted with her fair skin. He swept off his slouched suede hat in a grand gesture, and bowed. "I am-ah Antonio Giannini, an-ah you are-ah?"

"This is Joanna Garrett—the one you're here to photograph, Mr. Giannini."

"But-ah no!" he cried, his head tilting from side to side, eyes rolling in their sockets. "Issah no possible! So beautiful a woman, ownally teaching-ah school? Whats-ah wrong-ah weeth American men?"

Joanna didn't say a word. Doing so would only have encouraged him to say more—and she wasn't sure what that would be.

Mr. Giannini shook his head. "Ah woman like-ah you issah made for-ah man, no for-ah teach children."

Joanna felt the heat of a full-blown blush.

Lucy rolled her eyes, then closed them as she shook her head.

"Leetle-ah children very lucky, no? Maybe they learn-ah better weeth-ah teacher so nice-ah to look at."

"Mr. Giannini—you're wasting time." *She's not THAT pretty!*

"Excuse-ay," he said, surveying the classroom. "Where I'm-ah make-ah my picture of this so lovely lady?"

"At her desk," Lucy said, "surrounded by her books."

"I agree," Joanna chimed in, sensing Lucy's irritability and wanting this *interview* over with.

"Buttah, no...no!" Mr. Giannini cried out, his shoulders rising to meet his ears; his hands swirling in a circular motion. "She should-ah be by the window—where I can-ah make use of-ah the sunlight the goodah God in heaven issah sending us." He lifted the tripod and evenly positioned its three legs.

"Mr. Giannini—" Lucy started toward him. "I *want* Miss Garrett photographed sitting behind her desk." Had Mr. Giannini been looking her way, he would have seen the steely green-eyed look Lucy leveled on him.

Mr. Giannini spun around and, without warning, grabbed Lucy's shoulders. "Missah Sheppard, Missah Sheppard," he said beguilingly, "I am-ah artiste. I will-ah make ah picture of Missah Garrett that will-ah be *bellissima*—not-ah even the great-ah Matthew Brady coulddah do better!" He released Lucy and clapped his hands. "Now-ah we begin!"

The Italian looked at Joanna, then to the light streaming through the window; back and forth his eyes traveled, checking the sight line. Then, in a grandiose manner, Mr. Giannini flipped the black drape high in the air; it floated down, and covered the camera.

"I am-ah ready," he announced with serious bravado. "Missah Garrett, please-ah come..." he said, his hand extended to her.

Joanna obediently walked to the window and stood where the Italian pointed.

"We put-ah you shoulders back—like-ah thees, "he said, gently and respectfully positioning her, "we cross-ah you arms—like-ah thees, and—" he paused, scrutinizing her, "we brush-ah you hair away from-ah you *belissima* face-ah." His eyes swept over her. "*Perfezione!*"

He walked back to his camera, and turned around. "Missah Garrett, you stand-ah very still-ah until I say you cannah move." He ducked under the drape and held up his hand, signaling he was beginning the process. "Donnah move!" He was neither seen nor heard for several minutes.

Suddenly, the drape flew into the air, Mr. Giannini stood straight up, closed his eyes and kissed his fingertips. "*Perfezione...* perfect-ah!" He proudly pronounced.

Joanna was still reeling from the way the Italian had taken such liberties, posing her and touching her hair. Lucy stood quietly, her cheeks sucked in, her left brow raised in contempt for the brazen Italian. *If I have my way, your pictures will never appear in our paper again!*

"Now-ah, I will-ah move my camera and we make-ah picture attah the table with-ah ball."

He posed Joanna at the geography table, her hand pretending to spin the globe, her head slightly tilted as she smiled into the camera lens.

The clock chimed five times when Mr. Giannini finally began packing up his equipment.

"I had no idea it was so late," Joanna said.

"Neither did I, Miss Garrett," Lucy said. "I must be going, or I will be late for a dinner engagement."

Joanna brought Lucy's coat from the cloakroom and Mr. Giannini helped her don it.

"It has been quite a fascinating afternoon," Lucy said as she made for the door. "I believe I have all the information I need, but I do hope you will allow me to call again should I find any gaps in my story." With that Lucy was out the door and gone.

Little Mr. Giannini insisted on staying with Joanna until she was ready to leave. "Eet issah no proper," he said firmly, "for such-ah young and *belissima* woman to be alone so far-ah from town when night issah falling."

It was dark but for gaslights lighting the way as Joanna pulled up in front of the Morgan House. A shy young woman of about nineteen showed Joanna to a small table and handed her a menu. Joanna restrained a giggle when she saw the evening special: *Shepherd's Pie,* she said. *I've had my fill of Sheppards today, thank you!*

She had just ordered when Frances and John Lane walked up to her table. "Reverend Lane, Mrs. Lane, how lovely to see you again. Will you join me?"

"We don't want to inconvenience you, Miss Garrett, if you're expecting someone." Joanna smiled at John Lane's discreet way of finding out whether she was dining alone.

Joanna had been looking forward to being alone after having spent such a draining day, but she so enjoyed the Lanes' company that she quickly forgot her own concerns. She told them about the tests she had given and about Lucy's interview.

"A photographer came, too" Joanna said, "He was charming and funny."

"I don't think I would like having my picture in the newspaper, Miss Garrett," Frances said. "You're very brave."

"I didn't really like the idea either, Mrs. Lane, but I had nothing to say about it. Miss Sheppard was determined to have my photograph accompany her story."

"Miss Lucy can indeed be a force to be reckoned with," Reverend Lane said. He saw the quizzical look that came over Joanna's face. "You see, we've served on several church committees together and—" His wife gently tapped his hand and shook her head. He then beckoned to the serving girl, "We're ready to order, two servings of bread pudding, please. Will you join us, Miss Garrett? I can heartily recommend this bread pudding. Daisy Morgan makes it herself, and her hard sauce is something to dream about."

"I really couldn't, Reverend, but I would love another cup of this excellent coffee."

The Lanes lingered until they realized it was after six-thirty. The threesome walked to the stocky woman standing behind the front counter. It was Daisy Morgan, the owner, who had a natural gregariousness that found full vent whenever she left the kitchen for the dining room.

"Parson, Mrs. Lane, how glad I am to see you!" Daisy beamed. "I hope you found everything to your liking." Daisy's tone made clear that she expected their answer to be in the affirmative, and it was. "And who is this lovely lady with you?"

John Lane introduced Joanna.

At the mention of her name, Daisy clapped her hands together. "Lord love you! I should have known you was the new schoolteacher. My sister's boy, Freddie, goes to the school and he's been talking up a storm about you ever since term began. It's *Miss Garrett this* and *Miss Garrett that* pert near all day long."

John Lane took note of Joanna's humbled smile.

"No wonder the boy's so taken with you, as pretty as you are, not to mention all them new things you've got them doing."

Once outside, after a hug from Daisy and encouragement to *come back real soon,* Frances began to giggle. Her husband feigned displeasure, which only made her giggle that much more. Joanna was soon laughing along with her.

"A fine pair you make," John chastised them, as they walked up the church steps, "laughing all the way to an Ash Wednesday service." The twinkle in his eye belied his criticism.

There were no more than fifteen people in the sanctuary, so Joanna easily spotted Laura and Joe in their usual pew. Edgar, however, wasn't with them. On the way down the aisle, she nodded to Jim and Mary Langston, who filled a pew with their young family, including their new baby Alice.

Joanna slid in beside Laura.

"I see you survived your time in the lioness' den," Laura whispered. Joanna almost laughed out loud. She could not believe that she and Laura had shared the same thought.

"I'm alive and well... I'll tell you all about it later."

It was almost seven o'clock when the doors at the front of the church opened and Luke Goodman walked in, flanked by Edgar, Sam Bailey, and Harvey Greer.

Joanna followed the men processing down the aisle and realized one was Edgar. Luke went to his chair behind the pulpit and the other three took seats on the front pew. Joanna noticed that the Lord's table was set with the communion plate, cup and pitcher. *Edgar is an elder—why didn't I know that?*

The service was simple, brief and deeply moving. When it came time for communion, Joanna saw tears in Luke's eyes as he broke the bread and poured grape juice, representative of wine, from an earthenware pitcher into the chalice. He spoke the words of invitation, and her own vision blurred through her own tears.

I am unworthy, she thought, and not for the first time, *I am completely unworthy to receive the body and blood of my Savior.* Her lashes relinquished, and her tears ran down her cheek. *It's too much, too costly a gift for someone so undeserving.* Laura squeezed Joanna's hand when she began weeping profusely.

Edgar and Sam served the communion bread first, each taking one side of the church. When Edgar leaned forward extending the platen, Joanna smiled up at him, tears still glistening on her black lashes.

He whispered in the kindest, most gentle and loving tone, "The body of Christ for you, Joanna." The words he spoke and the sound of his voice, went straight to her heart.

Luke stood in front of the pulpit, his arms outstretched for the benediction, the end of the Lenten service. "May this time of introspection that we call Lent not only make you more aware of your shortcomings, but also lead you to deeper love for God, greater service to God, and abundant thanksgiving to God for salvation through Christ. May the Holy Spirit move in and through you, and may God grant you peace. Amen." He processed purposefully out of the sanctuary.

Joe, typical boy that he was, rushed to join Jimmy Langston and David Goodman, who were heading outside. Laura remained seated after Joe left, then rose herself, stood up, and turned to Joanna.

"Aren't you coming, Joanna?"

"In a moment," she whispered. "You go on ahead." She closed her eyes surrounded by the silence in the now empty church. *Lord, I need you. Help me, please.* She felt the presence of someone sitting down beside her and opened her eyes.

"Are you all right?" Edgar whispered.

She nodded.

"Would you like me to leave?"

Joanna shook her head, her eyes still closed.

They sat silently together in the tranquility of the sanctuary, eyes closed, hearing only the sound of each other's breathing. Edgar lifted Joanna's hand in his.

She hoped he didn't hear her sudden gasp.

When Joanna finally opened her eyes, Edgar's violet ones were trained on her. She started to speak, but Edgar gently placed his finger on her lips and smiled.

"Let's go home."

Chapter Fifteen

Joanna snuggled under the quilts, savoring the memory of those brief moments with Edgar. He held her hand as they walked to the rear of the church, only releasing his hold as they reached the narthex where Luke and Laura were waiting. Joanna thanked Luke for his message and Luke, in turn, had hugged her.

"It wasn't my message, just mine to deliver," he said, lifting Joanna's chin in a fatherly way. "I'm so glad you came to Appleton, Joanna Garrett. Go with God." Then he turned to Edgar and drew him in an embrace, which Joanna found deeply touching.

Joanna claimed joy this morning, almost floating down the stairs and rushing into the kitchen.

"Good morning!" Laura said. "Aren't you the little sunbeam this morning... and *why* might that be?" Her gaze was direct and knowing. "A good night's sleep, perhaps?"

Joanna crossed the room to give Laura a hug. "I slept very well and I feel wonderful." She paused and leaned into Laura's ear. "And because the interview with Lucy Sheppard is behind me."

"I don't think that's the only reason, but we'll have to discuss the other possibility later." She nodded toward the door where Joe stood, pulling up his suspenders as he walked into the kitchen.

He kissed his aunt, greeted Joanna, grabbed a biscuit from the warming pan, went into the lean-to, pulled on boots and a coat, and headed to the barn.

"Everyone seems to be in a good mood this morning." She motioned Joanna to join her at the table, where she leaned forward with a conspiratorial air. "Now," she said, "tell me—what happened between you and my brother last night?"

As the story poured forth, joy consumed Laura, who had felt for some time that Joanna was falling in love with Edgar. Her only fear was in thinking that Edgar hadn't done the same. *Ed enjoys Joanna's company, but he's still infatuated with Lucy Sheppard, though why, I'll never know.* She murmured a heartfelt prayer for the woman she had come to love as a sister. "Lord, please don't let Joanna get hurt—and please don't let my brother be a fool."

Only a blind person could have missed the look Edgar and Joanna exchanged when he and Joe came in from the barn. Their eyes locked for a brief moment, then Edgar said in a stiff way, "Good morning, Miss Garrett." It was all Laura could do to keep from whacking him with her spoon. *Perhaps, I can stop worrying about Joanna getting her heart broken when I hear you use her given name.*

As if all creation shared Joanna's joy that morning, the day was sunny and so warm that she unbuttoned her wool coat on the drive to school. Joe had taken his usual seat beside his father, but Joanna didn't mind. She wasn't sure she could have borne sitting beside Edgar that morning. Their closeness the night before, not just the physical nearness of him but also the spiritual bond they shared, had left her exhilarated and bewildered.

Admit it Joanna, you find him attractive. Oh, I do... very attractive, with that olive skin and thick brown hair, those broad shoulders and muscled arms. His eyes and that smile that— She smiled herself, *— makes me go weak in the knees.*

A little voice piped up inside her head. "So, he's attractive. So was Nicholas Brodie. Remember what happened with him?"

Edgar's not like Nicholas, she argued with herself. *He's... deeper than Nicholas. Edgar loves his son and is devoted to his sister, and he's not afraid to show his feelings.* Joanna remembered how Edgar had returned Luke's hug. *And he loves the Lord, too.*

"Are you going to teach today, or would you like to ride back to the farm with me, Miss Garrett?"

Joanna almost jumped at the sound of Edgar's voice. Her reverie was so deep that she hadn't realized they were at the school, much less that the wagon had stopped rolling. "I'm sorry.

My mind was elsewhere." She accepted Edgar's outstretched hand and climbed down. "I think I'd better go on in or I might lose my job." She walked up onto the porch and was unlocking the door when Edgar spoke again. She turned and found him standing so near that she felt the warmth of him.

"Wait a minute," he said. "I've wanted to talk with you since we left church last night, but we haven't had a moment alone together."

The very thought made Joanna's spine tingle.

"This isn't the time, but I thought maybe on Saturday we could ride over to Hanover and take in a livestock sale. There might be a good horse for you, and—" he paused, "and it would give us a chance to talk."

"I'd like that—" she said, dropping her gaze to the key in her hand. "I'd like that very much."

"Gosh, Miss Garrett, aren't you going in?" Joe pushed the door open and held it for Joanna.

Edgar came inside, just long enough to build a fire and check the tinderbox. When he left, Joanna resisted the urge to go to the window and watch him drive away. *You're acting like a schoolgirl,* she chastised herself, *not a schoolteacher.* She smiled broadly as her students arrived, unable to repress the lightness of her heart.

The day flew by and Joanna abandoned the usual routine as a reward for her students' hard work preparing for the examinations.

"There will be no drills in spelling, no arithmetic and no grammar exercises today." The students clapped their hands wildly.

"Instead, we'll spend our time with the globe and learn a little more about where you came from and where you'd like to go." She divided the students by age groups and let the younger ones have first crack at spinning the globe and searching for home countries. The older ones worked on art projects for the Open House.

After morning recess, Joanna did the unheard of and let the youngest pupils sit on the floor to color a large map of the world. In the afternoon, Joanna gathered everyone in a circle and read aloud from *Little Women.* "This is one of my favorite books, by one of our best known American authors, a woman named Louisa May Alcott."

"I don't want to hear no book by a lady writer," Jake Trimble said.

"*Any* book," Joanna corrected. "You don't want to hear *any* book written by a woman." *Makes no never mind,* she wanted to say, *because you're going to.* Instead, she simply began reading and soon the entire class was caught up in the story. No one was ready to stop when dismissal time came.

"I'll tell you what," Joanna said. "I'll read from *Little Women* for the last half hour every day and we'll finish the story before the end of the term, even if it is almost six-hundred pages long." A few students audibly gasped. "But," she added, "that means you will *really* have to focus on your studies. I can't let your other work fall by the wayside while we follow the lives of the March family."

Friday also came and went quickly, for which Joanna was grateful. Much as she loved teaching, her mind kept wandering to Saturday's trip to Hanover with Edgar. *Alone...* she kept thinking. *Alone together.*

Edgar had casually mentioned, during supper the night before, that he was going to take Joanna to Hanover for a livestock auction on Saturday. To which Laura nonchalantly responded, "Fine, I'll pack a lunch basket for you." On the inside, however, she was shouting, "hurray!"

Joe's response, on the other hand, had been vocal and animated. "Can't I come with you, Pa? I love to see the animals and I could help you and Miss Garrett pick out a real good horse. And I could help with the driving on the way back if you do buy a horse."

"I'd like to have you come along, son, but I need you here on Saturday. Mr. Matthews is delivering a load of lumber and someone's got to help get it into the barn." Edgar knew Stinson Matthews could manage the job alone, but he also knew Joe wouldn't be quite so upset about missing the trip if he felt needed at home. "And, if we don't find a horse on Saturday, you can go on the next trip. You do have good horse sense." Joe stopped wheedling and dug into his pumpkin pie.

Saturday morning dawned bright and clear. Joanna thought long and hard about what to wear for the trip to Hanover with Edgar; of course, she chastised herself for her vanity. She decided on the red and brown checked wool skirt and red blouse she had worn on her first day at the McGill farm. "It's comfortable," she told her reflection. And it answered back: *That's not why you chose it. You picked it because you always feel pretty in it!*

Joanna was downstairs, brewing coffee, when Edgar came through the kitchen on his way to do chores.

"You're up with the chickens this morning. You didn't think I'd leave without you, did you?"

"Of course not." She smiled "I just wanted to start breakfast for Laura. I won't be here to help with the bread baking and I don't like to shirk my share of the work."

He looked below her rolled up sleeves and saw that her hands were deep in biscuit dough.

"Your sister has been so good to me. I wanted to do something for her for a change."

"I know the feeling. Laura is a mighty fine woman. She's been a godsend for me and Joe. But no one could accuse you of shirking your duties. You're as hard working as my sister."

By eight o'clock, Edgar and Joanna were waving goodbye to Laura and Joe. For the first half hour, they made small talk—about the weather: "It couldn't be lovelier" and "It's warm for this time of year and not a bit of wind" — and about the farm – "I'm getting ready to plant corn" and "Is that a big crop for you?"

"This reminds me of home," she said, drinking in the wooded landscape of Jefferson County. "Raleigh has rolling hills like these and a lot of farms, too."

"It must have been hard to leave home and family and come to a strange place."

"I really haven't been homesick... maybe that's because I had already been away at school and at my other teaching positions." *The truth, Joanna. You should tell him the truth.* "And Indiana isn't completely foreign to me. I had a classmate, Abigail Wheaton, who's from the northern part of the state, and who told me a lot about her home here in Indiana." Joanna sighed. "If there's anyone I'm homesick for, it's Abby. She's my best friend."

Edgar clucked to Dolly, encouraging her to keep up her pace as the road began an uphill climb. "Where's Abby now? And why did she go all the way to North Carolina when we have normal schools here?"

"We didn't go to a normal school. We went to Peace Institute in Raleigh. After we finished college, Abby went back home to teach at the Hogue School in DeKalb County. She's about to be married, though, so she won't be teaching next year."

"You're a college graduate?" There was no mistaking the surprise in Edgar's voice.

"Yes. And you're the second person this week to be flabbergasted by that fact."

"Who was the first?"

"Lucy Sheppard, when she interviewed me for the

newspaper. She wanted to see my diploma, as if my word wasn't good enough."

"Well, you have to admit, a woman college graduate is a bit out of the ordinary. Lucy probably wanted to be sure of her facts before printing them." The moment she had mentioned Lucy's name, he saw Lucy in the gown she had worn to the social and felt her in his arms. The memory made his pulse race—then, he unfastened the coat's top buttons, and cleared his throat. "When is the article going to be published?"

"I don't know," she answered. Fear seized her, remembering how Lucy had grilled her about her past. "Perhaps in the next issue. I'm a bit nervous about it."

"Why nervous? Seems like a good way for people to get to know more about you."

That's what worries me, she thought. "I'm not important enough to be written about in a newspaper. I'm just an ordinary schoolteacher."

"Not with a college degree." He shook his head, then turned to her and smiled. "Tell me about Peace Institute."

"It was founded by Presbyterians almost 30 years ago and now it's a school for girls of all ages. They even have a kindergarten. I taught in it for a year."

"Kindergarten?"

Joanna explained the concept, her eyes dancing with the excitement of it. "I really believe in early education. The sooner we begin to teach our children, the more they will learn. Young minds are wide open, just waiting to be filled."

"Maybe you'll start a kindergarten in Appleton." He shook his head, "But I think you'll have a hard time selling the idea."

"Why?"

"Some folks don't like sending their children to school now— when they start at seven or eight—and at fourteen, a lot stop going to school so they can help on the farm." Edgar paused. "And some people don't think their daughters need to go to school at all. They may not say that to you, but that's how they feel."

"Then we need to educate the parents."

And you're just the one to do it, he wanted to say, then turned to her again. *You're quite a spitfire.*

"Maybe I could start by telling them Peace has a cooking school—that might seem less dangerous than Latin."

"You know Latin?"

"I studied Latin and French. But when Mr. Giannini came to take my picture, I wished I had learned Italian. I can just imagine how eloquent he is in his native tongue." They both laughed, thinking about how he fractured the English language.

"I'd have thought the school board would have let the whole township know we have a college graduate teaching in our little town. You must be very proud, as I'm sure your folks are, too."

They were... "I am proud. I loved going to college—it was exciting and challenging, and the professors were wonderful."

"Speaking of which," he said, pointing to a red and blue sign on the side of the road, "that's the entrance to Hanover College."

"I didn't know there was a college in Hanover."

"It was started by Presbyterians, too. Luke can tell you all about it. He graduated from Hanover and went on to their seminary in New Albany."

It was almost ten o'clock when Edgar pulled the wagon up to a hitching post outside the biggest barn Joanna had ever seen. "Let's get the list of horses from the auctioneer," he said, helping Joanna climb down. "Then we'll have a look around."

Minutes later, list in hand, Joanna and Edgar were in the sales barn, looking over horses chewing hay or pacing back and forth in their stalls. A small, black and white filly came to the end of her stall and nuzzled Joanna's hand when she reached in to stroke the horse's nose.

"I think she likes me."

Edgar looked at the list. "She's three years old and was bred by Samuel Larson from Ohio. Larson has good horses, but a filly this young might be a bit too frisky for you."

"I don't want a nag," she laughed. "I want a horse with energy, as well as good sense."

You want a horse like you, he thought. "We haven't seen a fraction of what's available yet. Let's keep looking."

They continued perusing animals, listening to comments from other potential buyers, and making notes on the sale list. By late morning, they had seen all the horses and had spotted several they agreed would be good choices, including the little filly.

He ran to catch up with her. "Say, the auction starts at one o'clock, would you like to look over the other animals, or have dinner first?"

"Let's eat—I'm famished! It must be all the fresh air and exercise."

He laughed. "I'm not sure I'd call this air *fresh*." He wriggled his nose as they passed a pen full of sheep. "But, I'm hungry, too. Let's get the basket and see if we can find a place to sit."

People milled about the tables and benches set up near a cart holding urns of coffee. Edgar took Joanna's elbow and guided her through the crowd. She liked the way his hand took hold of her arm and liked, too, the way he made her feel—safe and protected. They found places to sit and Joanna unpacked the picnic basket while Edgar fetched two mugs of coffee.

"Here we are, sugar and cream—" he said, handing Joanna a mug, "—just the way we like it."

I never would have guessed he even noticed. She filled a plate with chicken, deviled eggs, pickles and bread, handed it to Edgar, then fixed one for herself. She had her eyes closed in a silent grace before eating. They popped open when Edgar took her hand and began praying softly.

"Lord, thank you for this beautiful day and this food prepared by loving hands. Help us to find a good animal for Miss Garrett and bless our time here today. Amen." He released Joanna's hand and picked up his chicken leg.

"My sister," he said between mouthfuls, "is as good a cook as our mother was."

"I wish I had known your mother. Laura speaks about her often," she said, daubing her mouth with the the checkered napkin. "I can tell she was a kind and generous and loving woman."

"That she was... " he nodded, "that she was. Mama could be tough on the outside, but as soft as bread dough on the inside. And she had the most wonderful laugh." He grinned, staring down into space, as if hearing his mother's voice, then took a gulp of coffee. "That woman loved a good joke and wasn't above telling one herself. She was always teasing my father." He wiped his mouth and fingers with the cloth napkin. "Now, Pa had a good sense of humor, too, but he wasn't lighthearted the way Mama was. She would laugh so hard that she'd be in tears. Pa was more of a chuckler."

"Laura took after your mother because she's always laughing and seems to find the funny side of every situation."

"Laura wouldn't be above laughing out loud in church, if she took a mind to. If you scratched the surface of Laura, what would pour out would be pure joy." He reached for an apple turnover and dunked it in his still steaming coffee. "And can she cook!" He stared into her eyes. "'Course, I'd say she may have some competition now... those pies of yours make my mouth water just to think of them!"

They stowed the basket in the wagon and strolled around the sheep and cattle pens before heading back to the barn to pick up a bidding paddle and find good places to stand during the sale.

On the stroke of one the auction began. Joanna had never attended a livestock auction before and was fascinated by the way the auctioneer talked; well, it wasn't really talking, it was more akin to jabbering. An animal was brought forward, a starting price named, and bids flew from all directions, paddles popping into the air continually.

"How does he keep track of all the bids?" Joanna whispered. "I didn't even see a paddle go up for that last one."

"Some folks just nod. The auctioneer has to keep his eyes and his mouth moving all the time."

It was more than an hour before the auctioneer finished with the cattle and moved to the sheep. "I didn't realize the horses would be last," she said. "Is there a reason they do it that way?"

He nodded. "Most people come for the horse sale... they want folks to buy other animals, too, so if they started with the horses, half the crowd would be gone before they got to the livestock."

Joanna's heart began to pound when the first horse was brought forward. It wasn't one of the animals she and Edgar liked, but she was excited just the same. They had decided that Edgar would do the bidding, being taller and familiar with the process. He bid on the fourth horse, an Appaloosa, but the bids quickly exceeded Joanna's top price. This happened again with the next animal, and the one after that, and Joanna began to worry that she might not be able to afford to buy a horse. When the black and white filly Joanna wanted was brought forward, she clutched Edgar's arm.

He grinned and looked down at her. "You'll have to let go if you want me to bid on her." Joanna released his arm as the auctioneer opened the bidding again.

A flurry of bids hastened the round and Joanna noticed a tall, white haired man, standing off to the right of them, who seemed as eager as she to buy the same filly.

The round of bidding moved so quickly that only Edgar and the white-haired man were bucking each other's offer that was rapidly approaching Joanna's top price. She felt as if she couldn't breathe and, without realizing it, latched onto Edgar's arm again. He switched the paddle to his other hand and kept bidding.

The bids were now in small increases, back and forth between Edgar and the older man. Joanna looked over at the man and found him staring at her. She smiled; he smiled back.

Edgar's bid awaited the man's counter-offer. The auctioneer looked to Edgar, then to his competitor.

The old gent shook his head at the auctioneer, relinquishing his stand against Edgar's last bid. The auctioneer banged his gavel and hollered, "Sold to number twenty-seven and the pretty lady beside him!" Heads turned their way. Joanna lowered her head, and Edgar took her hand and led her to the payment table.

"I can't believe she's mine!" I was certain we—*you*, would be outbid!"

"And, to be sure, he would have been, ma'am—"

Joanna wheeled around and faced the man.

"—if your husband had come alone today. I liked that little filly right much, but I could tell you liked her even more," the stranger said, his blue eyes twinkling. "I couldn't break a pretty lady's heart over a horse."

"That was very kind... Thank you, sir." It suddenly dawned on her that he had referred to Edgar as her *husband*. "But this isn't my husband."

The stranger raised his eyebrows.

"I mean, we're not married."

He raised them even further.

Joanna was so rattled that she couldn't compose her thoughts.

Luckily, Edgar had his wits about him. "I'm Edgar McGill—" he said, tipping his cap and reaching to shake the man's hand, "—from over Appleton way. And this is Joanna Garrett, a schoolteacher staying with me and my family. She's in need of a horse and I came along to help her bid."

You don't have to make it sound as though you didn't want to come, but had to.

"She's had her eye on that filly ever since we got here this morning, and I thank you, sir, for yielding in the bidding."

"I see," the man said, bowing slightly. "I'm Jonas Taylor. I'm pleased to meet you both." He turned to Joanna. "I apologize for the misunderstanding. I thought from the way you were holding Mr. McGill's arm that you must be his wife." He smiled. "You take care of that horse, you hear? Don't let your pupils annoy her when your back's turned." He tipped his wide brimmed hat, said *goodbye*, and then sauntered off.

"I didn't expect to find anyone so gracious at a livestock auction," she said, following Edgar to the payment table. "I assumed it would be every man for himself."

"It usually is. Jonas Taylor's a real gentleman."

They paid for the horse and took the slip of paper given them to the stall to prove Joanna's ownership. The filly once again came straight to Joanna and nuzzled her.

"It's as if she knows me. Oh, I'm so happy I got her! I know she's going to be perfect for me!"

The young man tending the horse smirked, but stopped short of laughing when Edgar shot him a warning glance. "She's all yours," the stable boy said. "She's been well cared for at the Larsons and she's a fine little horse."

"Well, it looks like this was meant to be. Let's head for home." Edgar gave the lead to Joanna, who walked the filly to the back of the wagon, where Edgar tied her. "I don't want to make her work today. We'll hitch her up tomorrow and see how she does." He stroked his chin as he stared at Joanna. "Guess your next purchase better be a buggy— unless you want to ride side saddle to school!"

Joanna kept turning around to look at her horse, the filly easily keeping pace with Dolly, as they headed for home.

"What are you going to name her? I figure you'll want to come up with something special, no matter what the Larsons called her."

"Names are very important. I'm going to have to get to know her a little before I come up with the right one. Do you think Joe would help me name her?"

"He'd like that a lot, but be sure you let him know *you'll* do the deciding. Otherwise, that filly might wind up with some outlandish name from one of those books he's always reading."

"I might be the one who comes up with something peculiar..." She lifted her brow. "After all, I've read more books than Joe has!"

They drove in companionable silence through a village filled with brick houses topped with curved wooden roofs.

"I've never seen houses built like that."

"This is a German town. The folks here build their houses the way they did in the old country." He pointed to a small church, its front door painted bright red. "That's a Lutheran church. It's in an old tradition, dating from the Reformation. The doors of Wittenburg Cathedral, where Martin Luther posted his 95 Theses, were red. Other Lutheran churches were painting their doors red to show they were reformed and that the church was a place of safety and refuge."

"I never knew that, but then, we don't have many Lutheran churches in North Carolina."

"I think a lot of Martin Luther," he said. "I admire his courage and I respect his beliefs about how God wants the church to be. I just finished reading a biography about him and I'm now reading the 95 Theses."

"You're reading Luther—in German?"

Edgar grinned. "I'm reading Luther, but not in German, and not in Latin either. Luke loaned me his English translation."

Edgar loved the way curiosity lit Joanna's face.

"Luke is seminary trained and he, naturally, reads a lot. He's been loaning me books since I was ordained as an elder last year." He looked down at the reins, as if momentarily lost in thought, then continued. "I felt I needed to know more than I did about God and the church."

"I didn't know you were an elder, until you served communion on Wednesday."

"I guess you didn't expect to see me sitting there with Sam and Harvey," he laughed. "They're a lot older than I am and probably have more right to be a church elder than I do."

"It's not a *right*—it's a calling, Mr. McGill! You don't make a man an elder because he gave a lot of money to the church, or because he's the oldest member." She looked up and stared into his inviting eyes. "I'd venture a guess to say there isn't another elder in the church who's studying Martin Luther or feels any need to!"

His mouth dropped open and then he laughed. "Now you do sound like a preacher's daughter."

"I wasn't trying to be critical." She sighed, then hung her head. "Sometimes I speak too forcefully and without thinking. God must get very annoyed with me."

"Is that what you were feeling at church on Wednesday?" He posed the question gently.

"I'm not sure. I really can't explain what I was feeling... It just—well, it overwhelms me sometimes, to think God loves me and died for me and saved me. At times, especially when I take communion, it just hits me, as if a great flood is rushing over me." She leaned back against the seat. "I was really touched when Luke started crying as he said the words of invitation. He truly loves the Lord."

I've never had a conversation like this with a woman— not with Mama, or Laura; not even Bessie. Silence cradled him as he reckoned that this kind of talk revealed the soul, and he didn't like being vulnerable—except, it was Joanna who was revealing her vulnerability.

"Luke is not your usual preacher. And you're right, he really loves God." After another long pause ensued, Edgar chuckled. "He and I went fishing in the Ohio River one Saturday after he arrived in Appleton. I'll never forget what he said to me: 'Edgar,' he said, 'there are three things I love in this life. One of them is Jesus Christ and one of them is my wife and my friend,'-- he stopped there and put his hand on my shoulder— 'one of them is fishing.'" Edgar's deep laugh and Joanna's slightly higher pitched one rang out in unison, startling Dolly into a hastening pace.

How many times have we smiled and laughed together today? "I knew I liked Reverend Luke," she said, finally getting herself sufficiently under control to speak. "I'm eager to get to know him better."

"And he you."

Has he talked to Luke about me?

"I think you'll like his wife, too," Edgar said. "Carrie's a good woman, and a lot like Laura."

"I already like their children. David is so bright and such a hard worker. And Grace is just as smart as her brother, though she's much more talkative, but I think Grace could make friends anywhere in about five minutes."

"That's from her father. Luke never met a stranger. It's a real gift in a pastor."

"When I met him at the social, he held my hands as though he was genuinely glad to meet me. He made me feel welcome right off." *Unlike some other people that night,* she thought, disturbed that Lucy Sheppard invaded her thoughts.

They passed a barren field and Joanna saw a man and a boy working the soil. "Isn't that Mr. Langston—and his son, Jimmy?"

"Sure is," he said, then tipped his cap and both father and son responded with a wave. Jimmy shielded his eyes from the sun's glare as he tried to get a better look at the horse trotting behind the wagon.

"Toad's going to have a fit if he finds out Jimmy Langston knew about your horse before he did."

Joanna unconsciously laid her hand on Edgar's forearm and whispered, "Let's not tell him. Why don't we hitch up—whatever her name is—tomorrow, and let Joe drive to church? That will give him something to gloat about."

"Now, Miss Garrett." A frown furrowed Edgar's brow. "Is that any way for a schoolteacher to talk? Encouraging her students to be prideful!"

Embarrassment flushed her face and she lifted her hand, not realizing he was teasing her.

Edgar lifted her hand and replaced it where it had been. "I want to tell you how much I've enjoyed today."

"I have, too. I can't thank you enough for taking your whole Saturday to drive me to Hanover and help me buy a horse."

"It wasn't just to buy a horse... I wanted to spend some time alone with you." The words caught in his throat. "Not just a horse—*your* horse. That filly was waiting for you. I knew she was the one for you the moment she came up and nuzzled your hand."

"You didn't say that then, Mr. McGill!" Joanna cried through feigned indignation. "You told me she might be too young and frisky and I should see what else was available!"

"I also said that I liked the look of her." *I like the look of you, too, Joanna.* "She has a gentle nature, I could tell from the way she came right up to you. I have to admit, for a while there I thought you were in for a disappointment," he leaned close to her ear. "I thought everyone, including you, heard my sigh of relief when Jonas Taylor dropped out of the bidding."

"Well, you fooled me, Mr. McGill," she said, momentarily caught up in the way his eyes looked into hers. It was all she could do to quell what could not be defined. "I would like to thank Mr. Taylor for being so perceptive and thoughtful." She felt her face flush, remembering how Jonas Taylor had thought she and Edgar were married.

"Maybe you'll get that chance one day. But right now we'd better get your gift horse unhitched and into the barn."

They were back at the farm. She was glad to be home, though not at all accepting of the fact that their trip had ended. She turned to reach for the picnic basket. Edgar's arm went around her waist.

"It's been a long time since I had such a relaxed and fun day off," he whispered. "I'd like us to do this again sometime."

She felt herself trembling and wondered if he sensed it. "I'd like that, too." Her voice was so low, it was but a breath of fleeting joy that momentarily had her anticipating his kiss.

The sound of a squeaking door told her that he couldn't kiss her, even if he wanted to. They shared a smile that ended their day, and Edgar slowly slipped his arm from around her tiny form.

"Sometime soon," he whispered, his eyes saying more than his words of expectation.

"Yes, soon."

Chapter Sixteen

Joanna met Joe head-on as she walked in the door. "How would you like to drive the filly to church, Joe?"

"Really, Miss Garrett—can I really?"

"Yes, you *may*," she said." *I've turned into Papa,* she thought. *He drove us crazy, always correcting our grammar and insisting we speak properly.* A surge of melancholy swept through her. *I miss you, Papa.*

At supper Joanna and Edgar kept stepping on each other's sentences as they told about their trip.

"I was so afraid Mr. Taylor was going to outbid us," Joanna said. "I could hardly breathe, I wanted that horse so badly."

"And I lost all feeling in my right arm."

"Why, Pa?"

"Well, you see, Miss Garrett was clutching my forearm so tightly, it felt like a vise. I expect we were halfway home before I could feel my fingers."

"Why didn't you say something?" A truly surprised expression covered Joanna's face.

Laura held the napkin to her mouth, hoping to contain her composure. *Will wonders never cease? He's teasing her!*

"Well, maybe *some* feeling was back before that. But, then, my left arm was so stiff from holding up that paddle, the numbness didn't seem so bad."

"I had no idea, Mr. McGill!"

Joanna was so genuinely concerned that Laura wasn't quite sure how Joanna would respond if Edgar kept his performance going.

Joanna stood up. "I can get you some liniment..."

Edgar leaned back on the chair and shook his head, then looked up into her eyes. "I'm fine, Miss Garrett... I just got carried away with my storytelling."

'Pa! Did you make all that up?"

"Not *all* of it, son. I'm pretty sure I have a bruise on my arm where Miss Garrett was squeezing it."

"Oh, go on with you!" she said, shaking her head, her eyes dancing the joy of his humor. It was a side of Edgar McGill she had not known existed.

Bessie's death had devastated Edgar, and left him fearful. Laura understood that and was beginning to understand part of Lucy Sheppard's appeal. *Ed knows Lucy could never own his heart, but Joanna... Joanna is another story.* Joanna was a type of woman Edgar had never encountered before—and might never again.

Joe walked Joanna out to the barn to see the stall Edgar had fixed up for her filly. "Gosh, she's pretty, Miss Garrett," he said, stroking the horse's silky black mane. "She's like a dog in a horse's body."

Joanna leaned against the stall, squelching a laugh.

"What I mean is, she looks like Patches. If Patches were a dog, he'd look like this horse."

She looked down at the pup who had scampered into the barn after them. "Come to think of it, you're right, Joe. Maybe that's why I was drawn to her." She stroked the filly, who turned to nuzzled Joanna's neck. "That tickles, you silly horse!" She pulled back, but the horse followed. "Now, stop!"

Joanna's laughter brought Edgar from the other end of the barn where he was checking the wagon harness. He saw the filly nuzzling Joanna and thought, *that's one smart horse.* "Don't let her dominate you—" *Joanna;* he almost said her name.

"I won't. I know I have to show her who's boss."

Sunday, as hoped for, dawned clear and fair and Joe had the

filly hitched to the wagon and waiting at the front door before Joanna and Laura even had their hats on.

"That horse is as excited as Joe," Laura said. "Has she ever pulled a wagon before?"

Joanna opened the front door. "I don't know. I didn't think to ask Mr. Larson," she said following Laura outside.

"Where's Pa?" Joe's blue eyes raked the yard impatiently. "I don't want us to be late for church!"

"Luke will be delighted to hear how you couldn't wait to get to church, Joe," Edgar said wryly, coming from the side of the house. "Maybe you're ready for that confirmation class after all."

Joe gave his father a withering look as he climbed onto the wagon seat.

"All right, son, let's go!"

Joe released the reins, clucked to the horse, and the filly took off briskly trotting down the lane.

"Don't let her run, Toad. She has to know you're in charge."

"I know, Pa. She's not running, she's just frisky, like me." He spoke encouragingly to the horse. "Aren't you, girl? You're just frisky."

"That's the word for *you*, son."

Joe gave him that *look* again. "I'm sure glad that Mr. Taylor stopped bidding. I can't imagine a better horse because she matches Patches." He jerked a look back at Joanna. "Miss Garrett! That's what you should name her— *Match*."

"That's an idea, Joe."

Laura hiked her brows. "What kind of name is *that* for a filly?"

"I see what Joe's thinking," Joanna said. "The horse does have the same colors as Patches and their coats both look like patchwork quilts so—they match."

"That's it exactly!" Joe shouted.

"Let's keep thinking about it. I'm sure we'll come up with the right name, just like your father and I chose the right horse."

"No wonder your students love you," Laura said. "You're a natural born teacher." *And a natural born mother, too.*

Joe drove by the church on the way to the livery stable.

"He's hoping his friends will already be there," Laura whispered, "so he can show off."

Jimmy Langston, his brother Billy, Philip Werner, and the two Greer boys were outside, trying to break off the icicles dangling just out of reach on the church's steep roof. Wagon wheels crunching the hardened snow drew their attention. They all turned, dropped the sticks they were using to attack the icicles, and ran to the road. Joe gave them a formal nod and drove on. It was all Laura could do not to laugh.

"From the look on Joe's face," she whispered to Joanna, "you'd think he was Jeffrey Lee driving his hearse!" Both giggled and struggled to compose themselves as Edgar helped them out of the wagon.

"You can't fool me with that *butter won't melt in your mouth* look," Edgar whispered to Laura. "You're about to bust loose with a laugh."

"Shush," she said, her grin confirming he was right. Laura looped her arm through Joanna's and the two of them walked to the church, leaving Joe to tell his friends all about the new horse.

Lucy Sheppard, passing the boys on her way into church, overheard snippets of their conversation: "My pa and Miss Garrett," and "way over in Hanover" and "Saturday." Lucy's feminine intuition told her there was more to the trip than a mere horse purchase. She didn't really want Edgar McGill, but she wanted him to want her. She was as competitive as she was egotistical. It was fine with her if a man took second best, meaning any woman other than her pretty self, but she wanted to be the one who made him do it.

After worship, the congregation took advantage of the unseasonably warm day to gather outside and chat. Joanna was deep in conversation with Laura and Frances Lane when she felt a tug on her sleeve. She turned.

"Good morning, Miss Sheppard," Joanna said. "We were just discussing today's sermon. I've always been irritated by the story of Martha and Mary, and I was glad to hear Reverend Goodman's interpretation of it."

Lucy shook her head. "Irritated by the word of God, Miss Garrett? You, a child of the manse? I would think you of all people would find all scripture uplifting, as I do."

Frances Lane and Laura both turned and stared at Joanna. Frances found her voice first. "Is this true, Joanna? Is your father a pastor?"

"Yes, it's true," she said, "and it was my preacher father who taught me that God gave me a good mind and wanted me to use it, whether I was studying history or reading the Bible. I find that the more I wrestle with scripture, the more I make it my own."

"*Wrestle* with it?" Lucy snickered. "What on earth do you mean?"

"Read it. Think about it. Pray about it." Joanna used her

schoolteacher voice. "My father reads the Bible from Genesis through Revelation every year, Miss Sheppard, and he can say with Martin Luther, 'If you picture the Bible to be a mighty tree and every word a little branch, I have shaken every one of these branches because I wanted to know what it was and what it meant.'"

Lucy stood there with her mouth agape.

Good for you, Joanna, Laura thought. *You put Miss Lucy in the unusual position of being at a loss for words!*

"You may be able to quote Martin Luther," Lucy finally said, "but that doesn't make you a good Christian. I can quote Walt Whitman, but that doesn't make me a poet." She glared at Joanna. "Actions speak louder than words, Miss Garrett. You might want to remember that." Lucy nodded to Laura and Frances Lane, then flung her scarf over her shoulder and strutted off.

"That woman's tongue is as deadly as a viper snake," Laura said, then heard Frances Lane's gasp. "I'm sorry, Frances. I didn't mean to upset you."

"You didn't upset me, Laura. Lucy Sheppard did." The intensity of Frances' tone surprised both Laura and Joanna. "Proverbs says the tongue can be *a destructive and deadly weapon, sharp as a razor.* I am quite certain Lucy wouldn't find that verse uplifting!" Her round face flushed with indignation.

"Thank you, Mrs. Lane," Joanna said, putting her arm around Frances and hugging her. "Miss Sheppard seems to dislike me and I don't know why."

"You threaten her," Frances said. "You're intelligent and beautiful and you light up every room you walk into. Lucy is accustomed to getting all the attention; you, my dear, have stolen her thunder. She doesn't like that."

"But I'm not trying to get attention." *That's the last thing I want!*

"You don't have to try," Laura said.

"Why did she interview me for the paper, then? I should think that would be the *last* thing she would want."

"She probably didn't have any choice," Laura said. "Her father runs the paper, not Lucy. I'm sure he's the one who made that decision."

"What can I do? I don't want to make an enemy of her."

It's too late, Lucy could have told her. *You already have.*

"Be careful around her," Frances said. "And be as nice to her as you can."

"Kill her with kindness?" Laura shook her head. "I don't think that will work with Lucy."

"It may not," Joanna said. "But I don't see how I can do anything else."

Frances Lane was already gone by the time Edgar came out of the church.

"What took you so long?" Laura asked. "Joe said you were talking to Sam Bailey and Harvey Greer."

"I was, but not about church business. We were talking about Miss Garrett."

Joanna spun around. "Is there a problem?"

"Not unless you call having your house ready a problem. Sam says you should be able to move in right after Easter."

I feel as if I'm leaving home again.

"I wouldn't call it a problem, but it's not exactly good news either," Laura said. "I don't want Joanna to leave us."

"Me either!" Joe called over a rising wind. "Why don't you stay with us, Miss Garrett? If you're over there all alone, who'll help you with the filly and cut firewood for you?"

Alone... The word smote Joanna's heart. *I am alone, alone with my past and its secrets.*

"I'll miss you, too, Joe," she said. "But it's high time y'all got back to living without a guest."

"You're *not* a guest! I can hardly remember what it was like before you came! You're like my... like family," Joe said through tears he could not stop and ran off toward the livery stable.

I can't remember either, were the words stuck on the tip of Edgar's tongue.

Chapter Seventeen

Joe and Joanna were alone in the schoolhouse; she writing spelling words on the blackboard, and Joe sitting at his desk deep in thought.

"Miss Garrett, you won't have our wagon to drive if you move to that house."

Joanna was touched that Joe said, *if* you move, not *when*. "You're right, Joe. I don't think it would go over very well if I came galloping up to school, riding sidesaddle."

"Gosh, Miss Garrett! I don't know any ladies who ride right on the horse."

"Well, you do now. I'll ask your father at supper tonight where to look for a buggy. I'll want you to come along and help me buy one."

At the dinnertime break, Joanna went outside to move her horse to a spot where she could graze. Young hands reached to pat the filly's head and stroke her neck, but only little Emma Patterson remained by Joanna's side when the children ran off to play.

"What do you think of my horse, Emma?"

"She's beautiful. What's her name?"

"She doesn't have a name yet. Isn't that terrible?"

"Her name needs to be as beautiful as she is," Emma said in a surprisingly determined tone. "She can't have just any old name."

"That's how I feel, too. Will you help me think of one?"

The child nodded and went to sit on the schoolhouse steps. Joanna joined her. She knew something was bothering the little girl, but didn't question her. She simply chatted about the weather and told Emma she planned to buy a new Easter bonnet on Saturday.

"When's Easter?" Joanna saw anxiety in the child's brown eyes.

"It's in three weeks, Emma."

"My mama was supposed to be home by Easter." Emma's voice was barely above a whisper. "But now I don't think she's ever coming home." A tear rolled down her cheek and Joanna pulled her close, wrapping her arms around Emma's skinny frame. "Pa keeps telling us we have to be patient, she's going to get well, but I don't want to be patient anymore. I want my mama back."

"I know you do, Emma," Joanna whispered. "But it's not Easter yet." They sat in silence, and then Joanna said, "There's something you can do to help your mama, Emma, and it will help you feel better, too."

"What can I do... Mama's so far away?"

"You can pray for her. Do you know what prayer is, Emma?" The blank look on the little girl's face told Joanna so much.

"No, ma'am."

"That's when you talk to God, just the way I'm talking to you. You can tell God about your Mama being sick and you can ask God to help her get well. And you can ask God to help you not to be afraid."

"That's what that man said when he came to talk to Pa, but we never did it."

"What man?"

"I don't know his name. He said he heard about Mama being sick and gone off to Boston and he told Pa that God would help us if we asked, just like you said." She grabbed Joanna's arm. "But we never asked, Miss Garrett!"

"It's all right, Emma. We can ask right now, if you want to." Emma nodded. "Close your eyes, Emma." Joanna drew the little girl closer. "Father God, this child of yours, Emma, needs You. She is scared and asks You to take away her fear. Her mother is sick, Lord, and we ask You to send Your healing power through Emma's Mama and make her well and strong again so she can return to her family. And, Lord, we ask You to be with Emma's father. We ask all this in the name of Jesus Christ. Amen." Joanna felt Emma relax against her.

"Now," Joanna said, and stood up, "I think we better get back to work." She gave one pull on the school bell's rope and then turned back to Emma. "Would you like to ring it?" Most of the children begged for this job, but not Emma.

"I'll try." She stood up and gave the bell a weak but effective pull, and smiled up at Joanna.

"Thank you, Emma." Joanna said.

"Thank you, too, Miss Garrett."

The rest of the week passed with blessed normalcy, and with the filly still nameless. At supper on Friday, Joe declared the horse had to have a name before they went to bed.

"That's a great idea, son. Why don't you come up with one?"

"How about *Pepper*? The filly's black and white and pepper's kind of black and white, too."

"Sounds like a stallion's name, not a mare's."

"Well, what about *Speckles*? That suits a girl horse and she's speckled all over, just like Patches."

"Speckles doesn't fit... too tame."

"Well, what about—"

"It's Joanna's horse," Laura said. "She should name the horse." All three McGills trained their eyes on Joanna.

She sighed. "I've been *trying* to come up with one all week, and I'm still at a loss." She sipped her coffee and pondered. "I've considered *Dapple*, because of her different colored spots."

"Too ordinary," Joe said.

"What about *Beauty*?'" Laura asked. "She really is a pretty little thing."

Both Edgar and Joe said, "No!" and Joanna shook her head in agreement.

"Well, then," Laura said, "let's think about her disposition. She's a sweet animal but she's also very spirited. What about *Trixie*?"

"Not Trixie!" Joanna said firmly. "The little girl who sat in front of me all through primary school was named Trixie Hall and I'd hate to think of her every time I call my horse."

"Why not?" Joe asked. "Didn't you like her?"

"Not one bit," Joanna laughed.

"I thought teachers liked everybody."

"I wasn't a teacher then," Joanna said, getting a laugh from Edgar. "That girl thought she was better than everyone else because her father was rich. No, *Trixie* is out."

They sat in silence for a while, each pondering, then rejecting potential names.

Then Joe snapped his fingers. "I got it!" You want a name that sounds good when you call her, right Miss Garrett?" Joanna nodded as Joe came around to her. "Well, you know, we call our mare Dolly and I always thought it was a great name. How about *Molly*? I never know'd a lady named Molly who wasn't good natured and spunky."

"I like it, Joe," Edgar said, "but, then, I'm the one who named Dolly. What do you think, Miss Garrett?"

"I like it, too. It's a friendly name and it trips off your tongue. I can hear myself saying, Whoa, Molly, or giddy up there, Molly."

"Did you go to school with any girls named Molly?" Joe asked, his hands on his hips, as he leaned into her face.

Joanna laughed. "I did—and I liked her. In fact, I've liked every Molly I've ever met!"

Joe thumped his fist on the table. "Miss Molly, it is, then!" He pushed in his chair and headed toward the lean-to.

"Where are you off to, young man?" Edgar asked.

"Why, to the barn, of course! We all know Molly's name... she should know it, too!" The boy threw his coat on and was out the door.

Laura looked at Joanna and then at Edgar and all three started to laugh. *I'll miss this laughter*, Joanna thought.

After chores were done Saturday morning, they all set off for town. Edgar and Joe went into Hittle's Hardware, while Laura and Joanna headed straight for the general store. Neither could afford a new dress for Easter, but each hoped to find a pretty bonnet.

Joanna had just put on a pink straw hat trimmed with lavender ribbons, ignoring the tinkling bell at the opening of the store's front door. "What do you think?" she asked Laura, who proceeded to give it her serious consideration.

"It's a very pretty hat," a male voice answered, "but not nearly as pretty as the lady wearing it." Cal Turner, one of Joanna's many dance partners at the social, came up to them.

"You're very kind, Mr. Turner," she said. Cal's eyes lit up, surprised that Joanna remembered his name.

"Miss Garrett and I are shopping for Easter finery, Cal," Laura said. "What brings you to town?"

"Needed a new hammer and wanted to check wheat seed prices," he said. "Also thought I might see what baked goods Mrs. Werner has and pick up some of her canned peaches. A bachelor gets mighty tired of eating his own cooking." Cal gave Joanna a look that made her turn beet red.

"You won't go wrong with one of Celia's apple pies," Laura told him, intentionally raising her voice. "Celia's pies always sell out when the Ladies Aid has a bake sale."

As hoped, Celia overheard the remark and hurried to join them. "Now that's a high compliment, coming from you, Laura McGill. We all know who always wins the blue ribbon for apple pie at the county fair!" Celia beamed with pleasure. "But since Miss McGill isn't selling pies, Mr. Turner, and I am, why don't you come over here and sample a piece and see if you'd like to take one home with you?"

With Cal diverted, Joanna showed Laura an ivory straw bonnet lined with pink satin and trimmed with roses in three gradually darkening shades of pink.

Laura put it on and pursed her lips at her reflection in a hand mirror. "I don't know, Joanna. "Do you think this is too dressy?"

"How can an Easter bonnet be *too* dressy, Miss McGill?" It was the store owner, Richard Werner. "That hat looks like it was made for you!"

"Thank you, Mr. Werner. I'll think about it while we look over some shirt material." Laura bent over a table laden with bolts of fabric. When Richard Werner was out of earshot, she whispered to Joanna, "We got rid of Edgar and Joe so we could look at hats in peace, and then we get stuck with these two!" She shook her head and grimaced.

Joanna whispered back, "But Mr. Werner was right about that bonnet, Laura. It does look like it was made for you!"

"I think so, too, but I hate for Mr. Werner to think he talked me into it!" They were both giggling when Edgar and Joe walked in.

"Miss Garrett, I'm surprised at you," Edgar said with mock severity. "I'd think a schoolteacher would know how to comport herself in a public place." He focused his blue eyes on his sister. "But I'm not a bit surprised to find Laura cackling away."

"I'll have you know I am not *cackling*, Edgar McGill," she sassed. "Hens cackle. Ladies *chuckle*."

"Fine," he said, shaking his head. "Are you *chuckling* ladies ready to look at a buggy?"

"You found one already?"

"We found a great one, Miss Garrett. Pa and I looked it over and it's real nice, got black leather. It's just right for you, and—"

"Slow down, son. Why don't we let Miss Garrett look at the buggy and decide for herself? Are you two almost done?" He glanced at their empty shopping basket. "Doesn't look like you've even started."

Ten minutes later, two bonnets, a few yards of shirt fabric, and some dry goods were tucked into the basket and they headed to the livery stable. Joe was almost running in his eagerness to show Joanna their find.

"Slow down, son, Edgar chided. "We don't want Jeff Peters to think we're itching to buy." He pulled the boy to his side. "It's bad business to let a seller know you really want whatever he's selling. He might raise the price, or be less willing to deal." Joe nodded.

"I see you brought the ladies with you this time," Jeff Peters greeted them. "Mighty pretty ladies, too."

"Morning, Jeff," Laura said. "I think you've already met Joanna Garrett, our school teacher."

"Sure have. Nice to see you again ma'am."

"It's nice to see you, too."

"Who's looking for a buggy?"

"It's—" Joe started to say, but a look from Edgar hushed him.

"I wanted the ladies to see that buggy I looked at earlier, Jeff."

"Take your time... look all you want."

Edgar showed the women the buggy, with Jeff hovering around them. Every time Jeff said, "Now isn't this a nice little buggy?" and "I'll make you a good deal," Edgar pointed out a defect. "It's missing some paint on the box" and "there's a tear in the top."

After about five minutes, Edgar thanked Jeff for his time and ushered Joe and the two women back out to the street. Joe had a hard time keeping his mouth shut, until they were well outside of Jeff's earshot.

"What do you think, Miss Garrett? Do you like it? What about the price?"

"Land sakes alive, Joe," Laura said, playfully cuffing his ear, "give Miss Garrett a chance to answer one question before you ask her another!" She turned to Joanna, "What did you think? Looks like a sturdy, reliable buggy to me."

"I think so, too, but I had no idea a buggy would cost so much."

"Don't worry," Edgar said. "The price Jeff Peters quoted isn't what you'd have to pay."

"Why not?"

"Well, for one thing," Edgar said, steering the women toward the Morgan House, "the first price Jeff Peters names is always more than he expects to get." They went into the hotel, where Edgar ordered nut cake and drinks for everyone. "And, I happen to know who sold Jeff that buggy and what Jeff paid for it. If you want that buggy, Miss Garrett, I know we can get a better deal."

"I like it, but I don't need one right away and I'm not sure I want to buy the first one I see." She smiled at their waitress as she served three coffees, a glass of milk and four pieces of the freshly baked black walnut cake. "However, I don't want to pass up a bargain."

"Now, that's something our Scottish father would have said! Right, Ed?"

Edgar, his mouth full of cake, nodded agreement.

"Papa always quoted Benjamin Franklin— *a penny saved is a penny earned.*" Laura took another sip of her coffee. "But he wasn't stingy. Papa loved to buy presents for Mama, and he didn't stint on things we needed."

"Remember that cameo pin, Laura, the one he bought Mama for Christmas? She was so surprised—remember how she started laughing and the next thing we knew, she was crying."

"I remember," Laura said wistfully. "Then Papa said, 'Maggie, my dear, if I'd known it would make you weep, I'd have left it in the shop!'"

"That was the last Christmas they had together," Edgar said. "Almost ten years ago."

"Your mother is wearing a cameo in the photograph you showed me, Laura," Joanna said softly. "Is that the one your father gave her?"

"Yes, and I've often thought how glad I was that I talked Mama into wearing it. I had to talk her into wearing her best dress, too. Mama would have had her picture made in her house dress and apron."

"I like that picture," Joe said. "I like to look at my mama holding me." He sighed. "I wish I remembered her. If you didn't have that photograph, Aunt Laura, I'd never know what she looked like."

Joanna glanced at Edgar, who seemed in a daze, staring out

the window. *After all these years, he still misses her. He must have loved her very much.*

"Your mother was a wonderful woman, Joe," Laura said, breaking the heavy silence that suddenly enveloped them. "And you don't need the photograph to know what she looked like. Just look in a mirror. You look just like her, except you have your father's blue eyes." Joe smiled and Laura patted his hand.

"Mr. McGill, what do you think I should do about the buggy? You helped so much with buying Molly and I'd really value your advice on this, too."

"I tell you what, I'd let Jeff Peters stew a while. I'll come back into town one day next week and if the buggy is still at the livery stable, I'll haggle a little with him and get him to lower his price. Then, I'll bring you back to town, maybe on Saturday, and you can charm him into lowering it even more." His blue eyes twinkled as he teased Joanna.

"Why, Edgar McGill!" Laura pretended to be shocked. "Are you suggesting that Joanna use her feminine wiles on poor Jeff Peters?" She giggled. "Though if ever a man was susceptible to a woman's ways, it's Jeff. His wife has him wrapped around her little finger!"

Joanna was too embarrassed to join in the laughter that followed. She knew her cheeks were red and wished, not for the first time, that she could hide her emotions better.

"Good gosh, I almost forgot!" Joe said, pushing his chair back and jumping up. "Pa and I went to the post office before we came up to the store—there was a letter for you, Miss Garrett!" He pulled a slender white envelope from his pocket and handed it to her. She glanced briefly at the postmark, then quickly tucked the envelope into her purse.

"Thank you, Joe. Now, how about another piece of Mrs. Morgan's cake? My treat."

While Joe wolfed down a second piece of cake, Edgar and Laura glanced at each other, both wondering the same thing: *Why did Joanna stuff that envelope so quickly into her purse? And who wrote the letter?*

Chapter Eighteen

Joanna wasn't the only one keeping secrets about mail. Edgar had also received a letter but kept it tucked inside his shirt pocket until he was alone in his room after supper. He sat down on his bed, slit the envelope with a letter opener, and then sat for several minutes with the letter still folded in his hand.

It's not going to bite you. Go on, admit it—you're scared it might be a rejection and just as scared it might be a yes.

Edgar forced himself to unfold the letter; his eyes raced across the typed words. *We are pleased to inform you that your application has been accepted.*

He would have let out a *yippee,* but he settled for a vigorous thumping on his mattress. *I'm in! They want me to come to Philadelphia in the fall!* He read the letter through, then lay down, his arms behind his head, as he grinned up at the ceiling. *Just think—I'll be taking classes in drawing and painting and printmaking... I'll be with people who don't think, as Pa did, that art is a foolish waste of time. I can't wait.* The next thought came unwelcome and he shot straight up. *And how, pray tell, do you think you're going to do it? When there's no one else to run the farm, no one to watch over Joe and Laura.*

"Why, God?" he groaned. "Why did you give me this gift if I'll never be able to use it?!"

In her room above Edgar's, Joanna was reading and re-

reading her letter. When Joe handed it to her and she saw the Raleigh postmark, but no return address, her heart raced. *Why no return address? Is someone afraid I won't open the letter if I know who it's from?* It turned out that her anxiety was for naught. The letter was from Susannah York. *If I'd just looked at the handwriting, instead of fretting, I would have known it was from Susannah. Why, oh why, can't I learn not to borrow trouble?*

25th of February, 1885

Dear Joanna,

Have you forgotten that we have quite good mail service these days, or have you turned your back on us Rebels, now that you're up in Yankee land? I want to know how you are! Do you like the school? Do you have many students? Have you found a place to live? Are you happy?

I've been very busy this term as they asked me to teach a religion class along with my usual history classes. How I wish you were here to join in our discussions! The class includes three Presbyterians, two Methodists, and ten Baptists. You can imagine my challenge. We've already had heated discussions about infant baptism and I can't wait until we address predestination! But the girls are thinking about their faith, and that's so important— don't you think?

In February I took the train to Lynchburg, Virginia, to attend a meeting at the home of Ora Gray Langhorne. As you know, my sister Sarah resides in Lynchburg and she became acquainted with Mrs. Langhorne through church. It was a most interesting evening at which we discussed the plight of former slaves, as well as the suffrage issue. I was heartened to spend time with a group of women unafraid to broach the subject. Would that our own old North state had such a group!

I saw your brother Samuel last week. He was in town on business and we happened to choose the same restaurant for dinner. Samuel was quite cordial to me, which took me a bit by surprise after how your parents reacted to our trip to Petersburg and all that happened there. I wish I could tell you that Samuel asked about you, but he did not. I volunteered that you took a teaching position in Indiana and it seemed that was news to him. Did you not tell your parents where you were going? If not, I think you really must. They love you, you know, Joanna, even if they are angry and confused.

I must go and prepare for class. Dear Friend, please write soon. I endeavor not to worry and you are ever in my prayers.

Fondly,
Susannah

Joanna hugged the letter to her and, as Edgar had, she lay back on her bed, thinking over its contents. *Why didn't Samuel ask about me? He knows Susannah was my favorite professor at Peace and that we are now dear friends. Did Mama and Papa not tell him what happened in Petersburg, and about the newspaper article? Or did they tell him and now he, too, has disowned me, as Nicholas did?* She pondered Susannah's advice. *I should tell Mama and Papa where I am. It's wrong to make them worry and wonder. But I'm so afraid they won't write back... or, that they will and I won't like what they say.*

"Life," she said aloud, "is too hard, Lord."

As if God were proving her right, Lucy Sheppard arrived at church just as the McGills and Joanna did. Only Edgar thought this was good timing. Much to his sister's annoyance, he offered Lucy his arm as they went up the steps.

"Why, thank you, Edgar," Lucy said. "I can always count on finding at least one gentleman at worship." She stared at him from beneath the broad brim of her bonnet. Something in her expression made Edgar uncomfortable.

"You're kind to say so, Lucy, but I'm surely not the only man here with proper manners."

"Perhaps not, but you're the only one who will go out of his way to help a lady."

"I don't think you really need much help, Lucy."

"Oh, I wasn't talking about myself, I was talking about Miss Garrett. Everyone in town knows how you drove all the way to Hanover, just to find our schoolmarm a horse."

His smile faded. "I didn't realize everyone knew my private business."

"But people *should* know about your good deed," Lucy gushed. "It's wonderful of you to take time to help Miss Garrett. She's new here and boarding with your family and I'm sure she needs a—friend." Lucy wrapped her arm around Edgar's and widened both her smile and her eyes. "But soon she'll be moving into the old Gordon place and you'll be free of any obligation to her."

You make her sound like a charity case, he thought.

Lucy kept her arm entwined in his as they came into the sanctuary.

"Look at her," Laura whispered in Joanna's ear. "If you didn't know better, you'd think they were courting."

Joanna reluctantly followed Laura's gaze. "You would think that," she said. "They make a handsome couple."

"Lucy and Ed are *not* a couple," Laura said sharply.

Edgar led Lucy to the family pew.

"Good morning," Joanna said. "Let me find you a hymnal." She reached for one off the stack in the middle of the seat.

"Why, thank you, Miss Garrett," Lucy said. "As a schoolteacher, you must be accustomed to handing out books."

Joanna heard Laura catch her breath, but Edgar seemed not to have heard the exchange. *He's probably overcome by the attar of roses Lucy is wearing,* Joanna thought. *She was a bit heavy handed with it this morning.* Joanna immediately felt a pang of guilt. *Shame on you, thinking such a thing on a Sunday morning and in church, no less.*

When they stood up to sing, Lucy held one side of the hymnal and Edgar the other. Each time they sat down, Lucy edged closer to him. He found himself concentrating less on Luke's message and more on trying to identify the fragrance that kept wafting to his nose.

After service, Lucy proudly strolled up the aisle, her arm looped through Edgar's, when Sam Bailey motioned Edgar to join him down front. Laura covered her mouth with her handkerchief to hide her delight. The three women walked up the aisle together and Luke Goodman greeted them warmly at the door.

"Good morning, Miss Sheppard," he said. "You're looking especially lovely this morning." She accepted his compliment with a smile that quickly faded as Luke continued speaking. "I missed your father at worship. Is he ill? Shall I come to call on him?" Joanna sensed that Luke knew the answer to both questions.

"He's fine, Reverend Goodman, and though you're kind to offer, a call isn't necessary," she said.

The ice in in her voice would freeze a hen, Joanna thought.

"Father had pressing business in Madison and arrived home so late last night that he felt it wise to rest this morning. *His* work is quite demanding, you know." The intent of her sarcasm was not lost on any of her listeners.

"That I do, Miss Sheppard," Luke responded. "It is very important not to overtax ourselves." He smiled. "I do hope, however, that since he refreshed his body this Sunday, dear Mr. Sheppard will be able to refresh his spirit next week. Please tell him I asked about him." Lucy acknowledged his comment with a nod and swept down the steps.

Laura stifled a giggle and reached for Luke's hand. "Why, Reverend Goodman! You were mighty hard on poor Roscoe Sheppard. How dare you expect him to be in church on Sunday when he's so exhausted from making all that money!"

"I'm the shepherd of this little flock, Laura, and I want all of my sheep safely in the fold. Roscoe hasn't been in the fold for some time. I just wanted Lucy to let him know his absence hasn't gone unnoticed."

"Oh, Miss Lucy will convey your message," Laura said, "have no doubt about it! You'll probably find Roscoe in your study bright and early tomorrow morning!"

"At least he'll be in the church," Joanna said with a grin.

"I think you've been a bad influence on Miss Garrett," Luke said, raising his eyebrows as he lifted his chin.

"I've done no such thing! Joanna came up with that all by herself!"

Luke shook his head. "I'm glad to see you, Joanna. I wanted to tell you how much I admired the horse you were driving last Sunday. Mighty fine little filly." He refrained from voicing the very male thought that ran through his mind. *Much like her owner.*

"I'm pleased with her myself," Joanna replied. "Ed—Mr. McGill helped me choose her at an auction in Hanover. I'm getting ready to move, so I'm going to need a horse—and a buggy."

"Ah, ha," Luke said. "A very wise plan." *And an even better one if it gets you and my friend together—preferably alone!*

Edgar and Sam Bailey joined them on the steps and Laura saw Edgar give a quick look-see around the churchyard. *Hoping to spot Lucy, no doubt. Thank heavens she's already gone.*

"Miss Garrett, you're just the person I was hoping to see," Sam Bailey said. "As chairman of the school board, I am delighted to tell you we'll have the house ready for you right after Easter. All it needs is whitewashing and a good cleaning." He paused.

"You might prefer to clean it yourself, so it's done to your liking."

You don't want that house cleaned to Joanna's satisfaction, Sam Bailey—you're just cheap. Joanna will clean that house over my dead body! And Laura intended to tell Joanna so.

"That is good news, Mr. Bailey. Thank you for telling me." *Once again I'll be leaving people I love.*

Later that day, both Laura and Edgar were also thinking about Joanna's upcoming departure, though neither said a word.

I'll really miss her, Laura thought. *It's been wonderful having another woman in the house again. And what about Joanna and Edgar? She's obviously falling in love with him, but she doesn't stand much chance against Lucy Sheppard, if she and Edgar aren't seeing each other every day.* Laura knew full well what Lucy had been up to in church. *Once Joanna moves, I may be seeing a lot more of Miss Lucy. Heaven forbid!*

Laura would have been more hopeful had she been privy to her brother's thoughts. *I hate to see Joanna go. I enjoy her company and I like looking at her. She reminds me of... Bessie.* As soon as the thought entered his mind, he began pacing his room. *I am not going to fall in love again! It hurt too much when I lost Bessie. I never want to feel that kind of pain again.* Then another voice whispered: *But don't you want to be loved like that again? Don't you want a good woman to come home to, a good mother for your son?*

"No!" Shock overpowered him when he realized he had spoken out loud. "No!" He burst from his room and ran out the front door. The barn was the place for a man who needed to get his mind off a woman.

Lucy Sheppard, working on needlepoint in her richly appointed parlor, had her mind on a man and wanted to keep it there. The man, of course, was Edgar. *I've got to get him to pay more attention to me. I've got to get his mind off that schoolteacher.* Lucy didn't know what she wanted from Edgar McGill, but she knew Joanna Garrett was a threat to whatever it was. As she wove the silk threads in and out of her needlework, a thought dawned in her head. She pricked her finger, then sucked the tip, and smiled at her cleverness *Edgar McGill, get ready. You're about to be undone. And you, Joanna Garrett, are about to be done in.*

Chapter Nineteen

Joanna's nose poked out from under the cocoon of quilts and she realized it was freezing. She reached for her wrapper, scrambled into it, and hurried to the window. "Snow flurries! But it's almost Easter," she moaned. She dressed quickly and headed for the kitchen, where she found Edgar stoking the stove.

"Mornin'," he said, sounding surprisingly cheerful. "Did the snow wake you?"

"No. My nose did. It was so cold it felt twice its normal size."

Edgar reached out and lifted Joanna's chin and turned her head from side to side, appraising her cute turned-up nose. His fingers were warm and his touch gentle, and Joanna had to grab the sideboard to keep from falling into his arms.

"Looks the same to me," he said seriously. "It's a bit red, but not any bigger."

"Red!" She was halfway to the small mirror near the sink when she heard his muffled laugh. She wheeled around. Edgar was standing with the dishtowel over his mouth, repressing his uncontrollable laughter.

She waggled her finger at him and used her schoolmistress voice. "That was very naughty, Edgar McGill. You might just have to stay in at recess to atone for your conduct." They burst into laughter.

"I'm glad somebody can find something to laugh about this morning." Neither Joanna nor Edgar heard Laura come down the stairs. "I, myself, am a tad grumpy. I had planned to work in the yard this morning." She shrugged her shoulders. "Oh, well, that's March in Indiana for you. Didn't I tell you, Joanna, when we were shopping for bonnets, that it isn't unheard of for us to have snow on Easter Sunday?"

"Oh, surely we'll have nice weather by then!"

"It's only two weeks away, so there might still be snow on the ground." Seeing Joanna's downcast face, Edgar quickly amended his remark. "Then again, March is just about the most changeable month there is. And Easter's in April, so we'll probably have real springy weather by then." Joanna rewarded him with a smile.

I like what I'm seeing, Laura thought, *but I won't say a word,* she thought, walking into the kitchen. *They were made for each other, but will that pigheaded brother of mine ever see it? Not as long as Lucy keeps throwing herself at him. She'll stop at nothing...* she reasoned, as she prepared the coffee. *Knowing that minx, she might just succeed!"* Laura slapped the dishcloth on the edge of the sink, startling Patches from a nap on the rug beneath her feet. "Sorry, pup," she said, reaching down to scratch behind his little ears. "I didn't mean to wake you. But the thought of Lucy and Edgar together makes my blood boil. That is one woman I never want in my family!"

The snow that darkened Monday morning stopped by dinnertime and stayed away for the rest of the week. Edgar made a midweek run into Appleton, to the livery stable to see if the buggy was still for sale. It was.

"Is that pretty schoolteacher interested in it?" Jeff asked.

Edgar feigned ignorance. "Might be, might not be. It's hard to tell with a woman."

Jeff, married to an Irish girl known for her tongue and temper, guffawed. "It's not hard to tell with my Bridget. She tells me what she thinks every minute of every day, and she tells me what I think, too!"

"Joanna Garrett's not like that," Edgar said. "But I got the feeling she was put off by the price."

"It's a fair one."

"Didn't say it wasn't. Just said Miss Garrett seemed to think it was a bit much."

"Bought that horse, didn't she? Must have some money saved up if she could buy a nice animal like that."

"Maybe so," Edgar said.

Jeff was quicker on the uptake than Edgar expected he would be.

"Then again, Jeff, maybe she spent so much on the horse that she's got to pinch her pennies now." He roamed the stable, casually glancing back to observe Jeff; his brow was furrowed as he stood stroking his beard. *Got to you that time, Jeff, didn't I? Got you wondering if you lost a potential buyer.*

When Edgar told them about his conversation over supper, Laura was worried. "Are you sure you didn't queer the deal for Joanna? Jeff Peters isn't stupid, you know."

"Are you kidding, Aunt Laura?" Joe chortled. "Mr. Peters ain't exactly sharp as a tack, and Pa is!"

Edgar shook his head as both Laura and Joanna giggled.

"Well, Pa *is* a sight smarter than Mr. Peters!"

"Don't get in a dither, Toad, I'm not questioning your father's intelligence—just his judgment."

Joanna smothered another giggle, but Joe glared at his aunt.

"Don't look at me like that, young man," Laura said. "I know your father is one of the smartest men in Jefferson County. I also know no one would say that about Jeff Peters. I just don't want us to underestimate him, or Joanna might not get the best possible deal on that buggy."

"I'm not sure I want to buy it. I'll have so many expenses when I move and, well, I've been thinking maybe I should look for something less costly, like a buckboard."

"No one said you should buy that buggy." Edgar was quick to respond. "You may well want to look around in Madison or Hanover. I'd be glad to take you." Joanna's heart turned over in her chest. "I just wanted to get Jeff ready to dicker if you did want that buggy."

"You've still got time to look around before you go." Laura saw Edgar's blue eyes darken. She was pleased. *Think about her going, brother dear, and realize how much this woman has gotten under your skin in the last three months.*

When Saturday rolled around, it found the three McGills and Joanna up early, and on the road.

"I'm excited. This is my first trip to Madison."

"Mine, too, Miss Garrett, unless you count when Pa and Aunt Laura and me—I mean. Aunt Laura and *I*—went through there last year on the train we took to the state fair up in Indianapolis."

All of Madison seemed to be out and about when Edgar turned down Main Street. Joe almost fell out of the wagon as he went from side to side in his eagerness to see everything.

"Pa, is everyone here rich? I never saw so many brick houses, I just counted four different churches. And what is *that*?" Joe pointed to a brick building that took up almost a full city block.

"That's the Jefferson County courthouse, son. Our first stop is just beyond it." He turned off Main Street toward the Ohio River and pulled up in front of a frame building, its hand-painted sign, adorned with brightly colored birds and a heart, reading: *Koch's Buggies and Wagons*.

A gray bearded man wearing a tan leather apron over black pants and white shirt appeared at the doorway. He saw Edgar and hurried to greet them. "I'm glad to see you, my friend! It's been too long since we last met!" Jacob Koch pumped Edgar's hand. "And who are these lovely ladies with you, and this handsome young man?" Joe beamed the pleasure of being called a *young man*.

"I'm glad to see you again, too, Jacob. Let me introduce my sister, Laura McGill, and our friend, Joanna Garrett."

Jacob Koch bowed to each woman.

"And this is my son, Joseph," he said, putting an arm around Joe's shoulders.

"Your son?" Mr. Koch had hands the size of hams and extended the right one to Joe, who was caught off guard at being greeted as an adult. "But I thought your son was a mere babe! Has it been that long since we last met?"

"I guess it has, Jacob. I don't get up here often and you don't come down our way much either."

He's a delightful man, Joanna thought. *I'd like to do business with him.*

"So, what brings you to my little shop? You need a new farm wagon?"

"We're here because Miss Garrett, our new schoolteacher, bought a filly a couple weeks back. Now, she needs a buggy or she'll have to ride horse back to school."

"And why shouldn't she? God made that horse's back to hold a saddle and made us to fit in the saddle, didn't He?"

"That's a strange thing for a buggy maker to be saying, Mr. Koch." Laura said.

Jacob lifted Laura's hand and kissed it "You are so right, Miss McGill! I would be out of business if everyone rode on the horse!" He chuckled. "But, then, it's hard to fit a husband and wife and children on the back of a horse, not to mention a load of groceries or a bale of hay. So my livelihood is safe."

"What type of conveyance do you have in mind?" he asked Joanna.

"Well, I need something big enough to haul supplies and light enough for one horse to pull easily. *Miss Molly* is young and strong, but I don't want to hurt her."

"Your horse's name is *Molly*?" Jacob's expression made Joanna hesitate, but she nodded nonetheless.

The old German's hands flew up in the air and he burst into a jovial laugh. "*Ach du lieber!* She names her horse after my wife!" Jacob looked from Joanna to Laura to Edgar. He laughed so hard he had to make his way to a caned chair, where he sat laughing hysterically. His mirth was contagious, but Joanna could only manage a weak smile.

Jacob saw her distress. "My dear young woman," he said, urging her to come to his side. "Do not feel bad! It is wonderful my wife and your filly have the same name! My Molly, she will find it very funny," he said, patting Joanna's hands. She still looked doubtful. "Truly, she will. You see, Molly, is not her given name. Her real, Christian name is Amalia. Molly is my pet name for her." He chuckled again. "Your pet, my pet, both called the same. This is too wonderful!" Jacob said, wiping his eyes on his sleeve. "But we digress. You need a sturdy, well-built little buggy, just right for a young woman making her way in the world, teaching the children. Come, see what I have." He got up and lead Joanna into his workroom, filled with buggies and wagons of different sizes and shapes, some completed, some still in progress.

He pointed to a small buckboard. "Now, this might suit you, dear schoolmistress. It's small and not too high a seat, with plenty of room in the back. Or this wagonette," he said, pointing at what looked like a smaller version of the McGill's wagon. "This gate lifts down, like so, you slide things into it, like so. But she carries just two people." Joe tried his hand at raising the gate.

"It really does lift easily, Miss Garrett. And look how it lays flat on the wagon bed. Did you design it, Mr. Koch?"

"No one else in Madison builds one like it, Joseph." Joe, who rarely heard his full name, whistled softly.

Laura wandered around the shop and stopped to admire a gentleman's brougham. Jacob opened its doors to show her the leather upholstery better. "This is not what Miss Garrett requires, but isn't it fine?" Mr. Koch's pride was obvious. "My sons and I just finished making it for Dr. Taylor."

Joanna frowned, knowing she had heard that name before. Of course! The white-haired gentleman at the horse auction! "Would that be *Jonas Taylor*?"

"You know my old friend—but how can that be?"

"We don't really know each other, Mr. Koch, we just happened to be in the same place, at the same time, trying to buy the *same* horse."

"You mean Jonas wanted to buy Miss Molly?" Jacob laughed uncontrollably again, bent over, and slapped his knees. "Oh, this is too rich! My old friend trying to buy the horse named for my wife."

"But that wasn't her name then!" Joe said. "The horse didn't have a name when Pa and Miss Garrett bought her. It was *me* who came up with the name *Molly*. Goes real well with Dolly."

Jacob Koch gave the boy a blank stare.

"Dolly's *our* horse," Joe explained. "Dolly and Molly, see?"

Wise, kindly Jacob Koch understood more than Joe intended. *Why does this boy care so much that his teacher's horse has a name that goes well with that of his father's animal? He must think the father and the schoolteacher go well together, too.*

"Ah, ha. That explains it!." Jacob turned back to Edgar and Joanna. "And where did you and Jonas wage this bidding war?"

"Hanover," Edgar said.

"So, my friend did not roam too far from home. I thought as much. Jonas doesn't often leave Madison."

Joe's curiosity got the better of him. "Mr. Koch? Why does Dr. Taylor need a nice buggy like this if he stays in Madison all the time?"

"My friend and his lady ride around Madison quite a bit, young Mr. McGill, and they like to be protected from the wind and the rain when they do."

"Is Jonas Taylor a medical doctor?" Joanna asked.

"No, no. Jonas is a church doctor."

"What's that?" Joe asked.

"Mr. Koch means he's a preacher, Joe, like Luke."

"That is right," Jacob said. "My friend was pastor of the Madison Presbyterian Church. Just think, an old Lutheran and an old Presbyterian, best friends." Once again they were treated to his deep, rumbling laugh. "We are good friends who worship the same God in very different ways."

Jonas Taylor is a minister in my own denomination, Joanna thought. *No wonder he seemed so familiar. He reminded me of Papa.* Joanna's heart ached in the momentary memory. *Oh, Papa. Will you ever love me again?*

"But all this talk isn't getting you closer to finding the right conveyance, Miss Garrett. Would you like to get in one of my little wagons?"

"I would indeed." The foursome spent a happy half hour in the shop, and Joanna eventually decided to buy the wagonette.

"I like the simple design," she told Laura, "and it's easy to get in and out of."

"And," Laura added, lowering her voice, "the price is unbelievable – even less than what Jeff Peters wanted for that used buggy!"

"Did you want to drive it home today?"

'We can't," Joanna said. "We left Molly in Appleton."

"Then, when would you like to pick it up, next week maybe?"

Joanna looked at Edgar, who answered for her.

"We'll be here on Friday, if that suits you, Jacob."

"That would be—" Jacob began.

"Pa, we don't—"

Edgar gave him a stern look, but the boy was determined to speak. "Pa, that's Good Friday. Will Mr. Koch be working? And will you and Miss Garrett be back in time for church?"

Edgar could not believe his ears. His ten-year-old son was reminding him about a holy day when he, an ordained elder, had completely forgotten it.

"You're right, son, I clean forgot." He turned to the old German gent.

"Either day suits me," Jacob said. "Our Good Friday service is at one o'clock and I do no work afterwards. So, if you are here by eleven o'clock, we will have you hitched up and on your way well before I leave for worship." He turned to Joanna. "And do you have a preference? Would you rather not travel or conduct business on Good Friday?"

She smiled so sweetly at Edgar that Jacob could not mistake the feelings she held for Edgar and it made his heart ache, remembering how it was to be young and in love.

"Let's come on Friday," Joanna said, still looking at Edgar. "That way I'll have the wagonette to start moving my things on Saturday. And I'll be there to help Laura with preparations for Easter dinner."

"Friday it is," Edgar said. "We'll be here no later than eleven o'clock, and you'll get to meet the famous *Miss Molly!*" Everyone laughed as the group exited the shop.

Joe, however, had to ask Jacob Koch one last question. "Mr. Koch, why do you have this bird on your shop sign?"

"Ah, so you have never seen a hex sign, young Joseph? When we came from Germany, we brought our German language and customs with us." He pointed to the long-tailed bird. "This is a *distelfink*, Joe. He's a good fortune and happiness bird. See how he's perched on the heart bursting with tulips?" He traced the heart with his finger. "The heart adds love; the tulips add faith. All good things are rooted in faith."

"What a wonderful custom," Joanna said. "It's new to me."

"Look around Madison today," Jacob said, "and you'll see more of them."

"I thought a hex was putting a bad spell on someone."

"No, no," Jacob said. "You see the six-pointed stars on my sign? They are for good luck. In German, the word for six is *sechs*. People who do not speak my language thought it sounded like we were saying *hex*. And the name stuck."

Joanna tapped Joe's shoulder. "When you study geometry, Joe, you'll learn that six-sided objects are called *hexagons*. Our English word *hex* comes from the Greek word that means six."

"You can tell she's a schoolteacher, yah?" Jacob Koch reached for Joanna's hand once more. "Enjoy the rest of this day, my friends." He stood in front of his shop, waving until they were out of sight.

"What a charming man," Laura said as Edgar drove them toward their lunch stop. "Why haven't I heard you talk about him, Ed?"

"Maybe because it's been years since we met at that drawing class at Hanover. That man doesn't only make beautiful buggies—he also draws the most graceful ducks and geese you've ever seen."

"I didn't know you studied drawing, Mr. McGill." Joanna was obviously impressed.

"You couldn't really call it studying, it was just one class."

"Do you work in pen and ink, in oils, or pastels?

"Sounds as if you know a bit about art yourself, Joanna," Laura said.

"I know enough to admire other people who have that talent. I don't have a lick of it myself."

"You can say that again," Joe said.

"Don't be impertinent, Joe," Edgar said.

"He's telling the truth. Little Grace Goodman draws better animals than I do. At least you can tell what hers are!"

Edgar pulled off Main Street onto a long, tree canopied drive leading to a large white house.

"It's *Beech Grove!*" Laura said, clapping her hands. "I didn't know we were coming here!"

"I thought it might be a nice treat for us and Jo— Miss Garrett," Edgar said.

Oh, just say Joanna, brother of mine!

"There's no race today, but we can see the horses and buy drinks and sandwiches at the house."

After a small, but filling meal, they roamed the grounds and stables to view the racehorses, then leisurely walked down to the tree-lined river.

"I don't know much about beech trees," Joanna said, "they're not common in the south. What are they used for?"

"The wood is used for flooring and furniture, even railroad ties. It's good fuel, too, burns real well."

"I'll have to remember that when we do our nature studies," she said.

"If you forget," he said, lifting her hand, "you just come and ask me." They walked off, arm in arm. Laura caught Joe by his shirt collar when he started after them. Joe suddenly understood.

They had only been on the road a short while when Joe let out a thunderous yawn. "Would you mind trading places, Miss Garrett? I'd sure like to lean back and rest a while."

Edgar pulled off the graveled road. Joanna took the seat beside Edgar, while Joe, with a twinkle in his eye, jumped in the back beside his aunt.

Laura smiled with an appreciative nod, thinking: *What an odd couple of matchmakers we are!*

Joanna and Edgar had no idea there was a plot afoot. Both relished the proximity that allowed easy conversation as Dolly took them home.

And Laura thought, *If Joanna was a flirt or a temptress—or that vixen Lucy Sheppard—she would be pressing her advantage with Edgar and neither Joe nor I would even be here.*

However, Joanna sat contentedly beside Edgar, chatting and

laughing, relaxed and happy, as was Edgar, who had not been so in a long time.

There was a depth to Joanna, who understood the delicate balance that contentment played in one's life... and how short lived it can be...

Chapter Twenty

"I can't believe it's almost Easter," Joanna said, turning her spoon in her cup of coffee. "I've got to start getting ready to move into the school board's house."

"Would you please stop calling it the *school board's* house, Joanna? They may own it, but you're the one who's going to live there."

Joanna nodded, all the while thinking *But I don't want to live there. I like it right here.*

"I still think you should stay with us, Miss Garrett. I like having you here and I don't see why you have to go off and live by yourself."

Laura glanced at Edgar, who chose that moment to focus on his plate of stew beef and gravy.

"I know how you feel, Joe," Laura said, "and I'm going to miss her, too." *I'll say it even if you won't, brother dear.* "But Miss Garrett won't be far away. She'll be just a few miles up the road and we'll see each other often."

"I just don't like it."

Joanna reached across and patted Joe's hand. "Thank you, Joe. That means so much to me." She forced a light laugh. "Most boys who'd had their teacher living with them for three months would be packing her bag and offering to drive her to her next place of residence!"

No one laughed.

Oh, stop pretending, Joanna told herself, *and speak from your heart.* She folded her napkin and set it beside her plate. "I'm going to miss all of you, too. It's hard for me to believe that when I got here in January, I was upset that I couldn't move right into my own house. Now, I feel as if I'm leaving home all over again." Tears filled her eyes. "So, you'll have to promise not to be strangers when I'm in—" She looked at Laura and forced a smile. "—*my* house."

"You can count on that. "I'll be up there so often you'll hardly know you live alone," Laura said, glancing to her brother.

"Me, too." Joe said, tapping his fingers as he spoke. "And I'll keep my eye out for a dog for you! A good dog like Patches would be great company."

Only later, in her room, did Joanna realize that Edgar hadn't said a word when Laura and Joe promised they'd be frequent visitors at her new home.

He didn't even say he would miss me. She plunked herself down on her bed and covered her face with the feather pillow. *How so stupid I've been! Whatever made me think I might never leave this house, that Edgar might ask me to stay here and be his wife?*

Laura was also lying on her bed, writing in her journal:

At supper tonight, we talked about Joanna leaving and how we would miss her. At least Joe and I did. Edgar said not a word. Joanna probably thinks he doesn't care, but she's wrong. I know my brother better than he knows himself some times, and this is one of those times. Though Joanna doesn't know it, she has stolen his heart and that's why Ed won't say that he'll miss her. He can be such a mule of a man, too stubborn for his own good.

She put down her pen and thought for a moment.

But it's not stubbornness that has sealed his lips. It's his fear. He's so afraid to love, he's afraid to be loved, and he's afraid of losing love again. I don't know how to help him break free of all that fear.

If Laura had been at the schoolhouse the next morning, however, she would have had cause for hope. Edgar held onto Joanna's hand after helping her down from the wagon. "I didn't say anything last night—" He closed his eyes and shook his head. "I don't know why I didn't. My sister and my son aren't the only ones who've enjoyed having you in our home. I've liked it, too."

Joanna feared she might begin to cry, but Joe saved her.

"Miss Garrett, you better get this door unlocked because people are coming."

She nodded to Edgar and silently formed the words, *thank you* as he turned and climbed back into the wagon and left.

Joanna went through the motions of teaching that day, but her mind was elsewhere. She kept seeing Edgar's face, his eyes, and replaying his words over and over in her head. *He liked having me live with them. But does he want me to stay? Does he care for me, the way I've begun to care for him?* By the end of the afternoon Joanna was exhausted from her mental calisthenics.

Edgar, too, was distracted as he shopped for groceries at Werner's Store, so much so that only when a sweet fragrance overpowered the scent of the crackers he was scooping up did he realize Lucy Sheppard was at his side. The leap from thinking about Joanna to seeing Lucy standing beside him disoriented him.

"Why, Edgar, what a pleasant surprise. What brings you to town this morning?" Her green eyes were trained on him in a way he was not accustomed, a way that made him fully aware that he was a man and she was a very attractive woman.

"I had to come in for a few things, Lucy," he stammered, "like... sugar for Laura and... a new point for my plow." For some reason he could not get his mind and mouth working together.

"What a lucky coincidence. I usually do my shopping on Wednesday, but I just had to have some of Mrs. Werner's canned peaches for the luncheon I'm giving." A woman would have inquired about the luncheon, but Edgar just stood there staring at Lucy. And then, a voice intruded.

"Mees-ah Sheppard!" It was Antonio Giannini. "Just the lady I am-ah weeshing to see!" He swept his cap off his head and bowed.

"Good morning, Mr. Giannini. Why were you looking for me?" *I can't believe Father wouldn't fire him when I asked him to. That makes me so mad!*

"I have-ah the photographs, dear lady, an-ah they are bellissima, as-ah I thought they woulda be."

"What photographs?" Edgar asked.

"The photographs of-ah the so lovely schoolteacher, Mees-ah Garrett!"   In typical Italian fashion, Mr. Giannini's facial expression left no doubt he admired Joanna's beauty. "You will-ah be pleased, I am-ah sure." He reached into his black leather satchel and began to remove them.

"Mr. Giannini!"   Lucy's voice was so loud that a few shoppers turned in her direction. "I do not conduct business in the general store." *The last thing I want is for someone to see those photographs before they come out in the paper!*

"Butt-ah course, no!" Antonio Giannini's warm smile would have softened the heart of any woman but Lucy. "I meet-ah you at the office after you and you friend have-ah feeneeshed whatever it issah you are-ah doing?" Edgar nervously cleared his throat, rather than try to dissuade Mr. Giannini from assuming that he and Lucy were having a tryst in Werner's General Store.

"Very well. Meet me at the newspaper office in one hour." Lucy said and nodded when Mr. Giannini bowed again and, thankfully, left.

She bought her peaches and a few other items and when she reached the door, she pretended to lose her grip on her parcels. Edgar rushed to help.

"Let me carry those. I'll put them in the buggy for you."

"Oh, but I walked up town this morning," she said. "I can't ask you to walk all the way home with me. I'll manage."

Laura would have gagged at the syrupy sweetness of Lucy's voice, but Edgar was oblivious to Lucy's duplicity.

"Of course I'll walk you home. It would be my pleasure."

When they arrived at the two-story brick house she shared with her father, Edgar followed Lucy around to the side entrance to the kitchen.

"I'll take the packages now, Edgar," she said, with absolutely no intention of doing so.

"No. I'll carry them in for you."

"If you insist," she demurred, guiding Edgar through the narrow entry, where she made sure she entered at the same moment as Edgar. He was caught, squashed against Lucy's chest, so near to her face that he felt the warmth of her breath. She wiggled through a half-hearted effort to get beyond Edgar, which served only to force her body even closer to his—as close as her stays and hoop would allow. By the time she broke free, Edgar was practically panting. She sashayed into the kitchen and beckoned him to follow.

"Would you like some refreshment, Edgar?" she asked as Edgar placed the packages on a highly polished oak table. "I'm in need of some myself," she said, removing her hat and gloves." The words she spoke were totally proper; it was the look in green eyes that conveyed he could partake of more than coffee, if he so desired.

"I should be getting home. Maybe another time."

"Of course," she said, "but let's make it soon. Why don't you come to the luncheon I'm giving on Friday? I'm sure you would find the company entertaining." Once again Lucy's words conveyed a double meaning and Edgar felt the uncomfortable sense of being toyed with.

"I don't want to intrude on your party."

"It's not a *party*, Edgar, it's a business luncheon. Have you heard of Lydia Lewis?"

"I have. There was a story about her in a magazine... I believe she speaks against women getting the vote, doesn't she?"

"That she does, Edgar," she said, moving closer to him. "She's not one of those strong-minded women." She looked up at Edgar, arching her brows. "No man would want his wife involved with anything as sordid as politics, now would he?"

"I can't say that he would."

"That's what my father thinks, and that's why we want Mrs. Lewis to come to Appleton on her tour," she said, laying her hand on his arm. Her touch was electric. "The last thing we'd want would be to have one of those suffragettes come here, pushing votes for women, and who knows what else." She wrinkled her nose when she said *suffragettes*. "So, will you come to lunch on Friday?"

"I'll look forward to it. What time should I be here?"

Lucy gasped. "Time! Oh, my goodness, what time is it?" She lifted the watch she wore around her neck. "I have to meet Mr. Giannini!"

"I'll walk you back uptown."

When they reached the newspaper office on Front Street, she stopped him at the door. "Thank you, Edgar, and don't forget—noon on Friday!"

"I'll be there," he said and tipped his cap. He turned around and almost ran into Luke Goodman.

"Where will you be, my friend?"

"At a luncheon for some speaker Roscoe Sheppard wants to entice to Appleton."

"I see. Is Laura going with you?"

"No, Lucy just invited me."

"Did she issue this invitation today?"

"Yes, when I walked her home from Werner's Store."

"Ah, ha," Luke said. "Lucy seems more the engraved invitation type, not one for spur-of-the-moment propositions."

"I wouldn't call it a *proposition*," Edgar said, his face reddening. It was as if Luke knew what had gone on in the Sheppard's kitchen. "It's only for dinner."

"Uh, huh," Luke said. "If you say so."

"How are you coming with preparations for the Easter service?" Edgar was eager to change the subject. "Need any help?"

"The ladies have the decorating well in hand," Luke said, "and I've about got my sermon finished. But I'd appreciate your prayers, brother."

"You've got them," Edgar said, "as always."

Laura was bent over the cook stove stirring something in a large iron pot when Edgar carried in the packages from Werner's Store.

"It's about time you got back. I need the beef bones for this soup."

Edgar stopped dead in his tracks. There were no beef bones. Lucy had driven the grocery list right out of his mind. "I forgot them."

"What do you mean, you forgot them? You wrote out a list before you left this morning!"

"I know, I know. Something came up... I just forgot."

"Must have been mighty important if it made you forget why you went to town in the first place," she muttered, stirring the mixture in the pot. "What happened?"

There is no way I'm going to tell you I spent most of the morning with Lucy Sheppard. I don't need to feel worse than I already do. "I ran into that Mr. Giannini, and then I saw Luke... I just forgot about the bones." *Not the whole truth, but not exactly a lie.*

"All right. I'll just use the ham bone I was saving for beans." She playfully swatted Edgar as he passed her. "You can make it up to me by going to that butcher shop in Madison on Friday and buying us some nice lamb for Easter dinner!" Edgar abruptly stopped in his tracks. "What's wrong?"

Edgar stood locked in silence.

"If you don't have time for the butcher shop on Friday, don't worry about it."

He was furious with himself, though he remained silent and headed to the barn. *How could I have forgotten about taking Joanna to Madison on Friday?* Alone, and in his head, he could say her name; saying it out loud was quite another thing. *Now, what am I going to do?*

Chapter Twenty-One

The next morning was a continuation of his turmoil from the night before. *Maybe I can take Joanna to Madison on Saturday—that way, I can keep my promise to her and still go to Lucy's luncheon on Friday.* He shook his head, debating with himself. *But how can I let Jacob know about the change of plans? I can't send the man a telegram and scare him out of his wits.* He shook his head and nervously ran his hands through his tousled hair. *Maybe Laura could drive Joanna over to Madison on Friday... No, I want to be alone with her.*

He leaned into the mirror on his shaving stand. "This is why you haven't gotten yourself involved with women since you lost Bessie. They make life way too complicated." He nodded to his image. "That's right." He closed his eyes, "And that's why you're standing here alone, talking to yourself."

He threw on his clothes, stomped across the room, and out into the living room.

Laura heard his heavy footsteps; she knew him so well. *Something happened in town yesterday... I'd give anything to know what it was. Whatever it was, he's not happy about it.*

Edgar seemed *different* in a way Joanna could not explain. He pulled out her chair when she brought a basket filled with pumpkin muffins to the table, and when he guided the chair in for her, his hand brushed her shoulder.

That wasn't an accident, she told herself.

He sat down across from her, and their eyes met.

Thank God I'm sitting down. Those eyes of his melt me. I'm lucky I'm not a puddle on the floor.

"Does anyone need anything from town?" Edgar asked, layering butter on his biscuit.

"You're going *back* to town today?" Laura asked.

"I forgot to stop by the post office yesterday."

You're going all the way into town to get the mail? No... it's not the mail he's going for, Laura told herself. "Maybe you could stop by the church, and see if Luke needs any help. You know how busy holy week is for him."

"I saw Luke yesterday. He said he's got everything under control."

Edgar's heart was surprisingly light as he galloped toward Appleton. He knew exactly what he had to do. Everything had become clear to him out in the barn. He'd just tell Lucy he couldn't come to the luncheon. If she got mad at him, he would deal with it. Better making Lucy mad, than breaking his promise to Joanna.

He didn't often go inside the *Gazette's* office and had no idea where he'd find Lucy. He didn't have to look far, peering in the window. She was standing behind the counter, bent over a large desk, intent on something spread out before her. Her father was beside her, also leaning over the desk.

The bell over the door alerted them to his arrival. Lucy looked up, surprise was written all over her face. She quickly pulled some papers over whatever she and her father were scrutinizing and came to him.

"Why, Edgar! This is most unexpected. I didn't think I would see you until tomorrow!"

"That's why I came," he said, speaking softly. "Is there some place we could talk— privately, I mean?"

"My office; we can talk there." She walked down the hall and motioned Edgar to follow. "I'll be just a few minutes, Father," she said, closing the door to her office behind them.

"About the luncheon tomorrow—" He fumbled with his cap. "There's a problem."

Lucy simply raised her brows.

"I can't come. I completely forgot that I have to go to Madison tomorrow and there's no way I'll be back in time for dinner. I'm real sorry, Lucy. I don't know why I didn't remember this yesterday."

So I did distract you. You're so easy to manipulate! She hung her head in disappointment. "I am crushed," she said, looking back at him, her lips pouting. "I was *so* looking forward to your company, and now you won't get a chance to meet Mrs. Lewis." *And more's the pity, Mrs. Lewis won't get to meet you. Being seated next to a handsome man like you might have helped entice her to add Appleton to her next tour.* "Can't you change your appointment in Madison?"

"No, I can't. There's no way to get word to the person I'm meeting."

"Well, I'll just have to manage somehow without you." She sighed, moving closer to him, hoping her rose scent would send him reeling in the intoxication of its allure. "Maybe you can make it up to me."

"I'll do that. In fact," he said, without giving serious thought to what he was saying, "why don't you let me take you to dinner *next* Friday? We can go to the hotel or try that new place Mr. Giannini's wife opened."

"That would go a long way toward getting back in my good graces, Edgar, but are you sure you don't have another commitment next Friday? One that would take precedence over being with me?"

"I'm positive."

"I'm so glad." She snuggled against him, caressing his face and drawing it close to hers. She kissed him, the kind of kiss that suggested so much more.

Edgar was stunned as Lucy pulled away.

"Oh, I hope I didn't offend you," she said, still so near their bodies touched. "I'm just such a— passionate woman that sometimes I quite lose control."

"No, I'm not—offended," he felt himself stammering. "Surprised, maybe." *Try stunned! I've never known a woman to be so forward!*

"I will eagerly await our dinner engagement and, perhaps, surprise you again, Edgar."

"I'll come by for you at six o'clock, I promise." He opened the door, letting Lucy precede him into the front office.

Her father was holding up a photograph, apparently trying to see it in better light. Edgar thought it was Joanna's face. *So that's what they were looking at! I'll let Joanna know Lucy's article will be out soon.* Lucy rushed to her father and pressed his hand, photograph attached, down onto the table.

"Father, Mr. McGill won't be joining us tomorrow after all. It seems he had a previous engagement that *slipped his mind.*"

Roscoe Sheppard was not in the least concerned about Edgar missing the luncheon for Mrs. Lewis. The only people Roscoe wanted at his table were the town's movers and shakers—the Garners, the Greers, the Baileys. Edgar was far from a powerful figure in Appleton. He was only a dirt poor farmer and thus mattered not a whit to Roscoe. He could tell, however, that Edgar's absence mattered to Lucy, so he feigned distress.

"Now that's very disappointing," he said. "We want to encourage Mrs. Lewis to speak here in Appleton, and I was hoping for support from our town leaders."

Me? "I know it will be an engaging afternoon," Edgar said. "I regret having to miss it, but Lucy can tell me all about it when we have dinner next week." He bowed and left them.

Roscoe hiked his eyebrows ever so slightly. *So that's the lay of the land. Lucy has her eye on this dirt farmer. I can't imagine what she sees in him.*

Lucy was so exhilarated that she could think of nothing but Edgar. *Dinner alone with him!* She had set out to recapture Edgar's attention solely for the sake of her bruised ego, but the encounter at her house had left her wanting more. She liked the feel of his muscled chest against her and the feel of his warm and hungry lips. *Edgar McGill wants me more than I wanted him.*

Roscoe and Lucy returned to the photographs strewn across the work counter.

"Mr. Giannini has outdone himself," Roscoe said.

"They are quite good, aren't they?"

"Well, consider the subject. Even a jackleg photographer would have to work to make Miss Garrett look bad. She's a beautiful woman."

"I don't think she's beautiful."

Roscoe turned to his daughter and snickered. "You're jealous."

"I am *not* jealous of Joanna Garrett! Why would I be?'

"That beautiful schoolteacher is living with that hayseed and his sister, isn't she?"

"Edgar McGill is not a *hayseed,* Father. He's an educated man who just happens to farm."

"If you say so," he said, with an even deeper snicker.

"I do say so. And I am *not* jealous of Miss Garrett. If anything, *she* is jealous of me."

Roscoe laughed out loud. "I doubt it, Lucy. She's a college educated woman with a face that would make angels weep!"

Of course you do, Father. You never seem to find anything good about me. I'm as smart as Joanna Garrett and prettier than she is and I write well, but you won't even give me a byline. "Can we get back to the photographs and my story?"

"I'm not the one who made us digress. I think these photographs belong on the front page."

"Do you mean it, Father?" She couldn't believe her ears. Her father never ran what he called *feminine foolishness* on the front page. "My story, too?"

He smirked. "I will have to rework what you've written."

"I have edited that piece—three times already."

"And it needs one more," he insisted, "so I can run it under *my* name."

"I interviewed that woman and I got Mr. Giannini to drive all the way out to the schoolhouse— I wrote every word."

"I've told you before, Lucy, I will never give a woman a byline in this paper—and that includes you."

She wanted to scream. *I won't let you do this to me again. I won't!* "Do your editing, Father. Everyone in town will know I wrote the story anyway."

"But this story won't just be read in Appleton," he said, lifting Joanna's picture. "With these photographs in the feature, I wouldn't be at all surprised if some big city papers pick it up. And that, my dear, will mean some good money for us."

Making money is all that ever mattered to you. That's why Mama left you—and me—though I know you'll never admit it.

Chapter Twenty-Two

Friday morning dawned cold but clear and Joanna and Edgar set off for Madison before eight o'clock. Time passed quickly as Joanna regaled Edgar with stories from school and, before they realized it, the entrance to Hanover College loomed before them.

"Do we have time to drive around the campus? I'd love to see it."

Edgar checked his pocket watch and smiled and looked into Joanna's eyes. "Plenty of time."

It was a good half-mile from the main road to the college, along a narrow dirt alley that curved and dipped with the course of the Ohio River. Trees, though barren, arched above their heads as a grandiose arbor that nature willingly provided.

"This drive must be absolutely beautiful when the leaves are out, and a golden canopy in autumn."

The only other woman Edgar knew who would use a phrase like *golden canopy* was his sister. He told Joanna as much.

"My father used to tell me I spoke in poetry, but my brothers just said I talked all the time." Joanna laughed. "In fact, my older brother, Samuel, always told people I said my first word—dog—when I was one—and I haven't stopped talking since!"

"I bet your father is good with words, too, being a preacher."

"My father is one of the great pulpiteers of our time. He paints pictures with his words and you can't help but feel you're in Egypt or Israel, or wherever the scripture story took place. And when he prays, you feel God's nearness." She fell into a momentary silence. "My father is a great man, and a godly man." *And oh, how I miss him!*

"I'd love to hear him preach. It's a real gift to be able to proclaim the Word so powerfully that you don't just hear and understand it, but *feel* God's power in it."

They arrived in front of a massive red brick building. "I think that's Parker Hall, where some of the classrooms are," Edgar said, taking the left fork. Joanna gasped when a chapel's soaring steeple came into view.

"Isn't it lovely?"

"Would you like to go inside?"

"Could we—do we have time?"

"We can't stay long, but we can at least see what it looks like." He pulled the team up to a hitching post near a graveled walk leading to the church. They went first to double oak doors at the main entrance, but the doors were locked.

"Maybe there's a side door," Joanna suggested. "I never saw a church without one." Indeed, on the far side of the building, a run of steps led to a much less imposing entrance. This door opened. Edgar led Joanna into a dim hallway and paused to let their eyes adjust to the sudden change in light. As they did, a slight, spectacled man wearing a clerical collar came out a nearby door.

"Good morning," Edgar said. The man was so startled that he dropped the stack of books he was carrying.

"I'm so sorry," Edgar said as they both rushed to pick up the books he dropped. The gray eyes that returned Edgar's gaze were warm and friendly, with not the slightest hint of anger.

"It's quite all right," the man said, retrieving the books Joanna had picked up. "It's just that I wasn't expecting anyone until the service at noon."

"We're on our way to Madison and my friend here wanted to see the college. When she saw the chapel, we just had to come inside." Edgar suddenly realized he hadn't introduced himself. "I'm Edgar McGill, and this is Joanna Garrett. We're from Appleton."

"Appleton!" The several books he carried prevented his attempt to clap his hands. "Then you must know my friend, Luke Goodman!"

"Indeed we do, sir. We both attend Luke's church... he's a good friend of mine. Were you two in school together?"

The man laughed. "You flatter me, Mr. McGill! I was chaplain here when Luke came through the college. A fine man and truly called to God's service."

"Reverend, may we look at the sanctuary? We need to be on our way soon, but I covet a glimpse of what I feel must be a lovely place of worship." No one could have resisted the earnest appeal in Joanna's warm dark eyes.

"My dear, I would be delighted to show it to you!" He set his books on a small table and led them down the hall. "Bless me, I haven't even told you who I am! It's a good thing my dear wife isn't here or she would scold me for forgetting my manners. I'm Charles Middleton." Edgar reached to shake his hand as the three walked into the sanctuary.

Edgar had never seen such a church. It was much larger than Appleton Presbyterian and much grander, with curved-backed walnut pews, obviously hand-carved, with seat cushions and a red-carpeted floor. The stained glass windows took Edgar's breath away.

"I've never seen stained glass windows... whoever did these was a real artist. Just look at the detail in the faces of the children sitting at Christ's feet—and look how the ray of sunshine pour through, sending prisms of color all over."

Joanna was mesmerized, though less dazzled than Edgar; she had been in large churches before. "I feel God's presence here," she said. "I could bask in it, had we the time."

"I can see you're a woman of faith, Miss Garrett, and deep faith at that." Charles Middleton gently lifted her hand. "I also wish we had time to visit, so I might get to know you better."

"Speaking of time," Edgar said, looking at Joanna, "we really should be on our way. We don't want to keep Jacob Koch waiting, especially on Good Friday."

Jacob was standing outside, looking up and down the street as Edgar drew the wagon to a stop in front of Jacob's shop.

"We must be later than I thought," he said, pulling out his pocket watch. "No, we're right on time." He helped Joanna down and called out to Jacob. "Are you looking for us?"

Jacob waved vigorously. "No, no, Edgar, it's not you and your lovely Miss Garrett who have me in the street looking like an old fool." Jacob drew near to Joanna and lifted her hand, and kissed it. "My younger son—the rascal left here an hour ago on an errand and he hasn't returned yet. What is a father to do?" Jacob eyed the two horses now tied to the hitching post. "This must be the famous Miss Molly!" He looked the filly over and chuckled. "You picked just the right name for her, Miss Garrett. She is black haired, just as my Molly used to be!"

Joanna began to shiver in the last bite of winter's hold.

"Oh, please, come inside," Jacob said, putting his arm around Joanna in a fatherly way. "We will wait no longer for Willem Koch who can't tell time!" He led them into the shop.

Joanna drew a deep inhale of the fresh brewed coffee that mingled with the scent of leather.

Edgar sniffed, too. "Since when are you running a coffee shop, Jacob?"

"You make the joke, yes? It is because you are my friends and because it is Good Friday, and I will not see you on the glorious day of resurrection." He pointed to a small table set with cups and a napkin-covered basket. "My Molly made us *osterstollen*." He lifted the napkin and revealed the braided round bread, the center of which was filled with brightly colored eggs. "This is what we have for Easter, and I asked my wife to make one early so I could share it with you."

"How thoughtful," Joanna said.

Jacob moved the chair meant for Joanna, then brought the steaming coffee pot and filled their cups. "First we thank the Lord," he said, sitting down and reaching for Joanna and Edgar's hands. All three bowed their heads as Jacob prayed aloud. When he finished, he cut three thick slices of the sweet bread, serving Joanna first, and waited. She took a bite, closed her eyes, and *oohed* the delicious pleasure of it.

"This is heavenly! It's so soft and buttery and filled with—are these raisins, or currants?"

"Both," Jacob answered, beaming delight.

"Is this an old family recipe?"

"It is. My Molly's mother gave her the recipe which *her* mother had given to her."

While they drank their coffee and savored the *osterstollen*, the shop door opened and a young man entered. Joanna knew at once it was the missing Willem Koch. His beard was brown and his figure trimmer, but otherwise he was the spitting image of his father.

"So, there you are! Did you have to go to Hanover to find the wire?"

Willem laughed. "I'm sorry, Papa. I know you expected me long ago. But I ran into Mama on Front Street and she was struggling with parcels, so I walked her home, and then, on the way back, I passed Widow Schmidt and helped her put a bushel of potatoes in her wagon and then—"

Jacob raised his hand. "We will finish our *osterstollen* and then you'll bring Miss Garrett's wagonette out for her."

Willem's eyes widened. "*Osterstollen*? Today?"

"I know, I know, it's for Easter Sunday, not Good Friday. But our friends will not be with us for Easter so your mama made this special for them."

"Do you think she would mind if I have some today and on also on Sunday?"

His father laughed. "I won't tell on you if you won't tell on me!"

Willem quickly devoured a slice of the bread.

"Willem and I will go to the workroom and, Edgar, you and Miss Garrett will go outside and wait for us."

A few minutes later, father and son drew the wagonnette out through the shop's wide doors and into the street.

"Oh, just look at it! Which one of you polished it to a faretheewell?"

"That would be me," Willem said, flashing a shy smile at Joanna.

"Let us see how the wagonnette suits Miss Molly," Jacob said, motioning to Willem to give Edgar a hand with the horse. When she was hitched up, she began pawing at the ground, as though she was a racehorse at the starting gate.

"She is a spirited one, yes?" Jacob looked to Joanna, who nodded. "So, it is right that she is named Molly. My wife, she is a spirited filly herself!" Joanna giggled and Willem Koch blushed even more. Jacob pointed a warning finger at his son. "Now, don't you be telling your Mama what I said!"

"Give me another piece of *osterstollen*, Papa, and my lips will be sealed." Jacob laughed and clapped his son on the back. "I'm glad you mentioned the *stollen*, Willem," he said. "Run back into the shop and bring the package lying on the counter." Willem did as he was told and returned.

"My Molly, she wanted Miss Laura and young Joseph to try the *osterstollen*, too," he said. "This one is for all of you to share on Easter Sunday." Joanna thanked him, then impulsively hugged the big man. Now it was Jacob's turn to blush.

"Don't you be telling your Mama about that either, Willem Koch."

"I won't, Papa—at least not today!"

Jacob helped Joanna into the wagonette and handed her the reins. "You should have no trouble with this little wagon, Miss Garrett, but if you do, you come straight to me and I will make it right!" Joanna thanked him again and clucked to Molly, who took off at a brisk trot. Joanna wanted to turn and wave goodbye, but didn't dare take her attention from driving Miss Molly. Edgar followed close behind, and she heard him shout *Happy Easter* to Jacob and Willem.

About an hour away from Madison, as they approached the village of Rose Hill, Edgar urged Dolly forward so that he and Joanna were side-by-side.

"Do you want to stop for dinner? There's a nice little hotel that serves meals, and I've heard there's a new café run by some Greek folks who just moved here."

"I am hungry, though I shouldn't be after having two pieces of Mrs. Koch's wonderful bread! I would love some coffee."

Edgar passed her, leading the way to the eatery on Main Street. He hitched Dolly, then went to help Joanna, but she declined.

"I have to get used to doing it myself. You won't be there next week when I'm driving myself around."

It wasn't that Joanna was afraid to live alone—as a child she'd had an independent streak that had often frustrated her parents—but the ever-present reality of leaving the McGill farm began to settle in.

And Edgar, though he could never admit it, was hating the ever-constant reminder that Joanna would be gone... out of his life that began each morning with her lovely smile... the way she lightly tread on the staircase at night—and the lilting sound of her voice as she read *Treasure Island* when Joe had tired of reading

They finished their meal and cups of coffee, and left the café, wishing they could tie the wagonette behind the wagon and let the horses pull them in tandem.

It was four o'clock when both wagons pulled into the farmyard and headed to the barn. Joe was there, getting a head start on the evening chores. He ran to help Joanna down and she could not refuse him.

"Boy, it's pretty, Miss Garrett, and Miss Molly looks real good hitched up to it. How'd she do on the trip?"

"She did just fine, Joe. I think she liked it!" Joanna began to unhitch Molly, but Joe quickly stepped in and took over.

"I'll give Molly some hay and water, too." Again Joanna accepted his help. She was tired and hoped for a brief rest before helping Laura fix an early supper so they could get to church on time.

Joanna walked into the kitchen and saw a pot of soup on the stove, freshly baked bread on the table, and was pretty sure she smelled an apple pie in the oven. She sniffed in appreciation and climbed the stairs to her room. She dropped her coat and bonnet on the chair, unlaced her boots, and collapsed onto the bed. Within moments, sleep had overtaken her.

Chapter Twenty-Three

Saturday morning sky was laden with clouds that threatened to dump rain or worse down on Jefferson County.

Laura and Joanna, with needlework in hand, were sitting in the kitchen. Edgar came in from the barn and poured himself a cup of coffee, with Joe following after him.

"Joanna was telling me about that delightful pastor you met at Hanover College," Laura said. "I never heard Luke mention Charles Middleton... have you, Ed?"

"Some, but more about his days in the seminary, than at college." "We're lucky to have him in a little town like Appleton."

"Speaking of little towns," Joanna said, "Edgar and I had a delicious meal in Rose Hill..."

Thank You, Lord, she said Edgar's name! and it rolled off her tongue as naturally as if she'd been saying his name forever. As it should. Their trip alone was a good thing!

"...I just love that town's name. It makes me think of a hilltop covered with roses of all colors and hues, all smelling of nature's sweetness." Joanna closed her eyes and inhaled deeply.

A clap of thunder boomed overhead and Joanna's eyes popped open. "This is not an auspicious start to Easter," Joanna said.

"Don't fret," Edgar said. "It's not raining yet, it may even blow over."

"I hope so, because I planned to carry a few things over to my house today. Mr. Bailey said the work will be finished next week, and I should move in as soon as it's ready. I don't want the trustees to think I don't appreciate what they've done for me."

"We should head over there this morning," Edgar said, "in case it does rain—or snow."

The parlor clock hadn't chimed the next hour before the loaded wagon was on its way to Joanna's new home. Laura had insisted on coming along, assuring Joanna that preparations for Easter dinner were well in hand. "Besides," she said, "I really want to see what the place looks like now."

The sky remained gray with heavy-hanging clouds that seemed to droop lower as they neared the old Gordon place.

"The front porch doesn't sag and the steps are even," Joanna said excitedly.

"Still needs a fresh coat of paint," Edgar said, "but it looks a sight better than it did in January." He helped Joanna down and she hurried up the stairs to unlock the door.

Laura followed with a crate while Edgar and Joe toted Joanna's trunk.

Joanna walked inside. "Oh! It's just darlin'!"

Someone had been through the front room with a broom and mop and the windows sparkled. The kitchen, too, had been transformed. Joanna's eyes went straight to the shiny black object in the far corner. "And a new stove!"

"It's a nice one," Edgar said, inspecting it closely. "It's not new, but it is in good condition and was put in well, too."

"I suspect that was Richard Werner's doing," Laura said, "donating a good used stove he had in stock." Laura's guess was just slightly off the mark. Only the Werners knew their old kitchen stove would be cooking Joanna's meals, while Celia had a modern *Peninsular*.

The bedrooms had also had been spruced up. Joanna was sure the glass in the windowpanes was new and the room smelled faintly of beeswax.

"You're going to need some bed ticking," Joe told her, "cuz the ones on there are flat as griddle cakes. You'll want some curtains for your windows, too, I reckon, even though nobody's within lookin' distance."

"She'll want curtains anyway, son," Edgar said. "Women just plain like curtains at the windows. Your Mama made me hang them in every room of the house, and there's no one for miles around us." It was the first time Joanna had heard Edgar speak openly about Bessie, and it moved her.

"Aunt Laura says those lace ones in our front room were Mama's favorites. She said my Mama's mama hand knit the lace especially for her when you and Mama got married. Then Mama made it into those curtains."

"That's right, son." A fleeting sadness crossed Edgar's face. "Your Mama always treasured whatever folks made by hand. And she loved her mama." He drew Joe to him. "Just like your Mama loved you." Edgar withdrew his arm. "We'd best get the last boxes inside, Joe. It's starting to rain."

Joanna remained in the bedroom. *Why, God? Why did Joe have to lose his mother and Edgar lose a loving wife? I don't understand...* Immediately a thought came to mind. *You don't have to understand.* Papa always said that.

Joanna said a quick prayer for Joe and for little Emma Patterson, whose mother might never come home. She walked into the narrow hall and sniffed the air appreciatively; her nose told her coffee was brewing.

"I thought we'd all enjoy a snack in your new house, and brighten up this rainy day a bit," Laura said, pulling a red gingham napkin off a plate of thick slices of nut bread.

When Joe and Edgar came in with the last boxes, Edgar directed his *tsk, tsk* at Laura. "I thought we weren't supposed to eat between meals. I never dreamed you'd be such a rule breaker," he said with an exaggerated frown.

Joe nearly choked on his first bite of the sweet bread.

"I guess you and Eve have something in common, sister dear. You'd have tempted Adam with that apple of yours, too!"

"We'll *never* live that one down, Joanna," Laura said with a sigh. "But, then, the Bible is full of things men can be embarrassed about, too. Cain, for example, and—"

"And King David," Joanna added, "who made, shall we say, a big mistake with Bathsheba. And then there was Jonah and—"

"All right, all right!" Edgar laughed, bowing in mock surrender. "I should have known better than to mention Eve with two churchgoing women." He looked at Joanna with a sheepish grin. "And one of them a preacher's daughter, who probably knows more scripture than I ever will!"

Joanna cherished the moment. *What a wonderful way to christen my new home. It's exactly how I want my home to be, filled with friendship and laughter and seasoned with faith.*

A light rain fell through the drive back to the farm; all arriving a bit damp, though not soaked through. Laura immediately went to the kitchen to put on a fresh pot of coffee and stoke the stove while the men put up the horse. Joanna slipped into the front room to take a closer look at the lace curtains Joe talked about. The lace had been finely knit with a pattern of roses and vines, and the hemming was meticulously done in the tiniest and finest stitches. *Both Bessie and her mother had a true gift.*

The rest of the afternoon passed in a flurry of activity. Laura and Joanna did the last of the baking and prepared a leg of lamb to go in the oven before they left for church in the morning.

By nine o'clock all were in their bedrooms, though no one could asleep. Joe was reading Louisa May Alcott's *Little Men*, loaned by Joanna to make up for the fact that they'd be lucky to finish *Little Women* before the term ended. Laura was writing in her journal. Joanna was reading her Bible, and Edgar was lying on his back in bed, staring at the ceiling and thinking about Bessie. He had refused to allow himself to think about Bessie and, for months after her death, any memories of her had brought on a tidal wave of grief and anger. He had talked with Luke over and over again, and, miraculously, he began to accept Bessie's death and slowly began to heal. He still didn't welcome the times when a word or an event made Bessie leap into his mind; he doubted he ever would.

Today had been different. When Joe mentioned the lace curtains, Edgar felt neither anger nor pain. He was able to think of Bessie and to talk about her without the pain aching inside. *Maybe now it's time to get all my memories of Bessie and the baby out of that tomb I made for them in my mind.* He lay on his bed, the bed they had shared, remembering that long ago day they had met... how beautiful she looked on their wedding day and the inexplicable joy they shared the night Joe was born. It felt good to have her back as the part of him she always would be. And he realized that, finally, he was freeing some space inside himself—making room in his heart for someone else. He knew who that someone was.

Sunlight streamed into her room this Easter Sunday morning as Joanna lay in bed, savoring the peace and joy the unexpected brightness brought her. Then she jumped out of bed and began to dress. She took extra pains with her hair, twisting it in the new French knot style, then donned her pale lavender dress sprinkled with pink and yellow roses. She fastened her pearl earrings, the pair she had been given when she turned eighteen, and added her grandmother's mother of pearl cross. Her step was as light as her heart as she descended the stairs and went into the kitchen.

Laura was sitting alone at the table. She had risen very early, awakened by a dream and unable to return to sleep. The dream was so real that when she opened her eyes she expected to see her mother standing at the foot of her bed. She felt warm and loved, as if her mother had wrapped her in her arms. Nothing ever felt as reassuring and soothing as her mother's embrace. To feel it again, even in a dream, could only be a gift. She had reached for her journal and written about the dream—its joy, and the pain of missing her mother—until her fingers hurt. Then, just as Joanna had, she prepared herself for Easter Sunday, putting on her springtime pink silk dress, and smiling at her reflection in the mirror, wondering if her mother would approve.

"You two look just like Easter posies this morning!" Edgar said, gazing admiringly, first at his sister, then at Joanna. "And, dear ladies, you can wear those new bonnets today, too! We have sunshine and blue skies this Easter morning!"

Joe bounded into the kitchen. "What's for breakfast? We didn't eat all that nut bread at Miss Garrett's house yesterday, did we? I have my mouth all set for some!"

"And good morning and Happy Easter to you, too, Toad!" Edgar playfully tousled his son's hair.

"Awh, Pa! I just combed it!" Well, he had combed most of it, except for the strand that stuck straight up on the top of his head.

"Don't worry, Joe," Laura said, smoothing down the stubborn sprout, "I have nut bread warming, but you might want to toss down some eggs and bacon along with it. Dinner will be later than usual, so you'd best be well fortified to get you through the wait!"

Edgar ate hurriedly then excused himself to change his clothes, while Laura and Joanna cleared the breakfast table. By nine-thirty, they were on the road under a sunny sky. It was still cold, but it was the kind of cold that soon gives way to the warmth of spring.

"I think we can expect that services this morning will be crowded," he said, pulling up to the livery stable. There were buggies in line, more than Joanna had seen since the night of the social and the narthex was crowded with people, many of whom she had never seen before. Laura and Joanna maneuvered their way into the sanctuary. "I do like to see the pews filled on Sunday morning," Laura said.

208 *Melissa Warner Scoggins*

"You and every preacher in the world," Joanna laughed. "My father says he can count on having the church full on two days, Easter and Christmas. He likes it, but he says he'd rather folks came regularly, instead of being lilies and poinsettias." She waved at Frances and John Lane, who were seated with a young man they didn't know. Joanna and Laura slid into their usual pew, where Joe and Edgar soon joined them.

"Look at that lady's hat," Joe whispered to Joanna, discreetly pointing frontward. Joanna easily spotted the lady in question, a stranger wearing a yellow straw hat three times as big as her head and trimmed with flowers and feathers—*and* a stuffed bird. Even Joanna, who had years of training in proper church behavior, which did not include giggling, fought to resist chuckling.

Edgar leaned over Joe to Joanna. "She got her money's worth, didn't she?"

"My baby brother still doesn't know how to behave in church, especially on Easter Sunday!" His sister mockingly chastised him, "and what is so funny?"

He tilted his head and Laura leaned forward. Her hand flew to her mouth. "Now that," she said softly, "is a hat to behold!"

The pianist began playing and the congregation slowly quieted. Five minutes later, Luke entered from the side door and, with the full dignity of his calling, walked to the pulpit.

"Hallelujah!" he cried. "Christ the Lord is risen today!" Soon the gathered believers and seekers were hearing the Word, singing praises, and basking in the joy of worship on the most significant day in the Christian calendar.

Laura especially liked Luke's message based on First Corinthians:

"Oh, death, where is thy victory? O death, where is thy sting?" Luke read the gospel's words of hope, clearly and emphatically. *"The sting of death is sin, and the power of sin is the law. But thanks be to God, who gives us the victory through our Lord Jesus Christ."*

Somehow Laura's dream seemed part of the message meant especially for her. Her mother was still alive, just not visible to her. And the life they shared was an eternal one. She felt the tears rolling down her cheeks as she stood to sing the last hymn. Joanna put her arm around Laura's waist, offering comfort and support, as Laura had always shown her.

The service had ended.

The McGills and Joanna stopped to speak with Frances Lane, who introduced the handsome young man who had been sitting with them as their grandson, Michael, who was visiting from northern Indiana.

"Do you live near DeKalb County?" Joanna inquired of the young man.

"Yes, I do, ma'am. In fact, I live right on the DeKalb County line, near a little town called Laotto."

"Do you know Abigail Wheaton? She teaches in DeKalb County. We went to school together."

"I sure do, ma'am! She's about to marry my best friend, Dan Foote!" A delighted Joanna continued chatting with the Lane's grandson then followed Laura, Joe, and Edgar as they made their way to the narthex.

She saw Lucy Sheppard waving at Edgar from the pew where she customarily sat with her father—when she wasn't sitting with Edgar. Joanna couldn't help but admire Lucy's Easter attire, a stunning black and white striped silk gown and matching hat. She didn't want to admit it, but she felt a twinge of jealousy. She quickly halted a smile when Edgar nodded to Lucy, without any exchange of words between them, and kept on walking toward the front entrance.

Luke reached for his friend's hand, then kissed both Laura and Joanna on the cheek as they followed Edgar. "Other than my wife, you two are the prettiest sights I have seen today. I like seeing women decked out in Easter finery." He took note of Joanna's surprise.

"Some preachers think such self-indulgence turns Easter into a social occasion, instead of a holy day," she said.

"Why shouldn't we greet the day of a new beginning for humanity garbed in new clothes? Seems to put on the outside what I hope is on the inside."

"I like it, too, Reverend Goodman," Joe said. "Except when a lady's hat makes it near impossible to see you in the pulpit!" Edgar admonished Joe, but everyone laughed, knowing just which woman Joe was referring to.

Luke coaxed Joe to him; he knelt down, and lowered his voice. "It was a humdinger, wasn't it, Joe?" He patted the boy on the back and waved when Joe took off running after his father who headed for their wagon. Joanna lingered to talk to Luke and, together, they joined Laura at the bottom of the steps.

Carrie Goodman joined them, though her children politely urged her home for Easter dinner.

Edgar pulled the wagon to a stop. "I knew you'd all want to visit, but can we head for home? My stomach thinks my throat's been cut!"

The three Goodman children guffawed and applauded, thrilled to hear an adult echo their feelings. They said their farewells and Edgar drove home at a good clip, letting Dolly set as fast a pace as she wanted. The mare was in high spirits and trotted briskly, tossing her mane and giving an occasional whinny.

"I think Dolly knows it's Easter," Joe said. "Maybe we shoulda got her a bonnet!"

As soon as they were inside, Joanna and Laura quickly donned aprons and went to work in the kitchen. An hour later, they were seated at the table, covered with a white lace tablecloth and adorned with a vase of spring flowers. A platter of roast lamb graced the center of the table, flanked by bowls of creamy mashed potatoes and green beans, a basket of light rolls, and cut glass bowls sparkled with jams and pickles.

"This is truly a feast," Edgar said as they all joined hands for the blessing. And when it was said, he reached for the platter of meat; Joe took the basket of bread, and they began their meal in earnest.

After Joe finished his second piece of Joanna's pound cake topped with strawberry preserves, and Edgar refused a second helping of Laura's custard pie, dinner was over.

Joanna prevailed on Laura to go upstairs to change while she started on the dishes, promising they'd trade places as soon as Laura came back and Joe ran outside to play with Patches. Edgar came up behind Joanna, who was humming to herself.

"This is the nicest Easter we've had in years," he whispered, holding her shoulders and turning her to face him. "It's because of you." His eyes searched her, his heart almost desperate in its need to know. "You bring such light with you... you've made all our lives brighter, just by being here with us. I'm going to miss you very much."

Joanna was struck dumb and still searching for words when Edgar kissed her. It was a delicate but passionate kiss, in the fleeting seconds their lips touched. She opened her eyes with a smile that made clear he hadn't overstepped his bounds.

Laura came bounding into the room. "I'm back! Your turn, Joanna!" She took the dishcloth out of Joanna's hand and pointed her to the door. Joanna and Edgar exchanged smiles of regret and, when Laura turned to the sink, they both mouthed the word, *later*.

Chapter Twenty-Four

Joanna found her pupils difficult to contain on Monday morning for she, too, yearned to be out walking, instead of cooped up in a classroom. *Something different, we need to do something different today.* She had planned a practice spelling bee in anticipation of the upcoming Open House, but decided it could wait another day.

"Boys and girls..." Every eye turned her way. "I hope you all had a wonderful Easter. Would anyone like to tell the class what they did?" Hands flew up and to Joanna's surprise, Emma Patterson's was among them.

"Emma?" The child nodded. "Will you tell us about your Easter?"

Emma began to speak, so softly that Joanna could barely make out what she was saying. "My mama came home. Mrs. Higgins brought us some stew and bread and a cake and my papa cried. And we went to church and Mama and Papa both cried."

"Oh, Emma, that's wonderful! Easter is a time for great gifts, and you and your sisters and father certainly received one. I'm so glad your mother is home."

The next hour was spent listening to stories of family get-togethers, travel as near as Smyrna and as far as Indianapolis, long church services, and plenty of food. When everyone had had a chance to speak, Joanna announced they would spend the rest of the day exploring.

"What do you mean, Miss Garrett?" Caleb Matthews asked. "We can't get on a ship and sail away!" Joanna waited for the laughter to subside.

"You're right, Caleb. What I had in mind was taking a walk down to the creek." The school echoed the chorus of *yahoos* and *whees*. "But, we'll be looking for wildflowers and identifying trees along the way, and tomorrow we must get back to our regular studies."

Joanna stuck to her guns about the nature study but let the children run and even allowed the boys, and a few daring girls, to climb the trees lining the creek.

Emma Patterson came and sat beside her on the creek bank. "I did what you told me, Miss Garrett," Emma said. "You told me to talk to God and tell God about my mama being sick and ask God to help her get well. And I did. I wasn't sure I done it right because I didn't fold my hands or get down on my knees. I just said, God, this is Emma. My Mama's sick and I sure do miss her. Please help her get well and come home. Amen!"

That night, when they were washing up the supper dishes, Joanna told Laura that Mrs. Patterson was home.

"I'm so relieved," Laura said. "I was afraid Mae might never get well. And how those poor children have missed having their mother." She paused in her scrubbing. "I think I'll take them some bread and a pot of soup. Even if Mae's well enough to come home, she must still be pretty weak and tired."

"I'll send a jar of my peach preserves with you. I won't have time to make anything, what with getting moved into the house."

"When are you planning to leave?" Laura knew Joanna planned to move out that week, she just hoped it wouldn't be until the weekend.

"On Wednesday," Joanna said. "I just have to run into town to get some ticking and a feather bed."

"You'll do no such thing!" Laura dried her hands and turned to Joanna.

"Well, I can't sleep on the ticking that's—"

"Of course not, but you don't have to spend your hard earned money on bedding. We've got ticking and mattresses up in the attic, just waiting to be used again. We'll go up right now and pick some and I'll get Ed and Joe to haul them down for us. I'll air them out for you tomorrow and you'll be all set."

"I can't—"

Laura shook her finger at Joanna. "Don't you even think about telling me you can't accept them, Joanna Garrett! I won't hear of such nonsense. That bedding isn't doing anyone a bit of good up there in the attic."

"But—"

"Not another word, Joanna Garrett. As my mother used to say, *accept graciously.* After all, we're almost family!"

The two young women had no trouble finding ticking and a feather mattress, just the right size for Joanna's new bed.

"Forgive me for being curious, Laura... but why do y'all have so much bedding in storage?"

"Some of it is from when I was away at school and working in Chicago…"

"*Chicago!* I didn't know you'd been away from home."

"I spent six months in Chicago, two of them at a writer's institute and four of them working at *The Woman's Companion.* It's a magazine, a bit like *Godey's Lady's Book.* You've probably never heard of it."

Joanna plunked herself down on the nearest flat surface, which happened to be a trunk. "I've been surprised a few times in my life," she said, "but never like this. How did you talk your parents into letting you go to Chicago? What did your brother think about it? Why did you come back?"

Laura sat beside Joanna. "You poor dear," she said, patting Joanna's hand. "I didn't mean to shock you. I tell you what, let's get Ed and Joe up here to haul down this bedding, and then you and I will have a good long talk."

Once Edgar had removed the bedding, with the barest of help from Toad, Laura and Joanna each sat in the two extra rockers that had been stored away.

"You see," Laura began, "I've always loved to write. I made up stories to tell Edgar when he was little and then I started writing them down, and when I was in the upper level at school, I started entering essay contests. I even won one, with a story titled *A Girl's Life on the Farm.* She laughed. "'Write what you know,' that's what I've always heard, and the one thing I knew a lot about was life on a farm!"

"But how did you talk your parents into letting you go all the way to Chicago to school? It took me months to convince my parents to let me go to Peace, and Wilmington is a lot closer to Raleigh than Appleton is to Chicago."

"You never met Mama. She was a lady and she was educated. Her family lived in Philadelphia while she was growing up, and Mama went to school there before they moved here when Grandpapa's business failed. Mama was very artistic."

"I've seen evidence of that in her needlework."

"Some day I'll show you one of her paintings," Laura said. "So, it didn't take much to convince Mama—but Papa was another story. He finally came around, thanks to Mama."

"So, you lived in Chicago and you wrote for a magazine. That must have been exciting."

"It was, but I didn't *write* for the magazine, I was just an assistant, a very lowly assistant. I copied stories and I got dinner for all the real writers and every now and then I got to sit in on the meetings where they decided what they were going to publish. But nothing I wrote ever got into the magazine." She paused for a moment, fingering the lace on the table cover beside her chair. "It might have, if I'd stayed longer."

"Why did you come back?"

"Papa got sick, and Mama and Ed were trying to do everything, taking care of Papa and running the farm. I couldn't stay in Chicago when I was needed here at home."

"Did you ever think about going back?"

"Yes, but by the time Papa got better, Mama had gotten used to having my help. I decided I could write in Appleton just as easily as in Chicago. The weather was better here, too."

"If *this* weather is better, I don't ever want to live in Chicago!" They both laughed. "I remember you telling me that you wrote articles for the town newspaper, but I didn't know you'd had training in journalism. Couldn't you write for the newspaper in Madison or Columbus?"

Laura shrugged her shoulder. "I guess I could. I've never tried. Seems like a paper in another town would want to know why my hometown newspaper won't publish me. Lucy Sheppard is a little hard to explain, even if her reputation precedes her."

Joanna thought of the article Lucy had written about her. "I'm anxious about what she's written about me."

"I don't think you have anything to worry about. Lucy's stuck on herself; she's catty and not much of a writer, but she knows better than to lie in print. It's not as though she can reveal some deep dark secret about you. She can only write what you told her."

"But I do have a secret, Laura..." Her lids closed tightly over her eyes; a greater power had made her say aloud the words she meant to keep to herself.

Laura was almost afraid to ask. "It can't be a bad one, Joanna."

"Oh, but it can, Laura—and it is." She began to tremble.

Concern flooded Laura's face. "Joanna... what on earth—"

Joanna finally looked into Laura's eyes. "Can you keep a secret, Laura?"

"You don't have to ask that—of course I can, and I *will*."

Everything Joanna had kept bottled up for months came gushing forth, as a river overflows its banks. She began with Nicholas Brodie, then her trip to Washington, and then the fracas after Mrs. Stanton's speech in Petersburg. The most difficult part, which triggered another onslaught of tears, was the letter her father had written and the newspaper article he included.

Their shared tears flowed and Laura could only hug Joanna, offering comfort and concern to the woman she had grown to love as a sister.

"I have a great deal to fear from Lucy Sheppard."

Especially now that Ed is caught between two women —*one of whom will stop at nothing to keep him.* "I can't imagine how Lucy could find out about any of this, Joanna. She doesn't travel and only reads local papers—the possibility that she has heard anything about that convention or what happened in Petersburg—is really quite remote."

"I know it's far-fetched. But—" she daubed her tear-laden cheeks. "—I couldn't bear the thought of everyone here feeling about me as my parents do."

"We won't."

Joanna bit her lip, trying to restrain the tears that refused to obey. "*You* might not, Laura, but—"

"Edgar won't either—not if he hears it from you."

"I can't tell him, Laura. What we have is too fragile."

"You can't build a life together without truth. A good marriage needs a good foundation." Laura smiled and lifted Joanna's chin. "Yes, I'm talking about you and Edgar. Yes, I'm talking about marriage—and yes, I *want* you to be my sister."

"Oh, Laura." It came out a sigh. "I want to be Edgar's wife... to be Joe's mother, and I want to be your sister. I can't tell him what made me run away from Raleigh and my parents. He won't understand—as Nicholas wouldn't."

"My brother isn't Nicholas Brodie—and whether he's said the words or not—my brother *loves* you."

"I want to believe that. Oh, how I want to! I've ached to tell all of you the truth all these months, from the beginning. But, promise me, Laura... *please* promise me you won't tell him."

"You have my word. Only tell him soon, Joanna."

"I'll try."

"Try *very* hard, Joanna."

"Aunt Laura... Miss Garrett?" Joe's voice came from the floor below them.

Joanna wiped her face with the hem of her skirt and put on a smile.

"Come on up, Joe," Laura called out.

"I wanted to say goodnight," he said, his head appearing just above the opening in the attic floor, "and to ask Miss Garrett if she's planning to drive to school tomorrow."

"I am, Joe, unless you'd like to take the reins for me."

The boy's grin told her he'd like nothing better. His interruption sent the women back to the chores that originally led them to the attic. Laura went in search of Edgar to remind him to put the ticking and mattress outside in the morning before loading them on the wagon.

Joanna went to her room to take stock of what she needed for her house. "I've got linens and dishes and pots and pans and a broom and a bed and a stove and a table, plus all my clothes and toiletries, and all the books I brought with me. What else do I need?" She closed her eyes. *I need Edgar.*

"Oh, Lord, please help me," she whispered as she stood at the bedroom widow. "I love him and I think You want us together. Only You can give me the strength to tell him the truth and only You will let him hear it in love. And *please*, Lord, help him to forgive me."

The next morning, while Joanna was upstairs, Laura told Edgar and Joe that Joanna planned to move out on Wednesday. Joe's reaction was just what she expected.

"I don't want her to go! I don't think she wants to go either! But if nobody's going to make her stay here, I'm going to do all I can to help her and the first thing I'm going to do is look for a puppy for her. I'll feel a lot better if she has a good dog to keep her company and guard her house."

Spoken like a man, Laura thought, *and I'm not ready for you to be one!* She also predicted Edgar's reaction:

At first he said nothing. He blindly stared at Laura, as if she'd been speaking in Greek. Then he ran his hands through his hair and said, "Well, that's about what I expected." He turned on his heels and went out to the barn.

It's dark, brother dear, and you've already done the chores. I wish you would talk to me, but I guess you have to work this out for yourself.

On Wednesday morning Joanna was late coming down to breakfast; everyone else was already in the kitchen. She poured a cup of coffee and sat down at the table and immediately sensed something was amiss. She looked from Laura to Joe, and to Edgar, and set her cup down. "What is it? Why are you all looking at me?"

"We always look at you when you come into the room," Edgar said with a smile. "What else would we do?"

"Yeah," Joe said, "today's no different than any other morning. No siree, it's just a day like any other." When he began to whistle, Joanna knew something was going on. She gave Laura an inquisitive look, but Laura only smiled and reached across the table to take her hand.

"It's your last morning with us and we wanted to send you off in style." She nodded to Joe, who leapt from his chair and bounded into the lean-to. He came back carrying a pasteboard box covered in bright colored paper.

"This is for you... from me and Pa and Aunt Laura. Open it!"

Joanna just sat there, speechless, looking at each of the McGills in turn.

Laura slid the box closer to Joanna. "Look inside."

Joanna removed the lid and lifted out the treasures within. First came a lap robe knitted in shades of blue and lavender;. then came a coffee pot and a tin of coffee, and last thing she pulled from the box was a book—a copy of *Eight Cousins or the Aunt Hill,* by Louisa May Alcott.

"The coffee pot and the coffee are from me, Miss Garrett," Joe said. "When I come to visit, I want us to have coffee and read together, just like we did here."

"And the book is from me," Edgar said. "I know how much you like Miss Alcott's works... I've never heard you mention having this one. I thought you'd enjoy some new reading material when Joe comes to visit." There was an undisguised affection in his blue eyes that made Joanna tingle.

"I made the lap robe for you to snuggle under when you sit in your rocker and read to Joe."

Joanna's thick lashes caught the bounty of tears that refused to be held back. She was deeply touched and only Laura knew why.   Joanna's departure from Raleigh had been very different—hurried, with no one coming to say goodbye, much less to bring her parting gifts. "I will treasure these gifts, just as I will cherish the memories of the time I've spent in this home. I came as a stranger and you took me in and made me a part of your family. I will be forever grateful."   More tears fell and she brushed them away.

"Don't get your new book wet, Miss Garrett," Joe warned. "My teacher says books should be treated like friends and you wouldn't drip all over one of your friends!"

Joanna laughed through her tears and accepted the dainty hand-embroidered handkerchief Laura held out to her.

Joe followed Joanna upstairs. "May I carry something for you?" Joanna turned with joy.

"What?" he said. "What did I do?"

"You said '*may!*'"

"Well, I should know it by now. I have a really good teacher and she's been able to correct me all day, and all night, too."

After Joe left with Joanna's carpetbag, she walked around the room, taking a last look at the braided rag rug, the rose embossed curtains, the roll-top desk, and the china lamp. *I was so surprised when I first saw this room*, she thought, standing by the window, and said a prayer for the one who had made the room so inviting.

By the time she came back downstairs, Joe and Edgar already had her carpetbag, book box and gifts secured in the back of the wagonette.   Laura followed Joanna outside and handed Edgar another box.

"Just a little something for your supper tonight," she said. "This will tide you over until you can get to the store and do some baking." Joanna hugged Laura.

Edgar reached for her hand to help her into the wagonette. "I'm not going to say goodbye, because I'll be seeing you this afternoon when I come to pick up Joe."

"And I'm not going to say goodbye either," Laura said, "because I don't want to!" Joanna left the McGill house on a wave of laughter.

Joanna was not laughing later that afternoon when she unlocked the door and entered her new home, but she wasn't crying either. Someone had been there earlier.

The boxes of books she had left in the room were now neatly stacked in the far corner. There was a wonderful aroma coming from the kitchen. She followed her nose and, sure enough, there was fire in the cook stove and one of her kettles on the back burner. Her small kitchen table was covered with a blue checked cloth, a vase filled with tiny purple, yellow and white flowers sat in its center. There was a piece of paper propped against the pitcher.

Dearest Joanna, I hope you don't mind that Edgar and I borrowed Sam Bailey's key to your house at church on Sunday. We didn't want you to come home to a cold house, and Ed wanted to be sure your stove worked properly. Hope you enjoy your supper and sleep well. We miss you already. Love, Laura.

P.S. "Joe says to try your new coffee pot tonight."

Joanna smiled as she collapsed onto a kitchen chair. "I cannot believe they did all this for me, after everything else they've done." *And Edgar was part of it.* The gloom that had begun to descend on Joanna evaporated.

She hauled in her gift box, the box of food and her carpetbag, then went back outside to tend to Miss Molly.

"It's just the two of us now, girl," she told the horse, settling her into the stall and giving her water and oats. "But we're going to be just fine."

When Joanna walked into her bedroom to change out of her school dress, she found the room transformed. The old ticking was gone, the new one in its place, and the featherbed was fully made, topped with the bright patchwork quilt that had covered her bed at the McGills. Two plump pillows rested against the headboard. On top of a bedside table was one of Laura's kerosene lamps, filled with oil. A low rocker stood in the corner opposite one window and there was another note.

"I told you to sit in your rocker and sip coffee, but I forgot that you don't have a rocker. This was Mama's and I want you to keep it until you have one of your own."

Joanna started crying, but they were tears of happiness and they stopped as quickly as they had begun. She went back into the kitchen and put on a pot of coffee, thinking of Joe as she did, then busied herself unpacking her carpetbag.

"And where am I going to put all my clothes? I don't have a wardrobe!" She thought a while, then snapped her fingers. "I'll hang a rope across one wall and cover it with a curtain, and that will do until I can find an inexpensive wardrobe." She clapped her hand over her mouth. "Joanna Garrett," she said sternly, "you are not going to start conversing with yourself simply because there's no one else to talk to!" She laughed, remembering how her grandmother had frequently done just that, and what her grandfather always said: "It's all right as long as she's just talking to herself, but when she starts answering herself, she's gone too far!"

Joanna's first evening in her new home was a pleasant one. She read her new book while she ate supper, being careful not to smudge the pages. For dessert Laura had sent a piece of apple pie and a chunk of cheese to go with it. *Cheese to cut the sweet, Edgar had said when Laura served apple pie my first night at the McGill farm.* Somehow it seemed right to have the same treat her first night on her own. She washed the few dishes she had used, then sat at the table and corrected papers. When bedtime came, she climbed under the familiar quilt, said a thank you prayer, and fell soundly asleep.

Chapter Twenty-Five

Joanna was happily adjusting to her new home but the McGills were finding theirs empty without her. Supper on Wednesday night was less than cheerful; conversation was sporadic and no one mentioned Joanna's absence. Finally Laura could take it no longer.

"Ed, do you suppose Joanna liked what we did today? I've been trying to imagine the look on her face when she stepped inside."

"Me, too," he said. He had no trouble seeing Joanna's lips breaking into a smile and her dark eyes shining with joy as she discovered each of their surprises. "I hope she doesn't mind us going in without her permission."

Joe came forward on his chair. "What are you talking about? What did you do?"

"We borrowed a key from Sam Bailey so we could make the house more welcoming for Joanna."

"I would of gone with you if you told me what you were gonna do," Joe said, scowling. "I would of filled her coffee pot and had it all set up on the cook stove for her."

"Toad, if we had taken you out of school, Joanna would have

known we were up to something," his aunt said, "and it wouldn't have been a surprise."

"You still shudda told me!"

"Well, you know now. Maybe you and I can go over on Saturday and see if she needs any help getting settled," his father said. "She doesn't have a wardrobe in the bedroom and she'll be needing some furniture for the front room, in case she has company."

From the look on your face, Laura thought, *I think you'll make sure Joanna receives at least one guest soon. They say absence makes the heart grow fonder— I sure hope it's true for you, dear brother!*

Laura was hanging clothes outside in the crisp cold air when Edgar returned from taking Joe to school.

"I forgot to tell you," he said, picking up one of Joe's shirts to pin on the line, "I won't be here for supper tonight."

Laura removed the clothespins from her mouth. "Oh, and where might you be going?"

"I'm having supper in town."

Something in Edgar's tone made Laura turn and look her brother in the eye. "Alone?"

"No. Lucy Sheppard will be with me."

Laura could not believe her ears. *Here I am, sure you're not only in love with Joanna, but are ready to tell her so, and then you announce you're going out with that Sheppard woman!* She turned back to the clothesline. "When did you plan all this?"

"Last week."

Laura remembered how distracted and tense Edgar had been last week when he came back from town. *If Lucy's the reason you were so testy last week, then the prospect of having supper with her may not be a happy one.* She resisted the urge to hit her brother over the head with the laundry basket and call him seven kinds of a fool for taking Lucy out to supper instead of Joanna. "Well, I hope you have a good meal." *There's no way I'm going to wish you a good time.* "Where are you going?"

"I thought we might go to that new place Mr. Giannini's wife opened."

"You're becoming quite the international diner—last week Greek soup and German pastry, this week Italian cooking!" She deliberately mentioned his trip to Madison with Joanna—her ploy worked. Edgar went to the barn thinking of the dark haired beauty, not the blonde one.

When Edgar picked Lucy up that night, however, she had his full attention. His sister could have told him that Lucy's baby blue silk gown was cut in the latest fashion, and for a reason—to accentuated every part of her shapely figure. As he sat across from her at a corner table in Margot Giannini's little restaurant, he tried not to stare at the way her neckline plunged to her bosom. Lucy pretended not to notice, but was acutely aware of the effect she was having on him.

"This is a rather different kind of restaurant," she said as they waited for someone to come and take their order.

"It sure is. Not many places in Appleton have red silk curtains at the windows, linen covered tables, and bottles of wine out on the serving counter."

When a dark haired, buxom woman appeared at their table with menus and a pitcher of water, Edgar knew at once that he was facing the restaurant's owner.

"*Buona sera*," she said, "and-ah welcome to *Casa Giannini*." Her accent was as thickly European as her husband's. "I am-ah Margot Giannini and-ah I am-ah deelighted that you choose-ah to dine with us-ah tonight."

"Thank you, Signora," Edgar replied. "We look forward to a meal that is *bellissimo*."

"You speak Italiano?!"

"Not really, no" he quickly replied. "I just picked up a few words from a childhood friend."

"I weel-ah help you learn-ah more words," Margot Giannini said, "and I will-ah give you a taste of *bellissimo* Italian cooking, too!" She told them about the evening's specials, took their order, and disappeared into the kitchen.

"I didn't know you spoke Italian. What else don't I know about you, Edgar McGill?"

"Not much," he said. "Tell me about the luncheon. Is Mrs. Lewis going to add Appleton to her next tour?"

Lucy gushed the details of what Lydia Lewis wore, what dishes were served, and who was in attendance. The waitress interrupted her, setting bowls of steaming vegetable soup before them, and Lucy continued her accounting. Edgar, who still had no answer to his original question, took a spoonful of his soup.

"So, will I get a chance to meet Mrs. Lewis?"

"Indeed you will, if you come to her lecture in June."

Edgar was puzzled. "So soon?"

"She had a cancellation and this, as it turns out, is a good location for her."

Edgar raised his eyebrows in confusion.

"She'll be in Chicago two days before she comes to us, and then she goes to Tennessee. We were in route."

"I see," Edgar said, finishing his soup and smiling at the young waitress who returned to take their bowls. "Well, you'll be mighty busy getting ready for her. Two months isn't long to plan such a big event."

Lucy had been none too pleased when Mrs. Lewis offered them a spot in her current tour. It didn't give Lucy enough time to brag about bringing a famous person to Appleton, much less to advertise the program. She was telling Edgar about her father's advertising plan when their waitress reappeared with their main course. Edgar eagerly sampled his dish, but Lucy simply stared down at her plate.

"Tell me again, what it is we're eating?"

"*Chicken cacciatore*—chicken cooked with tomatoes, onions, black olives, and garlic. It's very tasty." When Lucy still didn't pick up her fork, Edgar picked it up, cut a bite of chicken from his own plate, covered it with some of the sauce and extended the fork to her.

Her eyes widened in surprise as she chewed.

Edgar laughed. "I told you it was good, didn't I?"

Lucy took her fork back, though she left more than she ate as they chatted through dinner and through their cream cake and coffee.

"So," Margot Giannini said, planting her hands squarely on her wide hips and looking intently from Edgar to Lucy, "deed-ah you enjoy you meal?"

"We did very much," Edgar said, lavishing his contentment with his smile, a smile that warmed the hearts of many women. He reached for Margot's hand, and kissed it. "It truly was *bellissimo*."

Mrs. Giannini neither blushed nor did she feign embarrassment. "That issah what I promise, and I do-ah what-ah I promise! I hope you and you lady weel-ah come to see me again soon."

Edgar and Lucy left the restaurant and met up with Harvey and Stella Greer, who had paused on the sidewalk.

"I thought that was you, Edgar," Harvey said in his deep lawyer's voice. "Wasn't that a splendid place to dine?"

"It was indeed," Edgar said. "As good a meal as I've had since Easter Sunday."

"Where did you dine then? At the hotel?"

"No, at home, like most folks do."

"Your sister must be a mighty fine cook," Stella Harvey said, "if her meal compares favorably with Mrs. Giannini's. And, I must tell you that I've never had such wonderful bread. I could have made a meal on it alone!"

"My sister is a good cook, but she had excellent help. Joanna Garrett was still with us and she and Laura cooked together."

Both Lucy and Harvey Greer picked up on the fact that Joanna was no longer at the McGill farm.

"So, has Miss Garrett moved into the school board's house?" Harvey asked. Edgar repressed a grin, remembering Laura correcting Joanna. "I hope she finds it to her liking."

"I think she will. It's been fixed up well and with a few more pieces of furniture, she'll have a nice home."

Lucy's excitement at learning Joanna was finally out from under Edgar's roof was tempered with annoyance. *He's a bit too concerned with Joanna Garrett's welfare,* she thought. "I'm sure Miss Garrett will enjoy being so near to the school," Lucy said. "I'll have to stop by and see her soon."

"Perhaps we could go together," Stella Greer suggested. "She might want to join our literary society, Lucy."

The *last* thing Lucy wanted was to have Joanna invading her territory but, again, she knew better than to voice an objection. "What a lovely idea, Stella. Stop by my office next week and we'll plan a day for our visit."

Edgar drove Lucy home, walked her to the door and remained on the doorstep.

"Won't you come in? I'm sure there's coffee in the kitchen and you might want something to warm you before your drive home."

"I can't, I've got to get an early start tomorrow morning." He didn't tell Lucy that he and Joe wanted to get their work done quickly and then stop by Joanna's house to see how she was doing.

"All right, then I'll thank you here. I enjoyed our dinner, though I can't say I'm quite as taken with Mrs. Giannini's cooking as the Greers were."

"It's good to try new things." He reached for her hand and Lucy thought he was going to pull her in an embrace and kiss her. She was prepared to put up a short, but ineffective resistance. However, Edgar simply took her hand and kissed it, much as he had Margot Giannini's.

How dare you! she thought. *You treat me no differently than you did that... tradeswoman. Next time, Edgar McGill, things will be different.*

Joe and Edgar were up with the chickens and had finished their chores before Laura had breakfast on the table.

"You two are sure in a hurry this morning. You'd think you had to be somewhere."

"We do, Aunt Laura," Joe said, eating so quickly that pieces of egg kept slipping from his fork. "We gotta go check on Miss Garrett!"

"Well, at least give her time to have her own breakfast and get the dishes washed before we land on her doorstep."

"We? Are you coming with us?"

"I thought I might," she said, looking from her nephew to her brother, "unless you two don't want me."

Edgar looked at Joe and the boy shrugged his shoulders. Laura was annoyed and a little hurt to think they'd prefer to go alone. Then she saw the smile creep across Joe's face; they were teasing her.

"You two beat all. I don't wonder, but what Joanna is relieved to have a break from your tomfoolery."

At that very moment, Joanna was, in fact, relishing being alone. She had risen very early, wrapped herself in a quilt and positioned herself in the rocker, where she could watch the sun come up over the horizon. It was her favorite time of day, the rising sun her silent companion during the half hour she read and prayed, and sought God's presence. Unless she rose very early, Joanna didn't have time for long morning devotions when she had to get ready for school, and while at the McGills, she had not wanted to be late to help with breakfast.

The sound of a wagon coming down the road drew Joanna's attention from the weeding she was doing. She shaded her eyes, trying to see through the sun's glaring light.

"Now, what brings you out so early on a Saturday morning?"

"Came to see how you was doing, Miss Garrett," Joe said, hopping down from the wagon.

Joanna was so touched by his concern that she refused to correct his grammar. "That's very sweet of you, Joe. I'm doing fine, and I'm mighty glad to see y'all... come on inside."

Joe raced ahead and let out a gleeful shout from the kitchen. "The coffee pot works fine... little bubbles are coming out the top!"

Joanna laughed. "I've already had two cups, and we'll have some in a few minutes." She turned to Edgar and Laura and reached for their coats. "I couldn't believe what you did for me," she said, putting their coats on a peg on the back wall. "I don't know how to thank you. I was dreading coming home to an empty house, and what I found was as warm a welcome as if the two of you were here with me!" She smiled again and reached for their hands. Laura noticed how warm her fingers were, despite the fact that she had been working outside when they arrived. Edgar just felt how small and soft they were and held them tightly. "God truly blessed me by bringing me to Appleton and into your—"

Joe burst into the room.

"What's keeping y'all?"

Laura looked at Edgar, then at Joanna, and Edgar looked from Laura to Joanna and together, brother and sister said, "*y'all?*

Joanna laughed.

"Well, it slips out every once in a while!"

Joe coaxed the three of them to the kitchen. "I want to see if Miss Garrett's pot makes coffee as good as Aunt Laura's."

"Better, I'll wager," Laura said, following her nephew into the kitchen. She watched Edgar watching Joanna as she gathered mugs, filled the cream pitcher and poured the coffee. What she saw in his eyes was something she hadn't seen in a long time—tenderness, mingled with happiness and a touch of longing. It did much to relieve her anxiety about what had gone on with Lucy the night before. He had come home in such high spirits that she feared he was getting involved with Lucy. Now, she wasn't so sure. Whatever stir Lucy created in Edgar, it was nothing compared to the hold Joanna obviously had on his heart.

The foursome spent a happy morning together. Laura helped Joanna measure the windows so they could go into town and buy curtain fabric. Joe found some wood in the barn and built shelves to hold Joanna's many books. And Edgar brought a rake and a shovel and busied himself cleaning up the yard. They stopped work at noon.

"I'll have dinner ready in a jiffy," Joanna said.

"You don't need to do a thing." Laura turned to Joe. "Toad, run on out to the wagon and bring in the basket." The boy hurried out the back door and quickly returned with the picnic hamper.

"You just never stop doing for others, do you?"

"No," Edgar said, "and she never will." Laura flushed demure humility as her brother kissed her cheek and reached for the hamper. "Let's see what's in here. Joe, why don't you help Joanna make some more coffee in that pot you're so proud of?"

Joanna stopped in her tracks. *He called me Joanna!*

Laura also noted Edgar's use of Joanna's given name and had to resist doing a little jig right on the spot. *Maybe now, I can stop worrying about Joanna getting her heart broken.*

Dinner was a merry affair as they munched on bread, cheese, leftover chicken, pickled eggs and apple turnovers. When Joe declared himself full after polishing off his third turnover, Laura offered to help Joanna with the dishes.

"No, ma'am," she said firmly, "you will not be washing any dishes this afternoon. You cooked and I will clean up— and that's final!"

"My, my! You don't have to use your schoolteacher voice on me," she laughed. "I'll sit down and talk while you work!"

"Feels just like home—" Edgar said, coming in to see if the women were ready to go into town. "—the two of you washing dishes and talking in the kitchen."

"Except I'm not washing and we're in a new kitchen."

"But it does make this house feel like home," Joanna said. "Wherever we are, when we're all together, I feel at home."

The full extent of what she said didn't dawn on Joanna until they were on their way into town. *Could I have been any more obvious about my feelings! I hope they didn't realize what I said.* In fact, both Laura and Edgar had heard and fully understood what she said, though neither mentioned it to the other.

Joanna was delighted to find red and white checked gingham at Werner's that was just what she wanted for her kitchen. At Seth Greenwood's shop, Laura was the one who found the right fabric for Joanna's bedroom curtains, a calico print that would pick up the colors in the quilt she had loaned Joanna.

"I like it, Laura. I think I'll get enough to make a skirt for my bedside table, too."

Joanna accompanied the McGills on a few errands of their own and was standing behind Edgar in Thomas Cook's Apothecary Shop when Lucy Sheppard walked in. Edgar was talking with Thomas, so he didn't see Lucy come in, nor did he see the look on her face when she caught sight of Joanna standing behind him.

Joanna *felt* Lucy's look, and almost recoiled from its vehemence.

Lucy headed straight for her. "Miss Garrett, how nice to see you. I rather thought you'd be at your new home unpacking all your books."

Joanna wondered how Lucy knew she had moved from the McGills. "I have been busy getting settled in, Miss Sheppard. That's what brought me to town. There were a few things I needed to feel really at home."

"And have you found them?" Lucy asked.

"Indeed I have, Miss Sheppard. Everything I needed is right here." Her words came lilting with the soft and delicate drawl that matched the look in her eyes.

Edgar finished talking with Thomas Cook about the liniment he wanted and turned around to Joanna. She smiled at him and he smiled back, unaware of what he had interrupted.

Lucy's eyes narrowed. Although Joanna had not meant to infer that Edgar was on her list of met needs, she didn't mind that Lucy interpreted it that way. Lucy stared at Joanna and Joanna stared right back at her and, without saying a word, both women knew they wanted the same man and that neither would give up without a fight.

Edgar was baffled by the tension between the two women and looked to Laura, whose expression said: *Oh, Edgar, you have no idea what you've started.*

Lucy moved closer to him and took his arm in a possessive way. "Why Edgar, I didn't expect to see you so soon after our lovely supper last night!"

Edgar blanched. "I didn't expect to see you either. I hope you're not here because you're ill."

"No, no, I'm fine. I just stopped by to pick up some lozenges for my father. I must say, though, I feared that spicy Italian food would keep me awake all night."

Great. Now Joanna not only knows I had supper with Lucy, she knows I took her to the newest place in town.

"You needn't fear Italian cooking, Miss Sheppard," Joanna said. "Garlic is supposed to aid the digestion. What did you have to eat?"

"Now, what was the name of that dish?" she said, placing her hand to her cheek as if in a quandary. "You'll have to tell her, Edgar. You're the one who's fluent in Italian!"

Edgar blushed. "What we ate was *chicken cacciatore*. The place is nice and very different. I wouldn't be surprised if folks come from all around Madison and Hanover to try it."

"Perhaps we should run an article about it in the *Gazette*. After all, Mr. Giannini does a great deal of work for us."

At the mention of the Italian photographer, Joanna remembered the story Lucy had written about her. "Speaking of Mr. Giannini, how did his photographs turn out?"

"You'll find out soon enough—you and everyone in Jefferson County."

Chapter Twenty-Six

Try as she did, Joanna could not dispel Lucy's enigmatic comment, until she set her mind to planning the school's first Open House, which took precedence. Joanna was concerned about the spelling bee for several reasons—because there had not been any community-wide Bees since she got to Appleton, and because, though she liked the idea of having everyone participate, doing so would rapidly eliminate many of her pupils.

"I wish I could talk this over with Edgar and Laura over supper, the way we used to." A dawning struck her. "But I can! I'll invite them to supper on Saturday... I'll have plenty of time to plan the menu and shop after school on Thursday."

A note went home with Joe on Tuesday and on Wednesday morning Joanna was at her desk perusing some papers when Edgar called to her from the door.

"Just wanted to tell you thanks for the invitation and we'll all be there for supper on Saturday." Joanna stood up. "Laura wants to know if she can bring anything."

"You tell that sister of yours she is *not* to bring anything but herself and her men folk," she said, walking to Edgar who propped himself against the door. "This is one supper she won't plan, or cook, or clean up after. You tell her that, Edgar McGill, and you let her know I mean business."

He stood at attention. "Yes, ma'am. I will," he said, his

brows lifting in worried anticipation, "Just don't make me stay after school if she shows up with a loaf of bread. I can convey the message, but I can't control the response!" Joanna swatted him with the book she was holding. "Ouch!" They were still at the door laughing when the children started filing in.

When the last student had left on Thursday afternoon, Joanna quickly gathered her things and walked the half-mile home. She rearranged her hair, picked up the list she had left on the kitchen table, then went to the barn and hitched Molly to the wagonette. Molly whinnied as Joanna put on the harness. "You're glad to be going for a drive, aren't you, girl?" Joanna leaned into Molly's ear. "Me, too."

Joanna pulled rein on Molly in front of Werner's and glanced in the window. Celia Werner, standing behind the counter, was surrounded by at least a dozen customers. All were bent over looking at something on the counter. Joanna opened the door. Several heads turned with the tinkle of the tiny bell above the door, and a woman pointed a gloved finger at her and almost shouted, "Look! It's her!"

Joanna's blood turned cold; she felt rooted where she stood, the door still ajar behind her. *Oh no!* and before reason had time to set in, the entire group surged toward her, enveloping her and firing off a barrage of questions. Joanna could hardly breathe. She saw Jim Langston, reached out and grabbed his sleeve.

"You're famous, Miss Garrett," he said, waving the newspaper above the heads of those who had closed in on Joanna. "You're the front page story in the *Gazette*!"

"That's right, Miss Garrett," Celia Werner said. "I saved a paper for you, in case you didn't get into town today. I don't think they'll be any copies left by tomorrow." She motioned Joanna over to the counter and handed her a copy. Sure enough, her photograph was on the front page below a humongous headline that read, *Not Your Typical Schoolmarm*. The photograph, nearly as big as life, showed Joanna standing at the window with the afternoon sunlight illuminating her face. Dismayed though she was, she recognized the photograph as a work of art. Antonio Giannini had more than done his subject justice.

"We had no idea you attended college, Miss Garrett," Celia Werner told her. "My husband is on the school board and if he knew anything about it, he certainly didn't tell me."

"I didn't know your daddy's a preacher," Jim Langston added. "Can't say that surprises me, though. You've sure been a churchgoing woman since you came to town."

All sorts of questions came fast and furious; Joanna tried to respond, but only competed with the clamor of impatient voices. When the shop door opened again, and Luke Goodman walked in, Joanna heaved an audible sound of relief and fled to his side.

"Reverend Goodman, I need to get out of here. Can you help me?"

Though Luke had no idea why Joanna needed to be saved, he immediately offered a graceful exit. "Just the woman I was looking for," he said, taking her by the arm. "Would you be so kind as to come with me to the church, Miss Garrett?" Without waiting for an answer, Luke gently propelled Joanna out the door, walked her down the block across the street, and into the church without saying a word.

"Now, Joanna, much as I like being a knight in shining armor, we knights like to know just what kind of distress our rescued damsel was in. Was Celia Werner trying to sell you last year's peaches?"

"I wish it was something that innocuous." She held up the folded paper.

Luke eyed the top half of the paper, above the fold. "Oh, my. It looks like you're the big news for the week—" He leaned a little closer and softly whistled. Antonio Giannini's photograph had captured Joanna's beauty from her figure, high bosom and narrow waist, to her luscious lips and her dark, heavily fringed eyes. "—*and* the picture of the week, as well. Oh, my dear, you're going to be the subject of a lot of supper conversations tonight!"

"I know—and I don't like it one bit!"

All of Luke's pastoral training came flooding to the fore. "What you need is a comfortable chair and a cup of tea and a chance to read this story from beginning to end. We're going to my house." Joanna protested, but Luke insisted. "You listen to your pastor, Joanna Garrett. I know you were raised to do that!"

If Carrie Goodman was surprised to see Joanna on Luke's arm, she didn't show it. "Joanna!" Carrie greeted her friend with a hug. "What a nice surprise! Come in and sit down." She threw a questioning look at Luke.

"A seat is just what Joanna needs, Carrie," Luke said, leading their guest to a well-upholstered armchair near the fireplace. "And a cup of tea and some of those cookies you baked yesterday." When Carrie returned with the tea tray, she saw Joanna's eyes frantically searching the newsprint, and Luke standing over her shoulder trying to read the print blurred as a result of Joanna's trembling hands.

"What's so interesting?" she asked, pouring three cups of tea.

Luke looked up with raised eyebrows. "Joanna is front page news... and let me tell you, my dear, this friend of ours has been hiding her light under a bushel basket!"

"I'm not that special, Reverend. Lucy Sheppard just made it seem as if I am."

"Not Miss Sheppard, my dear, her *father*."

"It was Lucy Sheppard who interviewed me."

"Well, it's Roscoe Sheppard's name on the story, and he's done a pretty fair job with the writing."

Carrie leaned over to look at the paper. "Who took your photograph? You look positively beautiful, Joanna—not just your physical beauty, but the inner goodness in you."

"Thank you, but it was all Mr. Giannini's doing. I wanted him to photograph me sitting behind my desk."

"The man knows what he's doing," Luke agreed. "And now, Carrie, you and I should let Joanna read this story in peace and quiet, which is why I brought her here in the first place." The Goodmans took their cups of tea and a cookie and sat beside each other on the horsehair sofa opposite Joanna. Ten minutes later Joanna put down the paper and looked up at them, her face nearly colorless.

"Well, now the entire town will know my life story. Miss Sheppard—or her father—printed everything I said, and then some," she said in a weak voice, then took a sip of tea.

Luke took the paper and flipped through the pages. "Take a look at this picture!" Together he and Carrie gazed at the photograph of Joanna posed behind the geography table, one hand pretending to spin the globe, as she smiled at the camera. Where the front-page photograph emphasized Joanna's beauty, this one conveyed her intellect.

"Oh, I like this one, too. And that's the globe the town's children have all been talking about."

"Mr. Giannini was fascinated by it, too." She didn't tell Luke and Carrie, but she was deeply disturbed by the article. There wasn't an obvious error or untruth anywhere, but the way the facts had been woven together created a false impression of Joanna as a woman determined to be independent from her family. *Lucy must never know the real reason I left North Carolina. It would destroy me!*

Joanna wanted to linger with the Goodmans but had to finish her shopping, which was the reason she had come into town in the first place.

"Thank you for the refreshments, Carrie; and thank you, Luke, for rescuing me. I came into town to get some shopping done," she said, looking at her pendant watch. "The stores will be closing soon."

Luke went to the window and watched as Joanna hurried down the street. "That is one good woman. I hope the Sheppards wrote a decent article about her. And, God forgive me, decency isn't the first thing that comes to mind when I think of Lucy and Roscoe."

"Why, Luke Goodman! I can't believe you're speaking that way about a church member. And I can't believe you're still here," she said urging him to the door. "I want to read that story myself!" She shooed him out the door, but he stuck his head around it and stole a kiss.

Joanna made her way to Hogg's Butcher Shop, having been stopped only twice en route, both times by ladies who told her how interesting the story was and how pretty she looked in the photographs. She politely and humbly thanked them as she paid for the pork roast and made a quick exit, deciding to alter her recipe so she wouldn't have to return to the general store. She crossed to the other side of the street. *Coward*, whispered the little voice inside her head.

She walked by Casa Giannini and heard a loud tapping on the plate glass window. Antonio Giannini was waving wildly, then ran to the door.

"Meesah Garrett!" Mr. Giannini rushed to Joanna, grabbed her free hand and kissed it. "I am-ah feeled with joy to-ah see you today! You see-ah my pictures?"

As anxious as Joanna was to get home, she could not be rude and hurry away from the kind little man who had taken such beautiful photographs of her. "I have, Mr. Giannini, and they are quite wonderful. You are a real artist."

"But-ah, Mees-ah Garrett," he said, rolling the "r's" in her name, "No one could-ah make a picture of you and no have it-ah be lovely. You are-ah beauteeful woman and the lens," he said, lifting his shoulders up the length of his neck, "it-ah captures what it-ah sees!"

"No..." Joanna blushed, shaking her head ever so slightly. "Mr. Giannini, you can't tell me the photographer's skill has nothing to do with how well a photograph turns out. You chose where I stood... you placed my hands just so, and you looked to see where the light was coming from. It is *you* who made the photographs beautiful, not me."

Now it was Antonio Giannini's turn to blush. "You are-ah

too kind, too kind," he insisted. "Wown-ah you come inside and meet-ah my wife? I know she would-ah be enchanted to know you." He gently pulled Joanna toward the door.

"I shouldn't, Mr. Giannini. I *really* must get home and put this meat in the cellar." She lifted the parcel.

"But you must-ah come in," Mr. Giannini persevered. "A few-ah more minutes will no hurt-ah the good meat and my wife, she be, how-ah you say, sick in-ah heart if I tell her you out-ah side our very door and no come in." His almost black eyes pleaded with her.

It was too early for supper customers, so the place was empty except for a young man sweeping the floor. Antonio Giannini led Joanna to the kitchen.

"Margot!" His call seemed unnecessarily loud. "Come here! *Venga qui*! It issah Meesah Garrett!"

Like Edgar, Joanna would have known Margot to be Mr. Giannini's wife had they met on the street. Everything about the woman bespoke her Italian roots, from the color and style of her dark hair to the cut of her clothes and the hoop earrings she wore, on a weekday. Margot reached for Joanna and patted her cheeks.

"I can-ah no believe you are here, on this of all-ah days, when my Antonio's so *magnifico* pictures of you in-ah news-ah paper for all-ah the world to see! Sit-ah down..." she said gently, "let-ah me look at you!" Joanna obeyed and for several moments Mrs. Giannini scrutinized her. "You are-ah so beautiful... an-ah I can see you are-ah a good woman, too, no just-ah pretty to look at on-ah outside." Joanna smiled and was rewarded with not one, but two kisses, one on each side of her face. "What issah you have there? From-ah English butcher?"

Only a newly arrived immigrant would have described Samuel Hogg as English, when his family had been in Indiana since just after the turn of the century. Joanna meekly admitted that the package came from Hogg's shop and opened it on request.

"You are-ah cooking all-ah that pork for you'self? Or-ah maybe, you have-ah the guests for dinner?"

"I'm having some friends over for supper on Saturday."

"You would-ah like some coffee, maybe?" The abrupt segue left Joanna feeling as if she were a character in a book whose dialogue had not yet been written. "An-ah then you tell Margot how-ah you plan to cook the pork?" Without waiting for an answer, Mrs. Giannini went back to the kitchen, and returned with three cups of coffee and a plate filled with long, hard cookies. "Eat," Mrs. Giannini said.

Joanna reached for a cookie and put it to her mouth.

"No, no!" Margot and her husband spoke in unison. "You must first-ah put-ah cookie in-ah coffee," Antonio Giannini explained. "This issah *biscotti* and if-ah you eat it without-ah making it soft in-ah coffee, you break-ah you teeth!"

Joanna carefully dunked one end of her *biscotti* into the coffee mug and bit off a chunk. It was delicious, tasting of almonds and cinnamon. "This is wonderful. I've never had anything like it."

"There issah no thing like it," Margot Giannini declared. "Only Italians make-ah the *biscotti*, unless-ah you know Italians, you donn-ah have it."

Joanna finished her coffee and placed the remaining piece of her *biscotti* in her sack of groceries. "I really must go," she said apologetically, explaining to Mr. and Mrs. Giannini that she had a pork roast to get home.

"An-ah how you fix-ah you pork?" Margot asked, but without waiting for Joanna to say, Margot explained that the *best* way was to rub the pork with a mixture of seasonings and roast it in the oven with potatoes and onions. However, Joanna lacked one critical ingredient. "Garlic," the Italian said, waving her hands and heading for the kitchen. "Here," she said, handing a packet to Joanna, "issah you garlic and I put-ah some oregano and basil for you, too, to make-ah the pork extra good!" Margot leaned over Joanna and kissed her on both cheeks. "You come-ah back and eat-ah my food...yes?"

Joanna smiled. "At the earliest opportunity I have."

"Mama mia! The supper people come and I have-ah no finish-ah my sauces!" Margot raced to the kitchen and Antonio walked Joanna to the door.

"So," he said, "you glad-ah I make-ah you come in and see my Margot, no?"

"I am very glad, Mr. Giannini. Thank you."

Joanna walked the short distance to the livery stable, allowed Jeff Peters to hitch up Molly, and returned home in high spirits. Luke and Carrie Goodman's ministrations and Margot Giannini's effervescence had erased the anxiety that consumed Joanna in Celia Werner's store.

Perhaps, I will sleep well after all.

Chapter Twenty-Seven

Joanna had hoped she might make it through the weekend without having to field questions about the newspaper article, but the first student who arrived Friday morning proved how fruitless that hope had been. Freddie Schmidt came running into the building.

"Miss Garrett, have you seen it? Have you seen the story about you in the *Gazette*?"

"I have, Freddie, and I gather you have, too."

"You betcha, Miss Garrett," the chubby boy replied. "My Pa always stops by the *Gazette* office and buys a paper on his way home for dinner on Thursday, so he and Ma can read it." Freddie's father worked as a teller at Ted Garner's bank. "I look at it after I do my afternoon chores. Gosh, that's a humdinger of a picture of you on the front page!"

Albert and Charles Greer ran in right after Freddie and they were waving a copy of the newspaper.

"Look at this, Miss Garrett," Albert shouted. "You're in the paper!"

"Right on the *front* page, Miss Garrett," Charles added.

Freddie Schmidt turned and scoffed at them. "She knew before I told her anyway!" He wished he had thought to bring in the paper, though he was sure his mother never would have let him.

As their classmates trooped in, Joanna quickly ascertained that only a few children had not yet heard the news. She sighed. *I may as well just read them the article and let them look at the pictures. Then we might be able to get on with our lessons.*

Reading the article had taken longer than she expected because she'd had to stop to explain words and concepts. "One of the many surprises Miss Garrett gave the writer was the news that she is a child of the manse," Joanna read.

"What's *that?*" more than one student asked.

"David, would you like to tell your classmates what a *child of the manse* means?"

"It means her father's a preacher, like mine. A *manse* is just a fancy name for a preacher's house."

"Fancy name," Phillip Werner chimed in, "but not a fancy place!"

"Well," David shot back, "preachers don't get paid a lot like shopkeepers, but they do a lot!"

Joanna quelled the mild uproar and continued reading. She had to explain what a *college* was, and she could tell from their expressions that some students didn't believe she had gone to one. Harry Jackson, who had been absent for weeks helping his father get in the spring planting, was among them.

"Come on, Miss Garrett," he said. "The only folks in town who went to college are Doc Peters and Lawyer Greer. Them places aren't for women."

Before Joanna could correct his grammar, Grace Goodman began waving her hand, desperately trying to get Joanna's attention.

"Harry's wrong, Miss Garrett. He forgot my papa. Papa went to college and he went to seminary, too."

"But he's a man!" Harry fired back. "Your Mama didn't go to college, did she?"

Grace glared at Harry. "No, but she could have! She's a lot smarter than you, Harry Jackson!" Several students stared at Grace in a mixture of admiration and fear. *Nobody* talked to Harry Jackson that way.

"Harry," Joanna said, "it is true that not many ladies go to college. Sometimes it's because the colleges won't admit them. In fact, I couldn't go to the University of North Carolina back in my home state." Harry shot Grace a triumphant look.

"But, Grace," Joanna continued, "you're right, too. There is a college near here that has many women students— Indiana University, up in Bloomington." Harry snorted and Grace almost bounced off the seat she shared with Samantha Akers.

"Did you get a diploma, Miss Garrett?" Grace asked. "My papa did."

"Indeed I did, and I can show it to you." Joanna went to her desk and retrieved her diploma from the bottom drawer, and held it high for all the students to see. "I wouldn't have said I graduated from college if I hadn't. That would have been a lie, and I don't lie. Now," she said, setting the newspaper aside, "It's high time we got back to work!"

Edgar drove to Joanna's house on Saturday, and before he tied off Dolly's reins, Laura tapped his shoulder. "I don't want us to bring up that newspaper story or the photographs. I'm sure Joanna is tired of talking about it."

"That's about all we did at school yesterday, Aunt Laura."

"Then I'm right. We don't talk about the *Gazette* business, unless Joanna brings it up—understood?"

Joanna had the table set and the food ready when the McGills arrived. They gathered at her small table and Joanna asked Joe to say grace. As soon as he finished, Joanna passed him the platter heaped with pork and potatoes and handed a dish of creamed peas to Edgar.

"Everything looks delicious, Joanna," Laura said.

"What are those white things in the meat?" Joe asked, poking one with his fork.

"That's a garlic clove."

"Where did you find garlic?" Laura asked. "Did you pick some up in Madison?" She had a reason for mentioning Madison.

"No, Margot Giannini gave it to me."

"When did you see her?" Edgar asked, remembering the episode with Lucy the other day in town.

"I passed by the restaurant on Thursday. Mr. Giannini saw me and came running out and said I had to meet his wife. He wouldn't take no for an answer."

"But why did Mrs. Giannini give you garlic, Miss Garrett? Is that how she says hello?" Joe was confused.

"No." Joanna laughed. "I had the package that Mr. Hogg wrapped for me, and Mrs. Giannini asked what it was and how I planned to cook it. She told me I needed garlic, and promptly went to her kitchen and wrapped some up for me before I left. She even kissed me on the cheek."

"She *kissed* you?" Joe was shocked.

"In the European way, Joe, on both cheeks—but her lips barely touched my skin."

242 Melissa Warner Scoggins

My lips definitely touched yours when I kissed you, Edgar thought and, feeling his face flush, rushed his next words. "I assume she was thrilled with the photographs her husband took of you—" He wanted to bite his careless tongue. *How could I be so stupid!*

Laura regretted her brother's tactless slip, but now that the subject had been broached, they rushed to share their views.

"Those photographs are spectacular, Joanna," Laura said. "Mr. Giannini not only captured your looks, but your spirit as well."

"The article was excellent," Edgar said, "and the photographs were the best I have ever seen." No one knew he had slipped into town to buy an extra copy of the paper, which he tucked away in his bureau. Just last night he had pulled it out and gazed hungrily at Joanna's image. She had taken hold of him, more than she could possibly know—and more than Edgar was willing to admit.

"I think the story and the photographs were fine, but I wish they had never appeared in the newspaper. You have no idea what it was like when I went into town on Thursday. I was almost crushed in Werner's store." She paused to take a bit of potato. "I dread going to church tomorrow."

"That's a strange thing for a preacher's daughter to say," Joe said. Edgar and Laura, however, knew what Joanna meant.

"You'll sit with us as always, Joanna," Laura said. "And if you want, we can pick you up."

"That's a sweet offer, and I'll sit with you, of course. But I'll meet you there." She stood up and began gathering the empty plates. "Who's ready for some dessert?" Over pumpkin pie and coffee, Joanna asked Edgar and Laura about the spelling bee, but it was Joe who solved her problem.

"Why are we having the Open House, Miss Garrett?"

"I want everyone to see our schoolroom and hear how well y'all are doing in your studies."

"If you want people to know what we've learned, the town folk shouldn't be spellers. Otherwise, they'll just find out what *they* know!"

Going to church wasn't as bad as Joanna feared, though heads turned as she walked down the aisle. She was thankful she went after hearing Luke's message. She felt as if he was speaking directly to her when he read from Deuteronomy: *"Be strong and of a good courage, fear not, nor be afraid of them: for the Lord thy God, He it is that doth go with thee; He will not fail thee, nor forsake thee."*

Reluctant celebrity though she was, Joanna accepted Stella Greer's invitation to talk about Peace Institute at the next literary society meeting and also agreed to attend the Methodist women's luncheon and tell what it was like growing up as a pastor's child.

Lucy Sheppard was also getting a lot of attention, but Lucy savored every bit of it. The only thorn in her flesh was having to share the limelight with Joanna. It irritated Lucy when someone said, "you did a fine job on that interview, Lucy," and followed it with: "and, my, isn't our new schoolteacher something!" Lucy's anger was only exacerbated when she saw that Margot Giannini had pasted copies of Antonio's photographs of Joanna inside the front window of her restaurant.

"If it weren't for me," Lucy muttered to herself, "that little Italian would have remained a nobody!"

Roscoe Sheppard, unlike his daughter, relished the attention the story had garnered for his paper. Just two days after the paper came out, the *Madison Courier* had asked permission to reprint the story, along with the photographs, and the next week, other requests came in from the *Indiana Gazette* in Corydon, the *Indianapolis Journal*, and the *Vincennes Sun*.

"With any luck," Roscoe had told Lucy, "the beautiful Miss Garrett will be known throughout the country—and making more money than anything we've printed previously!"

How wonderful for you, Father. Joanna Garrett will be famous and I'll remain the nobody you've made me.

* * *

11 July 1875

"Father, it's almost time for Sunday School," Lucy called up to him. "We better hurry."

"I'm not going to church today," Roscoe Sheppard shouted back.

"But don't you remember, Father, I'm playing the piano at worship this morning?" Lucy had been practicing for weeks, ever since the preacher's wife had asked her to play in her absence, when she went to attend her daughter's wedding in Indianapolis. "You're as good as I am already," Mrs. Bennett had told Lucy. "You have a real talent for the piano."

Roscoe came to the top of the staircase. "I've heard you play *Rock of Ages* and that other piece so often I think I could play them myself. I don't need to go to church to hear them again."

"But, Father—" Lucy paused.

"What, Lucy?"

But I want you to come, she yearned to say. *I want you to care.*

"I'm waiting."

Think! Lucy urged herself. *Think of a way to get him there.* "But you have to come, Father. Mr. Bennett is gone and someone has to tell the visiting preacher how we do things. Remember how that other preacher forgot the Apostle's Creed?"

Roscoe sighed. "That man was an idiot in a clerical color. You're right, no one else is capable of taking charge. I'll be ready in five minutes."

Lucy thought her heart would burst when she sat down at the piano. Her father was sitting in the front pew. Only Roscoe and the guest pastor knew Roscoe had abandoned his usual seat so he could maintain eye contact with the preacher. There would be no slip-ups today with Roscoe Sheppard at the helm.

The first hymn was *Rock of Ages,* followed by *Nearer My God to Thee.*

Lucy played them well, but it was her final piece that she knew would thrill her audience. She had practiced and practiced *At the Cross,* written by the great Isaac Watts, which had just been put to music by Ralph Hudson, a lay preacher and music teacher from Ohio. The closer it got to the end of the service, the more nervous Lucy became.

Calm down, she told herself. *You can do this. Breathe, for heaven's sake.* Even in church, it did not occur to Lucy to ask God for help. No Sheppard asked for help from anyone, even their Creator.

Lucy launched into *At the Cross* with fervor and played it better than she ever had before. There was even a brief outburst of applause, which was unheard of at Appleton Presbyterian.

Father must have liked it, she thought. *I can't wait to hear him say, 'I'm so proud of you, Lucy – you played beautifully.'*

But Roscoe Sheppard said nothing of the sort. In fact, he said nothing at all. Other worshippers told Lucy how well she had done and the visiting preacher said he liked the new hymn—but not one word of praise came from her father. She waited and waited until Sunday dinner at the hotel when she could wait no longer.

"What did you think of the music today, Father?"

"Music?"

"Yes... Did you like what I played at church?"

"I can't say I even noticed," he said, cutting his beefsteak. "I was too busy making sure that preacher didn't do something stupid."

Tears trickled from Lucy's eyes, but she quickly dabbed them away. *Don't cry! Father hates crying.* "One of the songs was brand new, Father. Reverend Gray said he liked it very much."

Roscoe sneered. "A man who stumbled over *every* other word in his text liked the song... how nice."

You've been a fool, again, Lucy Sheppard, she told herself. *Will you never learn?*

Chapter Twenty-Eight

The month following the story's publication was a whirlwind for Joanna. She spoke to the literary society, then to the Methodist church ladies, and then at a Grange meeting.

"I hardly see you anymore," Laura had said one Sunday. "Tell me where your next speaking engagement is and I'll come. We might get a short chat in afterwards! " Laura laughed, but completely understood the circumstances.

Joanna's social calendar wasn't just filled with public speaking; Edgar had filled her every spare moment, having taken her out to supper and to Madison to see Shakespeare's *Romeo and Juliet* at the Odd Fellows Building.

The day Joanna savored, though, was the Saturday she spent fishing with Edgar and Joe at Little Otter Creek. The day turned so warm that she left her shawl in the buggy, glad she had worn a summer dress. Edgar carried the fishing poles and Joe carried the can of worms and they found places to sit under an old elm tree.

"Joe, put the worm on the hook for me, will you?"

"No, ma'am."

Joanna looked at Edgar. "Then will you do it for me?"

"I'm afraid I can't help you either." Edgar bit his tongue to keep from smiling.

Joanna peered into the bait can, tentatively put her fingers inside, but immediately yanked them back. "Please?" she entreated them once more.

"You can't fish and not bait your own hook," Joe said. "That's for sissies and gir—"

"Oh, son, you're about to get in a peck of trouble."

"You were going to say *girls*, right, Joe?"

"Yes ma'am, but I—"

"Why should I take offense at that? I am a girl, and I want one of you non-sissy men to bait this hook for me!"

They fished for an hour before digging into Joanna's picnic lunch of sliced beef on rye bread she had purchased from the German bakery, pickled eggs, canned peaches and their favorite— Joanna's pound cake. After consuming his fair share and then some, Joe leaned back against a tree and promptly fell asleep.

Edgar reached for Joanna's hand, put his finger to his lips, then whispered, "Let's take a walk."

They strolled up and down the creek, talking and looking for wildflowers.

"I think that's trillium," she said, pointing to the bank beyond the creek.

"Want to pick some?" Joanna nodded and, with a handful of the delicate flowers, they made their way across the creek, slowly and carefully stepping on the rocks protruding from the water. Joanna slipped and would have landed in the creek, but Edgar grabbed her hand and pulled her; she landed flat against his chest. His blue eyes devoured the look in hers, and then their lips met, in not one, but several hungry kisses. She drew back breathless, yet wanting nothing more than to return to Edgar's arms.

They shared another kiss the following Saturday, when Laura declared the last Saturday in May as a workday at "Joanna's place." Her house was clean and habitable, but the yard and outbuildings were a mess.

"I'll bring lemonade and lunch and Edgar will bring his wheel barrow and tools and we'll both bring Joe so we can get the outside of your place looking as good as the inside."

Everyone went straight to work and by dinnertime the yard was neat and cleaned out, including the chicken coop. Joanna wasn't keeping chickens, yet, but Laura had insisted on scouring the coop anyway.

"It smells," was all she had said.

Joe and Edgar worked in the barn after dinner while Joanna went searching for the English hoe, hoping to finish planting the small vegetable garden with Laura. She waved to Joe up in the hayloft, but Edgar was nowhere in sight. She hunted for the tool and found it, then turned to leave and bounced off of Edgar, who couldn't see her through the towering load of hay he was carrying to Dolly's stall. The pitchfork landed with a thud and hay flew everywhere. Joanna burst out laughing and picked up the hoe.

Edgar glanced up to the loft, then suddenly dove on Joanna's lips, silencing her giggles. She dropped the hoe and Edgar yelped and Joanna began laughing hysterically.

Joe poked his head over the edge of the loft. "What's going on down there?"

"Your teacher thinks it's funny to make a man toss a load of hay all over and then stomp on his foot!"

"That's right," Joanna giggled, calling up to Joe, "so you best stay where you are!"

Joe leaned back, grinning from ear-to-ear, and rubbing his hands together. "Thank You, Lord," he whispered.

The day of the Open House arrived. Joanna spent most of her time calming anxious students—the girls who were going to sing, and Jimmy Langston, who was chosen to read scripture before Luke Goodman opened the event with prayer.

"I *can't* do it, Miss Garrett," Jimmy said, his eyes wide with fear. "I don't know what made me think I could get up in front of everybody—I can't do it! I'll mess up those big words, I just know I will!"

"I can do it, Miss Garrett," Agnes Werner declared, seizing her opportunity to garner a bigger part. "Why, I probably have that scripture memorized already!"

The child's going to grow up to be just like her mother, Joanna thought, *and that's not a good thing!*

"You know how to pronounce every word, Jimmy. I chose you for this part because you read with such feeling," She lifted his chin, forcing him to look at her. "Before you start tonight, take a deep breath and look at me. I know you can do this, and I know how proud your parents will be when you do." The boy flashed a toothy grin at her. "And, if you want, we can go over it one more time, just you and I."

Although Joanna told her students to be sure and eat a little dinner, no matter how nervous they were, she did not follow her own advice. Her stomach growled, but there was no time to eat. She had Molly hitched up by five-thirty and drove to the schoolhouse, relieved that no one arrived ahead of her. She wanted some time alone, to give the room a final once over and to pray, for herself and for her students.

She had just said *amen* when voices in the school yard drew her to the window. Edgar, Laura and Joe, and the Langston family were walking up the steps.

"You're here early!"

"Not too early, I hope," Laura called back. "We thought there might be some last minute things we could help you with." Edgar had insisted they be the first to arrive so Joanna wouldn't be alone when the town descended on her.

"If she felt suffocated in Werner's store," Edgar had said, "imagine how she'll feel when all of Appleton crowds into that schoolroom." His desire to protect Joanna had elated Laura. *The man is in love. I'm sure of it.*

"Land sakes, are they coming already?" Mary Langston said.

Indeed they were, and kept coming in a steady stream. Joanna stood on the steps to greet everyone, but soon realized her hand would be numb if she shook them all. She remained by the door, welcoming her guests, and leaned over now and then to pat a little girl's head or place a reassuring arm about a nervous little boy's shoulders. At six-thirty, to Joanna's delight, Emma Patterson walked up the steps with both her father and her mother. Joanna looked for Edgar and caught his eye as he helped Frances Lane out of her buggy. As soon as Frances was safely on the ground, Edgar joined Joanna at the door.

"Could you ask one of the men to give up his seat so Mrs. Patterson can sit down?" she whispered. "She's been ill, and can't stand through the whole program."

She's like Bessie, always thinking of others, he thought, and went inside, but Luke Goodman had already given his place to Mae Patterson.

Joanna walked to the front of the room to begin the program, realizing she had never seen so many people in such a small place.

"Welcome, everyone," she said, "and thank you all for coming." As always, Joanna's voice commanded attention. People expected a high-pitched voice, but Joanna's lower, mellow tone was a real asset for a petite, female schoolteacher.

"It's wonderful to have such support from the community," she went on, "and I want to tell you how glad I am to be in Appleton, and how very proud I am of the work your children have done this term. I know they're eager to show you what they've learned, so I will ask Jimmy Langston to come forward and get us started."

She held the Bible out to Jimmy, and no one saw that she gave his hand a little squeeze as he took the Book.

From Jimmy's clear and heartfelt reading from the Gospel of Matthew, to Emily Garner's closing recital of Samuel Goodrich's geography poem, *"The world is round, and like a ball,"* the program was a rousing success. Jenny Lind could not have gotten more applause than did Samantha Akers, Grace Goodman, and Sarah Bailey's rendition of Francis Scott Key's *The Star Spangled Banner.* The spelling bee was met with equal enthusiasm. Twice Joanna had to caution the grown-ups not to spell the words out loud when a young contestant wavered. Richard Werner actually sprang to his feet and shouted, "that's my little girl!" when his Agnes spelled down David Goodman on the word *ennui.*

The program lasted for almost an hour and a half. At its end, Joanna praised her student's efforts and invited everyone to the upper floor for refreshments furnished by the Ladies Aid Society.

"And, please, be sure to look at the artwork and geography projects before you leave."

"Where's that globe—" a man called out from the back of the classroom. "—the one that was in the paper?" There were murmurs of, "oh, yes, I want to see that, too." Joanna pointed to the geography table.

Edgar had maneuvered himself to Joanna's side when the program ended and stayed there as person after person came to shake her hand, congratulate her on the students' performance, and tell her how wonderful the newspaper article was.

"You're even prettier than your picture," one older lady told Joanna. Her husband, who was giving Joanna a look that would have enraged Edgar had it come from a younger man, added, "Never had a teacher that looked anything like you when I was in school. Might have gone beyond third grade if I had!"

Lucy Sheppard, who had come to cover the event for the newspaper, overheard the comments and bristled at them all. *If I'd known how popular she'd become, I might have thought twice about writing that story.* Seeing Edgar by Joanna's side had done more to enrage Lucy than anything any of the parents could have said. Lucy Sheppard couldn't stand having another attractive woman in town, much less have her catch the eye of the man who had previously danced to her tune. *I'll just have to knock Joanna Garrett off that pedestal Father put her on. Then Edgar will forget about her and come back to me.*

It was nearly ten o'clock when a weary Joanna locked the schoolhouse door as Edgar, Laura and Joe waved goodbye to the Goodmans.

"That was really something," Edgar said. "People will be talking about it—and you—all summer."

"I hope not! I've had all the fame I can handle, thank you... I'm even more thankful Mr. Giannini didn't come and take more pictures. I don't want to see my face in the *Gazette* ever again!"

You mustn't have seen Lucy standing in the thick of the crowd, Laura thought. *If looks could kill, Joanna, you'd have been dead on the spot.*

Chapter Twenty-Nine

Spring term had ended and the two women were at the schoolhouse for a cleaning party. Joanna's first Indiana June left her breathless.

"I knew winter would be much colder here, but I never expected summer to be so much milder," Joanna said, washing the blackboard. "Folks in Wilmington say spring sweeps through on a night breeze, dragging the dense heat of summer in its wake. But not here—the mornings and evenings are cool and the afternoons are just pleasantly warm."

"I never heard anybody call an Indiana summer *mild* or *pleasantly warm*. Just you wait until July." Laura tugged another desk toward the back wall, clearing the floor to be scrubbed and waxed. "I reckon you'll find Indiana every bit as hot as North Carolina—and humid! It's like breathing water."

"Then I'll feel right at home. When I cleaned out the school in Wilmington last year, I thought I'd melt right down into my shoes!" She said, setting the chalk-filled wet rag down and leaning against the wall with a sigh.

You're homesick. I expected you to feel that way in the winter, but not now, when school went well and you and Ed are seeing so much of each other.

Joanna sank into a chair, resting her chin in her palms. "I don't know what's wrong with me. Ever since school ended last week, I've been feeling low. Maybe I miss the children." She paused, staring at her shoes. "Maybe I need a tonic."

"Maybe you need a change of scenery—like an ocean and sand and some familiar faces?"

"You think I'm homesick?"

"You haven't seen your family in a long while. I can't imagine going a week without seeing Edgar and Joe, much less months." She paused. "Though many's the day when I thought I'd like to find out!"

"I haven't seen my family since Thanksgiving." she said, getting to her feet and grabbing the mop and bucket.

"Then, I'm sure they're missing you, too... no matter what that letter said."

"Do you really think so, Laura?"

"I do. I've known you only a few months and I'd be heartsick if you walked out of my life. Your parents and your brothers must miss you terribly." She paused. "Will you think about going home for a visit? You're free as a bird until August." *And my brother would find out just how much he likes having you around...which might not be such a bad thing.*

"I wish I could..." She fought the tears welling up in her eyes. "I just can't."

"I hate seeing you hurting so." Laura hugged Joanna. "I wish I could help."

"You have helped, Laura, more than you know! I feel... lighter somehow, with you knowing what I've been—" she stooped over and wrung out the mop. "—it's as if you took some of my burden."

"That's the work of the Spirit, and it's what friends do for each other. Now—back to work!

How I wish I could do more to help her, Laura thought. *I'd like to go down to Petersburg and give that newspaper owner a piece of my mind. The nerve of him, bending the truth like that and hurting innocent people!*

Joanna's thoughts were on the people she had come to love since moving to Indiana. *I can't imagine leaving Appleton—it would break my heart... not just because of Edgar, but also because of Laura and Joe, Luke and Carrie, and John and Frances... The only person I wouldn't miss is Lucy Sheppard.* She plunked the mop so hard into the bucket of water that it swamped the floor she had just cleaned.

Lydia Lewis' speaking event had absorbed Lucy in an unending mania for perfection. The great lady would arrive in Appleton the following Friday, just one week away.

"The Grange is booked," she said to herself, sitting at her desk. "Most all of the tickets have been sold and I've got a room reserved at the Morgan House." She rolled her eyes, recalling how Mrs. Lewis had refused to stay at the grander *Hotel Jefferson* in Madison.

"I always stay in the city—or town—where I am speaking," Lydia had said. "I give my all when I speak and, afterward, I find myself quite spent. The last thing I need is a long drive before I can put my head on the pillow." Lucy had then offered her home as an accommodation, but Mrs. Lewis had quickly declined that invitation, as well.

"I know how lovely your home is, since you were kind enough to provide me lunch there, but, again, I must refuse your generous invitation. Privacy, my dear girl, is something one never gets enough of when one is a public servant, and so one must insist on it whenever possible," Mrs. Lewis had said.

"Tea at the Morgan House, Mr. Giannini's photograph session," Lucy continued musing, "followed by a rest period and a *light repast* in Lydia's room." She had wanted to give a dinner in Mrs. Lewis' honor, but the lady, again, had said *no*.

"I simply cannot eat a large meal before I speak," Lydia had insisted, "I prefer to be alone to gather my thoughts and my strength." Instead, Lydia Lewis had suggested that Lucy organize a post-speech reception.

"I would welcome nourishment at that point, my dear, and I am quite sure the people will want to talk with me." Lucy had almost laughed at her phrasing. *The people.* Queen Victoria herself could not have been more imperious. Bringing the famous speaker to Appleton would be a feather in Lucy's cap, but a little of Lydia Lewis went a very long way.

Once Lucy was comfortable that nothing had been overlooked, she stopped pretending to work on her column and actually did so. She had avoided the piece because of its subject. Her father had insisted she write about the colleges that admitted women.

"But our readers don't care about that, Father," she had argued. "It's not a very womanly thing to do."

"Going to college *may* not be feminine," Roscoe had said, "but Joanna Garrett certainly is." If Lucy were a cat, she would have arched her back

Her father didn't share all his thoughts about Joanna with his daughter. If he had, there's no telling how Lucy would have reacted. Roscoe Sheppard considered Joanna one of the smartest and most attractive young women he had ever met. *She makes me feel like a man, and glad to be one. If that's not the epitome of a womanly trait, I don't know what is.*

"And you're wrong to say our readers aren't interested in the subject," Roscoe went on. "Thanks to my story about our Miss Garrett, they're very interested in colleges that admit women *and* the women who want to attend them."

How dare you call that woman 'our' Miss Garrett? She's not even from here—and I want her gone.

"Remember, Lucy, what gets people's attention is what sells newspapers!" Roscoe rapped his pipe on his desktop, for emphasis

Roscoe was right. The issue featuring Lucy's column, titled, *Colleges that Want Girls and Why They Do*, had sold almost as many copies as the edition with the story about Joanna.

"What business does a girl have studying physiology?" Richard Werner was heard to comment after Lucy's column came out. "It's not decent for a young woman to hear about such things—especially when the teacher is a man!" There were murmurs of assent from the men gathered in the shop.

Ted Garner chimed in with, "And mathematics? I don't employ women at the bank—if I did—it wouldn't be in a position requiring the need to know higher mathematics."

Stinson Matthews threw in his two cents worth. "It's educatin' women that's got some of 'em thinking they should get the vote. Doesn't do womenfolk no good to go to school beyond sixth grade." A few of his listeners covered their mouths to hide their smiles. They knew Stinson had stopped going to school long before that.

By the time Lydia Lewis got off the train that Friday in June, tickets for her talk were long gone and people were pushing Lucy to agitation, insisting that she add more seats in the hall.

"There's plenty of room at the back," Ruth Akers told Lucy. "Just move those tables out and you can fit in twenty more people."

"We could remove the tables," Lucy acquiesced, "but that might make it awkward for the ladies serving at the reception. Perhaps, Stella Greer could hold the punch bowl while Celia Werner ladles it out." Her sarcasm was lost on Ruth. When others suggested rearranging the seats, Lucy simply said, "You should have bought a ticket when they first went on sale! You'll just have to read all about it in the *Gazette*."

Edgar was all set for the big event. He had bought two tickets back in April and planned to take Joanna, assuming, of course, that the two would attend. "I have our tickets for this Lydia Lewis event," he said, driving Joanna home after dining at Casa Giannini.

"Oh, Edgar I wish you had asked me sooner.

"But we—"

"I've already made plans to go with Annie Campbell."

"I didn't know you were friends," he said, his disappointment clear. "How did you meet?"

"The same way everyone in Henry Township meets Annie Campbell—at the post office." Edgar rolled his eyes as he helped Joanna down from the wagon. "But we've gotten to know each other better through the women's circle at church. She invited me to go to the lecture with her a long time ago."

"I guess I'd better see if Laura wants to go."

"Oh, she can't go with you either," Joanna said blithely. "She's going with Luke and Carrie."

"Oh she is, is she? Why didn't she tell me?"

"You probably forgot to ask." They were now on Joanna's porch and she was fumbling in her handbag for the door key. "But I know someone who'd love to have that ticket."

"You mean there's someone I know who isn't already going?"

"Indeed there is." Joanna enjoyed her opportunity to tease Edgar, as he made a habit of doing to her. "Margot Giannini. She's furious because Lucy won't let her accompany her husband, who'll be taking pictures."

Edgar dropped his jaw and stood staring at her. It was all Joanna could do to keep from laughing. "Oh, sure, I'll take another man's wife to the lecture," he sputtered. "People would really like that!"

Joanna decided the joke had gone far enough. She had the door open now, and pulled Edgar inside. "I don't know about other people," she whispered, "but I'd be awfully mad." Edgar pushed the door closed with his foot and took her in his arms, guiding her to the horsehair sofa, where he pulled her onto his lap and began kissing her. Several minutes later she reluctantly broke free from his embrace and leaned back, trying to catch her breath.

"So, my lovely, Miss Garrett," Edgar said, his voice husky, "do you still want me to take Margot Giannini to the lecture?"

His eyes were as purple as she had ever seen them. "No," she whispered.

He pulled her close again, his lips pressing on hers, his kisses glazing her chin, then moving down her soft, smooth neck. Joanna gently eased him away.

"We can't... do this," she said, straining for breath. "We have... we have to stop."

It hurt so much to let her go, but Edgar knew she was right. He was a man, who had been a married man, and it took every ounce of self-control within him to release her. He ran his fingers through the long ringlets around her face. *What I wouldn't give, to see your hair down around your shoulders.*

"Joanna," he said, each syllable lingering on his lips and coming as a caress. "I didn't mean to... to do this. I... I got carried away." His finger traced the side of her face and along her chin. She shivered from his touch. "I'm sorry."

"I'm sorry, too—" she whispered through heavy breaths, her eyes fixed on his. "—sorry we have to stop."

Ladies don't say such things. The thought had barely registered before familiar sounding words took its place. *Oh, yes, they do—especially when they're in love.* The thought was his. The voice he heard was Bessie's.

She watched his face flush and then turn as white as his olive skin could get. "Edgar—" she said, gently touching his cheek. "—are you all right?" He didn't respond. "I shouldn't have said that... I've shocked you, and I'm sorry."

"Don't be..." His normal coloring returned and his voice was clear and calm. His hands slid around her tiny waist and he pulled her into his arms, stopping just short of their bodies touching. The look in his eyes showed a joy she had never seen before. "I love you."." Her own eyes widened in the reality of his words. "Do you hear me, Joanna Garrett? I love you."

"Oh, Edgar, I love you so."

They sat for what seemed an eternity, speechless and beguiled in the wonder of the love they professed for each other. Edgar caressed Joanna's face and eased her close for another kiss, a kiss unlike any they had shared before. Gentle, yet passionate, the kiss that happens just once, when lovers first acknowledge their love. Neither wanted it to end.

Joanna drew back and Edgar thought she had never looked more beautiful, or happier. The moon's soft light sparkled in her brown eyes and placed a glow on her cheeks, while her parted lips invited his.

"No..." Joanna whispered, again, gently easing him away. She saw the desire in his eyes and could only imagine that he was seeing the same in hers. *I can't give in to it.* She sat up, smoothed her skirt, and tucked her hair back into place. "I'll make some coffee."

"If you insist," he said. *Of course, she's right, we have to stop—but, oh, how I wish we didn't.* He followed Joanna to the kitchen, watching her stoke the stove with wood chips and strike the long stick match. She went to the pantry, lifted out the small sack of coffee, filled the pot with water, then reached into the cupboard for two mugs and plates. Her face radiated such happiness that every movement she made seemed infused with joy. *I wish I could paint you, right now,* he thought. *I want to remember how you look, now that you've told me how much you love me.*

"A penny for your thoughts," she said, kissing his forehead as she set their mugs on the table.

"I wish I had my sketchbook and some pencils."

"Why?"

"So I can draw you, of course! I want to capture how you look right now, this moment."

"And *how* do I look?"

"Like a woman in love—who knows her love is returned." Their eyes confirmed the almost magnetic lure between their two hearts.

"I have some paper in my room, and some pens and pencils; even some colored pencils that I brought home from the schoolhouse."

He stood up. "Tell me where—" but Joanna was gone in an instant, reappearing with a stack of paper and a handful of pencils in a tin.

"Will these do?"

"Yes—now go back to what you were doing. Pretend I'm not here."

As if that were possible, she thought, watching as he searched through the tin of colored pencils. *We both know our love has been confirmed tonight... and what we've felt all these months is real...* She went to the coffee pot, hardly hearing the sound of each scoop landing in the pot. *Here he is, sitting at my kitchen table, drawing a picture of me! Oh... how I'll cherish this moment for the rest of my life!*

She did her best to comply, going back into the pantry for bread and peach jam, filling a glass bowl with its golden sweetness, then slicing the bread, and laying it on a tin plate. Then, as silently as she could, she sat down at the table, facing Edgar.

"Ed—"

"Don't talk, my love—and don't move."

"But—"

"Shush."

She watched his hand moving rapidly back and forth across the paper, his eyes stealing momentary glances that seemed to devour her, then went down to the paper.

She lost all sense of time. He smiled at his creation and looked up at her. "You can move now."

Her eyebrows slid high on her forehead and she pointed to her mouth.

"Yes, yes, you may talk, too!" He laughed.

"May I see what you've done?"

"Not yet. Give me a few more minutes—but I'll take a cup of that coffee."

"Oh, my goodness! I hope it didn't burn!" She dropped teaspoons of sugar into the mugs, then poured the steaming brew. A flood of memories of her first days at the McGill farm warmed her.

"Now who's lost in thought?" He looked at Joanna with such tenderness that she thought her heart would burst.

"I was remembering when I first came here."

"To this house?"

She shook her head. "To Appleton... I was so scared and so alone—and then I met y'all."

Edgar slid his chair back and went to her, knelt down, and lovingly wrapped his arms around her. "You'll never be alone again, my love—not while this man has breath in his body." His lips took aim for hers, but her fingers caught his kiss.

"May I see the drawing now?"

He nodded and she went to the table and lifted the sketch. The likeness was unbelievable. Edgar had drawn her sitting, her arm extended, as if reaching to someone, one not drawn or seen. There was no mistaking that the look of love lighting her face was that of the person who had captured her smile, with lips slightly parted, as she leaned forward, conveying a tender intimacy. He had captured that mysterious and divine look in her eyes that revealed a tender passion... an innocence that questioned the actuality of it.

"My darlin'," she whispered, looking into his eyes. "I'm undone. It's... not... me..."

"Oh, but it is, Joanna. Every inch of you and every breath you breathe."

She looked back at the sketch. "It's beautiful, but so much

more... it's *luminous* and alive." Her hand hovered over the sketch, almost afraid to touch it.

"Her love is the light that shines through her eyes, and in the turn of her lips. It is you, Joanna. It is how I've seen you since the first moment your eyes looked into mine."

How she wanted to feel the strength of his arms around her again. "Oh, thank you, Father, for this gift you've given the man I love."

Edgar couldn't have been more deeply touched. It was all he could do to restrain the urge to feel the warmth of her in his arms.

"It is a gift, Ed," she said, looking up at him again, "a God-given gift—like Da Vinci and Rembrandt and Monet each had. You draw because you have to, just as they had to, that's the passion God gave you."

Edgar shook his head, all the while thinking – *She understands, just like Mama did.* "I'm nowhere near that talented, Joanna, though I'm flattered you think so. I don't have what those painters had."

"How do you know you don't? Do you know about Claude Monet—and how his mother encouraged him, then his aunt, and how he studied at the *École des Beaux-Arts*."

"How on earth do you know that?"

"I'm a teacher—" Her dimpled smile reassured him. "—I'm supposed to know things!"

"How do you know about Monet?"

"My father loves art and taught all his children to love it, too. We traveled to Washington, D.C., many times, to visit art galleries."

His eyes took on a faraway look.

"Oh, darlin,' there were so many wondrous works and pamphlets telling all about the artists. You could look at one painting for hours, if you wanted to."

"I know I would have wanted to. I envy you, Joanna, having a father who loved art. My father not only didn't love art, he didn't even like mine. 'I can't see the need for it,' I heard him say, time and again. 'Seems like a waste of time and paper to me.'"

"And your mother—didn't she love to draw, too?"

"Mama loved everything creative—everything from painting to sewing to building. And she always kept a sketchbook in her knitting bag, so she could draw a bit in between chores. Mama encouraged me to draw."

"Just like Monet's mother!" She took his hands in hers. "You *must* keep doing this. You have to draw and paint, and you *must* to see the works of the masters. We should go to Chic—" She caught her breath, realizing she was planning a life for them when all he had said was *I love you*. He hadn't proposed.

"I draw whenever I can, Joanna, whenever life lets me."

"We'll have to try to see to it that life lets you do a lot more of it, and more often."

It was many words, and several cups of coffee and slices of bread slathered with jam later that Edgar pulled out his pocket watch and bolted off the chair.

"Joanna, it's after midnight! I should go home."

Each had the same thought: *I'll be glad when 'home' is wherever we are, together.*

She walked outside with him and he embraced her one last time, willing himself to pull away.

He climbed into the buckboard. "Until tomorrow."

"Yes, tomorrow..."

Dolly started off and Edgar turned and blew a kiss to Joanna as Dolly carried him down the lane.

"Dolly, my girl, it may be late, but I'm in no hurry. I didn't want to leave Joanna. I hate putting one foot between us, much less two miles." He loosened his hold on the reins and Dolly slowed to a meandering pace. "Look at that moon," he said, drawing a long satisfying breath. "It's the full moon."

The dirt road wove its way through the hills, and the darkness appeared and disappeared as Dolly rounded each bend in the lane. At the edge of the road, a picket fence encircled a small clap-board farm house and beyond the little house was a mass of pink and red and white blooms dancing in the wind. "If I only had my sketchbook..."

He laughed. "First Joanna, now those flowers. Everything seems so... *alive*." He chuckled again. "It's you who's alive, Edgar McGill—alive for the first time since Bessie died." He suddenly fell silent, neither hearing the clip-clop of Dolly's hooves, nor the hoot of an owl in the distant pine. "Part of me died with Bessie—as if I'd lost my heart and my soul..."

You didn't want to live, Edgar—admit it... if it wasn't for Toad, you might have killed yourself.

"Yes, God help me, I might have." He rubbed his eyes and tears ran down his stubbled cheeks. "We were inseparable... people always said we belonged together. We loved the same things and Bessie believed in me—and my love of art... The night

Joe was born..." He wiped at his tears again. "We cried and laughed the joy of creating our child and Bessie told me I'd be a good father."

"I tried, Bessie," he said, looking up to heaven. "Toad loves Joanna and wishes she were his mother. I know he does. I see it in his eyes when he looks at her."

Joanna has given you a reason to live.

"She loves me. Wonder of wonders, the woman loves me! And how I love her. I really and truly love her, Bessie. Joanna has given me the will to *live* again, to let me *feel* again. And, God," he said, his eyes fixed on the heavens above, "you sent Joanna to show me the way. She's honest and true, like my Bessie was."

What a fool I've been over Lucy. She never really meant much, and she could never mean what Joanna means to me. And, God, my loving Lord, please... I beg you, please, don't take Joanna away from me... not now—or ever.

Edgar looked to the twinkling stars in the glowing heavens. "Thank you, God, thank you... THANK YOU, GOD!" he shouted.

"Things are going to be so good," he said, and Dolly whinnied as if agreeing with him. "We'll be married and she'll move back to the farm. And this winter won't seem so cold and empty." *She'll be my wife. We'll share a room...and a bed.* There was not a soul around but Dolly and that hoot owl, yet he could not dismiss the heat that flushed his face as he remembered the feel of Joanna's kisses. The passion, the tenderness—the answer to his long-held prayer.

"Joe will be so happy when I tell him; he loves Joanna so, and she'll be the mother he has always wanted. As for Laura — well, there's no mistaking she's crazy about Joanna, and loves her like a sister."

Dolly pulled the wagon around another bend in the lane. The farm sat in the peaceful distance, moonlight shining down on it as if it were a beacon, leading him home.

"Thanks for getting me home, girl," he said, then whispered, "and, Joanna, my love, if your heart can hear me... you and I are almost home, too."

Chapter Thirty

Edgar and Joanna were together again the following Friday afternoon, in Luke Goodman's study. *Something has happened,* Luke thought, the minute they walked in, *something good. Hallelujah!* He and Carrie had discussed the romance developing between their old friend, and their newest. He remembered what Carrie had said: "They're so right for each other, and Joanna obviously loves little Joe, too. She'll be a wonderful mother."

Luke looked admiringly at them, thinking: *They look so good together, she so tiny and fair and he so tall and dark. I wonder if they've come to talk about a wedding.*

"Do you and Carrie have supper plans tonight?" Edgar asked.

"Don't know about my wife," Luke said with a grin, "but I sure do. I plan to be eating."

Joanna and Edgar laughed. "We do, too, and we thought maybe you'd like to join us at Casa Giannini."

"I'm going to the lecture with Annie Campbell," Joanna added, "but Edgar and I thought it would be fun if we all got together for supper first."

Ah, ha. She regrets her previous commitment and this way she can honor it and still be with Edgar.

"It would be me and Miss Campbell and Edgar and you two and—" She stopped and gave Edgar a questioning look. "Who is using your other ticket?"

"Margot Giannini," he replied, and the two burst out

laughing. Luke smiled, though without understanding what was clearly a private joke. "She can't *join* us for supper because she'll be cooking it. She said she'll meet us at the hall and will come in *'like-ah the little church-ah mouse.'"*

"Mrs. Giannini?" Luke shook his head. "Never."

"So, will you come?"

"I can't imagine my wife saying no to a chance to have someone else fix supper." They agreed to meet at the restaurant at five, so they could have a relaxed meal and still get to the Grange early enough to get good seats for the seven o'clock lecture.

They were wise to do so. When they entered the hall at six-fifteen, ticket-holders were already lining up. Luke motioned their group toward the seats in the first row. "Just like at church," he told them, "always plenty of room down front!"

He guided Carrie and Laura to the center of the row, while Edgar took the aisle seat with Joanna next to him and Annie Campbell beside her. Annie Campbell had led a quiet life filled with church and her work as postmistress and voluminous reading. Hearing Mrs. Lewis speak was a major event for her and having supper out was an unheard of luxury. Edgar had insisted on treating her.

Annie and Joanna chatted as the hall filled with faces both familiar and strange. Joanna watched as a young man walked down front and began scanning the audience and jotting something on a writing tablet.

"I think he's a newspaper reporter," Joanna said, leaning to Annie.

"He is," Edgar said in Joanna's ear, placing his arm around her shoulders. "He's counting seats so he can estimate how many people are here." He sat back, but kept his arm where it was. Joanna liked it.

Well before seven o'clock all seats were filled   An undercurrent of excitement rippled through the crowd when Lucy Sheppard led Lydia Lewis to the podium.

Laura did not share the enthusiasm. *I'm not sure what I think about votes for women, but I've read Mrs. Lewis' articles and her arguments are poorly phrased and illogical,* she thought. *There's something about the woman that bothers me. If Lydia Lewis is against something, my heart says I should be for it.*

People applauded wildly when Lydia banged her fist on the podium and declared, "Women belong at home—not on street corners!" Some in the audience jumped to their feet and cheered when she held up a photograph of Amelia Bloomer and described suffragettes as "women who look like men and want to act like them, too."

Two hours later and despite Lydia's dramatics, Laura was still undecided on votes for women, but her mind was made up about Lydia Lewis. *I don't like her....she's pompous and loud and, for the life of me, I don't know why she has to keep pounding that podium.*

Laura turned on her seat and gazed around the room. *Almost everyone seems smitten with her, and though I hate to admit it, she is an effective public speaker. Her talk was well organized, her voice was clear and commanding, and she's fervent, I'll give her that.*

Annie Campbell was not one to be persuaded by pounding fists or rhetoric. *She's rude and spiteful and I bet she's never read anything the suffragettes have written or, I'll wager, never talked with a one of 'em. I need a book about this—but where will I find one? Bloomington, maybe?*

Had Annie shared her reaction, Joanna could have told her she had just what she wanted at home, in her carpetbag. Joanna had come to hear Lydia Lewis because everyone else was, not because she wondered what the woman would say. She knew exactly what Lydia Lewis would propagate, in fact, she could give chapter and verse of Lydia's arguments against woman's suffrage.

Edgar kept staring at Joanna and decided she didn't like the speech. He felt the way her body tensed and heard the sharp intakes of breath when Mrs. Lewis held up the picture of Amelia Bloomer. Lydia finished to a deafening applause; Edgar noticed that Joanna was not clapping. Neither, for that matter, was anyone else in his group.

They made their way to the refreshments and Edgar asked Luke what he thought of Lydia Lewis.

"Well, she's a powerful speaker. I know many a preacher who'd envy Mrs. Lewis her deep voice and her stage presence."

"I didn't like her," Carrie said. "She doesn't seem like a very nice person."

"Maybe not," Edgar said, "but what about what she said? Do you think women should vote?"

"That I'm not sure about."

"Neither am I." Laura and Annie Campbell spoke as one and smiled at each other. Joanna's silence on the issue went unnoticed; the loudness of the throng clambering for Lydia Lewis' autograph made it impossible to talk had anyone asked Joanna her opinion.

"Shall we get her autograph?" Luke asked Carrie as she stood sipping punch and munching *cannoli*, compliments of

Margot Giannini. "The children might like to have her autograph."

"The children never heard of Lydia Lewis," Carrie said, hardly impressed with her husband's idea. "I don't particularly want her autograph." She took a fierce bite of her *cannoli* and a dollop of its creamy filling punctuated her cheek.

Luke smiled, pulled a freshly ironed handkerchief from his back pocket and gently wiped the splotch of cream from Carrie's face. *That's one of the things I love about you, my dear—no one has to wonder where they stand with my Carrie!* Luke realized they were but feet away from the matriarch of the *status quo* for women.

"Mrs. Lewis may call herself a Christian, but she sure doesn't act like one."

"And what do you think of *this*?" Luke said, holding up his own *cannoli*. "What is it called anyway?"

"It is called *cannoli*, it's Italian, and it's scrumptious," Carrie said. She flashed Luke the smile that always seemed to beam straight from her heart. "But I get your intent... I'll be good from now on." After fifteen years of marriage she read her husband like an open book.

Edgar, Laura, and Joanna were at the food table, where Laura was complimenting Celia Werner on her new crystal punch bowl. Edgar felt a tug on his elbow. It was Lucy.

"Come and meet Mrs. Lewis," she commanded, pulling him toward her.

"Wait, and I'll get Laura and Joanna."

That's the second time you've used that woman's first name, and I like it less each time I hear it. "They can make their own way," Lucy said, pushing through the crush of people around Lydia, not bothering with an *excuse me*, until she was beside Mrs. Lewis.

"Mrs. Lewis, I want you to meet someone very dear to me. This is Edgar McGill, a gentlemen farmer here in Jefferson County. Edgar, this is Mrs. Lydia Lewis." Lucy's voice was unusually pitched, higher than usual, and agitated.

She's nervous, Edgar thought. *I never would have thought it possible!* He extended his hand to Lydia Lewis, and to the lady's surprise, he did a slight bow and kissed her hand. "Mrs. Lewis, I'm pleased to meet you. That was quite a speech you gave. Folks will be talking about it all summer," he said, smiling broadly.

Lydia Lewis may have been middle-aged, pompous and aloof, but she was a woman and few women failed to respond to Edgar McGill's enthralling smile. Laura would have said the lady *twittered* with delight.

"You are too kind, Mr. McGill, but I do hope people will keep talking until those suffragettes give up their foolish campaign." Her tone distinctly put the word *suffragettes* in the swear word category. "*Real* women," she went on, inclining her head toward Lucy, "do not want to stand in polls beside men—and *real* men," she said, underscoring the word with a smile, "do not want them to!"

"My dear Mrs. Lewis," Roscoe Sheppard said, stepping on Edgar's response, "I hate to take you away from your admirers, but there is someone here who must have a word with you before he heads back to Chicago."

The man Joanna had noticed before the lecture began was hovering at Roscoe's side. "He works for the *Tribune* and—" Lydia Lewis abruptly marched off with the reporter.

"Apparently, the lady places a high value on her press coverage," Roscoe said, then clapped his hands on Edgar's shoulder. "Mr. McGill, where is that charming little Southern belle who's been staying with you? My feature story has made her a celebrity, you know." Roscoe chuckled and side-glanced Lucy.

"Joanna's over there," Edgar said, pointing in her direction.

Roscoe peered round Edgar. "Ah... yes... where all the young men are gathered," again he chuckled. "I would wager you that the lovely Miss Garrett's photos are adorning a great many walls in town..."

He took hold of Lucy's arm, exerting the necessary force, and walked her to the opposite side of the room. "You are wasting your time, my dear," he said.

Edgar came up behind Joanna, Laura and Annie, who were talking with Sam Bailey and Cal Turner. *It's just like you, Cal, to be cozying up to the ladies, thinking every woman you meet will fall in love with you—but not my Joanna. No, sir, Cal—not my Joanna!* Edgar let out a burst of laughter. The entire group turned around to him.

"What's so funny?" Sam Bailey asked. "Did the famous speaker tell you a joke?"

"Far from it," Edgar said. "That is one very serious lady."

"How could she not be, looking like that?" Cal said. "She's built like a steamship and has a voice like a foghorn."

Joanna bit down on her lower lip to keep from giving Cal a piece of her mind, yet was delighted when Annie Campbell seized the moment.

"What a rude and mean spirited thing to say! You should apologize to all the women present, *Mister* Turner. I am sure we're all offended on behalf of Mrs. Lewis."

Cal looked from Joanna to Laura and then to Sam and Edgar. No one was smiling. His face flushed and he dropped his chin, looking down at his boots. "I uh... I uh... didn't mean to... to offend anyone. She's just... not the prettiest woman I've ever seen and—" He lifted his eyebrows apologetically and saw five pairs of eyes trained on him. "I *am* sorry. I didn't mean anything by it."

Sam clapped Cal on the back. "Of course you didn't! We all can tell that Lydia Lewis is a fine woman. And she does have a remarkably deep voice, doesn't she? Must be a big help to her, having a voice that makes people sit up and take notice."

"I like people to notice *what* I say, not just *how* I say it," Joanna said softly.

"So, Joanna" Edgar said teasingly as he drove his group homeward, "you didn't like Mrs. Lewis' message after all."

"No, Edgar. I didn't like her and I think she should get her facts straight before she gives that speech again."

Laura's eyes went wide. "What do you mean?"

"She shouldn't make her point by saying things that aren't true—or accurate."

"Such as?" Edgar studied Joanna's expression.

"She said no state has given women the vote. That's not true. Women can vote in Wyoming."

"I didn't know that," Laura said. "What else did she get wrong?"

"She mixed up Elizabeth Stanton and Susan Anthony. It's Miss Anthony who is a Quaker; Mrs. Stanton is the one who studied law and married a lawyer."

"How do you know all this?" Edgar had to ask.

"I learned about it in college," she said wryly, "which may be why Mrs. Lewis thinks women shouldn't go there!"

They were all still laughing when Edgar pulled Dolly up to Joanna's house. He walked her to the door, and though he didn't kiss her, the look he gave her warmed her from head to toe.

"I'll pick you up for church on Sunday."

"Until Sunday..."

Chapter Thirty-One

Had anyone asked Lucy to describe her feelings, following the encounter with her father, indignation or, perhaps, rage would have sufficed. Her father's deliberate intrusion into her conversation with Edgar and Lydia—and worse— the way in which he had belittled her, as if she were a schoolgirl, then dragged her off, capped the summit of her wrath. *This time, Father, you have pushed me too far... You treat me no better than you did my Mother, but I will not tolerate it. Never again will you look down on me and relegate me to the dung heap of society, where you place everyone.*

Lydia Lewis, on the other hand, was euphoric, basking in reflected glory. Lydia was anything but humble and was as distanced from reality as was the earth to the moon. She considered even her worst lectures, where she dropped her notes or spilled water on the lectern, to be complete successes. But she was right to pat herself on the back for a job well done in Appleton this evening.

It was a sellout crowd and I was at the top of my form, and I do believe I made some converts. More than one person told me I was "right as rain." So what if they were all men? Men still make the decisions. But Lydia was far from *spent* after her speech, despite what she had told Lucy Sheppard. The applause and cheers had exhilarated her and energized her beyond even her own expectations. When the reception ended and the crowd dissipated, going to her hotel room and being alone until morning was the furthest thing in her mind. Like an actress, she lusted for one more curtain call and all the adulation she could garner. So she asked Lucy to gather a small group and join her at her hotel. "You and your father, and a few others you think might enjoy a cup of coffee and some stimulating conversation, my dear," Lydia said. "Just an intimate little gathering of compatible minds."

I'll show you who can manipulate, Father! "Please come to our home instead," Lucy said. "The hour is late, and the Morgan House will have stopped serving. Father and I have a well stocked larder, Mrs. Lewis, and a staff more than ready to wait on us." Her *staff* was actually a local girl who came in to clean house once a week and a cook who normally would have been home and in bed by nine-thirty on a Friday night. However, Lucy had enticed them to stay late, paying a day's wages for the evening's work, on the chance that Mrs. Lewis would accept.

She recalled why Lydia had chosen to stay at the Morgan House in the first place: "Privacy, my dear girl," she had said, "is something one never gets enough of when one is a public servant, and so one must insist on it whenever possible." *Apparently, privacy is only a priority when acclamation is no longer available,* Lucy thought. *Another self-indulged hypocrite, like my father.*

Lydia Lewis accepted the invitation. The *intimate little party* had been Lucy's *fait accompli.* The Werners, the Garners and the Greers all came.

Cheese, prepared continental style with apples and grapes, and crackers imported from France were served. The cook also made meatballs in a white cream sauce and, for dessert, *petits fours* for those with a sweet tooth.

The beverages to serve had posed a problem. Lucy had bought sparkling wine on a trip to Vevay, but agonized over whether to serve it. Her father would not object, he drank on almost a daily basis. And she was confident that the Werners, as fellow Presbyterians, drank wine, though the Garners and Greers were Methodists and might be teetotalers. She was willing to risk offending them, but needed assurance that Lydia Lewis would not storm out of the house if wine was served. The matter was easily resolved after the lecture. A man had approached Mrs. Lewis with a punch cup in his hand and lifted it in a toast. "I would drink to your health with a fine wine, Madame, were it available to me."

"And I would join you, sir," Lydia Lewis had replied.

The party broke up before the midnight hour and Roscoe and Lucy walked Lydia the few blocks back to the Morgan House. Roscoe said his goodbyes in the lobby, but Lucy said she wanted to see Mrs. Lewis safely to her room. Actually, she hoped to be invited in to see Lydia's vast travel wardrobe.

"You cannot imagine," Lydia had said, "the amount of money one has to spend on clothing when one is in the public eye." But Lydia waved Lucy off as soon as the bellboy unlocked the door to her room, the largest in the hotel. "You have been most charming, my dear, and I thank you for the little *soiree*. But I am truly exhausted and must tell you goodnight and goodbye." Lucy slid her foot in the doorway.

"Good night it is, Mrs. Lewis, but not yet goodbye. I'll be seeing you off at the depot tomorrow morning."

"How kind. Until tomorrow morning, then." The oak door nearly closed in Lucy's face.

The train for Knoxville pulled out at ten o'clock and Lucy was at the station a half hour earlier, fearing Lydia might try to avoid seeing her. She watched the famed speaker sweep in, followed by two bellhops and her traveling companion, a mousy young woman, whom Lydia had not bothered to introduce. *Why do I feel this ridiculous urge to rise and curtsey to this woman?!*

"Good morning. I hope you rested well."

Lydia spun around. "Like a baby, my dear, like a baby." *Why do people always say that?* Lucy wondered. *Young mothers usually look like raccoons, their eyes ringed with dark circles from being awakened so often. The last thing I want is to 'sleep like a baby.'"*

"I brought something for your trip," Lucy said, extending a wicker basket. "You have a long journey ahead of you and I wanted you to have some refreshment and entertainment. Just a small token of our appreciation for coming here and broadening our horizons."

Two things happened to Lydia at that moment which were totally foreign to her—she was speechless, and she was truly touched. She was paid well for her lectures, people gave dinners in her honor, they sent flowers to her hotel room, but no one had ever packed her a picnic basket so she wouldn't be hungry on the train.

Tears did not betray her, but it was a long moment before she could speak. "This is really most thoughtful, Miss Sheppard. I shall look forward to unveiling this lovely basket as I travel." She paused, set down the basket, and took hold of Lucy's hand. "Thank you. Thank you very much. It was my pleasure to come to this charming town. I can't thank you enough for your most gracious hospitality." Lydia turned to her companion and pointed to the basket. "Put that in my compartment, Miss Davis, and see to it that you don't drop it." Lydia Lewis was herself again.

Lydia had Lucy's basket unpacked before the train pulled out of Appleton. The *refreshment* part included packets of the cheese and crackers that had been served at the party, a bunch of grapes, a half dozen *petits fours*, a loaf of what smelled like apple bread, some hard boiled eggs, a linen napkin and a flask of grape juice. The *entertainment* section was equally well stocked; a fan, a deck of playing cards, the most recent *Godey's Lady's Book*, and several issues of the *Appleton Gazette*. The inclusion of cards was risky, Lucy knew, but she guessed, correctly, that Lydia was open-minded about women playing card games despite her vehement opposition to voting rights for them. A game of solitaire kept Lydia well occupied for the first hour of her trip, after which she indulged in a short nap. During the long afternoon ride through Kentucky Lydia read the *Gazette*. When she reached the May issue, Lydia drew in a breath so sharply that Miss Davis would have sworn her employer hissed.

"I don't believe it! I just don't believe it!" She flung the paper at her companion. "Just look at that picture!" Miss Davis caught a brief glimpse of a dark-haired woman before Lydia snatched the paper back. "That woman is in Appleton and I never knew it! She's *teaching* in their school!" She muttered something under her breath, then said, "I *must* write the dear girl immediately. Fetch my writing case at once, Miss Davis!"

Mildred Davis reluctantly got up and made her way to the baggage compartment. "I hate trains," she muttered as she wobbled forward. "They're dirty and loud and I swear the engineer deliberately swerves every time I walk to the lavatory." Going all the way to the baggage compartment was torture. Mildred Davis was grateful, however, when the porter offered to fetch the case for her. She would have to tip him out of her own pocket, but it was well worth it.

Lydia drew a pen and a sheaf of paper from her writing case and folded the case down so she had a flat surface on which to write. "Let's see," she said, "How should I begin?"

1st of July 1885

"Dear Miss Sheppard,
Before I address the real purpose of this correspondence, let me say again how lovely it was to be in your charming town, and how well you arranged everything on my behalf. You treated me like a queen, and I thank you for that..."

"She really was most considerate, wasn't she, Miss Davis?"

"Yes, Mrs. Lewis, Miss Lucy had thought of everything you needed." *I wish someone would do that for me, just once,* Miss Davis thought, while Lydia continued speaking the letter as she wrote:

"I regard what I do as planting seeds and I can only pray that they have taken root and will bloom in your finest citizens and that the good people of Appleton will take a strong stance against this suffrage blight that threatens our country. It seems we have hardly healed since the War and all the hardships that followed. It is that blight which compels me to write you now..."

"Oh, I do hate to tell the dear girl what's happened in her town!"

Miss Davis held back her sneer. *Actually, Lydia, if the truth be told, you can't wait to tell Lucy Sheppard! You savor being the bearer of bad news—you hypocrite!*

Lydia Lewis came out of her contemplation and began her invective:

"I read the issues of your paper you so kindly placed in my travel hamper for which, again, I thank you. I was shocked to the core when I saw the photographs of and read the article about your new schoolteacher...."

Though, Lydia thought, *they truly are magnificent*

photographs. She chewed on the end of her pen and pondered her next words.

> *"My dear, I wish there were an easy way to say this, but there simply is none. Your fine town has, in the person of Miss Joanna Garrett, one of those radical vote demanding women!*
>
> *I knew that face the moment I saw it. Miss Garrett was in attendance at a suffrage convention in Washington, DC, a year ago last March. I saw her leaving the speech given by May Sewall. Several friends and I were there handing out pamphlets, trying to dissuade women from being fooled by Mrs. Sewall. I distinctly remember handing a pamphlet to Miss Garrett. She has a face that is hard to forget, but I also remember her because she smiled and thanked me..."*

Lydia paused to sip her grape juice, but the cheese and crackers were the greater lure. She consumed grapes, three *petits fours*, and an egg, then wiped her mouth and fingers, and picked up the quill pen.

"Miss Davis, did I mention that I saw Miss Garrett at that dreadful convention in Washington last March?"

"Yes, ma'am, I believe you did." *And, please don't tell me again!*

"I was handing out pamphlets with – let me see, who was with me? Agnes Porter and...oh, that–" Lydia waved her hands in the frustration of not remembering, "–that frumpy-looking girl who travels with Agnes—what is her name?"

"Margaret Johnson, ma'am." Margaret was her counterpart.

"Yes, that's right... we were handing out pamphlets after that Sewall woman spoke and saw three very well dressed women coming up the sidewalk. I marched up to them and said, 'You all seem to be ladies and you simply must read our pamphlet, that is, if you wish to remain so.' One of them, the oldest one, by the look of her, refused. I think she actually sniggered at me! But Miss Garrett took our pamphlet, looked me in the eye and said *thank you.* Can you believe it?"

"Courtesy was quite unexpected, then?"

"Yes indeed! Why, most of those suffragettes don't know the

first thing about etiquette, or even plain good manners. I'd like to know more about Joanna Garrett. I wonder... Miss Davis, where are my scrapbooks?"

Oh, no, Mildred Davis thought, *not another trip to the baggage compartment!* "They're in your small trunk, Mrs. Lewis."

"Fetch them immediately. I want you to see if you can find anything more about Miss Garrett."

Two hours later Lydia was back at her letter to Lucy:

"*My dear Miss Sheppard, I wish I could tell you that the news gets no worse, but I am afraid it does. I travel with scrapbooks of my speeches, as well as those of our opponents (in different scrapbooks, of course) and I asked my Miss Davis to look through them. It was an arduous task for us, but we struck gold. Miss Davis found several articles about Joanna Garrett and it seems she not only went to that convention, but also attended a speech by Elizabeth Cady Stanton in Petersburg, Virginia, just last November, where – can I say it? – she was arrested! It is simply too shocking — the woman is a criminal!*

As soon as I realized your children were being taught by one of these malevolent radicals, I knew it was my Christian duty to tell you. I am sure this is quite a blow, but I know you are a strong woman and that you also will do your civic duty. People must know about Miss Garrett!

I did not see Miss Garrett at my speech, but if that woman did attend, I can only pray she has seen the light and will mend her evil ways. I doubt however, that your school trustees will chance that possibility.

Should you require my assistance in this regard, I will do whatever I can to help.

My best to your dear father.

Sincerely,
Lydia Lewis"

"And now, Miss Davis, please write this over for me. I have blotted a page. Then we can get it on its way to Indiana."

"But—" Miss Davis caught herself just in time.

"But *what?*" *But it's late and I was hoping to rest! You try my patience, you slacker.*

"Nothing, Mrs. Lewis. Do you want me to use the cream stationery or the rose-colored?"

"The cream, of course! This is a serious letter, not a chatty note."

It was still dark the next morning when the train pulled into Hillsville, a tiny town deep in the mountains of Kentucky. Mildred Davis got off the train to post Lydia's letter. Lydia had mandated it. "There's a mail drop right on the train, but will that do? Oh, no," Mildred thought, mimicking her employer. She had worked for Lydia only three months, but already knew what it took to survive: *Do what Lydia Lewis asks, when she asks—whatever she asks—no matter how discourteous the request, or how difficult the task. Just do it!*

Luke and Edgar had worked hard to convince Carrie and Joanna to accompany them to Hanover for a presbytery meeting, enticing them with the promise of a leisurely picnic afterwards.

"I'll tell you one thing, Luke Goodman," Carrie had said. "I better not have my dinner at supper time because the meeting ran late."

"The lady is familiar with presbytery meetings," Edgar had said, grinning at Luke.

"This lady is, too," Joanna added. "I don't know how many times my father went off telling us he'd be back in a few hours and then was gone all day. He once called presbytery meetings 'the Protestant form of purgatory.'"

Luke had laughed until tears ran down his cheeks. "I've got to remember that one." He finally composed himself and said. "I promise you, Carrie, we'll eat right on time if you'll come with us. This is going to be a short presbytery meeting." Carrie rolled her eyes. "Really, it will be. All we're doing is approving calls to three pastors and reviewing the building plans for a new church near Corydon."

"Please come," Edgar pleaded with Joanna. "Just think how pretty it will be, sitting under all those elm trees on the banks of the Ohio River, smelling the roses, watching the birds, and munching on fried chicken and cornbread."

"I suppose you want us to fry the chicken and bake the cornbread?" Carrie asked.

"We could buy it in Hanover, I suppose," Luke had said, putting his arm around his wife, "but yours is so much better!"

When the day arrived Joanna and Carrie were glad to be with their men folk. It was a perfect July morning, sunny, clear and with almost no humidity.

Edgar drove, with Joanna beside him, looking pretty as a picture in her new summer frock. After the fourth time Edgar glanced sideways at her, Luke spoke up.

"The road gets a might curvy up ahead, so you might want to keep your eyes on it. Wouldn't want our fried chicken to wind up in a ditch."

"I'm doing just fine, thank you," Edgar laughed. "Let me mind the road and you just enjoy sitting back there alone with your sweet wife."

"Right," Luke said, snuggling up to Carrie like sweethearts instead of a man and woman who'd been married for fifteen years.

Joanna edged a little closer to Edgar and squeezed his hand. Luke would really have gotten nervous had he known that Edgar drove the rest of the way to Hanover College with one hand holding the reins.

When they emerged from the canopy of beech trees leading to the college, they saw the winding drive lined with buggies, wagons, and horses tethered to every available tree.

Luke let out a low whistle. "Looks like *everyone* showed up for this meeting," he said. "Hope this doesn't mean there's something on the agenda we didn't know about."

Carrie scowled at her husband. "Luke Goodman, if you brought me up here and this meeting lasts until dusk, I'll never forgive you." Luke hopped down and extended his hand to his wife. "Oh, but you will, my love," he said, his dimple showing. "You've forgiven me for much worse than that!"

An hour and a half later, four happy people were sitting on blankets spread at the Point, a bluff high above the Ohio River, where one could see all three bends in the river. They filled their plates with fried chicken, pickled beets, deviled eggs and cornbread. Joanna had brought what she called a *tea punch* and poured everyone a glass of the sweet tea with lemon slices floating in it.

"I've never had a more refreshing drink," Luke said. "And why haven't I had this before?"

"You've never been in the south. I've been drinking tea like this since I was a little girl. My Mama wouldn't think of serving anything else when the weather turns warm."

"Tell me more about your family, Joanna. The only thing I know about you is that you teach school and your father is a pastor," Luke said.

By the time they cut into Carrie's chocolate layer cake, he knew where Joanna was from, how many brothers she had, what her grandmother looked like and what she hated most about growing up in the manse. Luke even learned who her favorite college professor was, and why.

"I wanted to go to college," Edgar said, "but my father needed me to help on the farm. Not that I minded helping Pa—there was just so much more to learn." His blue eyes had a far away look.

"What would you have studied?" Carrie asked.

"Art," Edgar said.

This was the first Luke had learned of Edgar's love of art. "Is it drawing that you like, Edgar?" he asked. "Or painting?"

"Both. I've done a lot of pen and ink work and dabbled a little in water colors."

"I'd love to see your work," Carrie said. "Tell us more about your passion for art."

"I never thought of it as a *passion*," Edgar said, then looked into Joanna's eyes. "Though not too long ago, someone very dear to me told me it's a gift from God. It always came easy for me. I can pick up a pencil and start sketching and the next thing I know, an hour has passed. My mother was always drawing—she designed needlework and painted pictures on her *Hoosier* cabinet."

"I don't think I've seen that cabinet," Joanna said. "I'm sure I would have noticed it."

"It's in my bedroom."

"Then I'm glad you've never seen it," Luke said. Both Edgar and Joanna turned beet red.

After lunch the men walked the Happy Valley Trail down to the river; the well-worn path made their descent easy. They watched a flock of ducks drift to the water's edge, periodically bobbing their heads at something lurking under the surface.

"I envy wild animals sometimes," Edgar said. "They know just what they're supposed to do and when and how to do it. Everything's planned for them, right from the time they're born." He skimmed a stone across the still waters. "I know they aren't the only ones whose lives have a plan and a purpose. God has a plan for each of us, too. The trick is to not get in God's way when He's trying to reveal it to us."

"My friend," Luke said, clapping Edgar on the back, "that dog will hunt!"

They rejoined the women waiting on the bluff and Luke offered to drive back to Appleton, but Edgar insisted on taking the reins once more. The return trip was quiet, with all peacefully content to watch the sun making its slow descent and listening to the birds fluttering from tree to tree in search of their nests as nightfall moved in. *Godspeed, little birds,* Joanna thought. *Home is a good place to be when darkness descends.*

Lucy Sheppard was not at home, nor was she enjoying the beauty of nature. She was alone in her office at the newspaper, pacing back and forth, with Lydia Lewis' letter in her hand.

"I can't believe I am just now getting this," she said aloud. "Mrs. Lewis wrote it on the first of July and it's almost the end of the month! Whatever could have delayed it?" She continued her pacing, her smile growing broader and broader.

"Of course, there were all those tornadoes and that horrible train wreck in Ohio..." She held the letter aloft, waving it like a banner. "But it's here now! And I knew it, I just knew it! Little Miss Goody Two Shoes isn't so perfect after all." She spun around, whirling in a circle of sheer delight. "Oh, I cannot wait to share this news! I can't wait for the school board and that pious Luke Goodman—and especially Edgar McGill—to find out Joanna Garrett has been hiding something—" she snickered, "—something very, very bad."

She stared at the letter.

"But I'll have to wait. I'll have to plan this in such a way..."

She walked into her father's office, where he kept a Yale infallible safe and retrieved the key from its hiding place. She turned the dial, each number clicking, until the last number disengaged the locking mechanism. She shoved the letter under a mound of old newspapers.

"No one—not even Father—will be looking for the first issue of the *Gazette* anytime soon!"

.

Chapter Thirty-Two

A knock at the door interrupted a rare quiet time for Luke and Carrie, who were reading and catching up on correspondence long overdue for replies. Carrie went to the door and returned wearing a puzzled expression as she scrutinized the envelope in her hand.

"No one was there, just this lying on the stoop." Carrie held up a heavy ecru-colored envelope. "There's no name on it." She shrugged her shoulders and passed the envelope to Luke.

He slit open the flap with his pocket knife and pulled out its contents; a sheet of plain stock on which was written, *"You might find this interesting,"* and a page from a newspaper. "It's a page from the *Washington Post*, dated March 6, 1884."

Carrie came to his side to read along with him. There was an article about an upcoming election, a section on local events, and a story urging citizens to be cautious when crossing streets due to recent heavy rains.

"Why on earth would anyone send this to us?"

"To you, more likely," Carrie replied. "You're the preacher, after all."

"And what could this possibly have to do with me being a pastor? Or with me for *any* reason?" Luke was indignant. "Somebody's playing a joke on us, Carrie, and I don't much like it." He leaned over and kissed his wife on the cheek, tossed the two pieces of paper on the table, and headed to his study.

Carrie mixed up some bread dough and then sat down to have another cup of coffee. The envelope was still where Luke had flung it. She picked it up and removed the contents, ignoring the handwritten note, reading only the page of newsprint in its entirety, finishing with the announcements. Her mystified look grew more intense as she drank her coffee. "A church bazaar, a three-day revival, an auction and and article about the last day of the National Suffrage Association convention featuring a speech by May Wright Sewall titled, *The Forgotten Woman.*

"Hmm," Carrie stroked the cat as it sunned itself by the window, "I wish whoever sent this had also sent along the next day's paper. I'd like to know what Mrs. Sewall had to say."

Joanna also received an ecru-colored envelope that day, but hers came through the usual channels. It was the only piece of mail Annie Campbell had for her.

"Mighty nice stationery," Annie commented, passed the envelope across the counter. "Looks like an invitation of some kind."

Joanna smiled. Annie would never read another person's mail, but perusing the envelope was a necessity. Joanna read the return address, written in a fine script. "It's from Fort Wayne, Indiana, Annie. I don't know anyone there." She hesitated before tearing the envelope open. "Do you have a letter opener, Annie?"

Annie reached under the counter and pulled out what looked like a silver stiletto and handed it to Joanna. "It was a gift from Henry," Annie explained. "He thought a postmistress should have a fancy letter opener. But I just sort the mail and hand it out. Never get much myself."

"It's an invitation to Abby's wedding, on August 23 rd." She realized Annie didn't know the name. "She's my dearest friend from college."

"That's a month from today." Annie started to ask Joanna if she planned to go, but thought better of it; the postmistress was supposed to mind her own business.

Joanna headed for home. It had started out a surprisingly cool morning which encouraged her to walk into town but she regretted that decision now. It was just plain hot. She arrived home, changed into a dimity cotton dress and was sitting on her front porch, fanning herself and sipping a glass of tea, when she saw a wagon approaching. It was the McGill's and Joe was shouting and waving madly.

"Wait 'til you see it! You're not gonna believe it!" Joe said, leaping from the wagon before Edgar had even finished saying, *whoa* to Dolly. Joe leaned into the wagon bed, reached around, but came up empty handed.

"I can't get it, Pa. I need help!"

"Hold your horses, son. I'll be there in a second." Edgar came around the back of the wagon, lowered the tailgate and pointed inside. "Hop up. You've going to have to hunt for it."

Joanna's curiosity finally got the better of her and she joined them at the wagon. "Am I going to like it?"

"Nope," Joe answered, trying to retrieve something from under a pile of blankets. "You're gonna *love* it!" He raised his cupped hands and a tiny, coal black face peered up at Joanna. Its ears were lopsided, its black eyes blending into its fur, and Joe's hands completely covered its tiny body.

"Oh, it's a puppy!"

Joe handed her the dog, "Treat it gentle."

"*It*—" Edgar said, his smile matching the joy in his eyes at seeing Joanna's delight. "—is a *he* and we got him from Mary Langston. Seems their Sadie took up with a mutt down the road and this little fellow and four others like him are their happy offspring."

"The others aren't really like him, Pa. He's the *only* all black one. His brothers and sisters are mixed up colors."

"He's precious," Joanna gushed. "But won't Patches be jealous?"

Laura looked at Edgar and Edgar looked at Joe, and then all three looked at Joanna. She cuddled the puppy against her chest, her eyebrows raised. "What? Why are you all staring at me?"

"We thought... that is, *I* thought... well, I know how much you like dogs and now that you're out here all alone, well... I thought you might want him." Joanna looked at Joe, wide-eyed. "You've just got to take him, Miss Garrett. I was over to Jimmy's yesterday and his pa said he had to find homes for those durn dogs..." He heard Edgar clear his throat. "I mean all those puppies, by tomorrow, or he was gonna take them down to the creek and drown 'em. He said he had enough to worry about without feedin' a bunch of dogs. We can't let him get drowned, Miss Garrett!"

Everyone but Joe already knew the pup was no longer in danger. Joanna was not just petting the dog, she was crooning to it.

"It's not a baby," Edgar said through a laugh. "Put him down and let's see him move around a little."

Joanna complied, but hovered behind the puppy as he wobbled toward the house. He tried to climb the porch steps but tumbled backwards.

Edgar guffawed as the pup tried again and again. "You'll never make it, little fellow, but you've got the right idea. You've definitely come home."

Joanna picked up the puppy, walked up the steps and plunked him in Laura's lap, then went inside and brought out three glasses, a pitcher of tea, and a plate of gingersnaps.

"My father tried to pretend he thought dogs were useless," Joanna said, "but he loved the hound that showed up at our house one afternoon, wet and hungry. He and Mama still have one of Samantha's pups."

"That's like Patches," Joe said, "except Patches showed up at school and you wanted to keep him as much as I did, Miss Garrett!"

It was well past noon and Joanna invited the McGills to stay to dinner.

"We can't," Laura said. "I have to meet Carrie and Celia Werner at church to plan our fall bazaar, and Ed and Joe are supposed to help Luke and Richard in the church yard."

"But we gotta eat, Aunt Laura! You're not going to starve us, are you?"

"You're a long way from starvation, Toad," she said, "but, no, I didn't plan to deprive you of dinner. Carrie's bringing sandwiches and I've made deviled eggs and Mrs. Werner is bringing some newfangled thing called a *potato chip* they just got in at the store." She stood up and handed the sleeping puppy to Joanna. "You're sure you want him? A dog is good company, but house training one isn't much fun."

"What makes you think he's going to be a house pet? I thought he might stay in the barn with Miss Molly," she said with a wink, knowing that Joe couldn't see her.

"Miss Garrett! You can't make that little thing sleep in the barn! He's too young to be left alone!" He took the dog from Joanna and tucked him protectively under one arm.

"Relax, Toad," Edgar said, handing the pup back to Joanna. Their hands touched and Joanna felt the now familiar sensation that coursed between them. "This pup will be living in the lap of luxury. He'll be eating table scraps and sleeping on the bed, and will probably wind up reciting the alphabet and doing sums!" Joanna swatted him with the tin pie plate that held the cookies they'd eaten.

"Can't you tell when your teacher's pulling your leg?"

"No! I don't see her enough!"

"Come with us," Edgar urged Joanna. "I'm sure the ladies could use help planning the bazaar. Or you could work outside with us men."

He wants me with him. They had seen each other nearly every day since that wondrous night in June and had eaten supper together, just the night before. Joanna cherished every moment spent with Edgar, but she especially loved worshipping together. There was something powerful, even intimate, about praying together, sharing a hymnal, and taking communion.

Every Sunday when they said the prayer of confession, Joanna thought, *I have to tell him. I can't keep hiding my past.* But the thought of telling Edgar made her blood run cold. *He won't want me anymore... I couldn't bear the thought of life without him...*

The wagon pulled away and Joe waved furiously back at Joanna. "Start thinking of a name for him—but talk to me before you decide for sure. I'll help you pick a good one."

"I promise," she called back.

The McGills arrived at the churchyard and Joe couldn't have been more delighted when Carrie Goodman announced they'd have dinner before starting work. "I can't think on an empty stomach," she said, "and you men need energy for your work."

Joe ate more than his share of the potato chips. "I like 'em," he said. "They're crisp and crunchy and they go good with these sandwiches."

"Not me," Luke said. "They don't look like a potato, they don't smell like potatoes, and they sure don't taste like potatoes." He turned to Celia Warner with an apologetic look. "Sorry, Celia—I just don't think these things are going to catch on."

After dinner the women stayed in the cool basement to do their planning and the men headed outdoors.

"Some folks have all the luck," Joe muttered, "stayin' in where it's cool, instead of melting in the sun."

"Quit bellyaching, son. Griping won't get the job done any faster." Edgar was holding a tombstone upright while Luke packed dirt around its base

"The oddest thing happened this morning," Luke said, tamping the dirt around the headstone. "Somebody left an envelope on our stoop with a page from a Washington newspaper inside."

"As in the nation's capitol?"

"That's right. I told Carrie someone was playing a bad joke on us."

Richard Werner stopped scraping mold off a nearby tombstone and stood up. "Then someone's playing the same joke on me. I got an envelope this morning, too. Had a paper in it, just like yours, only mine was from Petersburg."

"Where's that?" Joe asked.

"In Virginia," Richard replied, "not too far from the North Carolina line. The date was sometime last November."

Luke shook the dirt from his hands. "Ours was from March, a year ago," he said, scratching his head. "This is very strange."

Joe ran to his father. "Wait a minute! Isn't Miss Garrett from North Carolina?"

"Yes, she is," Edgar said. He felt uneasy, the way he did when he'd forgotten to do something, like padlock the barn door, but hadn't remembered that he forgot. "But this can't have anything to do with Joanna."

Luke and Joe were accustomed to hearing Edgar use Joanna's first name, but it caught Richard Werner by surprise.

"Someone is trying to tell us something," Luke said, "and that someone is a sneak. I don't like sneakiness."

"After we finish up here, I'll run home and get my envelope," Richard said. "We'll look at both papers together and see if that helps any." The others approved his plan and went back to straightening tombstones and clearing away debris.

"This," Joe announced an hour later, "is not summertime work." His fair skinned face was red and sweat dripped from his brow.

"You're right, Joe," Luke said. "We wouldn't be doing it now if it weren't for the ladies from Madison coming to locate graves of men killed in the war." Luke didn't have to say "the Civil War;" Indiana wasn't even a state during the American Revolution.

"What are they gonna do with them?" Joe's eyes widened and his next question came out in a breathless whisper. "Are they gonna dig them up and perform some kind of secret ceremony?"

"I have never heard such nonsense, Joseph McGill," Edgar said. "Secret ceremonies have no place in a Christian's life. Those ladies want information, not bones." He gave his son's red suspenders a snap. "Just what've you been reading this summer?"

As promised, Richard Werner had fetched his letter. He, Luke and Edgar were pouring over the newspaper clippings in the church basement. After ten minutes, Edgar pushed his chair back from the table. Exasperation covered his face. "Doesn't make a bit of sense to me," he said, pacing the length of the room. "They're not the same date or even from the same place."

"And they don't have any of the same stories," Richard said.

"That's not quite true," Luke said, positioning the two clippings side by side. "Each has an article about votes for women."

Edgar stopped pacing, came back to Luke, and leaned over his shoulder.

"The article in the *Washington Post* mentions a speech by May Sewall at the National Suffrage Association convention." He pointed to the item in the announcements. "The paper Richard got, the *Petersburg Progress*, has a story about a talk by Elizabeth Cady Stanton." He pointed to that article and Edgar bent forward to read it better.

"Sit down, man," Luke said. "Read the whole thing." Edgar did so, then offered the paper to Richard Werner, who shook his head.

"You two better sort this thing out. I just remembered I promised Celia we'd go over the store accounts when we finished up here at the church and I'd best be getting home." He gathered his tools and when they could hear Richard's boots clattering up the basement steps, Luke turned to Edgar with a grin.

"Wouldn't want to be in his shoes when he gets home. Celia has a lot of virtues, but patience isn't among them."

"Aren't you supposed to love us, not judge us?"

"Whatever gave you that idea? Haven't you read your Bible? Jesus and his disciples were always pointing out people's flaws." He took the paper Edgar still held. "And besides, I do love my flock, warts and all. I'd hate to be the only one who has them."

"Pa?"

"Yes, son?"

"What are you two talking about?"

Both men laughed. "Women, and you'll never understand them."

Joe couldn't imagine ever wanting to. "So can we get back to those newspapers?"

"Sure."

"What do you think, Pa? What's somebody trying to tell us?"

"I don't know, Toad, but it's got something to do with woman's suffrage." Edgar picked up the Petersburg paper. "Let's look this over again."

The headline blared, "*Near Riot Ends Elizabeth Stanton's Speech, Many Arrested*" and he read:

> *Elizabeth Cady Stanton spoke on the subject of woman's suffrage at 7:00 p.m. this Thursday past, 27 November, at the Lyceum. Before an audience of nearly three hundred, including visitors from both Carolinas and Kentucky, Mrs. Stanton gave a speech titled, "The Bible and Woman's Rights." One hour into her talk Mrs. Stanton brought up the 15th Amendment to our Constitution, which gave colored men the right to vote, saying, "Women, white and colored, should also have this basic right." At that point people began shouting so loudly that Mrs. Stanton could not be heard. A wild fracas ensued, including the throwing of chairs and fisticuffs, and the police were called to quell the uproar. More than fifty women, all suffragettes, were arrested for disturbing the peace and Mrs. Stanton was led from the hall by armed officers. The City of Petersburg has asked Mrs. Stanton for a public apology.*

He looked wide-eyed at his father and Luke. "Gosh! I wish I'd been there!"

"Oh, no, you don't," Luke told him. "It's no fun being where things get so out of hand that people get arrested." He read through the article again. "Funny—it doesn't give the names of the women who were arrested. That's something readers would want to know."

"It's something I want to know," Edgar said firmly. "And I know how to find out." He reached into his pocket for his watch and discovered he had left it at home. "What time is it?"

"Can't tell you," Luke answered. "I left my watch in my study." Just then they heard the far-off pitch of a train whistle.

"Must be about five o'clock," Joe said.

"How do you figure that?" Luke asked.

"The only train that comes into town on Wednesday afternoons is the four-fifty-five from Indianapolis."

Edgar pulled his son to him. "Joseph, you never cease to amaze me!" Joe's smile reflected Edgar's.

You can tell they're father and son, Luke Goodman thought, *even if Joe's eyes are brown and his hair blonde.*

"And you've told me what I needed to know. The newspaper office closed a long time ago. I'll have to wait until tomorrow."

"Then let's get out of here and head to my house," Luke said. "If we're lucky, those womenfolk might just have supper started!"

No one said a word to Joanna about the mysterious envelopes or their contents. Carrie didn't tell her because she was distracted by the children's noisy squabbling over who got the biggest piece of spice cake. Luke never mentioned the articles because he didn't connect them with Joanna.

Edgar didn't tell her because...

.

Chapter Thirty-Three

Edgar walked into the empty newsroom of the *Appleton Gazette* early the next morning. He went to the metal bell sitting on the counter and laid a heavy hand on it. "Anyone here?

A young man emerged from the rear office, his young face flushed, his hands covered in ink. "I'm sorry," he stammered. "I didn't know you were here." His eyes darted from Edgar to the door and back again. "How did you get in?"

"Through the door."

"I left it unlocked—oh, no!" The young man pulled the towel hanging from his trouser band, frantically wiped his hands and practically ran to the front door, and turned the bolt, locking the door. "I can't believe I did it again. We don't open until eleven o'clock on Thursday since we're here late getting the paper out on Wednesdays. I come in early to clean the press, but Mr. Sheppard and Lu—Miss Sheppard don't get here before ten."

"I'm sorry. I should've looked at the sign, but I was so anxious to take care of my business that I burst right on in." His look was apologetic. "I'll be on my way if it's not convenient."

The young man shook his head, having recovered both his

wits and his manners, and extended a clean right hand to Edgar. "I'm James Taylor," he said; Edgar returned the introduction. "Since you're here, Mr. McGill, what may I do for you? Your business seems urgent."

"Not exactly urgent, more like perplexing." He explained about the letters and the newspaper clippings.

"I thought maybe I could get back copies of the Petersburg paper and read more about Mrs. Stanton's speech, and I thought somebody here would know how to proceed."

"I do, sir, but you'll have to pay for the papers and for the postage to get them here." Ten minutes later James had taken Edgar's order for a week's worth of papers from the *Petersburg Progress*. "They should be here in about ten days, sir, from the time they get our letter, that is."

"I appreciate your help, James, and don't fret about this morning. Neither Lucy nor her father will hear about that unlocked door from me!" James laughed, and Edgar heard the bolt click as soon as the door closed behind him.

Joanna invited the McGills to come for dinner after church. "Unless you've got something in the oven, Laura."

"There's not a thing in the oven except the rack," Laura laughed, "and it's a treat to have someone cook for me for a change."

"It's nothing fancy. In fact, you might find it a little odd."

"I like odd. How else do you think I stand living with Ed and Joe?" Peals of laughter and furtive glances in Edgar's direction brought him down the steps.

"For some reason, I think you're laughing at me."

"Not just you," Laura said. "Your son, too."

"*Toad?*" Edgar clutched his chest. "You mock my only child, dear sister? Say it isn't so!"

Laura shook her head and took Joanna by the arm. "See what I mean? This is the man you want at your house for dinner?"

Joanna's eyes met Edgar's. *Not just for dinner—forever!*

As soon as they arrived at Joanna's, Joe immediately went in search of the still nameless puppy, tracking his yelps of joy into the kitchen. Joe wrinkled his nose as he knelt to retrieve the pup. "He's made a mess, Miss Garrett."

"That's why I put the papers down," Joanna called back.

"Just roll them up and throw them in the barrel out back." Joe complied, holding the pup close to his chest with one arm and the rolled up papers as far away as possible in the other. Boy and dog remained outdoors.

"May I help with dinner?" Laura asked, following Joanna into the kitchen and noting just a single frying pan on the stovetop.

"No, you may not, Miss McGill. You may take this pitcher of tea out on the porch and stay there until you're called." Edgar poked his head around the corner. "And you too."

"Do we get to take glasses?" Edgar asked. He was rewarded with a pinch-eyed expression that said, *I'll get you for that.*

Several minutes later, Joanna called them back inside. Covering her round oak table were platters of sliced cold meat, cheese, a bowl of fried potatoes, and an array of marinated vegetables, along with a basket of bread, a plate of deviled eggs, and a crockery jar filled with butter. After they prayed, Joanna explained the meal.

"It's called *antipasto.* Margot Giannini told me her family has this every Sunday in summertime. Cold meat and just one hot dish."

"Makes sense," Edgar said, eagerly filling his plate. "The kitchen doesn't get hot, but everybody gets fed."

Laura stood to clear the table after they polished off Joanna's blackberry crumble, and nearly stepped on the pup dozing beneath her chair. "Goodness! I'd forgotten what it's like to have a puppy underfoot!"

"I'm forever stepping on the little tike, and yesterday I almost closed the bedroom door on him! He's like my shadow."

"That's it!" Joe snapped his fingers and jumped from the table, nearly knocking the chair to the floor, had he not had quick reflexes. That's the perfect name for him!"

Joanna looked confused. "I didn't say any name."

"You sure did, Miss Garrett. You called him your *shadow*! It's a great name for him. He's black and he follows you everywhere, just like your shadow. Let's see if he likes it." Joe dropped to his knees. "Shadow! Come here, boy!" The sleepy-eyed pudgy black pup wobbled toward him. "See! He came when I called him *Shadow.* Oh, please, Miss Garrett, can't we call him Shadow?"

"Son, it's Joanna's dog... *she* gets to choose his name."

Joanna did an affirming nod. "And I choose Shadow. Joe's right, it's the *perfect* name for the aggravating little thing." She bent over and lovingly patted the pup on his head. "Shadow, it is."

"How is the garden we planted doing?" Laura knew well enough, but thought she'd ask.

Joanna lifted her brows in an apologetic way. "I haven't checked it since we planted it."

"You can sure tell you weren't raised on a farm, Joanna." Edgar turned to Laura. "Why don't we look it over and see if it needs anything—like maybe a good watering from the rain barrel," and the two walked out the back door.

Joanna busied herself at the sink, while Joe sat holding Shadow, and staring out the window. He suddenly set Shadow down and went to Joanna's side. He stared up at her for a long moment. "Do you believe in Heaven, Miss Garrett?"

Though surprise caught her, she surmised Joe had a purpose for asking the question. "I absolutely do, Joe."

"Do you think my Mama is with Jesus?"

"Yes. I do," she said, sensing a deeper significance in his query.

"I don't remember my Mama, Miss Garrett."

"You were just a baby when your Mama went to Heaven, Joe."

"There's a picture of her—in Aunt Laura's room," he said, hanging his head.

The one Laura showed me, Joanna thought, *with Bessie holding Joe and looking at him with such love and tenderness.*

"I sometimes sneak into her room—" He paused and rubbed his eyes. "—I stand on a chair and stare at her and I try *so hard* to remember her." He wiped the tip of his nose. Joanna held back her own tears and knelt down to Joe.

Neither Joe nor Joanna heard the back door at the lean-to open.

"I should be able to remember... how she held me in her arms... maybe even kissed me," he said. He looked into Joanna's eyes, hesitating, then gently placed his finger on her cheek and caught the tear that slipped from her lash.

Edgar and Laura, with tears of their own, stood in the lean-to. Edgar opened his mouth to speak, but Laura silenced him, pressing her finger against her own lips.

"All babies know the love of their mothers, and not remembering could be God's way of easing her absence from you."

"Do you think Mama remembers me, even up in Heaven?"

"Yes, Joe, I do. I believe our loved ones who go on to be with God and Jesus know what we're doing — and that they watch over us all the time, like our guardian angels."

The pool of liquid that filled Joe's blue eyes gushed as he blinked awareness of what Joanna's words meant. "Then I don't think Mama would mind if I told you what I told her..."

Joanna looked questioningly into his sad eyes.

"If I could pick anyone—*anyone* in the whole wide world to be my Mother—I would pick *you*." There was no mistaking the pleading hope that filled the little boy and then, suddenly, he threw his arms around Joanna's neck and held her tightly to him. "I ask God every night before I fall asleep to make you like my Pa— and for Pa to marry you." He clung to her with all the strength he could force into his little arms.

Joanna thought her heart would burst in the love this little boy had for her, and she for him. She rocked him in her arms and kissed the top of his head. "If I could choose any young man—from *anywhere* in the whole wide world to be my son—" her hands tilted his face up to hers, "it would be *you*, my sweet Joe," she whispered.

He took a deep breath. "Would you keep a secret with me?"

"If you need me to, Joe."

"I'd like to call you *Mama*—just this once—until Pa marries you. Would that be alright?"

Joanna nodded through a sniffle.

"I love you, Mama."

"And I love you, Joe, more than you'll ever know." She settled his mussed hair as tears streamed down her face, and Joe hugged her again, placing his own soft, wet cheek against hers.

Laura choked her tears and pointed Edgar to the door. He wiped his own eyes, and the two carefully eased themselves back outside.

"He loves her, Laura. Joe *really* loves Joanna."

"I've known that long before today, Ed."

"I guess I just wasn't paying attention, or—maybe I didn't want to see Joe's feelings for Joanna, until—"

Laura shook her head as a smile crept across her face. "Until what, Ed?"

"Until *I* could admit to myself that I'm in love with her, too."

She threw her arms around her brother and kissed his cheek. "I've been waiting a long time to hear you say that and I hope you don't wait much longer before saying it to Joanna."

Something restrained him from telling his sister that he had. "I will, Laura."

"Don't wait too long, brother mine. You don't want to let Joanna Garrett slip through your fingers."

He nodded and together they walked back into the lean-to, deliberately slamming the door to alert Joe and Joanna they were returning.

Laura lingered before entering the kitchen. *Heavenly Father, that boy needs a mother; his father needs a wife—and Joanna needs them both.* She lifted the hem of her skirt to catch her own tears. *Please, let it be.*

Chapter Thirty-Four

Edgar made daily stops at Annie Campbell's over the course of the next week, but the package he expected hadn't yet arrived.

"If you tell me what you're waiting for, Mr. McGill, I'll have Henry bring it out when it comes. You're too busy to be making all these trips to town."

"No need for that, Miss Campbell, but thank you anyway." he tipped his cap and walked out the door.

"That's not like Mr. McGill," Annie told Elliott, preening himself in the ray of sunshine flooding the countertop. "He always stops to chat. Something's worrying him, Elliott."

As dusk settled in, Edgar was no longer worried—he was furious, and in anguish. He went out to the barn to find the sack of nails he'd bought at Hittle's. They weren't where he expected them to be, then he stomped out to the wagon and rummaged under the seat. The bag of nails wasn't the only thing he found.

This can't be good, he thought, glaring down at the ecru-colored envelope.

He walked into the house, went to his bedroom, where he shed his boots, and sat down at his desk. He held the envelope, staring at it and sensing nothing would be the same once he read the contents. He ripped open the envelope and pulled out the now familiar note. Along with it came a page from the December 1, 1884, edition of the *Petersburg Progress*. He took a deep breath and started reading:

> *Our readers will recall that last week Mrs. Elizabeth Cady Stanton, daughter of New York Judge Daniel Cady and wife of lawyer Henry B. Stanton, gave one of her talks here in Petersburg. Mrs. Stanton is a cofounder of the National Woman Suffrage Association and an adamant speaker on the subject. We reported that many ladies, some from Petersburg and some outsiders, attended the speech and surely rued doing so when their antics landed them in serious trouble indeed. The Petersburg sheriff reports taking thirty women into custody following the speech.*

His heart pounded as he read on:

> *Included among those reported to have been arrested were several well known Virginia ladies: Elmira Reaves Little, the wife of Professor Harold Little from the Washington and Lee University in Lexington; Letitia Guilford MacRae, whose family owns one of the Commonwealth's finest textile companies; Mary Sue Mottley...*

"What about the ones who were *not* from Virginia?" Edgar asked impatiently, standing and pacing the room. "Who were *they?*" He lifted the page, scanning the rest of the text, and there it was. He frantically began reading the list:

> *From our neighbor state, North Carolina, the following women were arrested: Susannah Hansfield York, a professor at Peace Institute in Raleigh; Roberta Scott Allen, a student at Peace Institute; Margaret Blake, also a student at Peace Institute; Joanna Garrett of Wilmington, a graduate of Peace Institute employed as a schoolteacher in Raleigh...*

He fell down onto the bed, the paper so tightly gripped that his knuckles went white. His mind raced, the blood pounded in his veins, he felt as if he were going to explode.

Why was Joanna arrested? Is she a suffragette? And the one question that would not go away: *Why didn't she tell me?* He crumpled the page and threw it, not caring where it landed, and lay on his bed, fuming, fretting and fearing—until exhaustion overtook him.

Saturday morning...

Laura awoke to the sound of hoof beats outside her window. She slid off the bed and pushed aside the curtains in time to catch a glimpse of Edgar astride Dolly, halfway down the lane. "And where is he off to in such a rush?" Her brow furrowed. "Something's wrong."

Joanna had just fastened the last button on her bodice when she looked out her bedroom window. Dolly's gallop was fast and furious. *Edgar's on horseback—something terrible has happened.* She raced outside to meet him. "What's wrong?" she called from the front porch. "Is it Joe—or Laura? What's happened, Ed?"

He said nothing. He dismounted, reaching into his shirtfront, advancing toward Joanna. His gaze was ironhearted, unrelenting in intensity. He took the steps, two at a time. "Nothing's wrong at home," he said. "The problem is here."

Joanna had never seen his eyes so steely cold, nor his jaw flexing anger, and then he stuck the paper in her face.

The Petersburg masthead froze her in silence as she sank into a rocker. "So you know," she said softly.

"Then it's true?"

Joanna nodded.

"When were you going to tell me—after I proposed? Or were you planning to tell me *after* we were married?" He slammed his fist down on the rail, the entire porch shook. "Or, maybe, not even then?" The muscles at his jaw continued to flex; Joanna could not say a word.

Edgar had only said *I love you*, he had never said, *Will you marry me?* Joanna knew she'd never hear either one again.

"I wanted to tell you, truly I did. I was just afraid—"

"*Afraid*— of what?" He leaned over her, bracing himself on the arms of the rocker, his face inches from hers. "*Afraid* that I might not want to be with a woman who has a criminal record? *Afraid* to find out she lied to me?" He heard her gasps.

Frightened and hurt though she was, anger propelled Joanna and she pushed him back, off the chair and stood up—undeterred by the fact that her petite size meant craning her neck to meet his gaze. She didn't realize that her low voice held the fire she so often heard when her father was in the pulpit.

"I *never* lied to you, Edgar McGill! I am *not* a criminal! And I am *not* ashamed of anything I've done. The only thing I am ashamed of is that I fell in love with a man who has judged me and found me guilty—without hearing *my* side of the story!" Her eyes, though full of tears, sparked a fury of rage he had never seen in a woman. "And if all you're here to do is accuse me, you can turn around and go straight back home!"

Edgar was shocked into silence. They stared at each other, violet-blue eyes locked on mahogany-brown, neither blinking nor flinching. Edgar picked up the news page that had fallen from Joanna's lap; he shoved it back inside his shirt and stormed off the porch. He kicked Dolly in her sides and galloped away at a breakneck pace.

Joanna ran down the steps and caught herself from begging: *Come back, Edgar... Please!* She turned back to the house, slumped in defeat, her heart leaden.

Edgar rode Dolly at full speed the half-mile into town and arrived at Werner's Store, panting almost as much as Dolly. Saturday morning shoppers filled the store and Edgar, without realizing or caring, burst through the door, pushing his way to the counter where Richard was weighing nails.

"I need to talk to you." His tone, along with his abrupt entrance, made clear that his business was important, if not critical. Richard finished weighing and bagging the nails, then motioned Edgar to join him in the stockroom, where Edgar shoved the newspaper at Richard, saying gruffly, "You need to read this." Confusion covered Richard's face. "Just read it. And then you'd best call a meeting of the school board." Edgar turned and left without saying another word.

Richard quickly glanced at the newspaper page. "From Virginia," he said. "Just like the clipping I got." Celia called to him; he hid the page under an empty crate before hurrying back to his customers.

It was late afternoon before Richard had time to retrieve the paper and read its contents. "I'll be," he said. "I never would've thought it." He scratched his jaw and shook his head. "Such a sweet, pretty little thing, too. Never would have taken her for one of them radicals." He sat for a while, then resolutely made his way to Ted Garner's bank. Richard wanted another school board member to help him break the news to Sam Bailey. Sam wasn't going to be thrilled about having to look for a new schoolteacher with the winter term a month away.

Edgar had ridden a mile toward home before he realized he didn't want to go there. "I can't face Laura. She'll ask too many questions. And what am I going to say to Joe? How can I tell him the teacher he loves isn't the person he thought she was?"

He wheeled back and found himself, without intending to, stopping at the church. The door was open; the sanctuary serene and cool in hushed stillness. Edgar stood for a moment before the Lord's table, then sat in the first pew. He didn't bow his head. He didn't fold his hands. He just sat there, listening to the beat of his heart and wishing it would stop. *I can't take this, Lord. I can't bear this pain—not again, Lord.*

Edgar didn't know how long he sat alone in the quietness before footsteps on a squeaking floorboard told him someone had invaded his safe harbor.

Luke wore his familiar, easy grin until he reached Edgar's pew. They looked at each other without speaking, then Luke took the seat next to Edgar and rested his hand on Edgar's shoulder. "Want to tell me about it?" Edgar shook his head. The two remained silent, until Luke tried again, "Want to pray about it?"

Edgar shook his head.

"You may not want to, but I need to pray." Luke removed his hand from Edgar's shoulder and raised both hands palms upward as he began. "Jesus, I know you are here beside me and my friend, Edgar, and I know you love and care for him. Something is hurting Ed. Only You, Lord, know what it is. He doesn't want to share it with me." If Luke's eyes had been open, he would have seen a shadow of a smile flicker across Edgar's face. "Help him, Lord. Help him to bear it, to share it—to be healed from the pain of it. We stand firmly on your promise to hear us when we pray, to comfort us when we mourn, to heal us when we are wounded. Thank you for your faithfulness. In Christ's name, Amen."

The two men sat a while longer, then Edgar turned to Luke. "Would your wife have a cup of coffee for a man who forgot to eat breakfast?"

"She'll do you better than that, my friend. Come over to the house and have a piece of the best coffee cake you ever tasted." *So, you're not going to tell me what compelled you to God's house today. That's all right. I'll know eventually.*

Sunday morning...

Luke stood in his usual place at the front door shaking hands and greeting people. His favorite seminary professor had told him something he remembered every Sunday morning. *"Watch people's faces as they leave worship. If there's a smile or a frown, you know you struck a chord with them. And if they won't speak to you, go visit them after dinner. God has work for you to do with that person."*

Sam shook Luke's hand and leaned into his ear, "I didn't see Miss Garrett at church this morning. Didn't expect to."

Luke showed concern. "Why, is Joanna ill?"

Sam didn't miss Luke's use of Joanna's first name. *So, they're friends.* He chose his next words carefully. "She's fine, as far as I know, Reverend. But the news that's all over town will probably keep her close to home for a while." He paused, then almost whispered, "Not that she'll have that home for long."

People were lingering behind Sam and Luke knew he had to let the elder move on. "Will you be home this afternoon, Sam?" The man nodded. "Then I'd like to stop by around two o'clock." Sam nodded again and left.

When Luke arrived at Sam Bailey's big brick house on Second Street, he also found Richard Werner, Harvey Greer and Ted Garner there also.

"Looks like I interrupted a school board meeting," he said, trying to keep his tone light. "You're just missing Doc Peters."

"Doc's out of town, delivering a baby," Sam said. "Otherwise he'd be here, too."

Their expressionless faces told Luke something was wrong, seriously wrong. "What's happened?" he asked, taking the chair Sam proffered him. "I know it involves Miss Garrett."

"It sure does," Ted Garner said. "It involves her up to her pretty little chin."

"What do you know that I don't?"

"A lot," Richard Werner said, and all three men started talking at once. Luke couldn't hear himself think, until he held up his hand urging silence. "Let me see if I've got this straight. Joanna Garrett went to hear Elizabeth Cady Stanton speak, got arrested at the speech, and went to jail. Is that the crux of the matter?"

"That's right, Preacher," Ted Garner said. "We've got

ourselves a suffragette schoolmarm, and a *convict* to boot. That's not the kind of woman I want teaching my daughter!"

"Not the kind I want teaching my boys either," Harvey Greer added.

"May I see the newspaper?"

Sam handed him the sheet Edgar had given him the day before and Luke sat down to read it. The murmur of the other men's voices was a distraction, but Luke soon rejoined the conversation. "Where did this come from?"

"Same place as those clippings you and I got, Reverend," Richard Werner said. "Edgar found an envelope—just like the ones we got— in his wagon with this newspaper page in it."

So that's what was hurting my friend, Luke thought. *Oh, Ed. Oh, Joanna.* 'I don't think we want to overreact here," Luke said. "We really don't know anything yet."

Ted, Sam and Harvey stopped talking and stared at Luke.

"The paper I got talked about a woman's suffrage convention. It didn't say a word about Joanna Garrett. The article Richard got said there was a riot after a speech Mrs. Stanton gave and some suffragettes were held at the Petersburg jail overnight for disturbing the peace. Again, that story doesn't mention Miss Garrett's name either. And this last article says Miss Garrett "*is reported*" to have been arrested. It doesn't say, for a fact, that she *was* arrested."

'Oh, come on, Luke," Ted Garner said. "You're picking at nits."

"I'm looking for the truth, Ted. We don't know that Miss Garrett is a suffragette or that she spent time in jail." He looked from one man to the next until he had challenged each one. "You're ready to fire the young woman, and you don't even know for sure that she did anything."

"I know enough," Sam said. "Where there's smoke, there's fire, my mama always said."

"Well, I'd really like to know who started *this* fire." *Whoever sent the anonymous letters and newspaper clippings wants more than an investigation of Joanna Garrett,* he thought, *and that someone must also have a vested interest in how such an investigation will end.*

"We've got less than a month until school starts," Harvey said. "We've got to act quickly if we're going to have a teacher in place by then."

Luke stood up. "You *have* a teacher in place, Harvey. Joanna Garrett is the best teacher Appleton's ever had and I, for one, want to hear her side of this story *before* we give up on her."

Laura did her best to get Edgar to talk to her. All she'd gotten out of him since Saturday afternoon were short answers to direct questions and a few comments on the weather. She was thankful that Joe had spent the weekend with Jimmy Langston. *I've seen Ed act this way before—angry and distant—but Joe hasn't. He was too little when Bessie died. He's never seen how Ed grieves.*

Joanna wasn't at church and when Edgar didn't mention her name, Laura knew that something had happened between them. *They've had a spat,* she thought. *This is just a lover's quarrel and it'll blow over.* They sat at the table, about to have dinner.

"You say the blessing." Edgar always said grace on Sunday and his break with tradition disturbed her. She prayed the blessing and handed him the platter of roast beef and potatoes, then passed the gravy.

"I wish you'd tell me what's wrong. I know it's got something to do with Joanna and I'd like to help."

Edgar pushed back from the table and stood up. "You can't help and I'd appreciate it if you stayed out of my business!" He stormed outside.

Laura didn't follow. *This is bad. Very bad. And only one person can give me the answers I need. I have to see Joanna.*

Chapter Thirty-Five

Joanna lay in bed, drained from all the tears she had shed. It was four o'clock, Sunday afternoon. The curtains were closed and Shadow lay snuggled alongside her. Every so often she petted his little head or stroked his soft baby fur...

The day before, after Edgar bolted away, Joanna had run into the house, thrown herself on her bed and cried until she ran out of tears. She had replayed the scene with Edgar over and over in her mind, until clarity took over, and she realized she had no idea what Edgar knew.

"What *exactly* did he say to me? I didn't even get a chance to read the newspaper, though I remember what the awful articles Papa sent me said. What did Edgar say... that I'm a liar and... and he called me a criminal.

She sat straight up, so abruptly that Shadow yelped.

"He thinks I was arrested, and put in jail, and that I'm a suffragette. Only one of those is true. Laura was right—I should have told him. If he knew the truth—"

"Was I wrong to fall in love with him, Lord? But I did, and it happened before I realized. I never felt this way about Nicholas, or any of the beaus who courted me... Not even Nicholas made me feel—loved." She closed her eyes. "I've hurt him, Lord, and betrayed him out of fear, the devil's tool... Oh, God! What have I done?" And, again, her tears overwhelmed her...

A pounding on the front door had Shadow trembling.

"Joanna... it's Laura! Please open the door, Joanna!"

Laura! She hurried to the door and opened it. When Laura smiled, Joanna burst into tears. Laura pushed the door closed, wrapped her arms around Joanna and held her until the torrent of tears subsided, then walked her into the kitchen, where she wet a towel and rang out the excess water.

"Wipe your eyes with your handkerchief," she directed. Joanna obeyed. "Now hold this towel on them for a few minutes." Again Joanna did as she was told. When she removed the cloth, her dark eyes were red and swollen.

"Thank you," she said, dabbing at her nose. "I'm sorry, that wasn't much of a greeting."

"It's better than what I've been getting at home. I can't stand the silent treatment. Edgar hasn't said a word to me since Friday, unless you count *please, thank you,* and *good night.* I know something happened between you two—something that's eating my brother alive. Should I guess what that is?"

"I should have told him, as you said, Laura... I should have told Edgar everything."

"How did he find out?"

"He had a page from a newspaper in Petersburg, Virginia."

"How on earth did he get that?"

Joanna shrugged her shoulders. "I have no idea. I was so upset and angry I didn't even look at the clipping, much less ask how he came by it."

"What did he say?"

Joanna recounted the entire scene for Laura, shedding more tears as she did.

"It sounds to me like my brother got his facts wrong about what happened in Petersburg, at least if I correctly remember what you told me."

"Do you want me to tell you again?

"Let's make a pot of tea and get you something to eat first. I bet you haven't had a bite since yesterday.

Several cups of tea later, Joanna was talked out.

"But, if you didn't do anything wrong, Joanna, and you weren't arrested, why all the fuss? Why did you have to leave home and family and find a new job?"

"The newspapers," Joanna said bluntly. "The press' perception of the melee wasn't true at all, but for people who weren't there, they believed what the press wrote. If you read it in the newspaper, you *assume* it's true, right?"

Laura reached across the table and squeezed her hand.

"I stayed with Susannah until she found me a position, and then I got on the train, and here I am."

Laura stood up. "We're going to do something about all of this, Joanna Garrett. I don't know what, but I am not going to let a pack of lies ruin your reputation—or keep you and my brother apart."

Practically everyone in Appleton knew Joanna's secret. With each telling, the story grew worse, so that by mid-afternoon on Monday folks gathered at Werner's Store were whispering, "*Miss Garrett broke out of a North Carolina prison where she was incarcerated for killing a suffragette!*"

Richard Werner overheard the scandalous talk and banged a hammer on a cook stove to get everyone's attention. "Now, folks, I want you to listen to me." He kept banging the hammer again, until silence reigned. "I'm on the school board and I know all about this business with Miss Garrett." If the truth be known, Richard Werner knew very little. "Miss Garrett was *not*—I repeat—*not* in prison, and she most certainly did *not* kill anybody. She *may* be a suffragette, she did *not* murder one." There were gasps and murmurs. "We believe she *may* have been arrested and *may*—I say again—*may* have gone to jail."

"Arrested? *And gone to jail!* And you men on the school board thought that qualified her to teach our children?"

"I doubt, sir," a woman's voice said, "that our very able school board knew anything about Miss Garrett's dubious past when they made the decision to hire her." It was Lucy Sheppard, splendidly attired in a red frock that no other woman in Appleton would have worn in the daytime. "The school board, no doubt, looked at Miss Garrett's paper credentials and they, we all know, are quite good."

Richard nodded appreciatively.

"However, the question is not what our school board did—but what they *will* do." Her green eyes leveled a challenging look at Richard Werner. His appreciation dissolved. "Just when does the school board plan to act, Mr. Werner?"

A chorus of, "*yeah, when are you gonna get rid of her?*" and "*when's the meeting?*" rang out. The storekeeper stood speechless.

"The board meets in private session on Friday," Sam Bailey

announced, "And in public session at seven o'clock next Tuesday evening. Come to the meeting and you'll see your school board in action." He made his way to the front of the store, leaned across the counter, and whispered to Richard: "Hope everyone can come on Friday. I had to think fast to pacify this crowd!"

Everyone in Appleton might have been talking about Joanna Garrett, but no one was seeing her. Joanna didn't plan to set a foot outside of her door until Friday, to catch the train for Fort Wayne , to go to Abby's wedding.

"Are you sure you still want to go?" Laura asked when she stopped by to check on Joanna in the afternoon. "Maybe you should stay here and work on your defense."

"My *defense*?" She shook her head and closed her eyes. "Now, I really do feel like a criminal."

"Oh, Joanna, I'm sorry, I—"

"I know what you meant, Laura. I don't think it will do any good. People believe what they want to believe. If everyone back home, including my parents, wanted to believe I was a wild-eyed suffragette and landed in jail, why should anyone here believe differently?"

"Luke thinks they will, and so do I. When truth speaks, Joanna, people hear it. You have to tell what happened that night. The truth is your defense."

"Would you have me tell the school board? I haven't found a single one of them on my doorstep asking to hear my side of the story. The whole town? No, thank you—no more mobs."

"Then, talk to Luke. He'll listen to you and the people in town will listen to him. And don't wait for the school board to come to you—go to them. Talk to Sam Bailey, he's a good man. Tell him what you told me and everything will be all right."

"I'll talk to Luke. But I won't go into town. I really am afraid of what might happen."

"Then write him a note and I'll deliver it."

Joanna did just that, asking Luke to come to her house, with Carrie, whenever he chose.

On Wednesday morning, Luke and Carrie's buggy pulled up in front of her house. Joanna waited at the door to greet them.

"Are you afraid to come outside, my dear?" Luke asked as he and Carrie walked in. "You can't keep living that way."

Carrie went straight to Joanna and enveloped her in hug, a motherly gesture that brought tears to Joanna's eyes.

What I wouldn't give to have my mother here with me right now!
"Please sit down. I made coffee for us, if you'd like some."

"Later," Luke said, "if that's all right with you two." Both women nodded. "I'd like to pray first and then I want you to tell us *everything* that happened back in North Carolina." Luke took Joanna's hand and drew her into a circle with Carrie. "Oh Lord, our Lord, wherever two or more are gathered in Your name, You promise to be with them. Thank You for being with us today. Keep Your loving arms around Joanna and let her lean on them for comfort and for peace. Give us Your wisdom, so that we may find a way out of this place of darkness and walk back into the light of Your love. In Christ's name, Amen."

Luke patted Joanna's hand and smiled. "Now, talk."

An hour later Luke and Carrie knew everything and were gathered at Joanna's kitchen table, sipping coffee.

"I still don't understand," Carrie said, "why someone sent us that clipping from the *Washington Post.*"

"Well, I was at the convention in Washington, but for the life of me, I can't imagine how anyone found out that I was. Susannah knew, of course, because we traveled together. The only people I told were my parents, and I can't imagine them publicizing it."

"Did you see anyone there that you knew?"

"Not a soul."

"Is there anyone in North Carolina who would try to hurt you, or who might be behind those notes to us and Richard Werner?'

"I don't have enemies back home, Luke, at least none that I know of."

"It has to be someone here, Luke," Carrie said. "The notes were hand delivered."

"That doesn't mean the mystery person is local. Someone could have come by train, or stagecoach."

When Luke and Carrie rose to leave, Joanna's heart was lighter than it had been in days. She walked out onto the front porch with them.

"That's the spirit," Luke said. "*Fear not,* God tells us. You cannot live in fear, Joanna, no matter what is going on in your life. Fear is of the devil, not of the Lord."

"You're right, my love," Carrie said, "but I still think Joanna should be cautious." She turned to Joanna. "Won't you come and stay with us? I'd feel so much better knowing you're not out here, alone, Joanna."

"I'm not alone," Joanna said and kissed Carrie's cheek. "God is with me, as your husband reminded me so many times this morning." She turned to Luke and smiled.

I know that look, he thought,. *I get it from my children when I get preachy at home. And, lately, I've been getting it from Edgar...*

Chapter Thirty-Six

Edgar walked the streets of Appleton feeling lost, alone and angry. If he were a drinking man, he would have spent the last four nights at Shipley's in Hanover. He had come into town for supplies, but found he didn't want to go back to the farm. He didn't want to talk to Luke either, and when the growling in his stomach reminded him that he hadn't eaten, he headed for Casa Giannini. The sight of its awning brought a flood of memories of Joanna. He pivoted on his heels and walked straight into Lucy Sheppard.

"Why, Edgar, what a delightful surprise!" She was lying through her fabricated smile—not about being glad to see Edgar, but about being surprised. She had been watching out the window at the newspaper when he exited Werner's Store. She grabbed her hat and dashed out the door, without a word to her baffled staff.

"Lucy," was all Edgar could say.

"Have you dined already?"

"No, I haven't"

"Would you like to have dinner with me? I've become quite fond of Mrs. Giannini's cooking."

Much as Edgar wanted to say, *anywhere but here,"* he couldn't, without explaining why. He opened the door to the restaurant and followed Lucy inside.

"Two of you for dinner?" Maria, the Giannini's daughter, greeted them. "We have a nice table by the window."

"That's lovely," Lucy said, "but we'd prefer one with a little more privacy, please." *The last thing I want is to sit by the window and have all of Appleton watching us.* Maria led them to a corner table and handed them menus.

"Try the special. It is one of Mama's best."

Now, Lucy thought, *just how do I get around to the subject of Joanna Garrett's fall from grace? I can't bring it up myself or I'll send Edgar running. I want him to run to me, not from me.* "I think I'll try the special," she said after a few minutes of uncomfortable silence. "Remember, we had the special when we first came here? Chicken, wasn't it? Chicken... *cacciatore?*"

Edgar stared at the menu. "If I remember correctly, you didn't like it."

"You're right." Lucy laughed lightly. "It had too many black olives. But I've grown to like Mrs. Giannini's cooking, so long as she isn't too heavy handed with the garlic. Do you think there's garlic in the special?"

Edgar raised his eyes, taking a good look at Lucy, her upswept blonde hair and her surprisingly low-cut red dress... and the seductive expression her green eyes held. "I doubt it, but we'll ask Maria to be sure." He signaled the girl, who confirmed the *veal piccata* had no garlic.

"Two specials, then," he said, "and a glass each of that white wine your Mama likes so much."

Lucy raised her eyebrows. "Wine, Edgar? At this time of day?"

"It's a special occasion."

"Is it your birthday?"

"It's our second dinner here, together... an occasion if I ever heard of one." When the wine came, Edgar raised his glass to her.

Lucy waited until the wine had sufficiently relaxed Edgar and she felt safe raising the subject of Joanna. "I had a letter from Lydia Lewis. She's home now, taking a break from her speaking schedule. So much has happened since then."

He took a sip of wine. "Have you heard about Miss Garrett?"

It's not Joanna anymore! It was all Lucy could do to hide her elation. "Why, yes, hasn't everyone? I was shocked, deeply shocked and—disappointed."

Edgar swirled the wine in his glass. "That's one way to put it."

"I was also surprised to discover you had chosen to be with a woman who wants to vote right beside you."

"What makes you think that?"

"Don't tell me you didn't know what happened back in North Carolina! I can't believe she would keep something like that from you, when you were growing so close." Lucy rested her hand on Edgar's. "You must feel so betrayed."

That's exactly how I feel, Edgar thought. *Finally someone understands.* "I hate being lied to."

"She lied to all of us, Edgar. Why, to think that she sat right there at Lydia Lewis' talk, as innocent as can be, when in truth she was one of those women we were being warned against! That was the same as lying."

Edgar nodded.

"Well, I agree with Lydia Lewis. I want absolutely nothing to do with ballot boxes and voting places. Politics is such filthy business." Edgar looked at her intently. "Even though I work with my father in what many people think of as a man's business, I don't want to be a man. I quite enjoy being a woman."

Maria returned to offer them coffee and dessert.

"Coffee sounds good, but I simply couldn't eat another bite. I'll never be able to wear this dress again if I keep eating like this." The stays in her tightly laced corset curtailed her appetite; she tolerated the discomfort, only to enhance the bosom she so daringly flaunted.

Edgar glanced at the low neckline of her red gown and then to Lucy's green eyes. "Now that would be a real shame."

Lucy dropped her gaze, feigning embarrassment. "Why, Edgar, shame on you!"

When the bills arrived, Edgar insisted on paying for Lucy's meal.

"This is the first time I've enjoyed myself in days, and I want to show my appreciation."

"Then I accept, but I *must* reciprocate—you must come to supper tomorrow evening."

"I'd like nothing better, Lucy. And now I'll escort you home."

"That would be lovely," she said, moving close enough for him to inhale her familiar rose scent. "But you'll have to escort me to the newspaper office instead. Father expected me back long ago, and I have work to do." They strolled down Main Street,

Lucy relishing in her conquest, and Edgar oblivious to everything but Lucy's blonde hair, sweet smell and apparent lack of controversial opinions.

Luke was on his way to the church and saw the two of them from across the street. He shook his head in disgust. "Edgar, Edgar, Edgar," he said under his breath, "you're making a big mistake, my friend." He rushed across the street and raced to catch up with Edgar.

"Good afternoon, Miss Sheppard, isn't it a beautiful day?" He abruptly turned to Edgar. "I'm glad I ran into you. Could you stop by the church office when you finish your business with Miss Sheppard?"

Lucy gave Luke the look that had made more than one copy boy turn tail and head back to the presses, but Luke ignored her. *I know it's not business that has you two together, but I'm not about to let you know I know.*

"I should get back to the farm. I've been here quite a while already." Lucy smiled and tightened her grip on Edgar's arm. Luke noticed.

"I just need a few minutes, so please come by." Luke tipped his hat to Lucy and departed, denying Edgar the chance to squirm out of the visit.

When Edgar walked into Luke's office ten minutes later, Luke quickly surmised that his friend didn't want to be there. "I know what brought you to the sanctuary last Saturday and I want to talk to you about it."

"There's nothing to talk about." Edgar hovered near the door. "It's over."

"If it is over, then that's what we need to talk about. But I don't see why your relationship with Joanna has to end."

"Because she lied to me, that's why!" Edgar pounded his fist on the door jam. "Because she's not the woman I thought she was—that's why!" He turned in the door's opening.

"You love her and you're hurt, *that's* why."

"Yes!" Edgar spun around to Luke, whose gray eyes were filled with care and concern. "I can't bear it—not again."

"This isn't anything like what happened with Bessie, Ed." He walked over to Edgar. "You haven't lost Joanna—not unless you choose to."

"There isn't any choice about it. I can't marry a woman who hid her past from me... who has done things I cannot condone."

"And just what has Joanna done that you can't condone?"

"She's a radical—she's been in jail, for heaven's sake! She's not the kind of woman I want raising my son. She's not even the type of woman I want *teaching* my son."

"And how do you know all this?"

"Someone sent me a newspaper clipping—it told me more than I wanted to know."

"When did you get your envelope?"

"Last week."

"And what newspaper was the story in?"

"One from Petersburg, Virginia, like the one Richard got."

"And what did it say?"

"Stop asking so many questions, Luke! It said enough to know Joanna's one of those suffragettes and has a very shady past."

"The articles I read didn't say anything of the sort," Luke's voice exuded more calm than he felt. "And Joanna told me a very different story."

Edgar's brows rose high on his forehead. "You talked to her?"

"I did, and you should, too."

"No, that can't happen."

"Give her a chance to explain what happened, Ed."

"I gave her a chance. She could have told me during all the months we were courting—she could have told me when I went to her house on Saturday. She did just what that newspaper said she did." *I can't believe this is happening all over again. I wait—how many years—seven, since I lost Bessie; waiting to give my heart to another good woman. And what happens? I fall in love with a mirage. I thought I knew Joanna, knew her through and through, but I don't know her at all. She's gone, just like Bessie. Joanna is dead to me.*

"Edgar, please," he persisted. "I spoke with Joanna and so did Laura, and we see a very different picture from the one you've painted."

"Joanna is good at painting pictures for people. What I want is the truth."

"I believe Joanna told me the truth. And I believe she's still the woman you thought she was, the woman you fell in love with."

"Well, Reverend—I don't."

"You'll regret it the rest of your life if you let Joanna go without hearing what she has to say." He hesitated, knowing his next words would be difficult for Edgar to hear. "And don't rush into Lucy Sheppard's arms. You say you don't love Joanna

318 *Melissa Warner Scoggins*

anymore because she's not the woman you thought she was, but I have news for you, Ed... you know exactly what kind of woman Lucy Sheppard is. She's not someone you love and cherish—much less someone who will love and cherish you."

"I'm not looking for love."

"Uhh-huh... then don't rush into Lucy's arms for that reason either. Just think about what you're doing. Think about Joe."

"Don't bring my son into this! I've been taking care of him for the past nine years and I'll keep on doing so, no matter *what* woman is by my side."

"You don't want Lucy by your side, Ed. You want her in your bed."

Edgar backed away, nearly toppling a table over in his haste to retreat. "I cannot believe you said that to me!" Edgar was more than just visibly shocked. His decency and morality were being challenged. "I'm not that kind of man."

"I know you're not, but Lucy is that kind of woman."

The two men stared silently at each other.

"Just be careful, my friend. Don't do anything in haste that you'll repent in leisure." Luke placed his arm around Edgar's shoulders, even though he felt Edgar's flinch. "And, remember, I love you, and God loves you. Don't leave God out of this, Ed. Promise me that you'll take this to the Lord in prayer. God might surprise you. It's happened before."

Edgar did not respond, which worried Luke more than he was willing to admit, except to God.

The men parted company and Luke took his own advice. He went straight to the sanctuary to pray.

Chapter Thirty-Seven

Friday ...

It was well before dawn when Joanna hitched Miss Molly to the wagonette and drove to the train station in Madison. Laura had again tried to talk Joanna out of going to the wedding, fearing that the townspeople would take her departure as an admission of guilt.

"They may, but I need to get away, Laura. I need some time to think and to be with friends."

Laura looked stricken. "You have friends here, too, Joanna."

"Oh, I didn't mean it the way it sounded," she said, and hugged Laura. "You and Carrie and Luke are the best friends anyone could hope for. I only meant that I need to be with someone who has known me a *long* time, like Abby."

"Do you want me to take care of Shadow?"

"I've already made arrangements for Shadow," she said with a soft smile.

"You have?"

"Yes—in the best possible hands."

Laura puzzled a look at Joanna.

"With Joe, in your home."

The Madison train station was near enough to the Ohio River to hear the deep-sounding burr of tugboats and even riverboats traversing the waterway. Joanna paid the stable owner to care for Miss Molly while she was gone and headed to the station.

Her train was on time and Joanna boarded it with a sigh of relief. *Maybe I am running away,* she thought, *just like I was the last time I got on a train. But this time it's different, this time I'll be coming back.*

While Joanna rolled farther and farther from Appleton, Lucy Sheppard was conniving to draw Edgar even closer than before. They had met for dinner again, at Casa Giannini, and Lucy had boldly advanced toward what she called *our table* without waiting for Margot to seat them. It was an outright affront to Margot, who shook in her loathing of Lucy's arrogance.

"Men are fools," Margot said to her daughter after the kitchen door closed behind them, "That nice-ah Mr. McGill with-ah that Sheppard woman! Where issah Mees-ah Garrett? Why issah she no here with-ah him, eating my pasta and holding hands, as-ah they did las-ah week?"

Maria Giannini knew her mother wasn't expecting an answer, but she gave her one anyway. "Miss Garrett has gone away, and soon she may be gone for good."

"Whatcha mean, gone-ah for good?" Margot turned, one hand clutching a wooden spoon, the other perched on her fleshy hip. "Why would-ah Mees-ah Garrett go away when-ah she so fine-ah teacher and she-ah in-ah love with Mr. McGill?"

In between serving customers, stirring pots and removing pans of bread from the oven, Maria brought her mother current on the town gossip. Margot was so incensed by what she heard that she could only glare at Edgar and Lucy when she brought their dessert, practically slamming the plate of *biscotti* on the table, then stalking off.

"What was *that* all about?" Lucy asked.

Edgar smiled and shook his head. "She's Italian," he said, as if that explained everything.

"Well, she better try to be a little *less* Italian if she wants to keep our business!"

It had only been three days since they last dined together, but Lucy already began to think of them as a couple. Edgar had come to supper the other night, but Roscoe Sheppard had spoiled her plans for a private *tête-à-tête* with Edgar. Tonight, her father unwittingly obliged Lucy and declined to join them in the back parlor for dessert and coffee.

Edgar followed Lucy into the parlor and sat at the small gaming table.

"Oh, do let's sit on the sofa, it's so much more comfortable." Edgar complied and Lucy sat down beside him, keeping a discreet distance until the serving girl had deposited the dessert tray on the table before them.

"I'm so glad you could come this evening." Lucy leaned forward and poured their coffee, then handed him the china cup and saucer. "I need your advice about something."

"And what might that be?"

"Father wants me to go to a newspaper convention in Chicago next month, but I'm just not sure about it."

"Why not?"

"Well, there will be hundreds of people there, from newspapers all over the Midwest. I've never been with so many strangers." *I can't wait*, she thought.

"Lucy, you blossom in a crowd. Remember when Lydia Lewis came and the Grange was packed? You loved every minute of it."

"Yes, I did, Edgar, but that was different. I was in my hometown and I knew just about everybody who came. This time I'll be all alone in a big city where I won't know a soul."

"Couldn't your father go with you?"

"Someone has to stay here and run the paper."

"Of course, I wasn't thinking."

"And then there's traveling alone on the train and staying in a hotel by myself. I've never done such a thing, and... it frightens me," she said, her lower lip quivering. It worked, as it always had; Edgar set his cup down and lifted her hands.

"I'm actually surprised that you're frightened. You never impressed me as the type to scare easily."

Lucy edged closer to Edgar, pressing her leg against his. "But it's so far away, Edgar," she practically purred.

"You'll meet lots of important people and you'll love seeing Chicago. Think of the museums you could visit and the plays you could see."

"But what about all that time on the train, all alone? You know the train will be full of men." *And, oh, how I'll enjoy that.* "I just don't think I can go so far away without anyone to... protect me." Her lips were still quivering and Edgar, well, he was fighting the overwhelming urge to use his lips to make them stop.

"Maybe someone else could travel with you, go up on the train and come back, and then go up to bring you home."

"Oh, Edgar, who would buy expensive train tickets and spend days on a train, just for me?"

"A friend would—like me."

"*You!*" Edgar was still holding her hands. She pressed them close to her heart. "I wouldn't ask it of you."

"But, I would, if you needed me to."

"Oh, Edgar," she whispered, placing her hand on his cheek, while the other remained at her bosom. "I don't know how to thank you!"

He suddenly pulled Lucy to him and kissed her. She offered no resistance, and his kisses continued, until her tongue slid into his mouth. It startled him at first, then inflamed him, and he pushed her back against the sofa. Again, there was no resistance. His lips devoured hers as passion overpowered him and, when his mouth slid to her neck, Edgar felt Lucy tremble beneath him.

This is just what I hoped for, she thought, *I wanted him to want me but, now, I really do want him.*

She slid lower on the sofa, her arms around his neck, pulling him down on top of her. He moaned through long, exploring kisses. Behind his lidded eyes, he saw only Joanna. Lucy reached for his hand and brought it back to her bodice.

Edgar got to his feet, trying to swallow through his panting breaths. "Lucy! I'm so sorry. I... I got carried away."

"I know," she said through her own pants, her face flushed, her lips slightly swollen. "but I liked it."

"It's wrong," he said, smoothing his hair, "I apologize."

"Edgar, I don't need an apology." *What I need is for you to come back here.* "Come—sit here beside me."

He yearned to do just as she asked. He stood staring at her while shock hammered his senses—not because of his bold behavior, but because he knew his desire was for Joanna. He shook his head. "That's enough."

"Perhaps you're right," she said, swinging her legs off the sofa and straightening her skirt. "But, *please* sit down and let's finish our coffee. There's no need for you to rush off," she said, patting the cushion beside her.

"Thank you for dinner."

Lucy rose and went to him. "Thank you for—dessert."

Edgar was speechless. "I'll be seeing you, Lucy. I'll let myself out."

When she shut the door, her emotions broke free: "Who do you think you are, Edgar McGill, to say *no* to me? What gives you the right to stop kissing me, when I wanted more? You're a fool, an arrogant fool." She paced the room, raving. "You're not in charge of our relationship—*I am* and *I am* the one who will decide things from now on." She plunked herself down in the wing back chair and smiled.

"But some things went just right tonight. I took your mind off Joanna Garrett, didn't I? And I made you feel protective toward me—as if I need any man's protection! You're as good as mine, Edgar McGill, and I can't wait for Joanna Garrett to find out she has lost you!"

Friday...

The five faces around Harvey Greer's conference table were resolute. Sam Bailey, as chair of the Appleton School Board, opened the meeting with prayer, as was their custom.

"Father, be with us as we work tonight. Guide the decisions we make and help us remember that our decisions affect many lives. Give us your wisdom, Lord. Amen."

Sam had barely opened his eyes before Ted Garner spoke. "I don't think we need much guidance. There's only one thing to do. The woman's got to go, and we've got to find us a new teacher before term starts."

"I agree," said Richard Werner. "I like Miss Garrett, but I won't have Emily being taught by a woman who isn't honest, no matter what her political beliefs are."

Doc Peters reached for the newspapers stacked in front of Sam Bailey and held one aloft, the one Edgar had given to Richard. "If this is where you got the idea of what her so-called political beliefs are, I wish you'd show me. I've read and re-read them and I can't find any place where they tell us whether Joanna Garrett is for, or against, votes for women."

"You must be joking!" Ted Garner grabbed the news pages, searched through them, and finally read aloud. "*From our neighbor state, North Carolina, the following women were arrested...Joanna Garrett of Wilmington, a graduate of Peace Institute employed as a schoolteacher in Raleigh.*" He slapped the paper down on the oak table. "You don't get yourself arrested for doing nothing, Walt!"

"But, Ted, that newspaper article doesn't prove she *was* arrested," Doc Peters said. "It just means *someone* said she was. We can't fire her without *proof* that she did something wrong."

"I agree with Doc," Sam said. "I'm concerned that we're of a mind to throw Miss Garrett out before we even know what really happened. I read those news stories, too, and as far as I can tell, that's all they are—stories. We need to know what happened before we do anything."

"We know something happened," Richard Werner said. "She's here, isn't she? Why would a young woman leave her family and take a school hundreds of miles away from home if she didn't have to?"

"But we've got to talk to Miss Garrett," Doc Peters urged. "We've got to hear what she has to say. I will not remove this young woman from her position—a position we thought she was perfect for when we hired her, let me remind you—unless I believe we have no other choice."

"That's easy for you to say, Doc." Ted Garner stood up to him. "Your children are all grown and on their way."

Walt Peters was a calm, kind man, qualities his patients appreciated. But when he was angry, it showed. This was one of those times. "Ted—" Doc Peter's voice was level but had an edge, "—you're wrong that I don't have any children being taught by Joanna Garrett. I've got more than any of you because every child in that school is a patient of mine. I'm responsible for more than just their physical health, you know. The person they spend eight hours a day with, who teaches them not just arithmetic but also right from wrong, is a very important person. Frankly, so far, I've believed Joanna Garrett was just the kind of woman I wanted teaching those children."

Harvey Greer squirmed in his chair. Doc Peters had made him recall how his boys had almost dragged him to the schoolhouse to show him that globe. He and Stella were thrilled that their sons went eagerly to school each day, and he'd been mightily impressed with Joanna Garrett. One recollection was how he had told Joanna: "*Continue in this vein and you'll have a long career here, if you want one.*"

"Doc and Sam are right," Harvey said suddenly. "Miss Garrett has been a mighty fine teacher, probably the best we've ever had here in Appleton. My boys learned more from her in one term than they did in the two previous years. Maybe those newspapers made a mistake. Maybe she was just in the wrong place at the wrong time. I want to hear what *she* has to say."

"And when are we going to do that?" Ted Garner nervously paced the conference room. "We've already called a public meeting for Tuesday night, and from what I hear, Miss Garrett has hightailed it out of town."

"She went to a wedding, Ted." Sam said, the look in his eyes was near disgust. "She didn't run away."

"She's gone, wherever she went," Ted replied. "We can't talk with someone who's not here, and I'm sure not going to tell people the meeting on Tuesday is off."

"Why don't we see if anyone knows when Miss Garrett is due back?" Doc Peters said. "Perhaps she told Reverend Goodman her travel plans, or maybe Laura McGill." He didn't say what every man in the room was thinking. *We sure won't be asking Edgar when she'll be back.* "And if she's back on Sunday or Monday, we'd have time to meet with her privately before the meeting on Tuesday." He faced Ted Garner. "I agree with you, Ted, postponing the meeting would be a bad idea. The town's in an uproar about this and the sooner we deal with it, the better."

Ted nodded and returned to his seat.

"All right, then," Sam said. "We'll find out if Miss Garrett will be back in time to meet with us *before* Tuesday night. If so, we'll hear her side of things, and then we'll come back into private session to talk about what we're going to do. Are we in agreement on this?"

Four heads nodded agreement.

Sam continued. "We'll have the public meeting Tuesday evening, vote on whether to keep her or let her go, and let everyone know our decision, right then and there."

"I don't know about that," Harvey Greer said. "Do you think that's fair, to make Miss Garrett sit there, surrounded by a bunch of angry people, while we deliberate? I think we should let folks know what's going on, hear Miss Garrett out, then vote the next morning, and post our decision."

"You can sure tell who the lawyer is," Sam Bailey joked. Everyone smiled and some of the tension lifted. "I think Harvey's suggestion is a good one." The others agreed, and after choosing Sam Bailey to contact Luke Goodman, the meeting adjourned.

Edgar's attempts at pretending that he didn't need Joanna, didn't miss her, and didn't love her had reached their pinnacle with Laura. She was prepared to discuss the matter with her brother after they'd eaten and Joe had gone up to bed.

"What's happening to Miss Garrett?"

Laura nearly dropped her ear of corn. "Nothing's happening, Joe. She's gone to her friend's wedding. She'll be back tomorrow."

"I know she went to the wedding 'cuz she asked me to take care of Shadow. Jimmy says she's done something real bad and she's gonna lose her job—" Fear filled Joe's eyes. "It's not true, is it? She's not gonna leave us, is she?" His pleading eyes moved from his aunt to his father, waiting for one of them to deny it.

I've been afraid this would happen, Laura told herself. "I'd like to tell you she isn't, Joe, but she might be."

Joe jumped up, his chair sailed backwards and slammed the stove. "She can't leave! She's the best teacher I ever had... all the other kids think so, too—even Emma Patterson can't stop talking about Miss Garrett—and she *never* talks to anyone! Doesn't that mean she's a good teacher?"

He turned to his father. "Well, doesn't it, Pa?"

Edgar didn't respond.

"I thought you loved her... you sure kissed her like you did—" Joe glanced to his aunt, then back to his father. "I saw you kissing her in her barn... when she bumped you with all that hay you were carrying... Don't you remember, Pa?" He waited, but, again, his father didn't say a word; he didn't even look at Joe.

"She loves you, Pa. I could tell—can't you, Pa?" Anger was building inside the boy, his aunt saw it in the way he kept looking at her, not understanding his father's refusal to converse with him. Laura let Joe have his say; it was time.

"I thought you were happy, Pa... happy like I never seen you before. I thought you were gonna marry her—so we could all be happy! I thought she was gonna be my mother!" Joe slammed his fist on the table; the barren ears of corn jumped on their plates.

"You don't want to be happy, Pa," he said in a low and steady voice, "and when you're not happy, I'm not happy and neither is Aunt Laura."

Laura was speechless, as was Edgar.

"You probably want me to say I'm sorry—but I'm not gonna say it, 'cuz I'm not sorry. And don't you ever think I'm ever gonna like that Lucy Sheppard. She hates Patches... she hates Miss Garrett—she hates everyboy—including you, Pa."

Edgar's eyes flew to his son's.

Joe nodded, his lips tilted in a smile of satisfaction that he'd finally gotten through to his father. "That's right, Pa. I saw the way she looked at you when you were dancing with Miss Garrett at the social..." His gaze went to Laura. "What's that you always say, Aunt Laura—*if looks could kill?* Well, Pa, you shoulda been dead that night."

Edgar pushed back from the table. "I won't have you talk—"

"You don't want me talking about Miss Sheppard, but you don't mind the way people are talking about Miss Garrett..." He began shaking his head. "I thought love counted for something, Pa."

Joe lifted his chair from the floor and ran up the stairs to his room.

Edgar let out a long and heavy sigh. "I'll have to punish him for talking to us like that."

"Punish him for what? For saying what he feels? And in case you don't know what that is, Ed, I'll tell you what's gotten into Joe. He loves Joanna and he knows she loves him and he's afraid he's going to lose her. It's tearing him up."

Edgar stared, astonished.

"Have you forgotten what we heard, hiding in Joanna's lean-to? He sees Joanna as his mother—he wants her to be his mother. And he wants her to be your wife. He prayed about it and asked Bessie for her blessing. And Bessie gave it to him, Ed."

'Don't tell me Bessie would like a woman who lies and deceives and isn't what she claims to be!"

Laura frowned, frustrated by her brother's blind stubbornness. "What's gotten into you, Ed?" There was enough chill in Laura's tone to frost a pumpkin. "You know who Joanna is and you know she's good, through and through. This... this *thing* that has come between you and Joanna is tearing at both your hearts—but will you talk to Joanna and find out her side of the story? Oh, no! Will you talk to me? Of course not. You just sulk around the house and refuse to speak, even when spoken to. You're acting like a child, Ed, and a badly behaved one at that!" Her stare punctuated her words. "Your son understands you better than you understand your son."

Edgar started to get up; Laura was quicker and pushed him back into his chair. "I don't understand you, Ed, and neither does your ten-year-old son, who said it very plainly: You'll listen to gossip and rumor, but you won't even talk to the first woman who's touched your heart since Bessie died. You'll jump to conclusions, but you won't try to find out if those conclusions are based on *fact*, or just puffs of smoke. And you'll go running to Lucy Sheppard, when a week ago you were on the verge of asking Joanna to marry you."

Edgar's violet-blue eyes became slits on a face that went void of color. "Did she say that? If she did, she was lying." He paused, his eyes drilling into Laura's. "But, then, she's quite skilled at lying."

"Don't you *dare* talk about Joanna like that!"

Momentary shock grabbed him, never having seen, or heard, his sister so angry.

"She's a good woman and she's an honest woman and she loves you—you fool—despite how you've treated her!"

The only sound that could be heard was the strained breathing between them.

"She told you I loved her?"

"Joanna didn't *have* to tell me you fell in love with her—anyone looking at you whenever you two were together—knew you were *both* in love. Joanna's never told you a lie, Ed. Maybe she didn't tell you everything about her past, but she didn't lie to you, which is more than I can say for Lucy Sheppard!"

"How... how do you know about Lucy and me?"

"There better not be a *Lucy and me*, brother mine. That is one woman with whom I will never share a house!"

Laura stalked out of the room, leaving Edgar to sit in stunned silence with no one but the dogs for company. Patches came and rested his shaggy head on Edgar's knee, while Shadow remained in the corner by the stove.

"She's right, you know," he said, petting Patches in an absentminded way. "And Toad's right, too. Loving and losing Joanna is killing me."

Patches licked his hand and Shadow meandered over to him and pawed his pant leg. Small comforts, but comfort nonetheless.

Chapter Thirty-Eight

Saturday ...

Sam Bailey was waiting on the church steps when Luke arrived.

"Morning, Sam. Did I forget a meeting?"

Sam shook his head. "No, Reverend. I just need a few minutes of your time, if you can spare it." Luke unlocked the side door and ushered Sam into his study, pointing Sam to an armchair near the hearth.

"I can tell by the look on your face, Sam, that this is important," he said, pulling a chair alongside of Sam's.

"The board met last night, and we need to talk to Miss Garrett."

Luke's heart sank. "The board decided to fire her?"

"No, no—at least, not yet. We want to hear her side of the story first. Trouble is, we've got that public meeting on Tuesday and she's not here and we don't know when she's due back." Sam drummed his fingers on the arms of the chair. "We know you and Mrs. Goodman are friendly with Miss Garrett, we were hoping she might have told you when she's coming home."

"Joanna will be back late tomorrow." He leaned toward the elder. "I'm glad the board wants to hear from Joanna, Sam. I'm sure that when you do, you'll want her to stay on."

Sam shook his head. "I don't know about that. A few board members were set to get rid of her last night, I don't know if anything will change their minds."

"Well, all I can do is pray that you all wind up on Joanna's side."

Luke remained at his desk after Sam had gone. He was fiddling with a piece of chestnut he kept for that purpose. Then, he slapped the desktop so hard his ink well jumped. "I'll pray all right, but I'll act, too!" He got out a piece of paper and started writing.

The one responsible for all the trouble, at that moment, was reading a newspaper story she hoped no one else in Appleton would ever see. Lydia Lewis' assistant had sent it to Lucy with a note: *"This story came out, as you can see, last April. I remembered Mrs. Lewis asking me to go through all our scrapbooks to find articles about Miss Garrett and thought you should see this one, although you did not specifically request it."*

Lucy read the headline aloud: *"Sheriff Admits Error, No Arrests Made at Mrs. Stanton's Speech; Women Cleared."*

She fell into a chair, then read on.

> In November of last year, this newspaper published two articles about a fracas at a speech by the woman's suffrage leader, Elizabeth Cady Stanton. We reported that a group of Mrs. Stanton's followers was taken into custody after a riotous outbreak and clash between pro- and anti-suffrage attendees and the local police. We also reported that a group of women was held overnight in the Petersburg jail, including several "ladies" from outside the Old Dominion.
>
> We regret that the earlier stories were in error. Sheriff Hector Pruitt has advised the editor that he was "encouraged" to investigate fully what happened at Mrs. Stanton's speech. Mrs. Stanton's National Woman Suffrage Association asked for the investigation, as did Mr. Alfred White Benson, a senior senator from Lynchburg. Mr. Benson's sister is Margaret Benson Keenan, whose husband is a professor at the Washington and Lee University. Mrs. Keenan attended Mrs. Stanton's speech. As Sheriff Pruitt told the writer, Mrs. Keenan's family was "hopping mad about having her name in the paper."

> *Sheriff Pruitt's investigation showed that the*
> *twenty-six women taken into custody after the speech*
> *were "wrongly detained." We deeply regret this*
> *serious error and apologize to all the ladies who were*
> *wrongly accused. We regret that we inadvertently*
> *caused them to suffer public embarrassment and to*
> *become the target of malicious gossip. Sheriff Pruitt*
> *asked the Progress to print the names of the ladies*
> *wrongly vilified, which we are glad to do. They are:*

Lucy skimmed through the list and there it was, smack in the middle of the article:

> *"... Miss Joanna Katherine Garrett, daughter of*
> *Reverend Matthew H. Garrett of Wilmington, North*
> *Carolina..."*

Lucy threw the paper up in the air and began pacing the floor. "I just can't believe it! Why did that meddling Miss Davis have to send me this? *'You didn't request it,'* she says. I wish I'd never seen it!" She fumed in fury. "Think, Lucy, think! There has to be some way to deal with this." She suddenly concluded:

"No one needs to know about this. Who's going to find out about it? No one up here reads the Petersburg paper. Certainly not Edgar McGill." A little voice inside her head whispered, *Are you sure? Can you risk it?* She thought a while longer, then smirked. "You bet I can risk it. No one here needs to know anything about Joanna Garrett's name being cleared—at least not until *after* the school board fires her and sends her back down south where she belongs."

Annie Campbell closed up shop at one o'clock on Saturday, as was her custom, except this Saturday, as Luke Goodman burst through the door.

"Am I too late, Miss Annie?" Luke was breathless, having clearly run from wherever he was, to the post office.

"You just made it, Reverend," Annie answered with a smile, gladly staying open late any day for Luke. "What may I do for you?"

"I've got three telegrams to send, and a letter to post by special delivery."

This was a red-letter day in the Appleton post office. Annie Campbell didn't send three telegrams in a month, much less in one day. She calculated the charges, then asked Luke if he wanted to stay while she sent the telegrams.

"No," he said, flashing his warm, wide smile, "I'll trust you to get them off." He handed Annie a dollar bill and as she made his change, she ventured a rare inquiry into a customer's business.

"Must be mighty important to be sending so many telegrams," she said, handing back his change.

"You could say it's a life or death matter." He stroked Elliott, who, as always, was perched on the counter. "It's about Joanna, Annie. I'd covet your prayers for her."

"I've heard about her troubles, she's been in my prayers. If there's anything else I can do, Reverend, please tell me."

"Come to the school board meeting on Tuesday night, Annie. Joanna will need to see as many friendly faces as possible."

Sunday ...

Everyone attending worship services at Hope Presbyterian Church this Sunday morning knew Luke Goodman was fired up. He began preaching without once glancing at his notes, and what he had to say poured straight from his heart and his soul.

"Brothers and sisters," his rich voice rang out, "I must begin by telling you that the wrong text is posted at the front of the church." There was rustling and murmuring in the pews. "No, the sexton didn't make a mistake. I fully intended to preach on Mark 9:1, until the Lord gave me a different text, and a different message, just yesterday morning." He paused to let his words sink in. "And when the Lord takes the time to come to me on Saturday morning and say, *'Brother Goodman, I have a word for you,'* believe me, I listen. And I want you to listen, too."

Luke held his Bible aloft. "Take your Bibles, if you will, and read our Old Testament lesson with me. It is Genesis, Chapter Two, verses twenty-one through twenty-three. Hear the word of the Lord. *'And the Lord God caused a deep sleep to fall upon Adam, and he slept: and he took one of his ribs, and closed up the flesh instead thereof; And the rib, which the Lord God had taken from man, made he a woman, and brought her unto the man. And Adam said, 'This is now bone of my bones, and flesh of my flesh: she shall be called Woman, because she was taken out of Man.'"*

"And now, hear what our Lord said in Galatians, Chapter Three, verses twenty-eight through twenty-nine. *'There is neither Jew nor Greek, there is neither bond nor free, there is neither male nor female: for ye are all one in Christ Jesus. And if ye be Christ's, then are ye Abraham's seed, and heirs according to the promise.'"*

Luke then began to preach a message unlike any his congregation had heard before, though they'd often heard him on fire for the Lord. He talked about men and women, how all were God's children and all were equal in the eyes of God. He reread the Genesis passage, proclaiming that God's intention before the fall was *equality* between men and women, not that man should be dominant over woman. "Only after sin entered in," Luke said, "was there inequality between male and female. This was never God's plan and is *not* His desire for His children."

Equally startling was Luke's interpretation of the Galatians passage. "Let there be no doubt," Luke expounded, "that Jesus Christ came to save men *and* women, both of whom are *equally necessary* in His kingdom."

He talked about the women at the tomb and about Sarah; he talked about the women of Hope Presbyterian Church and their "tireless efforts on behalf of those in need"; he talked about the many times Christ reached out to women. "Whatever the Bible tells us about man's role as leader of his family, and of the wider church family, do not for an instant believe this means our womenfolk are less worthy, less important, less capable than the men who lead them. Our Savior died for *all of us*, friends, every man, woman, and child. Remember this, and live according to it."

Usually, the congregation began chatting as soon as Luke left the pulpit. Not so this Sunday. Luke heard nothing but breathing until he stopped at the pew where his wife and children sat and motioned Carrie to join him. They walked arm-in-arm to the door, where Carrie remained by his side.

"That was some sermon," Edgar said, shaking Luke's hand. "I'd wager more than one parishioner is going to say you've stopped preaching and gone to meddling."

"And will you be one of them?" Luke's frankness caused his friend's blue eyes to widen, and then he smiled.

"Don't know yet, but you sure gave me food for thought. You're up to something, my friend, I just don't know what that something is."

Laura and Joe followed close behind, and Laura hugged Luke. "I've never heard a pastor talk about equality between men and women, Luke. I thank you for it." She leaned close to whisper so that just Luke and Carrie could hear. "It took courage for you to do this, and I hope you don't pay dearly for it!"

When Joanna walked into her house late Sunday, she found four notes waiting for her. One from Luke; one from Laura, one from Joe, and one from Sam Bailey. She laid her hat and shawl on a chair and went into the kitchen to boil water for tea. At least one of those notes would be better read with sustenance at hand.

Sam Bailey asked her to meet with the school board on Monday at four o'clock. He suggested they come to her home, which surprised Joanna. She liked his idea, not having to face Harvey Greer's imposing office, or the stares of anyone who happened to be on Main Street. "I'm not a coward, but I'd rather deal with the public *after* the board decides my fate—not before."

Laura wrote that she was eager to hear about the wedding. She promised to stop by on Monday afternoon and enclosed a devotional "*a friend gave me long ago and which I find especially appropriate for my schoolteacher friend at this time in her life.*"

Tears filled her eyes as she read: "Remember, in Christianity, as in education, there are three R's: Relax in God's peace, Refresh in God's energies, Relinquish to God's wisdom and will." "Thank you," she whispered, to both the absent Laura and the very present God.

Joe's note made Joanna laugh.

> *Deer Miss Garrett, Shadow is fine. I fed him and played with him and am about wore out. I will bring him to your house tumorow. Aunt Laura is coming, two. Be ready to be licked. Your frend, Joseph McGill.*
>
> *P.S. Shadow will do the lickeng.*

Luke's equally short note said he and Carrie were keeping her in their prayers and "*had every confidence that all will be well.*"

Joanna sipped her tea and rifled through the stack of paper. Despite her fears, the words of support and encouragement affected her more deeply than did Sam's terse request for a meeting. For the first time since Edgar had showed up on her doorstep and confronted her with the newspaper article, she felt hopeful. And she liked it.

Monday ...

Laura and Joe stopped by Joanna's house, as promised, and Patches scampered into the house, slid all the way across the floor to Joanna, and licked her face, her neck, and her ears.

"See! I told you, Miss Garrett!"

After a cup of tea and a few cookies, Laura announced the plans to accompany Joanna to Grange Hall. "Joe and I will be here at five, and we'll pick up Luke and Carrie, and then we'll all go to the meeting together."

"You don't have to do that. It's a short walk and I'm quite sure I'll be safe."

"I insist." Laura's tone left no room for argument.

"Do we have to go so early?" Joanna sat with Shadow nestled in her lap, where he had collapsed after giving her the head-to-toe licking Joe had warned of. She stroked the pup over and over, unwittingly revealing her distress.

"We do," Laura insisted. "But you don't have to spend two hours sitting on the front row. There's a little room off the main hall where you can wait. Carrie and Joe and I will get seats, and Luke will stay with you until the meeting begins."

"We'll be right there waiting for you, Miss Garrett. You just look at me and Aunt Laura and don't you pay no attention to anyone else."

"*Any* attention," Joanna automatically corrected. Both Joe and Laura laughed.

"See, even now you're trying to help me talk right. I told Pa you're the best teacher I ever had."

And what did your father say to that? Joanna wanted to ask.

"I told Pa I wanted you to be more than my teacher, too. I told him I want you to be my mother. You'd be a real good one."

Joanna saw the love and longing in Joe's eyes, and felt a thickening in her throat. *I can't tell him that will never happen, I won't hurt Joe.* She knelt down, motioning Joe to get a hug.

"That means so much to me, Joe, you're a boy any woman would be proud to have for a son." She kissed his cheek and Laura saw her wipe a tear as she stood up. "It will make things easier for me, having you there— and you, too, Laura."

And what about my brother? Laura wouldn't voice the thought. *Will he be there tomorrow night? And if he is, will it be as Joanna's supporter, or as her detractor?* She went to stand behind Joanna, her arms around her waist.

"It's going to be all right," she said in a soothing but determined tone. "Everything is going to be all right." Both women knew Laura was not just referring to her job.

At exactly four o'clock, the school board members arrived. Joanna offered them coffee when all five were seated in her front room, but they declined.

"We're not here on a social visit, Miss Garrett," Ted Garner said curtly. Joanna noticed that both Doc Peters and Sam Bailey cut their eyes at him. It gave her a flicker of hope that, perhaps, not every man in her home wanted to see her leave it.

Sam Bailey explained what they knew and asked Joanna to tell her side of the story. She told them what she had told Laura and Luke and Carrie.

Sam Bailey looked her in the eye, as did the other four men. "Is that your full accounting of the events, Miss Garrett?"

"Yes. It is the complete chronology of the events, as they happened."

"Then this meeting is over." The other four men followed Sam's lead. Only Doc Peters smiled at her before he closed the door behind him.

"Well," she said to Shadow, "that's that."

Chapter Thirty-Nine

Tuesday ...

The town of Appleton buzzed with an energy and excitement that rivaled the day a newly-elected governor waved from a train's caboose when he passed through town.

Luke Goodman felt it when he walked home for lunch; Richard Werner felt it in his store, and Lucy Sheppard thought she could almost see it from her office window.

"The whole town's agog," she told her father, "and the school board meeting is still five hours away."

"We better get to the Grange by six, if we don't want to stand through the whole meeting."

"Better make it five. That way Mr. Giannini can get his camera set up down front."

It was a little after five o'clock when the McGills and the Goodmans pulled up in front of the Grange, just in time to glimpse Lucy Sheppard disappearing through the front entrance.

"Don't worry," Luke shouted from the rear seat. "We don't have to face that lioness yet." Carrie and Laura tittered, Joe guffawed, and a smile made a fleeting sweep across Joanna's face.

338 Melissa Warner Scoggins

"There's a back door, I have the key here, somewhere," Luke said searching his pockets.

Ten minutes later a puzzled Edgar watched Laura, Joe and Carrie emerge from the side door beside the stage. He was holding a first row seat for Lucy, who had run back to the office to grab the writing tablet she had forgotten in her haste.

"Hey, there, Toad." Edgar stood as Joe came over to him. "I didn't expect to see you here this early."

"We brought Miss Garrett. She's waiting with Reverend Goodman in a little room back there." He pointed to it.

"Luke didn't want Joanna to wait alone," Carrie said, "and she didn't want to sit out here while the whole town poured in."

"Whole county is more like it," Edgar said. "From what I hear, there'll be more folks here tonight than came to hear Lydia Lewis speak."

"Wonderful," Laura said, her voice dripping with uncharacteristic sarcasm. "Like Romans in the coliseum."

"Not all of them are coming to gloat or be entertained, Laura," Carrie said. "A great many are here for the same reason we are, to support Joanna."

"Is that why you're here, Ed?" His sister's direct question caught him completely off guard. "I wasn't sure we'd see you at all, much less in the front row."

Before he could answer, a commotion at the entrance drew their attention. Antonio Giannini was banging his way through the door, a camera bag clutched in one hand and a huge stand in the other. Directly behind Antonio came his wife, and behind her was Lucy Sheppard. At the sight of Lucy heading their way, Laura knew why Edgar was waiting on the front row.

"Let's go sit down," she said quickly. "I don't relish making small talk with Lucy Sheppard."

"Why can't we sit here, with Pa?"

"Somehow I don't think we want to, Joe," his aunt said. "We might not like the company." Joe and Carrie both looked confused as Laura led them to seats at the far end of the first row. Laura counted out five seats and then took the one on the aisle. "Joe, you sit by me, and Carrie, if you take that fifth seat in, we'll put Luke by you and Joanna beside him." Joe and Carrie did as directed, but Joe never took his eyes off his father. When Lucy Sheppard sauntered up and sank down beside Edgar, Joe groaned, closed his eyes, and shook his head.

"Aunt Laura," he whispered, "how come Pa's sitting with *her*?" He spit out the word as if it were venom.

"Only your father can answer that question, Joe."

"Why does Pa want to be with Miss Sheppard when he loves Miss Garrett?"

Carrie and Laura exchanged quick glances.

"Not so loud, Toad," Laura said. "Somebody might hear you... love's a very private matter. Of course, folks are about to find out a whole lot about Joanna's private life, aren't they?" She leaned toward Joe. "Your father's confused and angry right now, and he's doing a stupid thing because of it. Even grown-ups make mistakes when we're hurt or mad."

"I'd like to go over there and tell Pa what I think of him!"

Laura stifled her grin. "I think you've already done that, Toad."

Antonio Giannini began setting up his camera equipment near their seats. He bowed and smiled, but kept to his work, and when he had finished, he came over to them.

"I am-ah charmed to see-ah you both-ah thees night," he said in his usual courtly way. "Though I would-ah rather no be here," he shook his head emphatically. "No for thees-ah reason." His black eyes were doleful and his expression somber.

"Are you taking pictures for the newspaper?" Laura asked.

"I am. Mees Sheppard, she cann-ah be very persuasive." He looked to where Lucy sat beside Edgar. Her blonde head was tilted toward Edgar and his arm was draped around her shoulders. Laura followed Antonio's gaze; her gasp spoke volumes. When she turned back, Antonio's eyes were warm with sympathy. Laura shrugged her shoulders and Antonio Giannini shook his head.

"People in-ah love... they can-ah be very-ah stupido, No?" He bowed and returned to his camera.

Joe tugged Laura's sleeve. "How does Mr. Giannini know about Pa and Miss Garrett?"

"He's Italian, Joe. Italians know a lot about love."

Over the next hour Laura and Carrie and Joe made small talk and watched the people filling the Hall. Roscoe Sheppard claimed the seat beside his daughter and when John and Frances Lane joined Carrie, their row was full. Frances leaned close to Carrie. "The friendly faces outnumber the hostile ones, at least on the front row!" Carrie wondered in which Frances had counted Edgar.

By six-forty-five, the room was full and people were overflowing into the entranceway. At ten minutes to seven, the school board ascended the steps onto the stage and took their places in the six chairs behind a long imposing table. Laura suddenly realized why there was a sixth chair ; she leaned over Joe to speak to Carrie.

"They mean for Joanna to sit up there with them," she whispered. "They're putting her on display!"

"Luke expected that," Carrie whispered back, "If I know my husband, he's taken care of it!"

Sure enough, when Luke and Joanna came out the side door five minutes later, he led Joanna down the steps and waited until she had taken the seat beside Joe before he went back on the stage to speak with Sam Bailey.

"I'd like Miss Garrett to sit with us until you need her to speak," Luke said quietly. Sam shook his head, but Luke persisted. "Be fair, Sam. She can't sit up here, all eyes on her, for the entire meeting."

"Luke's right, Sam," Doc Peters said in a low voice. "That poor girl shouldn't be made to sit in front of all these people. She's not on trial, for heaven's sake!"

At precisely seven o'clock Sam walked to the center of the stage. "Good evening. I'm glad to see all of you here tonight. I'm pretty sure this is the biggest turnout we've had for a public meeting of the Appleton School Board. It's good to know so many folks care about our schools."

Lucy leaned into Edgar's ear and spoke loudly enough so that others could hear her. "That's not why they're here, and Sam Bailey knows it." Edgar nodded and shifted uncomfortably in his seat.

Sam continued. "I'm sure you all know why this meeting was called, but I'm going to tell you anyway, in case some folks haven't heard. We're here because of a concern about our school teacher, Miss Joanna Garrett. After this meeting, the Board is going to vote on whether Miss Garrett will be teaching in Appleton next term." An undercurrent of murmurs began. "We won't be announcing our decision tonight, though."

Several in the crowd called out, "Why not?"

Sam pressed on. "We'll talk privately after this meeting and make our announcement in front of Lawyer Greer's office tomorrow at noon." There was another wave of murmuring.

"Now, folks, to get us started, I'm going to ask Doc Peters to tell you what's happened so far." Doc joined Sam, but put one hand on his shoulder to stop him from returning to his seat.

"Sam, I think you've forgotten something," Doc Peters said. "We always start our school board meetings with prayer, and I think we should do so tonight." Sam nodded, as did the other board members. "Usually our chairman leads us in prayer, but we've got a lot of clergy here tonight and I know one of them would love to intercede for us." Walt pointed to John Lane. "Reverend Lane, could I impose on you?"

John stood and said in his pulpit voice, "Let us pray." Every head bowed and Antonio Giannini and his wife made the sign of the cross. "Father, be with us in this place. The work of this night is so important, not only for our sister, Joanna Garrett, but also for our schoolchildren and their families and for our entire community. Give us wisdom, Lord, and keep our tongues from harsh words and our minds from unkind thoughts. Guide the board in its decision and may all that happens here tonight be pleasing in Your sight. Amen." *And please, God*, he added silently, *give Joanna Your courage and strength and stay close to her this night.*

Doc Peters cleared his throat. "First, let me tell you how this meeting's going to be conducted. I'm going to talk and then you'll hear from Miss Garrett and perhaps from my fellow trustees." There was another undercurrent of murmuring. "Then we'll open this up for comments from the public. Wait for me or Sam Bailey to acknowledge you, then speak loud enough for everyone to hear you. When you're finished, sit down. We'll take turns and there'll be no yelling out. Then I imagine Miss Garrett might want to respond again and we'll finish up for the night. Everybody clear on how things are going to be?" He paused to look over the audience, then turned to the Board members at his back. "All right then. I'll begin."

"You all know the Board brought Miss Joanna Garrett here from North Carolina back in January to take over teaching at the Henry Township School. We were pleased with Miss Garrett's teaching during the spring term, mighty pleased." He looked straight down at Joanna and nodded to her. "I know I'm not the only one here who attended the Open House back in May and came away impressed. And I bet most of you read the fine article Mr. Sheppard wrote about Miss Garrett and saw Mr. Giannini's handsome photographs in the *Gazette*." Antonio Giannini popped his head from under the drape.

"We're not here tonight because Miss Garrett did something wrong during the spring term, or because we've had any complaints about her teaching. On the contrary, the Board members have heard more compliments about Joanna Garrett than about any other teacher we've had in my time here." He paused and looked across the first rows of people. "No, we're here because of some things we've learned about Miss Garrett just recently, things that have nothing to do with her teaching credentials." Doc Peters looked down at Joanna. "Her credentials are excellent. She's the *first* college graduate we've ever had teaching in Appleton, and she was at the top of her class."

There was a smattering of applause, during which Dave Calhoun whispered to Cal Tuner, "I thought this meeting was to fire Joanna Garrett, not to tell us how wonderful she is!"

Doc Peters continued. "We called this meeting because we obtained copies of pages from some North Carolina and Virginia newspapers that had stories about Joanna Garrett in them, stories some of us found shocking."

Edgar felt Lucy draw in a breath and when he glanced sideways, he reached one conclusion. *She's enjoying this.* He slid his arm from the back of Lucy's chair; she didn't even notice.

Doc Peters held up the Raleigh news page. "This talks about a speech Mrs. Elizabeth Cady Stanton gave in Petersburg, Virginia, in November of last year. Mrs. Stanton, you may know, is the founder of the National Woman Suffrage Association."

Some in the crowd pitched their *boos.*

"We'll have none of that," Doc said sternly. "There was a disturbance at Mrs. Stanton's speech and a group of people, all ladies, were taken into custody by the police. One of them was Miss Garrett."

The revelation touched off widespread murmuring and Luke squeezed Joanna's hand. She closed her eyes, wishing with all her heart that it was Edgar doing so.

"The Board met with Miss Garrett privately," Doc Peters said over the crowd, "and Miss Garrett confirmed that she did attend Mrs. Stanton's speech, and that she was taken to the jail in Petersburg afterwards."

The crowd erupted into near chaos:

"I don't want no jailbird teaching my little girl!"

"What lies has she been telling our children?"

"She's one of 'em women what wants to be a man—get rid of her!"

"Send her back to North Carolina!"

This must have been what it was like in Petersburg, Edgar thought, *only much worse... it must have been terrible for Joanna.*

"Silence!" Doc Peters' voice thundered. "I told you we're not going to have any of that and I mean it! The next person who shouts out is going to be removed from the premises!" He stared into the audience until every person was seated again.

"The newspaper articles report that Miss Garrett was arrested at Mrs. Stanton's speech." More muttering began, but

Doc glared the audience into silence. "Miss Garrett tells us this is not true. I think it's time you heard what she told us." He motioned Joanna to join him on stage.

Luke squeezed Joanna's hand. She stood up, smoothed her skirt, and slowly climbed the stairs to the stage. The air crackled with tension as she began to speak.

"I'm used to talking in front of my pupils," she said, "but this is the first time I've addressed such a large gathering of adults. I must say I liked it better when I talked before many of you at our Open House back in May." She paused and took a breath. "I will do my best to speak clearly and loudly, and I hope you will grant me the courtesy of listening to what I have to say." She focused her gaze on a spot in the center of the audience, avoiding eye contact with anyone, especially Edgar in his front row seat beside Lucy.

"I did attend Elizabeth Cady Stanton's speech last November. I was there at the invitation of one of my professors, Susannah York, who teaches history and religion at Peace Institute, the college I attended in Raleigh."

"Professor York and I, and several of her students took a train to Petersburg and went to the Lyceum, where Mrs. Stanton was scheduled to speak. We arrived almost two hours early and found seats down front at the foot of the stage. By the time Mrs. Stanton came out, the hall was so packed that people were standing in the aisles."

"Just like tonight!" someone shouted. Joanna ignored him.

"There must have been at least five hundred people there, a very large number even for the size of that lecture hall. At first, people were well behaved—quiet and listening to Mrs. Stanton—but about an hour into her talk, some men in the crowd became quite angry and started calling her awful names and yelling at her to leave town."

"I'd of done the same thing!" Another man shouted and jumped up. "She's crazy!" Several people mumbled agreement.

Doc Peters pointed his finger at the rabble-rouser. "Sit down, sir! If you yell out like that one more time, you'll be removed. Do you understand, sir?" The man sneered and sat down. Doc nodded to Joanna to continue.

"The shouting got louder with horrific comments and men started throwing things at Mrs. Stanton. I was so afraid they were going to hurt her." She shuddered briefly and Edgar felt a wave of protectiveness surge over him.

Joanna continued: "People began climbing over the seats behind us, and forcing us out of our seats. I lost my balance and went down on my knees. If Susannah York hadn't pulled me up, I would have been trampled." She paused and took a deep breath. "You can't imagine how frightening it was, being in a hall with hundreds of people gone mad. We were pushed down to the very edge of the stage as men lunged every which way, trying to climb on to the stage. I looked up and saw some men encircling Mrs. Stanton. If they had not done so, I'm sure she would have been hurt." Joanna focused on the front row long enough to see Frances Lane wipe a tear from her eye and Carrie Goodman lean her head against her husband's shoulder.

"I was frightened... no, I was absolutely terrified, and so were the women with me—some really just girls in their first year of studies at Peace. Many were crying and clinging to Susannah. Then we heard police whistles and almost immediately there were police officers everywhere, brandishing billy clubs. Someone grabbed my wrist and pulled so hard that I thought it would break."

The room grew very still and those close to the front could see the pain in Joanna's face.

"It was a police officer tugging on me..." Joanna sighed and those on the front row knew she was reliving the terror of that night. "I felt so relieved that help had come. *We're safe now*, I remember thinking." She shook her head and looked directly into the audience.

"But, we weren't safe. The police dragged us out a side door and into the street and then they—" Her teeth caught hold of her lower lip. "—they handcuffed us, like common criminals and acted as if *they* were in danger from us."

Her face took on a pained expression. "The police in danger... from a few women? When there were dozens of men climbing over seats and throwing things and knocking people down? I'll never understand why they grabbed any of us, instead of those men."

"Because you're such a pretty little thing!" a man yelled. Joanna thought it was Cal Turner's voice.

"Instead of protecting us, the police held us out there in the street—that bitter cold winter night—until a police wagon came. You can't imagine how brutally they handled us. One girl's skirt was torn, caught on a nail or a shred of wood, as they shoved her inside their wagon." She breathed deeply again. "It was humiliating. Totally and horribly humiliating. They handcuffed us and threw us into that wagon, and hauled us downtown, where for hours, we kept telling them, over and over again, that we had done nothing wrong."

Joanna paused and looked into the audience. "They

wouldn't listen." She wiped at the tear that started to run down her cheek.

"So, some of what these newspaper articles reported is true. I did go to Mrs. Stanton's speech and I was taken into police custody."

"Then you need to go back where you came from! Get outta here!" The shout came from the man who had yelled out earlier.

Doc Peters and Sam Bailey both jumped to their feet. "I told you, there'll be none of that!" Doc shouted. He motioned to two men standing at each end of the first row, who ran back and grabbed the heckler by both arms, hoisting him up off his feet, and carried him out out of the building.

"This isn't going to be another Petersburg," Sam Bailey announced, shaking his finger at the crowd. "No one's going to be hurt or scared here tonight. There'll be no jeering or heckling and there sure isn't going to be any running up front to attack *our* speaker." He and Doc flanked Joanna. "Please, Miss Garrett, go on," Sam said.

"I was taken into custody, but I was not arrested, nor was anyone else in our group." For the first time, Joanna made deliberate eye contact with people in the audience, Edgar included. When he smiled at her, she felt her knees go weak. "We had to identify ourselves and answer a lot of questions, but the police did not arrest us. We were finally released, long after midnight, and allowed to go home."

Joanna fell silent, momentarily looking around the room. "I did nothing wrong that night in Virginia," she said softly. "I went only to hear Mrs. Stanton talk about a subject that upsets a lot of people, and got caught up in a mob of angry men. But for a lot of people back home, I was guilty by association. I left North Carolina because of what newspapers reported had happened that night. Everyone believed what the newspapers wrote, even—"

Laura knew Joanna was remembering the letter from her father.

"—even my family. I hope I don't have to leave Appleton for the same reason." She turned to Sam Bailey, inclining her head toward her empty seat. He nodded and Joanna went back to her chair.

"If anyone wants to ask Miss Garrett a question, or make a comment, now's the time," Sam said.

Several people jumped to their feet and one started talking. "Remember the rules! Wait for me to recognize you, say your piece and sit down. And *no* yelling!" He pointed to Harold Akers.

"I'd like to know if Miss Garrett agrees with Mrs. Stanton's views."

Joanna stood up to answer, but Sam Bailey motioned her to stay seated. "Harold, the Board thinks Miss Garrett is entitled to keep private her personal views on voting rights for women." There were more *boos* and catcalls.

Harold Akers spoke again. "I think what she believes affects her character, Sam, and so do a lot of other folks." He turned to the audience for affirmation. "Am I right about that?" Heads nodded and hands clapped.

Sam started to speak, but Joanna stood up this time. "Mr. Bailey," she said, loudly enough for all to hear, "I'd like to answer Mr. Akers' question, if I may." Sam looked to the other trustees and everyone nodded.

She turned to face her questioner. "You're right, Mr. Akers. What we believe is important. I am who I am because of *how* and *where* I was raised, *what* I was taught, what I've experienced, and what I *believe*—especially what I believe about the God who made me."

"Amen!" several voices shouted.

"I'm a southern girl and for many of you that may not mean much—but it's different being raised south of the Mason-Dixon line—especially for girls. We're sheltered and protected and aren't often as—." She paused, considering her next words. "—as independent as many ladies in the Midwest. But, I'm also a preacher's daughter, and I was raised in a home where God came first, family came next, and work came last. I have two brothers, one older and one younger than I. My parents let me do almost anything my brothers could do. I ran and climbed trees and learned to ride a horse, side saddle. And my parents sent me to school right along with my brothers."

"My father went to seminary and though my mother never attended school, she received a good education at home. Mama and Papa both love to learn and they instilled that love in me. I loved reading and studying, and I yearned to know everything. I sometimes think I drove my father a little crazy with my questions."

A titter ran through the crowd and Laura leaned toward Joe, "Sounds like you and Joanna have something in common."

"It was that yearning—that need to know—that led me to want to learn more about woman's suffrage. It's not something that's talked about back home. Indiana has had a suffrage organization for many years, but there isn't any such group in North Carolina, even today. I don't know anyone besides my friend, Susannah York, who has gone to suffrage events." She took a deep breath. "Mrs. Stanton wasn't the first woman I heard speak about woman's suffrage. Nine months before that, Mrs. York and I went to Washington, DC, and heard May Wright Sewall speak at the annual meeting of the National Woman's Suffrage Association."

Lucy poked Edgar in his side. "Did you hear that? She did go to that convention!"

"Be quiet. I want to hear what Joanna has to say."

So it's Joanna again, is it? How wonderful...

"You may not know that Mrs. Sewall is a Hoosier, who lives in Indianapolis. After I heard her speak, I went home and started reading everything I could lay my hands on about votes for women—pro and con. I wanted to know why the idea frightened some people and why it made so many people so angry. I thought about how my parents raised me, telling me God had given me a good mind and wanted me to use it... telling me that in the Garden of Eden men and women were equal, and telling me that Christ died for men *and* women, and calls *both* into His service. I began to think that it didn't make sense that women can read and understand scripture and read and understand mathematics and science and history, but they can't read about government and politics and make an intelligent decision about elected officials."

"I went to hear Mrs. Stanton and Mrs. Sewall speak for the same reason most of you came to hear Lydia Lewis, because I was curious about this important issue. I didn't go to their lectures as a follower."

"But are you one now? Tell us!" someone called.

"Let the lady speak!" To Joanna's surprise, John Lane stood up and turned to the heckler. "Miss Garrett will answer that question in her own way, in her own time." He sat down and Frances gave his knee an approving pat.

Joanna smiled appreciatively at Mr. Lane. "What happened in Petersburg made me furious, but I was also embarrassed. I didn't want to be lumped in with what some writers call *those strong-minded women,* but I do believe that women should have the right to vote, the right to help make the laws that govern them, as well. If Mrs. Helen Gouger can defend people in a court of law up in Lafayette, why can't she vote?"

"If Dr. Mary Thomas from Richmond—a member of the American Medical Association—can practice medicine and save lives, why is she thought *not* capable of voting?"

"I believe I should have the right to vote. But I haven't been willing to say so. I haven't been willing to risk my reputation, until tonight, and to risk being hated for my views. I remember telling my parents that if everyone already thought I was a suffragette, I might as well be one." Joanna grimaced at the memory. "And I stand before you now, saying I am one."

She sat down amid heckles and scattered applause, until Ted Garner stood up to speak.

"I've heard Miss Garrett tell her version of what happened twice now, and I'm still not satisfied. Those newspaper articles in North Carolina said she was arrested; they got their information from somewhere. With all due respect for Miss Garrett, it seems like someone is lying here, and the only person with reason to lie is her."

"That's right, Ted!" someone cried out.

A tall, gray-haired woman who had come in late and was standing near the entrance came forward to speak. Sam Bailey acknowledged her.

"You're quite right, sir, someone *is* lying," the woman said, "and I will gladly tell you who it is." At the sound of her voice, Joanna's hand flew to her mouth as she craned her neck to see over the crowd.

"I was with Joanna Garrett in Petersburg last November," the speaker continued, her voice assured and clear. "I am Susannah York..." There were gasps from the crowd and many heads turned toward the back where she stood. "And I had the great pleasure of teaching Joanna when she was a student at Peace Institute. I also had the pleasure and the misfortune to accompany her to Elizabeth Cady Stanton's speech last year." She paused until the audience calmed down. "I say *pleasure* because Mrs. Stanton is an articulate and engaging speaker. I say *misfortune* because the outrageous conduct of some men in the audience had forced Mrs. Stanton to end her talk prematurely."

"You're one of them suffragettes!" someone shouted from the middle of the audience, "You don't like men!"

Susannah York stopped midway down the aisle, turned, and stared into the section with a look that could only be described as withering. "My late husband, sir, I hope would have disagreed with you."

Laughter erupted and Carrie and Laura applauded.

"And you have no idea whether I agree with Mrs. Stanton or with Lydia Lewis, whom I understand spoke here not long ago." More applause erupted, and Susannah continued her march down the aisle. "As I was saying, I was with Joanna when a group of men swarmed Mrs. Stanton and the police came in to calm the uproar. Although the police *may* have been well intentioned, they rounded up about thirty women that evening, but not one of the men who threw tomatoes at Mrs. Stanton, and forced her to leave under armed guard."

"We were *brutally* handcuffed, just as Miss Garrett told you, and we were herded like animals into a police wagon. They took us to police headquarters as if we were common criminals—which *we were not*—and treated us as anything but ladies, which I assure you we were, and remain. But we were never, I repeat, *never* arrested. Those newspaper articles were wrong." Susannah was guided to the far wall, where she waited until a man gave up his seat.

Her short, impassioned speech had the audience in an uproar. Sam Bailey kept stomping his foot to get their attention.

"Thank you, Mrs. York. Now, would anyone else like to speak?"

Lucy stood up. "Mr. Bailey, I feel compelled to speak, as a representative of the newspaper industry, and as a citizen of Appleton." She held aloft a sheaf of newspapers. "I have listened to both Miss Garrett and Mrs. York, and I have heard them contradict what these newspapers reported about them."

She waved the newspapers above her head. "But I must agree with Mr. Garner. The newspaper publishers have no reason to lie. My father wouldn't print a lie in the *Gazette*." Lucy had started to say, *and neither would I*, but caught herself. "However, Miss Garrett and her professor have good reason to do exactly that. Their careers, not to mention their reputations, are at stake. If what they have both said is true, they would have pressed their cause in Virginia and surely their names would have been cleared by now. Why, it's been almost a year! I think, Mr. Bailey, that our schoolteacher does indeed have something to hide, and that something is that she is a criminal—just as the *Petersburg Progress* says she is!" Lucy waved the newspapers again and mayhem appeared to be the next order of business.

"Quiet!" Sam grabbed the gavel and pounded the wood block. "Silence! Quiet, I tell you!"

Lucy took her seat and turned to Edgar with a triumphant smile. He grabbed the short stack of newspapers out of her hand, shook his head in disgust, and went to a vacant seat behind Laura.

What a fool I've been, he thought, *a complete and total fool. How could I have doubted Joanna? And how could I go running to Lucy? Luke was right about her...* He slouched into the seat and rubbed his forehead, then glanced down at the newspapers. He suddenly sat straight up. *Wait a minute...* He unfolded the *Petersburg Progress* to its full length and his eyes raced over the front page.

The din lessened and Doc Peters came to stand beside Sam, whispering and pointing to a thin woman who had walked to the side of the stage.

"Mrs. Patterson?" Doc Peters said. "Did you wish to speak?" Mae Patterson nodded.

Lucy Sheppard had been bold and Susannah York confident, but Mae Patterson looked scared to death. At first her voice was so low that even those seated on the front row strained to hear, but with John Lane's encouragement, Mrs. Patterson took courage.

"I don't know nothin' about this votes for women business and them newspaper stories and what happened down south," Mae Patterson said, "but I know somethin' 'bout Miss Garrett. She's a good, Christian woman, and I'm glad— more 'an glad, I'm thankful to God she's teachin' my little girl." Mae choked up. "I was real sick this year and I had to go back east. My Emma took it hard. But Miss Garrett helped her. She gave Emma somethin' to eat when she didn't have nothin' in her lunch bucket, and she talked to Emma and she prayed with her. I say that's the kind of teacher we should hang on to, not get rid of." Mae was trembling, but she smiled and nodded to Joanna and saw the tears running down her face.

"I agree." All heads turned to where a slight, spectacled man wearing a clerical collar stood in the very last row. It was Charles Middleton, the kind reverend from Madison, and Joanna smiled through her tears. *Friends on the front row, friends on the last.*

"I know Joanna Garrett," Charles said, "not as a schoolteacher and not as a student, but as a friend. She's a fine person, a true Christian and as honest as the day is long. If she says she was not arrested down south and did nothing wrong—a fact confirmed by a college professor, I might add —you good people here in Appleton can believe her."

As soon as Charles sat down, a woman sprang up in front of him. Joanna heard Ted Garner groan. The woman was his wife, Julia. "I feel moved to speak," Julia Garner said, "because I came here tonight sure that Miss Garrett had done something shameful and deserved to be fired. We've talked about her at our house all week and some of the things we've said weren't very nice." Ted Garner seemed to slouch further into his seat. "But now I think I was wrong. I think she's a good person, and I've always thought she was a fine teacher. My Emily thinks the world of Miss Garrett. So, I want to apologize to Miss Garrett and tell her I hope she'll stay on despite how she's been treated."

Edgar was on his feet before Julia Garner stopped talking.

"Mr. McGill?" Joanna's head popped up in surprise. "Do you have something you wish to say?"

"Not yet," Edgar said, "but I may have a lot to say soon." He walked across the aisle and tapped Roscoe Sheppard on the shoulder. "Come with me," he said in a low voice. "There's something you need to see."

Roscoe hesitated.

"Please, sir, just come with me." He headed up the aisle to the back of the room. Lucy looked questioningly at her father, who shrugged his shoulders, then followed Edgar.

Chapter Forty

"Everybody here knows Joanna Garrett is a friend of mine," Luke Goodman said, "and of my wife, as well as a member of my congregation. And if you think that influenced my attitude toward this matter, you'd be right." Luke moved to the front of the hall so he could face the crowd. "It takes a lot to convince me that one of my friends has done wrong, and I wish I could say that about more people in this town. This past week I've heard gossip and unkind statements about Joanna Garrett from folks who didn't have the first idea of what they were talking about. All week I kept thinking how disappointed our Lord would be if he were eavesdropping on conversations in our little town." Luke was in full preaching form and he had a lot of people squirming in their seats.

"Remember what Christ said? *'He that is without sin among you, let him first cast a stone at her.'* I wish more of us had taken that scripture to heart these past few weeks. We've been so busy throwing stones at Joanna Garrett that we lost sight of what's really important—*Truth*, my brothers and sisters, Truth. We know the truth about Joanna Garrett, folks." He turned back to face Joanna and the board. "She did no wrong, and she's just the kind of person we want teaching our children and living in our town, whatever her views on woman's suffrage might be."

He looked into the faces in the audience. "And about woman's suffrage. Do you know that some people you probably admire think women *should* have the right to vote? Like one of my favorite authors, Louisa May Alcott? More than a decade ago, she asked for justice and equality for women, for civil rights, as she put it, for *"us, and our daughters, forever.* And Mark Twain? He said it's ridiculous that all we require of a voter is that he *"wear pantaloons instead of petticoats."* This man might be useless, he might be a scoundrel, but, as Mr. Twain put it, so long as he can *"steer clear of the penitentiary,"* his vote is as weighty as that of *"a president, a bishop, a college professor, a merchant prince."*

Roscoe Sheppard stopped listening to Edgar and looked toward Luke. *I told Lucy that man was in favor of votes for women,* he thought, *but would she believe me? Of course, not. Now, even if Miss Garrett keeps her job, Reverend Goodman has given me a front-page story!*

"Do you want to take care of this, sir, or shall I?" Edgar stood his ground.

Roscoe's face showed more than anger, it was pure rage. He pointed to the newspapers. "May I have these? I will give them back to you when I'm—finished." Edgar nodded and Roscoe folded the papers, stuck them under his arm, and strutted back to his seat.

Roscoe took the seat Edgar had vacated. "What was that all about?" Lucy whispered. "What did Edgar want with you?" Lucy could feel her father's tension.

"Whatever made you think you could get away with it?" he whispered. "What were you thinking?" He drew the newspapers from under his arm; she saw that several were not the ones she had brought with her. *Oh, no,* she thought.

Laura was asking the same thing of Edgar. "What was that about? Since when do you cozy up to Roscoe Sheppard?"

"I did it for Joanna... wait and see."

Luke had almost finished and turned back to the trustees. "I think this Board knows, as I know, that keeping Joanna Garrett here is not just the right thing for Appleton, it's the *best* thing for Appleton." He swiveled to face the audience. "Am I right? If you agree with me, stand up and be counted!"

Joanna watched, dumbstruck, as person after person rose to be counted among her supporters. Lucy Sheppard, of course, remained seated, as did her father. Joanna heard Margot

Giannini's loud voice calling "Hooray for Mees-ah Garrett!" and saw Joe put his two little fingers to his mouth and issued a piercing whistle.

Sam Bailey stamped his foot on the stage and the entire Board stood up, shouting for quiet. When the noise level returned to normal, Luke spoke again.

"Sam, you and the Board asked the public to come here tonight and tell you whether they thought Joanna Garrett should remain in Appleton or go. I think you know the answer to that question as well as I do. Let justice roll down like waters, gentlemen. Keep Joanna Garrett here in Appleton, Indiana!"

Sam Bailey had to calm the crowd one more time before he could be heard. "This has been quite a night, folks. I think it's safe to say it'll be a good long while before a public school board meeting draws a crowd like this again, much less has such impassioned speeches." There was more applause and even some laughter. "Now I think it's time for this meeting to come to an end, and we'll end the way we began, if Reverend Lane is willing."

But before John Lane could rise, Roscoe Sheppard was on his feet.

"Mr. Bailey, may I address the Board? I assure you I will not be long and that our townspeople need to hear what I have to say."

Sam nodded, though utterly perplexed.

"I came here tonight," Roscoe began, "feeling much as Mrs. Garner did. I was ready to send Joanna Garrett packing. I started feeling a little differently when I heard the many voices raised in her defense—but I still thought, 'What about those newspaper articles? What about that story in the *Petersburg Progress* saying Joanna Garrett was arrested?' I'm a newspaperman and I value the integrity of the press. If a quality newspaper prints something, I believe it to be true."

"Integrity," Laura whispered to Edgar. "Now, that's a word I didn't think was in his vocabulary."

"You may change your mind," Edgar whispered back putting a finger to his lips.

"A short while ago Edgar McGill asked to see me about a matter of great importance. *What could he have to say to me?* I thought. I had nothing to do with trying to get Joanna Garrett fired or, for that matter, trying to keep her here. Something about Mr. McGill's manner, though, made me follow him to the back of the Hall." Roscoe paused and looked straight at his daughter, his gaze icy and unrelenting.

"What Mr. McGill wanted, ladies and gentlemen, wasn't to say something to say to me—it was to *show* something to me—" He held up the stack of newspapers. "The newspapers we've heard so much about tonight."

"No," Lucy whispered so softly that no one heard or even saw her lips move. "Don't do it, Father."

"A lot of these stories came from one paper, the *Petersburg Progress*. But what Mr. McGill noticed, and which I saw immediately, was that they didn't match. Most of you don't know what a masthead is, but—" he held up a front page. "—it's the big heading at the top of the front page, the name of the paper. The mastheads on these newspapers don't match—but they're supposed to, because they were allegedly printed the *same* week."

A few in the audience gasped and Laura pulled on Edgar's sleeve. "You figured that out?" Edgar nodded. "Oh, the evil of it," she said.

Roscoe shook the paper above his head, as Lucy had done. "What happened here, is that someone made up what we in the business call a *dummy page*. It's a *fake*—it looks like a real newspaper, but it isn't. Whoever did this wanted to spread vicious lies about Miss Garrett. Whoever did this knew how to lay out a newspaper page," he said, walking toward Lucy. "And whoever did this had access to a printing press."

Roscoe stood over Lucy and yanked her up from her chair. "I can't swear to it yet," he said, his voice trembling with anger, "but I believe my daughter is the one responsible."

The crowd erupted. "Oh, the vixen!'... "Why'd she do it?" and "What a terrible thing to do!" were heard all over the Hall. Sam Bailey pounded his gavel and called for quiet.

"I believe Lucy did this, though *why* I cannot fathom. And I assure you, if I find this to be true, you will not have to worry about such a thing ever happening here again. I'll not only discharge my daughter from the *Gazette,* but I will turn her out of my home."

He turned to face Joanna and bowed to her. "I hope you will accept my apology, Miss Garrett, for the wrong done you through the instrument of my paper, albeit without my knowledge or approval. I will fully understand if you bring charges for libel against us."

Lucy could stand it no longer. She jumped to her feet and began shouting. "He's lying! You think he would let me anywhere near his precious printing press? And why would I care about Joanna Garrett? She's a nobody, just a poor schoolteacher from a poor preacher's family."

When Lucy paused to take a breath, Roscoe clamped his hand over her mouth. "Not another word," he ordered, and pushed her, causing Lucy to stumble. She regained her balance and raced up the aisle. Roscoe was right behind her and Edgar on his coattails.

Sam Bailey blew out an exaggerated sigh and ran his hand through his hair. "Are we finished now, folks? Or does anyone else have something to say?"

No one spoke.

"Apparently we're done," Sam said. "So, Reverend Lane, the floor's all yours." John blinked his eyes several times and then nodded.

Joanna bowed her head. *Edgar left... why? I've lost him, haven't I, Lord?*

"I'd like Reverend Middleton and Reverend Goodman to join me, if they will," John Lane said in the voice his congregations had come to love. "And any other pastors who might be with us as well." Luke joined John and waited with him as Charles Middleton and two other men worked their way down front. Joanna felt a lump rise in her throat when she saw one of the men. Jonas Taylor, her friend from the horse auction.

"Lord," John began, "earlier this evening we asked You to be with us in this place, and You answered that prayer. Thank You for Your presence. Thank You for the courage You gave to those afraid to speak and the comfort You brought to those afraid to hear. Protect us all from harm, O Lord, and bind the wounds that can tear families apart."

Yes, Father, Joanna prayed silently, *protect Lucy from her father's wrath and heal their relationship. And, please, heal the hurt in my family. Help Papa and Mama forgive me. And Edgar, too.*

"The work of this night is done now, Father," John Lane went on, "but the work of the morrow awaits this Board. Continue, Lord, to guide their actions, we pray, and may all that we do be pleasing in Your sight." And all said, "Amen."

"This meeting stands adjourned!" The words had barely left Sam Bailey's lips before pandemonium broke out. The four preachers surrounded Joanna, who caught Luke by the sleeve. "I want to see Susannah, but I'm afraid to go into that crowd."

Luke looked incredulous. "*Afraid?* Joanna, you're surrounded by friends, not by enemies."

"That may be true, Luke, but I'm still surrounded."

"I tell you what. Let's get you into the side room and I'll come get you when the crowd thins." Luke guided her to the waiting room, but not before Antonio Giannini pled his case.

"Please, do no take Mees-ah Garrett away. I wannah to make-ah picture of her."

"Yes, yes, of course, Mr. Giannini," Luke said, "but let's wait until the crowd thins."

When Luke opened the waiting room door ten minutes later, Joanna came out to a stage filled with well-wishers: Laura and Joe, of course, Carrie, the Lanes, Charles Middleton, Jonas Taylor, Susannah York and Mae Patterson, whom Joanna hugged through tears that began anew.

"Now issah no the time for tears, Mees-ah Garrett!" It was Margot Giannini, holding a lamp where her husband and his camera waited. "Now issah time for smiles, so my Antonio make-ah beauteeful picture of you an' all-ah you good friends."

Twenty minutes and several beautiful pictures later, Joanna was in the Goodman's parlor, sipping coffee and chatting with Susannah York.

"But how did you know about the meeting?"

"A friend of yours sent me a telegram," Susannah said.

"Sent me one, too," Charles Middleton announced from the sofa. "Gave me quite a fright when it came."

"Special delivery letters get one's attention, too," Jonas Taylor said, seated at a table with Frances and John Lane.

"But who—?" Joanna saw Luke staring out the window, though it was almost ten o'clock. "Luke..." She said his name as if it were a prayer. "It was Luke who wrote you?"

All three nodded and Luke turned to face them. "I had to do something. I prayed and I preached, but I had to do *something* more."

"He had Annie Campbell dying of curiosity," Carrie laughed. "Can you imagine? Three telegrams and a special delivery letter, all in one day!"

Joanna counted. *Jonas got the letter, Charles and Susannah had received telegrams, but to whom did the third go?* Luke seemed to read her thoughts.

"Apparently the third came to naught," he explained, "though I still haven't given up hope."

"But what more does Joanna need, Luke?" Carrie asked. "The trustees can't possibly need more evidence to decide in Joanna's favor."

"Maybe not," her husband replied. "But there's another fish in need of frying, and that's what the third telegram was about."

Chapter Forty-One

Come Wednesday, just before noon, the sidewalk in front of Harvey Greer's office was overrun with people spilling over into the street. Many were there hoping to catch a glimpse of Joanna's face when she learned her fate. Joanna, however, was already inside Lawyer Greer's office, with Luke by her side. Sam Bailey had taken them in through a back door a half hour earlier.

"No reason for you to hear the news outside, Miss Garrett," he said, ushering her into Harvey's vestibule. "You deserve some privacy for this." Joanna's heart lurched in her chest and Luke gave her a reassuring nod.

Ten minutes later, Harvey asked her to join the Board in his conference room and as soon as she walked in, Joanna knew she could stay in Appleton if she so decided. Doc Peters, grinning from ear to ear, walked up to Joanna and grasped both her hands.

"My dear Miss Garrett," he said, "we have what we hope will be good news for you." Sam Bailey was on Doc's heels and echoed his sentiment.

"Yes, Miss Garrett," Sam said. "The Board wants you to stay and teach this term. In fact, we'd like to offer you a two-year contract," he said, extended the legal piece of paper to her. "We've put that offer in writing." He paused, flushing slightly.

"We are awfully sorry to have put you through such turmoil, Miss Garrett. Like the preacher said last night, we hope you can forgive us and stay here in Appleton."

"It's a good town, Miss Garrett," Doc Peters added, "and most folks were never out to get you. They were just concerned about the children, you understand."

"I am so thankful," she said. "Thank you, all of you, very much." She sighed and for a moment Luke thought she might faint. He pulled a chair near to where she stood but Joanna declined it with a smile and a slight shake of her head. "I want the Board to know I'm not angry and I'm not going to carry a grudge about this. I'm glad, truly glad, to be teaching in a place where people really care about who teaches their children—though it was awful to be talked about behind my back, and to have people saying things as if they were gospel when they were nothing but lies and half-truths." She paused and caught her breath.

"But I owe you an apology. I should have told y'all about it when you hired me. I was just too afraid." She turned to Luke and slipped her arm in his. "My pastor gave me some good advice, just last week. He said, 'You cannot live in fear, Joanna, no matter what is going on in your life. Fear is of the devil, not of the Lord.'"

Luke patted Joanna's arm in a fatherly way.

"And, I'm going to follow that advice. So I can tell you right now that I accept the Board's offer and I'll gladly stay in Appleton for as long as you'll have me."

Four of the five Board members rushed to shake her hand. Ted Garner hung back and Joanna realized she would never know if he voted for or against her.

Sam Bailey offered to let Joanna out through the back door but she declined. "I don't need to skulk out the back, Mr. Bailey," she said firmly. "Why don't we go out together and I'll stand with you and the Board when you make the announcement?"

"Shall I tell them you've agreed to stay?"

"Yes, please do. The sooner everyone knows, the sooner we can all get back to normal." *At least some things will get back to normal. Just not me and Edgar...*

The crowd erupted in cheers when Sam announced the Board's decision and a throng of people followed Doc Peters and Richard Werner as they went to post the announcement at the general stores and the post office.

"Maybe I should have gone out the back door after all," Joanna said to Luke. He had her by the elbow, steering her toward his house, when Antonio and Margot Giannini ran up to them. Luke didn't try to stop Margot from throwing her arms around Joanna.

"I am-ah so happy," Margot cried. "You come-ah to supper tonight, and we celebrate! I make-ah you something special, on-ah the house. You come!"

Joanna accepted and received Margot's most affectionate Italian hug with double kisses.

Carrie and Laura were waiting for them, and as soon as Luke opened the door, Carrie clapped wildly. "Joanna's staying! I can tell by the look on your face."

"I am." Joanna's smile lighted her eyes, showing a joy Laura had not seen in a long time.

"Oh, Joanna," Laura said, coming to hug her. "I'm so very happy."

The Goodman children and Joe rushed from the kitchen, clapping their hands and shouting *hooray!* Joe almost knocked Laura over in his haste to reach Joanna. He grabbed hold of her and held her in a hug.

"I knew it would be all right," Joe said, "I just knew it! Me and Grace and David have been praying and praying and praying. I knew God wouldn't take you away from me—us, I mean!!"

Joanna held tight to Joe, even after he released her from his hug. "Thanks for believing in me, Joe," she said. "I couldn't have gotten through this without you and all of my friends."

"Have you seen my Pa?"

"No, Joe. Not since I saw him in the audience last night."

"He was with Miss Sheppard at the start, but then he came and sat with me and Aunt Laura. I was sure he was going to come find you after the meeting broke up."

I was, too, Joanna also thought.

When Laura and Joe left the farm that morning, Edgar desperately wanted to say, "I'm coming with you." But the words caught in his throat and all that he could do was stand at his window and watch as they drove away.

"I've been such a jackass, and so hard hearted. I wouldn't blame Joanna if she never spoke to me as long as she lives. I believed that newspaper, instead of trusting the woman I love." He paced the room. "Maybe she knows I tried to help."

He was still pacing, running his fingers through his hair until it stood on end, when a thought suddenly came to him. "How do you know you've lost her? Are you sure?"

How could she want me?

Edgar grabbed his hat and raced halfway to the barn before he remembered that Laura and Joe drove Dolly into town.

"Then I'll walk," he shouted to the sky. "Serves me right!"

By the time Edgar got to town, everyone who had gathered outside Harvey Greer's office had long gone. He saw the posted announcement of the Board's decision. "Thank you, Lord!" he said, and went straight to the home of the only One who could assuage his heartache and loneliness.

The peace of the sanctuary engulfed him and Edgar sat in silence, not even praying, simply soaking in the feel of the holy place. He had no idea how long he had been there when he felt a gentle tap on his shoulder. He looked up and saw a slender, gray haired woman.

'I don't want to intrude," she said. "I came in to pray and when I saw you, I felt I had to let you know you were not alone."

"But I am alone." The words slipped out before the thought had fully formed.

"What do you mean?"

"I've lost the woman I love." And that, too, had slipped out of his mouth before he realized it.

She sat down beside him. "That must hurt very much."

"It's unbearable," he said, his voice catching. "But it's all my fault."

"Do you want to tell me about it?"

"You don't need to hear my problems."

"Maybe I do. Maybe that's why I was drawn into the sanctuary."

"Are you Presbyterian?"

"No," Susannah said, laughing, "but my friend Joanna told me a lot of my beliefs fit her denomination better than my own."

His eyes went wide as saucers. "Joanna Garrett?"

"Why, yes. I taught her in Raleigh, and now we're friends."

"Of course!" Now he recognized Susannah York, from the meeting. "I was there last night, too. It was when you spoke that the tide began to turn in Joanna's favor."

"And how do you know Joanna?" *I just might know the source of his pain*, she thought.

"I should have introduced myself. I'm Edgar McGill. Joanna lived with me and my family for a while."

"And you fell in love with her."

He leaned back in the pew and sighed. "Yes. And then I was stupid enough to let her go."

"Tell me about it."

Edgar poured his heart out to this woman who also loved his Joanna.

"I've known Joanna a long time, Mr. McGill. She's smart and she can be stubborn and she's as feisty a woman as I've ever known."

"That's her, all right."

"And she's also the most generous, kind hearted, loving friend I have." She slapped his forearm. "Go talk to her! If she loves you—which I am certain she does—she's waiting for you to come back to her. She'll forgive you."

"But what if I can't forgive myself?"

Susannah rose and tapped Edgar's shoulder. "Then you're in the right place to ask for help doing just that." She exited the pew, then leaned back to him. "We all left Reverend Goodman's home—" Susannah paused and looked at her pendant watch. "—over an hour ago, she should be home by now..." Susannah headed up the aisle and over her shoulder said, "God bless you, Edgar."

Chapter Forty-Two

Lucy was almost the only person who had stayed away from Harvey Greer's office. Going into the meeting last night, she was sure the board's decision would be a resounding condemnation of Joanna Garrett. Today, however, Joanna's world was entirely different, as was Lucy's.

Lucy steered her horse down the outlying roads of Appleton to skirt the tumult in the center of town. She kept looking in all directions, fearful of someone seeing her, or her trunks on the back seat of her carriage.

"He actually put his hand over my mouth—and pushed me out of the Hall—in front of everyone. I was humiliated, totally humiliated, but did Father care? Oh, no!" *He never cared about you—what he did today made that very clear.*

"He threw me out! He'll die a lonely, old man, as he so justly deserves!" Lucy gritted her teeth, willing back the tears that wanted to spill forth. "No, I'll *never* cry," she told herself, holding her head high to catch a breeze, but even that was denied her. "Tears are for the weak." And for the weak minded, as Lucy so often consoled herself. "I should have burned your house down,

Father— with you in it! You betrayed me to save your precious business! You'll see how indispensable I really am, oh yes, you'll miss me soon enough!" She pulled at the collar on her dress. "And, *you*, Joanna Garrett, will rue the day you came to Appleton!"

Her horse and carriage passed the school house at a quick trot,. "All this started at that damn schoolhouse," she reminded herself. "How well I remember sitting in that schoolroom, while you spewed your lies... I should have seen through your manipulation, you—" Lucy drew a deep breath. "I certainly can't leave town without paying my respects..." A deep-throated laugh choked her parched throat.

"I'm the one who gave you such prominence— you holier-than-thou *phony*." Her lip curled contempt. "And that syrupy-sweet Southern drawl that slips from your lying lips at all the right moments—you *phony*!" Lucy shouted the word and cracked the buggy whip over the horse's hind quarter, screaming, "Move! I'll sell you to the glue factory when I get to Madison, I will!"

Lucy sat waiting in her buggy in the thicket of trees across from Joanna's house. She felt the run of perspiration drop from her chin. Hell couldn't be much hotter, but hell was the furthest thing from Lucy's mind. In fact, the idea of hell never entered Lucy's mind, despite all the scripture she'd memorized at Sunday school.

"Finally!" she said, catching sight of Joanna's buckboard coming down the road. "It's nearly three o'clock," she said, folding the lid on her pendant watch. She slid out of the buggy and watched Joanna pull alongside her house. "Hurry! I have a train to catch, you wench!" and then she smiled, watching Joanna hitching her horse to a post, and running into the house. "And do change that pathetic frock," Lucy said, making her way along the wooded boundary of Joanna's property.

Joanna stepped out of her dress and into the pale pink dimity cotton one she removed from her wardrobe. She hurried to button the bodice front and then ran her comb through her hair and felt the cool air on her neck. "I'm thankful to You, Lord, for this day that has ended as I prayed, and which You have lovingly blessed. Thank you, Lord... Amen." Joanna's heart was light and her smile a testament to the joy that filled her as she ran out the front door to Molly, after first giving her full attention to Shadow, who would not rest without Joanna's loving touch.

Lucy followed Joanna at a safe distance and could hear her sweet talking *Miss Molly* and *Shadow* as she led them to the barn.

"How disgusting, talking to animals as if they had feelings." She removed the pistol from her cloth purse, then set the pouch down, beside the barn. "This will be the last truly happy day you live..." She stepped into the opening in the barn. "Miss Garrett..."

Joanna knew the voice. Her lids closed down over her eyes. *Oh, dear God...* Her tongue swiped her lips, as she slowly turned around. "Hello, Miss Sheppard," she said, refusing to court the fear that knocked on her soul when she saw the pistol in Lucy's hand.

Lucy snickered. "Still maintaining your illusion, Joanna?" She moved deeper inside the barn, her gun in plain view.

Joanna could hardly breathe facing the loaded pistol.

"You really didn't think you were fooling me—did you?"

"I wasn't trying to fool you, Lucy."

"You succeeded—at least for a *short* while—with poor dear Edgar.

Joanna considered her options. *No, I won't discuss Edgar with you.*

"Your arrival in Appleton was a *curse*, right from the start." Lucy said, moving her head in a slow side-to-side motion. Her taut lips parted with an unexpected grin. "I thought it only fair to repay you for ruining my life."

"I won't have this conversation with you, Lucy," Joanna said, then turned and started for the open barn door.

"Stop!" Lucy screamed. Shadow bolted into the air and scampered inside Molly's stall. "Don't you *dare* walk away from me! I haven't finished with you yet."

"You want to torment me with that gun, is that it?"

"*Torment* you? Heaven's no. I'm here to kill you, Joanna."

Joanna abruptly stopped and slowly turned back to Lucy. "You're here to *kill* me? And how will you live with that on your soul?"

"Quite well, I should think."

Joanna slowly advanced toward Lucy. "It will be your eternal damnation—a far worse existence than the one you believe you have here."

"How could I be blamed for killing you—*you*, who destroyed my life?" An almost evil resonance charged Lucy's voice, frightening Joanna more than the pistol.

"I have done nothing to you, Lucy."

"So you say." Her green eyes bored into Joanna's. "You are a *fraud*. You thought by luring Edgar that you'd force him into marrying you."

368 *Melissa Warner Scoggins*

"I did no such thing! I taught his—"

"Yes! And you took full advantage of *that!*"

"I understand why you—

"You understand *nothing!*" Lucy screamed and cocked the hammer on her pistol. "Edgar is *still* mine— *if* I want him." She eyed Joanna up the length of her, then back down to her hem. "*You* mean nothing to him," she sneered, "so eliminating you would be no loss to Edgar. In fact, one less suffragette would be a blessing to society!"

"Lucy." Joanna could not believe how calm she sounded. "You and I are not so unlike. I know you're going through a great deal of —"

"You *know nothing!*" Lucy screamed through her gritted teeth and pointed the pistol in Joanna's face.

Joanna thought her breath would never catch. "I know about being alone— and being lonely..." Joanna, as everyone else, had heard the way Lucy's father disavowed her. Justly so, in her father's eyes, but Joanna's heart ached for Lucy at the moment when Roscoe Sheppard tossed his daughter to the wind.

"My father turned his back on me, too, Lucy. I *know* what that feels like... I was devastated."

"You don't know what you're talking about—my father loves me!" Lucy punched the air with the pistol. Her hand was trembling.

"Yes, I'm sure he does love you, in his own way..." Joanna continued advancing toward Lucy. "But you are alone, Lucy. And you're terribly frightened, just as I was, and sometimes still am..."

A strange silence fell over Lucy while her eyes remained fixed on Joanna's.

Whether Joanna realized she had struck a nerve in Lucy mattered not. Joanna was speaking from her heart, sharing things she had not spoken to anyone else.

"Whether we realize it or not, fathers are the ones from whom we seek approval— not our mothers. They're our steady beacon in all our storms, the anchor that steadies us throughout our life. When my father turned out that light, I felt as if all was lost. All I could do was pray." She edged still closer to Lucy. "But it seemed God wasn't listening... I thought that He had cast me off abandoned me, too—as my father had done."

Lucy stared at Joanna, as if mesmerized.

"But God *was* listening, Lucy. He *never* left me. It was God who brought me to Appleton, Lucy." Joanna was but inches away from Lucy and slowly reached for the pistol.

Lucy's eyes had filled with such pools of liquid that she couldn't see Joanna's hand moving for the gun.

"You're running away from God, Lucy, when you should be running to God." Joanna folded her hand over Lucy's. "And you don't need this, Lucy. It's only for defense, and I'm not going to hurt you—I never wanted to hurt you," she said in a near whisper, lifting the gun out of Lucy's hand, then casually dropping it into the pocket in her skirt.

Lucy clung to every word Joanna said, even though her eyes never registered cognizance of what Joanna was conveying.

"Can you forgive me, Lucy—"

Lucy opened her mouth sa if to say, "What?" but no words came.

"—I never saw the pain in you when you came and spent that day with me, Lucy..." she said, still in a whisper, and holding Lucy's hands. "My only concern was to protect myself."

Lucy's breathing intensified, though her stare remained fixed and unyielding.

"We all need love, Lucy, we need to give it and to receive it. There is only one way to rid ourselves of the obstacles of pain and fear. We have to give them to God, putting all our worries and fears in His hands, and walk away from them." She tried a smile, "It was the hardest lesson I ever had to learn."

Questions filled Lucy's mind in the quandary of facing the truth. And then, she fell forward, her forehead landing on Joanna's shoulder. "Oh, Joanna... I came here to *kill* you!"

"No, Lucy. You may have thought you did," Joanna said, cradling Lucy in her arms in what was, perhaps, the only truly compassionate love ever shown Lucy Sheppard.

"I'm so very sorry, Joanna," Lucy whispered through a sniffle. "You won't tell any—"

"No, Lucy, I won't," Joanna said, settling the loose strands of hair at Lucy's temple. "This will be our—"

"*Secret.*" Lucy said, and she shook her head. "Can you ever forgive me, Joanna?" Her voice sounded as Joanna had never heard it, gentle and innocent. "*Will* you... forgive me?"

"I already have, Lucy, but it was never *my* forgiveness you sought."

No further words were spoken as Joanna and Lucy walked in silence back to Lucy's carriage. The two young women waved goodbye to each other with a loving smile as daughters of a merciful God who had intervened in their lives, as He surely would again.

Edgar was closeted in Luke's study.

"You warned me about Lucy, but I wouldn't listen to you... Laura told me Lucy was no good, but I didn't listen to her either... Even Joe told me about Lucy—and you know I didn't listen to him! Edgar hung his head and Luke just shook his.

"My friend, you must   know that Joanna was deeply wounded." Luke was politely telling Edgar that any sympathy he sought was in small commodity.

Edgar looked up, fear in his eyes. "Do you think she can forgive me?"

"You're asking the wrong person, Ed. Joanna is the only one who can answer that question. But—" Luke came from behind his desk to put a hand on his friend's shoulder. "That's a big hearted woman you're in love with. I'd give it a try."

"Do you know where Joanna is?"

"She went back to her house a while ago."

"Alone?"

"Yes."

Edgar leaped up and ran out the door, but abruptly returned. "I've got a problem."

"I thought we just talked about that."

"No," he said. "This is another problem—I need a horse."

Ten minutes later Edgar was astride Luke's horse, galloping to Joanna's.

Joanna had barely composed herself after the emotional encounter with Lucy and had just gotten off her knees from thanking God for His guidance. Her promise to Lucy was true; she would never tell another living soul about Lucy's visit, and the conversation God had led her through.

She didn't hear the gentle knock on the door until it became a heavy rapping.

When she opened the door and found Edgar on the other side, her mouth dropped open. The delicate pink dimity cotton of her bodice jumped with each beat of her heart. Silence hung heavy between them and then Edgar began, his words gushing forth as a schoolboy with his first love.

"I...I came to apologize. I'm sorry, Joanna... I'm sorry I doubted you—I'm sorry for all those awful things I said to you. I'm sorry I let you go through these last few weeks alone and—."

"But, I haven't been alone. Luke and Carrie and Laura and Joe have been right beside me."

His look was pure anguish. "I've been seven kinds of a fool,

Joanna. I have no right to ask you to forgive me. But I am. Please, Joanna, forgive me." His violet-blue eyes pleaded more eloquently than his words.

She frowned and her teeth caught her lower lip. "Just *seven* kinds—are you sure it wasn't more like seventy?" There was no smile, just the tiniest hint of a glint at the corner of her eyes.

"I'll admit to *seventy* times seven! Only say you forgive me." He ventured his next move, hesitatingly, "Please say they're forgiven..." Suddenly, Joanna's cheeks were awash with tears and her smile confirmed forgiveness. But before she could say the words, Edgar pulled her into his arms and held her so tightly she could scarcely breathe.

She nestled in the comfort of his embrace, sitting on his lap on the sofa, when the sound of a horse and buggy alerted them that someone was approaching.

"You're not expecting another beau..." His brow furrowed. "If that's Cal Turner, I'll just have to shoot him."

Joanna smacked his arm and rolled her eyes. "You'll do no such thing. You don't even carry a gun!"

"No, Miss Garrett, but you do."

"Oh, go on with you. Whoever it is, is *not* another beau," she said, kissing him. "You may not believe it, but you're the only man I've ever loved."

Edgar's lips made aim, and Joanna's accepted them with tender passion. "We should see who it is," she said, easing off his chest.

Reluctantly, Edgar released his hold and Joanna walked to the window and pulled the curtain aside.

"It's a man," she said, "but I can't tell who it is. Oh... as I live and breathe, it is Ca—" Joanna shrieked, and ran out the door, quick-stepping it down the porch. Edgar was right behind her, in time to see her fling herself into the man's outstretched arms.

"Oh, Papa!" She wrapped her arms around him so tightly, she couldn't let go. "I can't believe it's you!"

"It's really me, Josie. I'm here."

Joanna burst into tears. "I was afraid I'd never hear you call me Josie again."

Matthew Garrett gently eased his sobbing child from his chest, and looked deep into her eyes. "For that, my one and only daughter, I must ask your forgiveness. I acted rashly and spoke harshly and I'm truly, truly sorry."

Don't worry, she's pretty good about forgiving men who act the fool, Edgar thought.

"Forgive *you,* Papa?" She could barely speak. "I should ask... your forgiveness. I defied you and Mama... and embarrassed you so terribly."

"No, Josie," he said, shaking his head, recalling the memory. "I read the newspaper article Nicholas brought and, I don't know what happened to me. It's not like me to leap to conclusions and make rash decisions." He lifted her chin. "Will you accept my promise to listen to you first before I jump to any conclusions?"

"That's my promise, too."

Matthew Garrett looked up with surprise. "And who might you be, sir?"

Joanna wiped her eyes and coaxed her father toward the steps. "Papa, this is my... friend, Edgar McGill."

Matthew took one look at his daughter's face as she smiled up at Edgar, and he knew Edgar McGill was more than a friend— much more."

Edgar extended his hand. "I'm pleased to meet you, sir. Joanna has told me a lot about you."

Joanna? Oh, yes, they're more than just friends, using first names. "She has, has she? I am pleased to meet you as well, Mr. McGill, though Joanna has said not one word about you to me."

"Well... I would have, Papa, that is, if we had been communicating."

"We seem to be communicating now, sweetheart. Why don't we go inside and you can tell me everything."

Oh, Joanna, don't tell him everything... or your father will be running me out of town!

Joanna walked inside and turned to her father. "How did you know where I was?"

"Samuel told us."

"That's right, Susannah told him I had taken a school in Indiana. But Samuel didn't know the name of the town, did he, Papa?"

"No, that we found out later," he said, sitting on the sofa.

Her eyes questioned him.

"One of your friends sent me a telegram. It gave your mother quite a fright."

"Luke!" Joanna and Edgar spoke at the same time.

Joanna was stunned. "I saw him this morning... he never told me he had written you!"

"You're not the only one who can keep a secret, Josie."

"Well, sir, I'd like to take you and Joanna to supper tonight," Edgar said. "We have several fine restaurants in town, sir."

"Restaurants!"

Matthew Garrett and Edgar looked quizzically at each other, then at Joanna.

"I almost forgot! I'm supposed to be somewhere for supper."

"But I was hoping we could... celebrate," Edgar said.

Matthew Garrett might have been in his fifties, married nearly half his life and the father of three children, but he had not completely forgotten what it was like to be young and in love. Joanna and Edgar clearly needed to be alone for whatever celebration was in store. "I will pass on the invitation tonight, if you don't mind. It was a long trip from Wilmington and what I really need is some tea and toast and a comfortable bed. Maybe you can show me to a hotel on your way to supper," he said, and stood up.

"Absolutely not!"

"But, where would you have me stay, dear daughter?"

"You're staying right here, in my guest room."

Matthew Garrett raised his eyebrows. "My daughter has a guest room? They must pay schoolteachers better up here than they do down home."

"The house is part of my pay, Papa."

"A part she first yearned for, then didn't want," Edgar added.

Matthew smiled and shook his head. "Before you tell me anymore, I need that tea."

An hour later Edgar and Joanna were dining at Casa Giannini. Margot had practically done a dance upon Joanna and Edgar's arrival.

"I have-ah been praying all-ah day," she said, "asking good-ah God above to bring-ah you *both* to my restaurante. And God, He answer my prayers!"

Margot led them to the table they had shared on their previous visits, the one where she had refused to seat Edgar when he dined with Lucy. There were candles and flowers on the table, and Margot disappeared back into the kitchen, leaving the two young lovers alone, and reappeared in what seemed record-breaking time.

"I am-ah back!" Margot laughed setting two round wine glasses and a bottle of Chianti before them.

Edgar poured their wine and Margot told them her menu. She had their mouths watering before they took the first bite. Veal, lemons, spinach, zucchini, and crusty bread— and for dessert, she promised them chocolate. "But I no tell-ah you how it weel-ah be fix-ah! I say on-ally issah chocolate, the sweet of kings—an-ah lovers!" She winked at Joanna and left Edgar blushing to his shirt collar.

"Only an Italian could use that word in public, to an unmarried couple, and mean nothing improper by it," Joanna said. "I've never known anyone like Mrs. Giannini before."

"I've never known anyone like *you* before," Edgar said, his blue eyes swallowing the sight of her. He reached across the table and lifted her hands. "I love you, Joanna Garrett. I want to be with you for as long as you'll have me—" He had promised himself he would say those words before another day separated them. "—preferably forever."

"Edgar, my love..." Her voice trembled. "I will *always* love you."

Edgar came to Joanna and knelt beside her. "When I say *forever*, Joanna, I mean I want you to be my wife," he said, gently wiping her tears. "Will you?"

"I will, but only if it is forever."

Edgar placed a kiss on Joanna's upturned palm, in front of God and everybody, and slipped his mother's wedding ring on her finger.

From her place at the kitchen door Margot Giannini beamed her approval.

Epilogue

January, 1886

Winter blew in cold and hard.

Joanna stood at the bedroom window, scratching at the frost to see the moonlit landscape of white-tipped evergreens, their boughs outstretched as arms to the farmland blanketed under drifts of pristine snow.

Edgar carefully tiptoed his way across the room, wrapped his arms around her waist and nuzzled her neck. "What's so interesting out there, Mrs. McGill?" he whispered.

"Snow," she whispered back, cradling herself in his arms. "Lots and lots of snow."

"I'll know you're fully settled in Indiana when you stop thinking of every snowstorm as a gift."

She turned in his arms and kissed him. "But they are a gift," she insisted. "Remember how it was snowing that first day we met?"

A knock sounded on their door. "It's me, Pa. I want to say goodnight."

"Come on in, Toad," Joanna called out.

"Do you *have* to call me that?" Joe playfully groused, joining Joanna and Edgar at the window. "That's a baby name."

Joanna kissed the top of his head. "Remember when you told me how you got that name, and how it was snowing then, too?"

"What is it with her and snow?" Joe laughed, looking up to his father, his face shining happiness. "You'd think it was a big treat or something."

Joanna drew Joe close in a hug. "Your father just said the same thing. But I love the snow! Good things happen to me when it's snowing."

"It didn't snow when you and Pa got married, and that was a good thing."

She kissed the top of his head. "Indeed it was."

Joe frowned. "It was snowing when we put Aunt Laura on that train to Chicago."

"Yes, Joe, it was. And in a way, that was a good day for your Aunt, too."

"*Good*—when Aunt Laura left us!"

"Yes, but not good *because* she left us... good because of where she was going and what lay ahead of her."

He lifted his brows knowingly. "Like when you got on the train and came here?"

"Just like that," she said. *And I pray Laura finds love waiting for her, as I did.*

"Time for bed, son"

"All right." Joe hugged them both and Joanna kissed his cheek. "Goodnight Pa," he said, and headed for the door. He turned and ran back into Joanna's arms and kissed her cheek. "Goodnight, Mama."

"Sleep tight, my Joe," she said, walking him to the door. "I love you." She closed the door behind her and drew a deep breath. "I hope he'll love his new brother or sister," she whispered, her eyes slowly rising to meet Edgar's.

He stood thunderstruck, his mouth ajar.

Joanna went to him, reached up, and gently closed his gaping mouth. "Darlin', I was waiting for the right moment to tell you..."

Edgar lifted her up into his arms and twirled her around the room. "Did you say what I think you said?"

"God's miracles continue," she said, running her hands into the thicket of his hair as he placed her ever-so-gently on the bed. "The 4th of July should be an even bigger celebra—"

He silenced her lips with a tender kiss and when he opened his eyes, Joanna caught his tears, and he daubed at hers. "You came into my life and revived my soul," he whispered.

"My darling, it is our Heavenly Father who deserves the credit for saving us both..."

The moon's light illumined the falling snow that danced outside their window...

Edgar nuzzled Joanna's neck and she snuggled in his arms, recalling the moment of that October day when Luke pronounced them man and wife and the bells tolled from every steeple that *Joanna was home...*

Melissa's Lecture

Melissa Warner Scoggins holds a Juris Doctorate and is a practicing appeals attorney in Virginia.

Her interest and studies in the woman's suffrage movement began when she attended college. Her family hails from Indiana and she is married to a Tarheel preacher from Wilmington, North Carolina. Both places carry warm memories and provided the backdrop for *Joanna's Crossroads*.

Mrs. Scoggins' style is a delightful, and sometimes humorous excursion for her audiences—men, as well as women, teens, and young adults—who will have the rare opportunity to learn about another time when life was innocent and true. There is no finer, nor educational, approach to learning about the early women's movement, than to engage Melissa Warner Scoggins for a delightful two-hour presentation.

Contact:

FW Publishing
P.O. Box 93
Marietta, GA 30061—0093
Email: fwpublishing@mindspring.com
Phone : 678.773.2674

fW Publishing Current Titles

LOST IN YESTERDAY
A 70th Anniversary Commemoration of
Gone With The Wind
by Peter Bonner

STEPPING ON MEMORIES
A Sister Remembers the Great Depression & WWII
by Marge Griffin-Glausier

AWESOME WOMEN
Some Famous... Others Infamous... and
Those Lost in History
by Leslie "Nicki" Sackrison

THE CIVIL WAR IN ROSWELL, GA
And the Ghosts It Left Behind
by Connie M. Treloar

WHORE OF MADNESS
The Hoax of the Century & the
Secret Alternative Fuel
Dani Dubre'

Upcoming Titles:
BETRAYED
by Dani Dubre'

Printed in the United States
209815BV00004B/79-315/P